Silent Trail

Other Books By
Mark A. Biggs

Operation Underpants
Claudia
St. Mary's Dating Agency
Operation OBE
Operation Origami: The Ire of Claudia
Operation Snowflake
Love Letters from Dresden
Isn't it Madness
Mia Bella
In Search of Daniel
Above and Beyond

Silent Trail

Mark A. Biggs

A CIP catalogue record for this book is available from the
National Library of Australia.
First Published in Australia 2024.

by
mbkbooks
62 Sunnybrook Ave
Warragul Victoria
Australia

www.markabiggs.com.au

Dedication

The Way of St. James

Silent Trail is a fictional piece crafted from the author's transformative experience walking the Camino in 2023 with his wife, Lacy. Inspired by the remarkable individuals they met along "The Way," aspects of the story draw from these interactions. The espionage plotline within the narrative is fictional.

Silent Trail

Prologue

William Marshal waited on the platform of the Eurostar station in London, staring blankly ahead, his mind occupied with memories of his late wife, Hannah. They had planned to embark on "The Way of St. James," the Camino, together, but their dream was cut short when Hannah suffered a stroke and passed away.

At age sixty-seven, he had been a professor of physics and Hannah, a year older, a nurse. They'd been married for forty years and never been separated for more than a few days at a time. Hannah had been William's anchor, his constant companion, and the one person who understood him. As he waited for his train to arrive, he reflected on their life together.

They had met as young students at Oxford University, where William was studying physics and Hannah nursing. Over late-night conversations about science, religion and philosophy, they fell in love and became inseparable. After completing their studies, William stumbled into a career in the defence industry, where he would become one of the UK's leading experts in nuclear submarine design. Meanwhile, Hannah devoted her life to raising their only child Samantha, and working as a nurse in hospitals and clinics.

Despite their varied interests and personalities, William and Hannah complemented each other. Hannah was outgoing, eager to meet new people and explore new places, while William was an introvert, preferring to explore the mysteries of physics. When Samantha left home, they dreamed of travelling the world together, experiencing different cultures to imprint lasting memories.

William's work at BAE Systems, with its demanding security requirements, made it difficult to fulfil their dream. Foreign travel needed prior approval, and altering an itinerary was restricted. After an unsatisfying pilgrimage to Türkiye to visit Christian holy sites, a trip the British Security Service had objected to, they delayed their travel plans until after William's retirement.

Boarding the train, William felt a pang of guilt. He had promised Hannah that he'd retire when he turned 60, but his work on the Astute class replacement, known as Submersible Ship Nuclear Replacement (SSNR) before being renamed SSN-AUKUS, under the AUKUS trilateral security pact, had delayed his departure. If he'd kept his promise, Hannah would be alive, and they'd be walking the Camino together.

As the train left the station, a wave of sadness overpowered William. Dealing with his emotions had never been his strong suit and the death of Hannah had hit him hard. The months prior to his trip, he'd felt like someone cast adrift, uncertain of his future now that his life partner was gone. As a practical man, he knew he had to pull himself from his melancholy. It was Samantha who suggested that he embark on the journey. Despite his initial reservations, he had agreed, recognising the opportunity it provided.

"The Way of St. James" is a challenging pilgrimage, stretching across northern Spain, starting in South Western France, St. Jean- Pied-De-Port in the Pyrenees and ending in the Spanish city of Santiago de Compostela, a distance of 790km. William was aware the journey would test him physically and emotionally and the idea of embarking on a journey spanning hundreds of kilometres across challenging terrain was incredibly intimidating. Deep down, part of him viewed the upcoming endurance walk as self-punishment, a way to atone for not retiring as promised, and he hoped the physical strain would ease his guilt.

Speeding through the picturesque French countryside, William retrieved the antique puzzle jewellery box from his travel case, a precious item containing secret compartments, entrusted to him by Samantha. This heirloom was from Hannah's side of the family and was borrowed by Samantha after the funeral. It carried an air of mystery, its origin a subject of conjecture. Hannah believed that her great-great-grandfather brought it back from China, while others in the family thought that Hannah's great-great-grandfather created it. Unlike simpler puzzle boxes, this one relied on a series of intricate movements to operate, a sequence explained by Hannah to Samantha as it prepared to journey to the next generation. Inside, Samantha had placed cherished items from her mother. William sighed as he remembered the bond between the two women, unconditional love, shared secrets and a comprehension only they could understand. Losing her mother had floored his daughter, and William felt a duty to carry Samantha's memory of Hannah with him on his pilgrimage. Had his wife been cremated, he'd have carried her ashes - not to scatter along the way. More so that she could share his journey.

Turning the box over in his hand, he wasn't tempted to solve the item's puzzle, merely to wonder at the memories hidden inside. *A photograph of Hannah perhaps*, he thought, *but which one would Samantha have chosen?* He stroked the box and whispered, 'I miss you, Hannah.' Recognising the duality of his nature, he added, 'Hannah and Samantha, I'm so sorry. I didn't expect the walk to take this turn.'

Putting the box away, the flickering light from the windows and the hum of the train on the tracks made his eyes heavy. He closed them, intending to rest for a moment, but when he reopened them, he saw the Eiffel Tower in the distance, soaring over the city of Paris like a sentinel. He felt a sense of awe, marvelling at the engineering feat from the 19th century.

Stepping off the train at Gare du Nord he checked his watch. He had two hours before the train to St. Jean-Pied-De-Port departed from Gare Montparnasse, a short train ride or a nine-minute taxi ride away. Making his way through the bustling Parisian station, the chaos, the noise of rushing footsteps, the blend of different languages, and flurry of activity was overwhelming. Something was amiss.

Chapter 1
Train Strike

William Marshal

Stepping onto the platform of Paris Gare du Nord, my travel case in tow, a sense of urgency overcame me as I searched for the departure point for the train which would take me to Gare Montparnasse, where my journey to St. Jean-Pied-De-Port would begin. To my dismay, the railway station was in disarray, with people scurrying in every direction, a barrage of unintelligible announcements echoing over the PA system. Being unfamiliar with French, my unease burgeoned, unsure if something grave had occurred. A potential terrorist attack, perhaps. If it were, I was oblivious to crucial safety instructions blurting from the speakers. Amidst the chaos, my eyes fell upon a railway employee engaged in conversations with passengers disembarked on the platform. Determined to gather some clarity, I dashed towards her and said, 'Excuse me, what is happening?'

She shook her head, her reply laced with inconvenience, '*Je ne parle pas anglaise*. No English.'

I stared at her blankly. With a shrug, she turned her attention to another passenger, leaving me isolated and bewildered.

She was of no help. Now what do I do?

'Excusez-moi, Monsieur,' a female voice said from behind, her romantic French accent unmistakable. I turned amidst the sea of hurried travellers to witness a French woman in her sixties gazing at me and smiling. She had a presence, a timeless elegance, reflecting a refined taste that defied her passing years. Wearing a tailored unbuttoned charcoal grey coat, gently draping over her petite frame, the soft fabric with subtle hints of silver threads shimmered in the dull light. Beneath the coat was a cream coloured blouse adorned with delicate lace detail, complemented by a knee-length skirt in a muted shade of lavender. Her clothes, much like when Hannah and I would go out, contrasted with my own. I knew I was going hiking but, for the train trip, I'd worn my favourite suit. It had been of quality in its prime, but time and use had left their marks. Hannah would say, I had a dishevelled style, one I was comfortable with.

The French woman reminded me of Hannah. Oh, did every woman? My gaze shifted towards her face and I noticed her features, delicate, softened by the embrace of age. Her countenance carried a patina of wisdom, highlighted by fine lines, telling stories of a life well-lived. Deep set hazel eyes, framed by slender arched eyebrows, betrayed an undeniable spark of intelligence, still possessing the curiosity of youth. She wore a natural thin smile as she clutched in her right hand a folded umbrella, its fabric a collage of vibrant reds, blues and yellows, mirroring my perception of her personality, a burst of joy amidst the chaos of the station. Interrupting my thoughts, she repeated, 'Excusez-moi, Monsieur. You seem lost. May I assist you?'

'You speak English.' The silly statement slipped out before I could stop myself.

'Oui, Monsieur.'

Glancing about at the frantic movement of people, I said. 'What is happening?'

'Monsieur, it is the railway employees. They have gone on strike.'

'Without warning?'

'Oui, Monsieur.'

'Oh, how awful!'

The woman shrugged. 'In Paris, there have been many instances of major protests and strikes throughout the years. Some say it's the fiery personality of the people.'

'I have a train ticket for St. Jean-Pied-De-Port, departing from Gare Montparnasse in two hours.'

'I'm sorry Monsieur. You *had* a ticket.'

'There are no trains?'

'That is correct, Monsieur. There are no trains across all of France.'

Confused, I said, 'I have just arrived on the Eurostar from London.'

'I cannot say, Monsieur. However, this is a snap strike.'

Once more, words slipped from my lips before I could stop myself. 'When will the strike be over?' It was a silly question. How was this elegant woman to know?'

'Who can say, Monsieur? Who can say?'

My mind raced as I was on a strict timeline.

How was I going to get to St. Jean-Pied-De-Port in order to start?

Many pilgrims walked the Camino Frances with no lodgings booked, enjoying the freedom of movement each day and the ability to stop and stay whenever their heart desired. I'd read that with the number of pilgrims walking to Santiago growing each year, many pilgrims in a race for a bed started walking in the dark, some as early as four thirty in the morning.

The woman, seeing concern sweep across my face, asked if everything was okay. I explained I was walking the Camino, "The Way of St. James," starting in St. Jean-Pied-De-Port and had booked my overnight stays for the thirty-four-day trek in advance. Although the explanation required nothing further, in a sign of my nerves, I added, 'Unlike many Pilgrims who like to stay in Albergues, with their dorm-like sleeping arrangements, you know, bunk-beds in a large open room and basic facilities, including shared bathrooms, that's not for me. I've booked single rooms with a private en-suite.'

'Oh, dear Monsieur, that is a dilemma. The Camino is a walk that I've wanted to do myself, so share in your disappointment. You were planning to leave St. Jean-Pied-De-Port tomorrow?'

'No, I have given myself two nights in St. Jean-Pied-De-Port before starting the walk.'

'Monsieur, do not be distressed as you have time yet. A hire car, perhaps?'

I felt a twinge of anxiety as I'd not driven on the right side of the road before. 'Yes, a car, perhaps.' I paused and gathered my thoughts. 'I need to find a hotel first, a place where I can organise myself. Do you know if there is a tourist information office here at the station?'

'Oui, Monsieur. But it is closed because of the strike.'

'Oh!'

'Don't worry yourself, Monsieur. We will go to a cafe and I will help you find a hotel. Oui?'

'That is most generous of you. Yes, thank you.'

'Good. There are... *de nombreux* hotels, how do you say in English.... many hotels, near the Gare du Nord. *Venir.*'

She gestured for me to follow. Pulling my rolling backpack behind me, we passed a Starbucks before exiting the station onto a busy street. There were long queues at the Taxi rank and the bus stop, people trying to find a way to their next destination. Across the road was a Burger King, "The Home of the Whopper", the accompanying sign, read. Next to it, LE ZINC DU NORD Cafe and Restaurant and then a McDonalds. To my relief, we turned left, away from the Fast-Food chains.

Where are we going?

As if she could read my thoughts, the lady halted and turned toward me, saying, 'I'm taking you to the Paris Nord Cafe.' She pointed, and not far away, I spotted our destination. To my delight, above the array of shops that adorned the street were several hotels. The Tim Hotel, Richmond Hotel and above the Paris Nord Cafe, a sign proclaimed, "New Hotel."

Leading me inside the cafe, the woman said, pointing to her ear, 'Too much traffic noise to sit outside.'

I nodded as we were greeted by a server dressed in traditional attire, wearing black trousers and a crisp white shirt. My companion said, '*Une table pour deux, s'il vous plait.*'

We settled at a cozy table for two. The lady turned to me, inquiring about my drink preference. Before I could answer, she declared, 'I'm going to have a glass of wine.'

'That would be lovely.'

Addressing the waiter, the elegant lady said, '*Deux verres de Sauvignon de Touraine, s'il vous plait.*'

I recognised the word "Sauvignon," so knew she'd ordered white wine.

I smiled at her before saying. 'Thank you for being so kind and helping me. I'm William Marshal. William Marshal from the UK.'

Extending her hand, she introduced herself, 'Pleased to meet you, William Marshal from the UK. I'm Anna Dupont, from France.'

Why did I feel compelled to add 'William Marshal from the UK' How silly of me? Is it nerves?

'Pleased to meet you, Anna.' I experienced a mental blank and unsure of what to say next, blurted out. 'Do you often rescue hapless individuals at railway stations?'

Anna burst into laughter. 'No, this is my first time. I overheard you ask the station employee for help and was ashamed by her response. It is difficult if you don't speak the language. That's why I asked you if you needed help. I check now on my phone for news of the strike... maybe it says when the trains are operating again.'

Using her smart phone, Anna scrolled through the news. As she read, the server returned with our drinks. I lifted my glass to say, 'cheers', but she didn't notice. I took a sip, savouring the taste.

'Good news, Monsieur Marshal. It is a snap strike; trains will operate from midnight on.' She drank from her glass before saying. 'We must find for you a hotel near Gare Montparnasse. That is where the train to St. Jean-Pied-De-Port departs.'

I thanked Anna, and we chatted while she searched hotels on her phone. I thought the hunt would take a couple of minutes, but the demand was high because of the strike. Twenty minutes later, with no booking, we ordered a second glass of wine.

'You are a brave man, Monsieur Marshal. When I walk the Camino, I will start from Pamplona. In my sixties, I fear crossing the Pyrenees is beyond me.'

'It is still a challenging walk from Pamplona to Santiago.'

'Oui, seven hundred kilometres. I must not delay longer.'

I nodded and took another sip of wine. 'Will you walk it alone?'

'Oui. My friends are not keen and my husband passed away ten years ago. Are you a religious man, Monsieur Marshal?'

I asked myself, *Should I tell her about Hannah?* but decided against it. 'Am I undertaking a pilgrimage for religious reasons? I'm not sure. I've read that many people experience a profound spiritual journey. While I'm open to a religious experience, I'll be pleased to arrive at the Cathedral.'

Were we to meet in Pamplona, I would tell her about Hannah.

'You have chosen the best time to walk, Autumn. The weather is stable and not so hot as summer. But many people go on the trek, which is why you book ahead, yes?'

'Yes.'

Pointing to my travel bag, she said, 'Your rucksack with its wheels is not ideally suited to be carried long distances. Are you having it transported?'

I smiled. 'Absolutely. A day pack is all I'm carrying.'

'Walking poles, Monsieur. I've read they are an essential item. Will you be purchasing them?'

'I have telescopic poles in my bag.'

'Monsieur, you are an organised man and all you need now is a place to stay for the night.' She smiled and held her phone for me to see. 'Will this do? It's three-star, one block from the station.'

I would have accepted a backpacker hostel with a shared bathroom, let alone a three-star hotel. 'The Château Belle Montparnasse is perfect, thank you.'

'I will book it for you, yes?'

'Please do.' I took the credit card from my wallet and held it for Anna Dupont to use. She shook her hand. 'No. I will call them and make the booking. You will pay at the hotel. I can also call your hotel in St. Jean and let them know you're arriving a day late'

'You are most kind.'

With my night's accommodation secured, Anna suggested we order some tapas to accompany our wine in honour of my Spanish quest. As we indulged in the delightful flavours, we engaged in a conversation about the reasons people embark on the Camino. Some sought it for exercise, fun or adventure, while other pursued it as an ethereal journey, to disconnect or reconnect, perhaps as therapy to help them confront personal challenges. Anna and I kept our own motives private, an unspoken agreement resonating between us. Except, when Anna mentioned her late husband, we refrained from prying into each other's personal stories. A passing remark by her suggested Anna had experience of cyber security and I inadvertently raised my eyebrows; she noticed, but let it pass. We spent an hour and a half in comfortable conversation and as we left the cafe; I felt sad knowing that our time was drawing to a close.

Anna arranged for a taxi to take me to my hotel and as I stepped into the cab, I said, 'Try not to wait too long before embarking on your own pilgrimage.'

She smiled warmly. 'I won't, Mr Marshal. Perhaps I will see you on "the way" I knew that this was a shorthand reference to "The Way of St. James," or the Camino de Santiago.

As the cab pulled away from the curb and I waved goodbye, her words lingered in my mind, hinting at the possibility of a shared destiny. Despite our brief time together, it left me with a sense of connection, and I found myself hoping that our paths would cross once more.

Chapter 2
Hotel Château Belle Montparnasse

William Marshal

The taxi driver navigated the busy streets until he reached the convergence of Boulevard Edgar Quinet, Rue de Odessa, and Rue Du Montparnasse. He pointed to the hotel nestled in a vibrant corner, betraying the pulsating energy of the district. After I'd settled into my room, I resolved to indulge in a brief thirty-minute slumber before embarking on my exploration of the city, my heart set on witnessing the majestic allure of the Eiffel Tower, a mere couple of kilometres away, a distance that Anna had assured me was a leisurely stroll in Camino terms.

Stepping into the reception area of Hotel Château Belle, a wave of nostalgia mixed with disappointment washed over me. The peculiar blend of quirkiness and weariness in the space made it clear a transformative touch was long overdue. The tired wallpaper, once adorned with vibrant floral motifs, now faded and worn, carried secrets of the hotel's former opulence fading into history. As the edges peeled back, hinting at the original hues beneath, I glimpsed a faint echo of its past splendour, now a mere whisper in the corridors of time. Before me was a reception desk, its dark wood worn, the surface bearing the marks of years of use, with scratches and faded spots telling stories of long-forgotten guests and their check-in rituals. The desk was unmanned, and I waited, expecting someone to appear in the doorway leading to an office behind the counter. After a minute or two, I spotted the brass bell, tarnished but intact, beckoning me to announce my arrival. I hit the bell and its chime resonated through the reception area. As I waited, my gaze wandered to the carpet. Its faded hues and frayed edges betrayed the countless footsteps it had endured. To one side was a worn-out velvet couch, above which was a cracked mirror, capturing my own flawed reflection. Yes, it begged rejuvenation, but the hotel's ambiance spoke of a bygone era and the murmurs of forgotten stories.

'Monsieur.'

I turned and found myself face to face with someone behind the reception desk who embodied the essence of the establishment. The man had a groomed moustache, silver hair swept to the side, and wore a sartorial ensemble that could have been plucked from the pages of a vintage fashion magazine. A tailored waistcoat in a deep shade of burgundy adorned with intricate golden patterns caught the light with his every movement. A crisp white dress shirt peeked out from beneath the waistcoat, adding further elegance to his attire. He sported well-fitted trousers in a muted grey tone and polished leather shoes that I imagined echoed with each step as he walked the worn-out carpet. Completing his ensemble, he wore a burgundy bow tie with a subtle pattern. The name tag attached to his waistcoat read Pierre Moreau - Propriétaire.

'Good afternoon, Sir. My name is Mr William Marshal. I have a booking for the night.'

'Oui, Monsieur Marshal.'

In keeping with the hotel's ambiance, I expected Pierre Moreau to retrieve a large dusty guest registration book from under the counter, place it next to the antique brass bell and rifle through its pages. Instead, he opened a draw that harboured a keypad and, like any modern establishment, tapped in commands to display my details on the screen in front of him. He stared at the screen for what seemed an eternity. With the air heavy in silence, I was forced to intervene.

'With the train strike, will you be busy?'

Pierre Moreau shrugged and, without raising his eyes from the screen, said, 'It is difficult to say, Monsieur. Maybe we will or maybe we won't.'

His response was strange; after all, it had been difficult to find a vacancy.

'Ah, Monsieur William Marshal. You are staying with us for the one night. We have you in room 404, on the fifth floor.'

The fifth floor. How strange!

'One moment Monsieur, while I retrieve your key.' He vanished into the office.

A real key, I wondered, *not a swipe card*?

Pierre Moreau reappeared moments later holding a tag which read 404. Attached to the tag hung an old-fashioned key with its weighty metal body and ornately engraved head.

'Will you be dining with us this evening, Monsieur?'

'No, thank you. I will visit the Eiffel Tower and will have dinner nearby.'

Pierre Moreau shook his head. 'Monsieur, you must be careful of the pickpockets near the tower. In an instant, they will pick you as a solo traveller and be all over you like flies. It is not wise to carry items of value. It would be safest to leave them here. If you wish, I can put them in the hotel safe. As I say, if you wish.'

I smiled, 'That is most kind of you, but I have little of value and will hold on to my wallet tightly.'

'As you wish, Monsieur.'

'Is there an elevator?'

'Oui, Monsieur Marshal.'

I waited, expecting Pierre Moreau to point out its location. After fifteen seconds, I asked, 'Can you direct me to the elevator?'

He pointed to the corner of the reception area to a sign written in English: *ELEVATOR*, below which were sliding metal Bostwick gates.

In moments of unrest, why is it we often overlook what lies right before our eyes?

***

Stepping out of the lift and onto the fifth floor, I was greeted by an eerie silence. It felt as though I was the only guest, but I doubted that could be true. My room, like the rest of the building, resonated a faded elegance. Kicking off my shoes, I laid on the bed, which embraced me with its inviting softness and within moments of my head touching the pillow; I drifted into a restful sleep. In my dream, I was seated in my study surrounded by stacks of papers and files, a testament to my demanding career. I glanced at the family photograph on my desk and my mind filled with memories of Samantha growing up. A pang of regret coursed through my heart as I realised the moments I'd missed because of my relentless dedication to my work. I watch her first day of school and recall the excitement in her eyes as she donned her tiny backpack, eagerly waiting to be driven. Of course, I went to work leaving Hannah and Samantha to share that mile-stone without me. I remember the school plays and concerts I'd missed over the years and of Hannah telling how Samantha, overflowing with talent and grace, had taken to the stage with her classmates, performing with enthusiasm and passion. Hannah was a pillar of strength and support, filling the gaps left by my absence, always there to cheer Samantha on, to applaud her accomplishments and wipe away her tears. Their close relationship became a constant reminder of the moments I'd missed, and it comforted and saddened me.

In my dream, I see the day Samantha received her acceptance letter from Oxford University and relive the pride I felt when I held the letter in my trembling hand, marvelling at the woman Samantha had become. My eyes well up with tears, not just because of her achievements, but also because I recognise Samantha's success had been nurtured by the love and dedication of her mother.

The sound of a car horn outside woke me. At the moment before the dream faded, I vowed to make amends. It was too late for Hannah, but it was not for my daughter. Now awake, I said, 'I will proudly bear the puzzle box as my standard, a symbol of Samantha's cherished connection with her mother.' I laughed at my pomposity as I added, 'I will photograph it at the Eiffel Tower, the beginning of my journey.'

Let's do it William.

Leaving the lift, I wondered if I was to hand in my key at reception, but that decision was made for me. The desk was unattended, so I put the key in my pocket and headed for the exit.

'Monsieur Marshal,' Pierre Moreau's voice called from behind me. I turned. 'Are you walking or taking a taxi, Monsieur?'

'Walking.'

'Your day pack Monsieur Marshal. It would be wise to wear it on your front until inside the Eiffel Tower.'

After making the alteration, I thanked Pierre Moreau and left the hotel.

***

Pierre Moreau

I waited for the door to close behind Monsieur Marshal before using the phone. 'He's just left. You can't miss him; he's wearing a blue day pack on his front.'

'Well done,' said Odette of the DGSE, the French secret service. 'Is he walking to the Tower?'

'Yes.'

'That is very good. Very good indeed.'

***

William Marshal

Standing before the Eiffel Tower, I looked up. It was a moment Hannah had dreamt of for years, and now I was here.

'Are you ready?' I whispered to myself.

Ascending the stairs to the 2nd floor, I queued for ten-minutes for the lift to the top where, from the tower's heights, a breathtaking panorama stretched before me.

Hannah, this is how you imagined it would be.

I reached inside my day-pack for the puzzle box, but when I had it in grasp, the idea of taking a photograph of it felt in poor taste. I resolved to tell Samantha where I had been and that I had described the scene to her mother.

'Hannah,' I whispered, the name hanging in the air like a secret between us. 'I can see it all. Paris sprawls out before me like a carefully woven tapestry, each thread spun with history and romance. The streets below form intricate webs leading to charming buildings that seem to call out to me. The Seine River winds its way gracefully, reflecting the soft light of the setting sun. In the distance atop a hill, stands a church, its silhouette a beacon against the evening sky.'

'That is the Basilica of Sacré Coeur de Montmartre,' a French voice said to my left. I turned to see a Catholic priest, and I acknowledged his statement with a nod. He pointed. 'And there, that's the Grand Palais.'

'Thank you. And where might I find the Avenue des Champs-Élysées and the Arc de Triomphe?'

He gestured to our left.

'You must excuse me for talking to myself,' I added with a sheepish smile. 'It must have sounded strange.'

'Not at all. I thought perhaps you were using Bluetooth to converse with your phone, and I hoped I wasn't being presumptuous in adding to the description you were giving. The young nowadays, they all seem to have something hanging from their ear, talking vaguely into space as they walk. Technology, it is getting away from me. They call it the generation gap.'

'Yes, I'm no fan of ear pods either.'

'Ah, is that what they are called?' the priest remarked with a hint of curiosity. There was a brief pause before he continued, 'May I point out some of the other sights of our wonderful city you can see from here?'

As we strolled the viewing deck, day gradually gave way to night, and I watched as the city transformed with a dazzling display of lights, the Eiffel Tower also becoming a beacon of radiance, its iron lattice adorned with fathomless twinkling bulbs.

My guide, Father René Char, bore the same name as a renowned French poet and WWII resistance fighter. As our conversation unfolded, we agreed to dine together at a restaurant he knew near the Tower. During the meal, I told him about my pilgrimage and how I'd embarked on the journey to honour Hannah's memory. René enquired if Hannah was the person I had conversed with on the Tower and I confirmed his assumption. I discovered that Father René had served as a soldier before embracing his calling as a priest. In 1986, he was part of Operation Epervier in Chad, a mission aimed at safeguarding Hissène Habré regime from the advancing Libyan forces and their rebel allies. Although René had not witnessed direct combat, the experience left him disillusioned with the meddling of France and other foreign powers in the affairs of other nations. 'We were dispatched to assist a dictator, a man who would later be convicted as a war criminal. France sought prestige through exerting influence and projecting power onto foreign soil. I returned from Chad, relinquished my role as a soldier and embarked on the path to priesthood.'

When Father René asked about my career, I winced. Not because of the secrecy that surrounded my work. I was accustomed to telling people I was employed by BAE Systems and not add more. I realised I represented the life Father René had rejected.

'You must have had an interesting career,' Father René said before hesitating. 'I'm not sure what to say next. I don't want to give you the impression that I'm probing you.'

'My career was always a party stopper. The funny thing is that much of what I did is in the public domain. Type the phrase, "Active Sonar Stealth Submarines", into a search engine and you get a deluge. The South China Post recently ran an article purporting that the Chinese had developed a new coating device that helped their submarines evade enemy sonar by mimicking water. It described tiles that analysed sonar frequency to generate misleading waves to confuse a sonar operator into mistaking the submarine for water. It even provided technical details, the decibels and frequency. Government boffins prefer you remain mute, even if technically nobody is breaching the Official Secrecy Act. After all, a secret isn't a secret when it's available via Google and YouTube.'

What I didn't disclose to Father René, my mission when in BAE Systems, was the clandestine pursuit of a revolutionary technology: a magnetohydrodynamic drive, or MHD accelerator, a marvel promising ultra-silent propulsion. That project mandated the strictest of security protocols. To safeguard the project's confidentiality, critical data had to be impervious to digital threats. Every detail had been painstakingly transcribed onto paper and then safeguarded within a fortified safe. This priceless knowledge had to remain beyond the reach of online hackers.

Father René nodded. 'I recently read an article on "Open-Source Intelligence"—that's what you're alluding to, stuff in the public domain.' He sighed, 'We live in interesting times, if that is not a trivialising statement. Russia, China, Iran, the fracturing of the USA, war in Ukraine, the weaponizing of energy and trade, these are uncertain times. And how do we respond? First your country and then Germany announced their biggest investment in the military since the cold war. A treaty allowing British forces to be stationed in Japan, Australia to get nuclear submarines. My country is doubling its military spending. All this is happening when our focus should be on global and social issues. The climate emergency, refugees, cost of living, the affordable housing, to name a few. I am a man of peace.'

I nodded. 'These are uncertain times.'

Father René shrugged. 'Even as a man of the cloth, I recognise similarities between now and the lead up to World War II. Once I did not support the old cold war proposition of peace through strength, but these are unusual times.'

'You are well read, Father René,' I said.

'Yes... You and I are of the generation that take an interest in such things. I like to read the daily newspaper while enjoying a coffee, not on a tablet, but in the old-fashioned manner, something you can spread out on a table.' He shook his head. 'But that's enough of dark topics. Let's talk about happier matters. Tell me about your daughter. You have one child, Samantha. That is what you said her name was.'

I don't recall saying her name was Samantha... I must have done, didn't I?

'Yes, her name is Samantha. Like many fathers, I am immensely proud of her. She followed in my footsteps and embarked on a journey to Oxford to pursue her passion for physics. Currently, she immerses herself in the captivating realm of quantum physics, diligently shaping her career in the field.'

'It must be truly enchanting to share such a common interest.'

I acknowledged the sentiment, concealing that her work ethic mirrored the dedication I had once possessed. As life afforded me more time, Samantha had become engrossed in her own ambitions, leaving little room for anything else. I doubted I would ever have grandchildren.

As the last morsel disappeared from my plate, Father René asked me if I'd like some company on the way back to my hotel. 'It's never wise to wander these streets alone at night,' he said.

Grateful for the offer, I nodded in agreement. It had been a remarkable evening, and I was looking forward to continuing our conversation. As we walked, conversation flowed effortlessly, covering topics ranging from history and religion to aspects of the human spirit. Without warning, the night's tranquillity was shattered by two figures who emerged from the shadows, faces obscured by dark hoods. Gleaming knives glinted in the street-light; their intentions were obvious as they blocked our path. Fear was my first emotion, the weight of uncertainty gripping me like a vice.

'Your pack,' one of the hooded men growled in English, his voice laced with malice. 'Hand it over, or else.'

With little choice, I began removing the pack, but Father René stepped forward and said to the hooded men, 'My Son. It's best that you leave.'

The man who'd demanded my pack said, 'Piss off, Father, we don't want to hurt a priest.'

With a swift and calculated movement, Father René lunged at the assailant doing the talking. The Father's body moving with an agility that defied his age. A surge of adrenaline coursed through my veins as I watched, my heart pounding. Father René's bravery commanded my respect, and fleetingly, I glimpsed the warrior lying beneath his priestly robes. The surprised hooded man stumbled backwards as Father René disarmed him, causing his weapon to clatter to the ground. The accomplice, witnessing the defeat of his comrade, hesitated. Father René beckoned him to step forward, but the man remained rooted to the spot. Father René's voice commanded authority as he said, 'Leave now, or suffer the consequences.'

Their bravado evaporating, the hooded men turned on their heels and fled as I stood frozen.

'The army training. It never leaves you,' Father René said.'

A weight of gratitude settled on my shoulders. 'Thank you.'

In a reassuring voice, Father René said. 'You're welcome, William. Come now, we are near to your hotel.' We resumed our walk as the echoes of the encounter dissipated into the night.

Chapter 3
St. Jean-Pied-De-Port

Pierre Moreau

'Have a safe journey, Monsieur Marshal,' I said as I watched him leave. After the door closed behind him, I dialled my contact.

'This is Pierre. William Marshal has departed the hotel to catch the 07:08 train to Bayonne, from where he will board the 12:23 train to St. Jean-Pied-De-Port, scheduled to arrive at 13:40 this afternoon.'

***

William Marshal

Montparnasse railway station was a grand structure, teeming with the energy of travellers embarking on their personal adventures. Finding the platform, I was filled with anticipation as I boarded the TGV train and nestled in my seat, ready for the journey. Seated next to me was a woman in her forties of Asian heritage and possessing a solid build.

The journey started with a gentle sway as the train picked up speed, gliding through the picturesque French countryside. Verdant fields stretched out on either side, their lushness broken only by the occasional rustic farmhouse or charming village. The soothing rhythm of the train lulled me into a state of relaxation, the passing scenery providing a soothing backdrop to my thoughts. I reflected on the warm-hearted individuals I had crossed paths with over the past day, Anna and Father René. Not one to be labelled a "people person," I found comfort in their kindness and longed for more such encounters. Summoning my courage, I turned to the woman beside me and offered a simple, "Hello."

She remained resolute; her gaze fixed ahead, lost in her own world. Undeterred, I tried to catch her eye, hoping to elicit an acknowledgment. But she remained steadfast, paying me no attention, as if my existence held no significance.

Oh dear. That was a mistake. I wish I hadn't done it.

As the train rattled on, I wondered about her; the experiences that had shaped her, joys and sorrows that marked her path. I glanced at her profile, noting her stern expression.

Was that the appearance of a person at peace, or focused on her own thoughts?

People would often tell me I looked fierce. 'Dad, don't look so grumpy,' Samantha would tell me when taking a family photograph. But I wasn't feeling grumpy. I was happy. Is this woman like me?

The stranger beside me didn't resemble my daughter, except for their shared gender. Yet, in that moment, my mind conjured an image of Samantha immersed in the world of quantum cryptography, a realm where encryption was fortified by the principles of quantum mechanics, safeguarding information from eavesdropping. I stole another glance at the enigmatic woman. There was an undeniable poise to her, a strength radiated and her presence commanded respect, spoken words unnecessary. Like Samantha, here was a woman who'd forged a unique path, unapologetic for her choices, and resolute in her determination.

With the pleasant sequence of fleeting encounters that had marked my journey since departing England in my mind, the stranger's silence unsettled me but, respecting her choice, I closed my eyes and my thoughts were consumed by Samantha. She'd recently shared fragments of her work, revealing that the military and defence sectors were pouring substantial resources into quantum cryptography research. Although Samantha was bound by secrecy, unable to divulge intricate details, she'd hinted at a remarkable breakthrough. 'A realisation of quantum communication's potential to enable flawless data transmission, impervious to any hacking attempts,' she'd told her father. 'Qubit,' I murmured softly to myself, contemplating the possibilities it held.

A commotion erupted in a nearby carriage, abruptly interrupting my deliberations and shattering the tranquillity as a ripple of unease spread along the carriage. Whispers and anxious glances were exchanged as rumours circulated, each traveller speculating on the cause of the disturbance. I overheard talk of a confrontation between unruly passengers, others insisting that a danger lurked beyond our compartment doors. I glanced at my neighbour, who remained unmoved, though her manner was now guarded. Or was I imagining it? After what seemed like an eternity, the train pulled into Bayonne Station. Passengers, some abuzz with curiosity and concern, disembarked. I felt a mixture of relief and trepidation amongst my fellow travellers. Pausing on the platform, I turned, seeking the woman who'd travelled next to me. She was nowhere to be seen.

Changing trains in Bayonne, I found myself surrounded by fellow Camino travellers, backpacks aplenty, many adorned with the Scallop Shell or "Viera", a symbol of the Camino. As we boarded the next train, there was a palpable sense of unity among us, a shared anticipation of the experiences that lay ahead. As the train sped along its tracks once more, the landscape transformed. The rolling hills and distant peaks of the Pyrenees came into view, announcing our imminent arrival in St. Jean-Pied-De-Port. As I alighted onto the platform, my heart brimmed with a mix of excitement and relief. The rumours and commotion on the journey faded, and I inhaled deeply. Soon I would embark upon the pilgrimage.

'Should I take a taxi to my hotel or walk?' I said to myself and answered with, 'Walk!'

With my smartphone as my guide, I checked into a cosy bed-and-breakfast on the outskirts of town. After leaving my backpack in the room, I felt excited as I set off to explore the surrounds. I soon passed under the sturdy Porte d'Espagne, the grand entrance gate to St. Jean-Pied-De-Port in the foothills of the Pyrenees, the starting point for the French Way. The cobblestones beneath my feet were polished smooth by the footsteps of countless pilgrims who'd trodden the ancient streets before me. Awed by the rich history that surrounded me, I wandered into Rue de la Citadelle, a captivating street lined with picturesque houses adorned with vibrant window shutters. The charm exuded by these dwellings had withstood the relentless passage of time. Lost in the beauty of my surroundings, I glimpsed the towering spire of the Church of Notre-Dame-di-Bout-du-Pont. I envisioned its stone facade and imagined it carried the marks of centuries. Looking about, I felt the weight of faith and devotion that had shaped this region for generations. Following the sound of bubbling water, I was drawn towards the Nive River. Spanning it was the ancient Roman bridge, Pont Romain, a testament to the engineering of the past. Pausing, I allowed the tranquillity of the scene to envelop me, the whispers of the water sharing stories of the pilgrims who'd crossed there throughout the ages. Continuing my exploration, I entered the bustling hub of Place Charles de Gaulle, a vibrant square adorned with market stalls where locals and visitors alike perused the offerings of fresh produce and artisanal crafts. The aroma of freshly baked bread reminded me of my neglected hunger, prompting me to purchase a baguette to satisfy my appetite. Consulting my phone's map, I directed my steps towards the Citadel, a fortress that once guarded the town against potential invaders. Its commanding presence atop the hill offered a panoramic view of the town and the idyllic landscape. A patchwork of rolling hills and verdant valleys stretched out before me as nature's tableau. As I retraced my steps, I spotted familiar faces from the train, fellow pilgrims exploring the town before embarking on their odyssey. I was sure that our paths would intersect again along the arduous journey ahead of us.

When I returned to my lodgings, exhaustion tugged at my weary bones and I sank into a soft bed, allowing myself a few moments of respite before venturing downstairs to the restaurant. Prior to my departure from England, I'd seen snippets that hinted at the later opening hours in France and Spain, inconvenient for Camino pilgrims like myself, with our need to rise early. It didn't surprise me to find the restaurant teeming with patrons, nearly at full capacity as I arrived. The proprietor directed me towards a vacant seat at a table already occupied by a solitary diner: Jonathan Swindon, a striking thirty-four-year-old hailing from the state of Oklahoma, in the United States. He had undeniable good looks. His piercing blue eyes and chestnut hair suggested a man accustomed to capturing the attention of those around him. As I engaged in conversation, Jonathan's melodic accented cadences were refined with an elegance reminiscent of a BBC broadcaster. With each word that spilled from his lips, I was captivated. His pronunciation was precise, diction impeccable and his intonation carried authority.

Jonathan told me he was on a working holiday and held a master's degree in Business Administration from a place called Oral Roberts University. Curiosity piqued by the unfamiliar institution, I resorted to my trusty smartphone and a surreptitious search revealed that Oral Roberts University was a private evangelical university. As I unearthed this titbit, Jonathan excused himself and made his way to the restroom, exposing a man of imposing height and sturdy frame. I delved deeper, uncovering the university's devout reputation. I reckoned Jonathan must have possessed an ingrained sense of faith to choose this institution.

Upon his return, our conversation drifted towards the reason for his working holiday and the Camino pilgrimage. His mission, he confessed with a glimmer in his eyes and a playful tone in his voice, was to find his future Mrs. Swindon. 'Spiritual enlightenment and love are my primary goals,' he said with a chuckle.

With a warm smile, I said, 'You've lofty expectations of the divine, whereas I merely ask for a small favour from Him. No blisters upon my weary feet.'

Jonathan's laughter filled the air. 'You seek a miracle.'

Chuckling along with Jonathan, I said. 'You have a point, my friend. Perhaps it's wiser to keep your expectations within reason.'

Our chatter continued as we ate our meal. 'Tell me Jonathan, when did you begin your working holiday?'

Jonathan's expression turned thoughtful. 'Ah, it's been approximately a year and a half, give or take a few weeks.'

'What sort of work do you engage in during your travels?'

A mischievous glint danced in his eyes. 'My most unconventional asset lies hidden at the bottom of my rucksack. I carry with me a polyester and rayon business suit. When my financial resources dwindle, I unfold my suit, transforming myself from a humble traveller to a professional seeking contract work. It hasn't failed me yet.'

Chapter 4
Claudia

William Marshal

I woke to the sound of rain gently tapping against the windowpane of my snug room. Today marked the eagerly awaited commencement of my Camino pilgrimage. Hastily dressing, I wandered downstairs to the dining area, anticipating the lively chatter and camaraderie of fellow travellers preparing for the day's trek. Yet, as I descended the worn wooden staircase, an unexpected silence greeted me. I found myself the sole guest at breakfast. The innkeeper welcomed me with a kind smile, though the absence of fellow pilgrims left an unspoken question lingering in the air.

'Please, choose your seat, Monsieur,' she said with a gracious smile.

A few minutes later, she returned, delicately placing a steaming cup of coffee before me.

Glancing around the empty room, I inquired, 'Am I early?'

'No, Monsieur,' she replied, her gaze lingering on the solitary figure before her. 'The other pilgrims departed early this morning.'

'Really, before breakfast!'

'Oui, Monsieur. The first day on the Camino, especially through the Pyrenees, presents a formidable challenge regardless of one's readiness. Today's conditions with the possibility of snow only compound the difficulty. The first pilgrim set out at five this morning.'

'In the dark?'

'Oui, Monsieur. They all left in the dark wearing their head lamps. Where are you walking to?'

'Roncesvalles.'

'Roncesvalles! Walking twenty-five kilometres in the challenging terrain will make for an adventurous first day. Will you be joining us for breakfast?'

'In for a penny, in for a pound,' I replied with a shrug, noting her puzzled expression.

'Excuse me, Monsieur. I'm not familiar with that expression.'

'Ah, it means I'm committed now, so I might as well go all the way. So, yes, I'll be having breakfast.'

'I'll bring it shortly. And Monsieur, if your luggage is to be transported, you must leave it in the lobby now.'

***

Claudia

Speaking aloud to myself, I muttered, 'Surely he's already departed and I must have missed him.' Glancing at my watch once more, I dialled the control room at MI6 headquarters in London. The duty officer, Jemimah Raj, informed me that my target, William Marshal, was still inside the accommodation, enjoying his breakfast.

I chuckled. 'He has no clue about the challenge that awaits him.'

'Indeed,' Jemimah responded coolly. 'Stephen Walls wishes to speak with you. Please hold, Claudia, and I will connect you to him.'

'Good morning, Claudia.' Stephen said.

'Good morning, Sir.'

'How is the walk progressing?'

'We are yet to start. I am still at St. Jean-Pied-De-Port. It seems Mr Marshal is keen to have a hearty breakfast before setting off.'

'He won't make this mistake again, will he?'

'I assume not, Sir. Jemimah said you wanted to speak with me.'

'Yes, there are two things. The first is about your ex-boyfriend, Monya.'

'Monya! For a man who lived in the shadows, he's become quite the showman.'

'Indeed, Claudia, indeed. He pulled his mercenaries out of Ukraine on what he's calling a "march of justice", against the Russian military over allegations they had fired on his men. There are reports of soldiers in army trucks being moved around the streets of Moscow, reinforcing key facilities such as television stations and energy infrastructure. Putin fears an armed mutiny from Monya and his Keiser mercenaries.' Stephen paused before continuing. 'Claudia, you know Monya better than anyone. Do you have any insights into his thinking?'

I exhaled heavily, gathering my thoughts. 'I'm not surprised, Stephen. Monya's public comments have become more brazen in recent days. When he told the Russian people that Putin was wrongly advised on the need for the Ukraine war and that NATO was never a genuine threat to Russia, he has been moving closer to an attack on Putin himself. The Keiser group has fewer than 25,000 men, so there'll be no direct confrontation between Keiser and the Russian military. Not yet, anyway. However, the seed of discontent has been sown and if not Monya, someone else will make a play for power. The endgame for Putin starts here. I don't think you need the resources of MI6 to see the deep fractures in the Russian elite around Putin. Putin is brutal, but I expect he'll do as he always has, eliminate those he deems a threat'

'Indeed, Claudia.'

I sighed. 'Some things are difficult to interpret and I wouldn't be surprised if Monya is back in favour with the Kremlin next week. What we know, Stephen, history has proven one thing, never march on Moscow.'

'Yes, never march on Moscow, which is why I believe this is will be the end of Monya.'

'A likely outcome.' I paused before adding, 'Monya and Putin are similar.'

'How so, Claudia?'

'Both suffer from self-delusion, supercharged by their own echo chamber... Oh, thank goodness, Stephen. William Marshal is on the move finally.'

'Well, it leads nicely to the second thing I wanted to speak to you about, William Marshal. There's a mount...'

I interrupted Stephen mid-word, saying 'Darn. Marshal's gone back inside.'

Stephen chuckled.

'Sorry, Stephen. You were saying?'

'I was saying, Claudia, that there's evidence that William Marshal is not the unwitting mule we first thought.'

'Before I left, you weren't certain that Samantha had stolen state secrets. Has this changed?'

'The truth, Claudia, is we don't know. What we know for certain is that William Marshal is carrying something given to him by his daughter and that she has access to classified information. The rest is conjecture.'

'Do you suspect they are working together?'

Stephen signed, 'Samantha has access to sensitive information that would be prized by our adversaries, as did her father. We need to know what is unfolding, which is why you are there. Are we facing a security breach or, worse, a den of vipers in our midst?'

'I'll transmit an encrypted SMS to you, revealing what we uncovered on William Marshal's computer. It implies he secretly plans to meet someone at the Parish Church of Rabanal del Camino, suspicious in itself.'

On cue, my phone vibrated, signalling the awaited text message.

⊳∨<∨✕∨◊,

As I scrutinised it, a wave of uncertainty washed over me. Before commencing this assignment, I'd studied William Marshal. Prior to retiring, he'd been entrusted with classified information regarding the British Nuclear Submarine program. He'd led a team working on a combat effective magnetic pump, an ultra-silent propulsion system with no moving parts. His team had overcome limitations with the system and taken it from science fiction to a workable technology that could replace the propellers on the future SSN-AUKUS submarine. Because of his work, the intelligence services had maintained a valiant watch over his activities.

Mindful of the spectre of cybersecurity breaches, particularly the ominous threat posed by SNDL (Store Now Decrypt Later) tactics orchestrated by foreign adversaries, Marshal's involvement in the SSN-AUKUS endeavour, the vanguard of nuclear submarine technology for both Great Britain and Australia, had been relegated to the realm of hard copies. With a meticulous eye on security protocols, Marshal's interactions with sensitive documentation were choreographed under the watchful gaze of closed-circuit surveillance. Every encounter with classified files was an orchestrated affair. Marshal, flanked by security detail, would retrieve the paperwork from the fortified confines of BAE Systems' impregnable safe, transferring them into a locked briefcase. Throughout this dance of security, British Intelligence agents observed as vigilant sentinels, tracing the briefcase's every move as it traversed from one location to another. The documents were never left unattended, their custodian forever tethered to a state of perpetual scrutiny. Such was the gravity of their contents, and the stakes inherent in their safekeeping, that Marshal was subject to relentless surveillance, ensuring that the secrets the documents harboured remained hidden from prying eyes.

'Stephen, I'm still of the opinion that it is improbable that William Marshal pilfered classified documents. He was constantly monitored.'

'I don't disagree Claudia, however we can't dismiss what has been uncovered, or that he is working in concert with his daughter.'

'William Marshal has an impeccable track record; nothing in his past suggests he posed a threat to national security.' A brief pause lingered in the air before Stephen, perceptive as ever, noticed my hesitation and inquired, 'What is it, Claudia?'

'Well, he's a wealthy man. I assume his finances are tracked as part of his security clearance, yes? Were alarm bells rung?'

'You assume correctly, Claudia. William Marshal has been subject to continuous vetting. We know how he made his money. He is a skilled equities trader and a savvy property investor. When asked about his wealth, our records show he joked, saying, "Well,

I'm not gonna lie to you. I'm a high-end gigolo". He is wealthy, but it is not unexplained wealth.'

Despite Stephen's attempt to explain Marshal's affluence, my doubt persisted. 'Thank you, Stephen. I side tracked you from the encrypted message.'

'Yes, I was saying. The cypher implies that he's colluding with Samantha or operating autonomously from her influence. There's a possibility he's entangled in a broader scheme. Regardless, we can no longer view him as an unwitting pawn.'

I examined the message again, before adding, 'If William Marshal is involved, what is he involved in?'

'What's on your mind, Claudia?'

'The old Knights Templar cipher code is a far cry from the level of encryption either William Marshal or Samantha is capable of. His use of it and the ease with which you found it raise questions. Is he playing with us, and why the Templar? Could Marshal be guaranteeing that we are tasked with ensuring his safety during the pilgrimage? After all, the Knights Templar held a similar responsibility on the Camino.'

'The cipher doesn't sit comfortably with us either, Claudia. Unfortunately, the realm of espionage is a convoluted dance of contradictions, causing one to question the very notion of intelligence itself.' Stephen paused. 'If you're correct, William Marshal will expect our presence, your presence, Claudia.'

'What about Samantha?'

'She's under surveillance. We are allowing her some freedom until we know what William Marshal has in his possession.'

'You're confident he has something of significance?'

'Indeed. I'll be candid, Claudia. Our fear is that he's smuggling plans for the AUKUS submarine. We have intercepted communication that tells us he's under surveillance by foreign players. It's possible that an adversary will try to intercept him before he reaches Rabanal del Camino.'

'Why not apprehend him now, or at least have him searched?'

'If we have a den of vipers, identifying who's involved is important to us. No, Claudia, it's vital for us! Giving William and Samantha Marshal some rope is a risk we will take.'

'If a nest of vipers exists, Stephen.'

'Indeed, Claudia, indeed. We must be certain.' Stephen paused. 'You are well equipped for the assignment?'

'I take nothing for granted, Sir. Given that I must carry everything I need for the walk and have limited space, I have only what is essential.'

'Very good. We will talk again soon… Oh, Claudia, one more thing. Last night, using William Marshal's phone as a listening device, we learned he met a man about your age named Jonathan Swindon. He's an evangelical Christian on a quest, walking the Camino in search of his future Mrs. Swindon. He might be useful to us.'

'Has a security check been conducted?'

'It's in progress, Claudia.'

'Thank you, Sir.'

***

William Marshal

Donning my raincoat, this time in readiness for the weather, I hoisted my daypack onto my shoulders and set off again from the bed-and-breakfast. The day's journey started with a steep ascent of the mountains, the rain-soaked ground making each step treacherous. The path wound its way through a lush landscape and when the mist lifted, offered breathtaking views of the surrounding valleys and mountains. Because I was late leaving, the trek was a solitary but awe-inspiring start to my journey. As I continued, covering several kilometres along the uneven path, my ears caught the faint rhythm of voices carried on the breeze. I quickened my pace, eager to join the company. Turning a corner, I was greeted by the sight of a young couple. They had no walking poles and were sheltering under a shared poncho, bodies huddled close together; they looked ill-prepared as they trudged forward in the challenging conditions. We exchanged greetings. Their names were Emily and Cable, pilgrims from Canada on their way to Albergue Orisson, a refuge between St Jean and Roncesvalles. Protected from the elements in my raincoat, I offered them the use of my emergency poncho I carried in my pack, which they gratefully accepted. We fell into step together and as the conversation flowed effortlessly between us, I was distracted from the cold and wet and the discomfort coming from my feet.

Emily radiated joy even on this miserable day and beneath the poncho, her auburn hair cascaded in loose waves around her shoulders. I imagined it fluttering in the wind on a warm and breezy day. Her fair complexion complemented her expressive blue eyes, exuding determination and curiosity, a woman undeterred by the arduous pilgrimage. Despite her slight build and the obvious strain of the trek, her warm smile remained ever present. Beside her stood Cable, her strong and sturdy companion. His rugged features bore the marks of countless adventures and the determination of a seasoned traveller, although this observation was in contrast to their preparations for the Pyrenees, which was inadequate. A groomed beard framed his square jaw, accentuating his toughness. His hazel eyes, tinged with warmth and intensity, scanned the terrain ahead, broad shoulders hinting at his physical strength.

Maybe it was the discussion I had with Jonathan Swindon last night about finding love, him on the search for his future Mrs. Swindon, that stirred my curiosity about Emily and Cable's history. The first time I laid eyes on them, their affection and commitment radiated so vividly as they shared a poncho. Yet, presently, it appeared, physically at least, they were contrasting figures.

The air was moist and heavy with drizzle, causing the ground to become slick and unforgiving. Each step required precision to maintain balance. As we ventured forward, our eyes were fixed on the path ahead. To quench my curiosity, I turned to Emily and asked, 'How long have you known Cable?'

Emily glanced at me to answer, and that was all it took. Her foot landed on a rock which slid, causing her to lose her footing. As if in slow motion, gravity pushed her helplessly towards the ground. Cable reacted, aiming to stop her fall, but it was too late. A cry of pain escaped Emily's lips as she collided with the unforgiving surface. The jagged edge of a rock scraped mercilessly against her leg, leaving behind a deep crimson stain on her hiking pants. Cable and I knelt down beside her.

'Are you okay?' Cable asked.'

Placing her hand on her leg, Emily answered, 'I don't know.'

Cable started to roll up her trouser leg, but halted abruptly as Emily cried out in agony.

I suggested he cut the material away, so we could see the extent of her injury.

'How?' he inquired.

'Do you have scissors or a knife, perhaps?'

'No. What about you?'

Shaking my head, I responded. 'I brought a first aid kit, but I shipped the knife with my luggage, not wanting extra weight on today's climb. Try using your teeth?' It was a ridiculous thing to say, but the words escaped my lips before I could stop them.

A woman's voice from behind us said, 'I have scissors and a first aid kit.' Turning, I saw a blonde-haired woman of athletic build, probably in her thirties, dressed in full wet weather hiking gear. Placing her walking poles on the ground, she removed her day pack, unzipped it, and retrieved the first aid kit. Leaving her pack on the sodden track, she crouched beside us and, with scissors in hand, said, 'Hello, do you mind if I have a look?'

Emily nodded.

'I'll be careful, sweetie. With the precision of a surgeon, the woman cut the trousers away from the wound. 'Oh, that's good, the cut isn't deep.' Staring at Emily, she said, 'I'm going to stop the bleeding by applying direct pressure to the wound with some sterile gauze I have in my first aid kit. I'll get one of your friends to maintain pressure on it while I check if anything is broken. Is that okay?'

What luck, she sounds like she's from the medical profession.

Emily nodded her permission as the woman applied the gauze. She turned to Cable and told him to apply pressure before easing her hands down Emily's leg. As she reached the ankle, Emily yelped in pain.

'When you fell, sweetie, did you hit your head?'

'No.'

'That is good. Now, while...' She looked at the man helping her.

'I'm Cable,' he said.

'And?'

'Your patient is Emily.'

'Excellent. While Cable applies pressure, Emily, I'll remove your shoe and look at your ankle. I think you have a sprain, well, at least I hope you do.'

Emily nodded as I watched the blonde-haired woman assess Emily's injury. Satisfied, she plucked a bandage from her first aid kit and strapped the injury. As she worked, the woman kept Emily distracted by engaging her in conversation. Once complete, she took over from Cable, checking the bleeding. It had stopped, so she cleaned the cut using a saline solution before applying antiseptic ointment and a dressing, securing it with adhesive tape.

With a reassuring smile, the woman said to Emily, 'You're as good as new. Let's see if you can stand.' She held her hand for Emily to take and, with Cable's help, Emily rose to her feet, stumbling as she put pressure on the ankle.

The blonde woman offered Emily her walking poles, allowing Emily to limp forward. After a few tentative steps, her confidence grew, and she said, 'That is better, much better. I'll make it, I'm sure.'

She took another step, then grimaced in pain.

'Are you okay?' the woman asked.

'Yes. It won't be easy, but with help I will make it.'

Cable expressed his gratitude to the woman, who responded with a slight bow of her head. 'Oh, goodness,' she exclaimed, realising her oversight. 'Forgive me for not introducing myself. My name is Claudia.'

'Hello, Claudia. I'm William,' I said.

Claudia's smile conveyed her acknowledgment. 'I'm headed towards Roncesvalles. What about the rest of you?'

Cable and Emily told Claudia that they were making for Albergue Orisson. I said, like her, I was heading for Roncesvalles.

Claudia nodded her head. 'Orisson is a wise choice, Emily. Roncesvalles would be difficult. You'll need a couple of days' rest for your injuries to heal. If you don't mind, I'll accompany you to your destination.'

The journey to Orisson became a collective effort as we aided Emily.

Is this what it means to walk the Camino?

Perched on a hillside, Orisson revealed a breathtaking panorama of rolling hills, its viewing deck and restaurant offering refuge to tired pilgrims. Claudia offered Emily her walking poles to keep and, after ensuring that Emily and Cable were settled in their Albergue, decided that she would pause for a meal and drink at the bar before continuing the journey. I was disappointed because I would have enjoyed her company. With seventeen kilometres still to travel, I was determined to forge ahead, so embarked on the steep asphalt road, my footsteps echoing in my solitude.

With rain relentlessly soaking the landscape, I stopped to capture a photograph of the enigmatic Virgin of Baikorri. The mist veiled a breathtaking backdrop, concealing its magnificence. After catching my breath, I pressed forward towards the Thibaud cross, an essential landmark on the perilous mountain crossing. It was where the trail diverged from the beaten road and ventured into the wild embrace of an untamed grassy path. My research had forewarned me of the dangers of this stretch, a narrow crevice nestled between the imposing peaks of Pic de Leïzar Athéka and the treacherous Col de Bentarte. Tales of unfortunate souls meeting their demise in the face of deteriorating weather clouded my thoughts.

Amongst my scribbled notes, before departing Britain, I'd jotted down the location of an emergency shelter along the trail, a potential lifeline, should I find myself ensnared by the elements. Standing alone at the juncture, a rift in the clouds revealed a fleeting ray of sunlight piercing the gloom to cast a golden glow upon the path ahead. I hesitated, uncertain of my first step. A wave of longing for Claudia's presence overwhelming me. I cast my gaze back along the path I'd travelled, hoping to discern her silhouette in the mist, but she was nowhere to be seen.

Where are you, Claudia?

After a deep breath, I stepped out, the words escaping my lips, 'You have to do this, William. No turning back now.' Forty minutes into my journey, the weather turned for the worse. The sunlight was obscured by dark clouds and the air grew heavier with mist carrying the scent of an impending torrent. With every step, the fog thickened, cocooning me in an ethereal prison, visibility a mere arm's length, temperature dropping markedly. I shivered, nature conspiring against me, panic clawing as I feared freezing, losing my way or fatally falling.

Disorientated, I strained my eyes, seeking respite when the ground gave way and I stumbled. Unable to regain my balance, I fell face-first onto the muddy ground, motionless for a moment as I summoned the will to get up. As I tried to rise, it seemed an immense weight held me down. Prostrate, I closed my eyes, seeking comfort from the surrounding chaos.

From within the mist, a voice reminiscent of my departed wife, Hannah, called out to me, 'William, William, stand and come to me.'

I lifted my gaze, my heart pounding with hope and disbelief. I replied, my voice trembling, 'Where are you?'

'Here I am.'

Through the veil of fog, I caught sight of a figure, faint and elusive. With determination, I stood, using my walking poles for balance. I stumbled forward towards the apparition. 'Is that you?'

'Yes.'

Hannah beckoned me forward. 'Follow me.'

'I can't see you!'

'Here I am William.'

Guided by divine intervention, an outline emerged from the hazy surroundings, tiny, barely discernible. I felt a surge of relief; the emergency shelter. It was in front of me. Hannah had led me to this beacon in the desolate landscape. Empowered by a newfound determination, I forged ahead towards the shelter just as the storm erupted, its rage unfurling. Upon seeking refuge within, a sense of gratitude flooded over me for evading nature's tempestuous onslaught. Eyes shut, I murmured my thanks to Hannah and the divine. My weariness must have taken over because as I awoke, the only greeting was serene silence. The storm had passed, the sky cleared, and the plateau was bathed in brilliant sunshine. Despite being damp underfoot, the conditions were perfect to continue my journey to Roncesvalles. As I left the hut, I pondered whether Claudia had been caught in the same storm.

I hoped she's alright.

Something inside me told me she was.

The rest of the journey was torture and, just as I thought I had depleted every ounce of energy, the medieval church of Santa Maria materialised before me in Roncesvalles. Arriving at my lodging, I was welcomed into a courtyard with inviting benches, where fellow travellers who had arrived earlier were indulging in food and drink.

'Hey there, William!' called out the familiar voice of Jonathan Swindon. Seated alone on a bench, he was savouring a glass of wine.

I turned to face him and a faint smile escaped my weary lips.

He raised his glass towards me and said, 'I looked for you this morning. Did you sleep late?'

Shaking my head, I replied, 'No, I had breakfast at the B&B.'

'Well, I'll be darned! I wish I shared your confidence. I wanted to cover a few miles before eating. Care to join me for a drink?'

Every bone in my body ached and my feet throbbed as if they were on the brink of explosion. All I yearned for was a hot shower and the comfort of taking the weight off my feet, welcoming some rest.

I need to lie down!

Despite my discomfort, I summoned a response for Jonathan, forcing the words from my mouth. 'Sure, that would be great. Give me fifteen minutes to check in and freshen up.'

Oh, to be young.

Chapter 5
The Path to Pamplona

William Marshal

Despite the gruelling walk to Roncesvalles, I didn't sleep well, kept awake by throbbing feet and the fear of the trek to Zubiri. The guide book described an easier walk ahead with the next stage downhill across the fertile plain of the Rio Erro flowing southwards. It told of woodland shade and plenty of drinking fonts on a delightful section of the Camino.

Learning from my mistake of the day before, I left early to walk to Espinal where I intended to stop for breakfast. Unlike the prior day, the conditions were perfect.

Leaving Roncesvalles behind, in front and off into the distance, I could see the outline of other pilgrims already treading the well-worn path meandering through the picturesque countryside. Wanting to close the gap, I picked up my pace, hoping that walking with company would take my mind off my hurting feet. After ten minutes and with the figures in the distance pulling away from me, I slowed. Still, in under two hours, the village of Espinal emerged on the horizon.

My stomach rumbled with anticipation as I meandered through the streets adorned with ancient stones. A few steps away, tucked along a side street, I spotted an eatery. 'This will do,' I told myself. With a creak, the cafe door swung open, inviting me into a welcoming atmosphere. The soft murmur of conversations and the clinking of cutlery provided a backdrop as I searched for a table. The rustic interior had exposed wooden beams and walls hung with faded photographs of past pilgrims. Sunlight filtered through the lace curtains, casting gentle shadows across the polished wooden tables. I found a seat near the window, allowing me to absorb the lively ambiance of the cafe while I indulged in a well-deserved breakfast. The menu enticed me with an array of delectable options, from flaky croissants and crusty baguettes to hearty Spanish omelettes with freshly squeezed orange juice. Opting for a steaming cup of cafe con leche and a warm buttery pastry filled with home-made jam, I savoured each bite, all the while observing my fellow pilgrims as they shared stories and hearty laughs. Their camaraderie was infectious, and I wished my American friend from St. Jean Pied-de-port and Roncesvalles were with me. Almost as if summoned, the cafe door swung open and there stood Jonathan Swindon, accompanied by the woman I'd met the day before, Claudia. Their being together unexpectedly disappointed me. Jonathan was on a quest to find the future Mrs. Swindon and was now in the company of the unquestionably captivating Claudia.

'Hey there, William,' called the towering American in a friendly voice as he spotted me. With Claudia at his side, he strolled over. 'Do you mind if we join you?'

'Not at all. You are both welcome. Hello again, Claudia.'

Jonathan's eyes widened as he regarded me. 'You two know each other?'

Claudia nodded with a smile. 'We crossed paths on the trail yesterday. It's a pleasure to see you again, William. I was concerned about you when the weather took a turn. But it seems I needn't have worried. You appear to be in good shape, excellent shape, in fact.'

I let out a drawn-out groan. 'Only on the outside, Claudia. On the inside, an already old man has aged considerably.'

Claudia and Jonathan laughed in unison.

'Are you having breakfast?' I asked.

Jonathan answered with a question, 'If we do, will you wait for us, William? We could all walk together to Zubiri.' He looked at his female companion. 'Is that okay, Claudia?'

Claudia smiled warmly. 'Sure. I would like to walk with you both.'

By Claudia's response, I realised that Jonathan and she were not paired, although Jonanthan's interest in her was obvious. 'Yah, I'll wait while you eat and enjoy your company, as long as you both promise not to walk too fast. I'm twice your age, and probably some.'

***

With breakfast finished and our bellies full, Jonathan, Claudia, and I embarked on the next leg of our journey. The path led us to the village of Viscarret-Guerendiain nestled at an altitude of 790 metres. The panoramic views encouraged us to pause and marvel at the beauty of the nature surrounding us.

'What's that?' Jonathan asked, pointing to an old building.

Without hesitating, Claudia replied, 'That's the parish church of Saint Peter which dates to the 13th century.'

'I can see it's a church, the spire and bell are a giveaway, but how do you know its name and when it was built?' I asked.

'That's easy, William. It's in my Camino guide book as one thing to see on today's stage. Shall we take a gander inside?'

Eager to explore, we strolled to the iron gate set within a weathered stone arch. I tried pushing the gate, but it remained firmly locked, preventing us from reaching the church door on the other side.

***

Claudia

That the church was locked piqued my curiosity. It also presented an opportunity to see what length Jonathan would go to impress me. On the walk from Roncesvalles and before we met William in the cafe at the village of Espinal, Jonathan had shared with me his faith in God and that he was an evangelical Christian. Although I didn't know if he would be of any use to me, my training taught me to treat every encounter as offering potential. I responded with a quote from Romans 10:9-10 that suggested to Jonathan that I shared his beliefs and values. 'If you declare with your mouth, "Jesus is Lord," and believe in your heart that God raised him from the dead, you will be saved. For it is with your heart that you believe and are justified, and with your mouth that you profess your faith and are saved.' From the look in his eyes, I knew he was hooked and that I could reel him in anytime.

'Darn,' I muttered, disappointed. 'This is one place on the walk I wanted to see.' I grinned playfully and added, 'Surely you can pick the lock, Jonathan? It dates back to the 13th century, after all.'

We exchanged amused glances as Jonathan replied, 'Are you implying the lock is old and therefore easy to pick, or that I look like someone from the 13th century who should know how?'

I grinned playfully. 'Definitely the former.'

Reel him in, girly.

'What would I even pick it with?'

William chimed in, 'Hey, come on, guys, we're pilgrims, not burglars.'

Keeping the mood light, I smiled and retorted, 'We'd only be burglars if we get in, and I doubt that's happening anytime soon.'

Jonathan recognised the challenge and said, 'Well, technically, if we gain access, we'd be trespassers, not burglars. Burglars steal something. Wait here a moment.' He strolled up to the five-foot stone wall surrounding the courtyard, placed his hands on top, and leaped over, landing softly on the other side. Through the wrought-iron gates, William and I watched as Jonathan turned the handle on the wooden door of the entrance to disappear inside. A moment later, he popped his head out and called, 'Well! Are you coming?'

I'm impressed by your ingenuity. You looked beyond the locked gate.

Turning to William, I pointed to the stone wall and asked, 'Do you want a boost up?'

With a wry grin, he shook his head, but then chuckled and said, 'Why not?'

Well, Mr William Marshal, before this, I would have described you as being as dreary as an old painting hanging above a fireplace in an English cottage—but that is certainly not the case.

Inside the church, rays of sunlight streamed through the glass windows, casting a glow on the worn wooden pews. The stillness of the building caressed us, our footsteps echoing in the silence. When we spoke, we did so in hushed whispers, as if paying reverence to the sacred space, though there was no need for such quietude.

The final ten kilometres to Zubiri flew by and any discomfort we felt from the walking was masked by the flow of our conversation. As we strolled on, William mentioned that he'd booked to stay at the Casa Rural Txantxorena, a tastefully renovated mountain home with a rich history dating back to the 17th century. He was surprised when I told him I was staying there too, adding that we had both chosen well. William had planned for luggage transfers throughout the entirety of his walk, which had made it easy for MI6 to identify where he was staying and book me into the same accommodation. As the walk progressed, it would become essential for me to stay in the same places as William without exposing my intentions. Jonathan was staying at an Albergue near the Casa Rural Txantxorena and I knew he held the key to embedding myself with William for the duration of the Camino. Jonathan was a man, after all, and I am an attractive woman.

As we walked the last part of the scenic path to Zubiri, I feigned the need for a nature break, creating the perfect moment for Jonathan to approach William and enlist his help to keep our walking trio together. The espionage world had taught me to be cautious, so I took the opportunity of my absence to have MI6 conduct a background check on Jonathan. It was a standard procedure, and I needed to ensure that he wasn't a foreign operative, using me as a pawn to access William. In counter-intelligence, nothing was ever as straightforward as it appeared, and deception lurked around every corner. Trust was a rare commodity. My instincts told me Jonathan was genuine, but I knew appearances could be deceptive.

***

William Marshal

Claudia excused herself and stepped away, leaving Jonathan and me alone.

'She's a God-fearing woman, William, and could be the future Mrs. Swindon. What do you think?'

'I haven't spoken to Claudia about her faith, but if she is a Christian, she may well be your future wife. It might be a little too early to say?'

'Oh, I agree William. That's my problem. It's too soon.' Jonathan paused. 'But it would be great if we could walk together for a few more days. It would give me more time. I'm worried though.'

'Why, Jonathan?'

'As it stands, we're each going our own way in Zubiri, well at least I am. You and Claudia are at the same hotel and if I don't see you on the trek to Pamplona tomorrow, who knows when our paths will cross again, if at all?'

'I see your concern.'

'Would you help me, William?'

'How?'

'Oh, I don't know... Um, how about you invite us both to have dinner with you? If Claudia declines, then I'll suspect she's not the one for me.'

'When?'

'Um... tomorrow night, in Pamplona.'

I saw Claudia approaching and hesitated for a moment before agreeing to assist.

Smiling to myself, I mused.

Maybe I could write a novel? A book title sprung to mind: "Jonathan Swindon Walks the Camino in Search of the future Mrs. Swindon." Inwardly I chuckled... Oh, the folly of youth.

As we entered the town of Zubiri, we halted at a road junction. One path led to Casa Rural Txantxorena, while the other led to Jonathan's Albergue.

Turning to Jonathan, I said, 'I've heard that the Cafe Iruña in Pamplona is the place to eat. How about we rendezvous there tomorrow night, in case our paths don't cross on the trail tomorrow?'

Jonathan's face lit up with enthusiasm as he responded, 'Sure, William! Count me in!'

I glanced at Claudia, who nodded in affirmation.

Curious to know their accommodation plans for tomorrow night, I asked. 'Where will both of you be staying in Pamplona?'

Claudia shrugged and replied, 'Finding somewhere to stay is on my to-do list for tonight.'

Jonathan chimed in, 'Same here. I'm yet to book anywhere.'

Keeping the future Mrs. Swindon in mind, I offered a helpful suggestion. 'My hotel, the Europa, is close to the Cafe Iruña. Perhaps you could both seek accommodation nearby or at the Europa?'

Claudia rubbed her chin before saying, 'That's good thinking, William. I'll start by checking the Europa. What about you, Jonathan?'

'Sounds like a plan.'

Jonathan's eyes brightened with gratitude as Claudia offered, 'When I make my reservation, would you like me to find something for you too?'

'That would be fantastic. Thanks, Claudia.'

Claudia inquired where I was staying the following evening and I told her the name of my hotel in Puente La Reina. Claudia nodded thoughtfully. 'I'd like to ship my pack, like you're doing. It would be easier if I book a couple of days in advance. Do you mind if I try to book Jonathan and I into the same place?'

I saw a glow illuminate Jonathan's face. He couldn't believe his luck.

'No, it would be great to have you both there. If you can get in, that is.'

'I can only do my best.'

Claudia turned to Jonathan. 'Meet me at the Casa Rural Txantxorena at six o'clock tonight, and I'll let you know what I've arranged. I'll wait for you in reception.'

I noticed the joy in Jonathan's expression.

Chapter 6
Up In Smoke

Claudia

The security assessment of Jonathan Swindon revealed no red flags, confirming what I had already learned about him as we'd walked together. He was a thirty-four-year-old man from Oklahoma and a graduate of Oral Roberts, an evangelical university. The office had said that while evangelicalism was not a monolithic group, students at the university were likely to share a commitment to their faith and core beliefs. According to MI6, Evangelical Christians emphasise the authority of the Bible as the Word of God and believe in salvation through faith in Jesus Christ. Their devotion is reflected in regular church attendance, personal prayer, Bible study, and a dedication to evangelism, sharing their beliefs with others to encourage them to embrace the faith. Being politically active, they often engaged in matters concerning social and moral issues. What I heard warned me to be cautious when discussing politics and religion with Jonathan, and these topics were likely to arise. It was a call from MI6 later in the evening that raised alarm bells.

Jonathan was waiting in the reception area when I arrived promptly at six in the evening, as we'd arranged. I greeted him warmly and informed him we would all be staying at the Europa tomorrow night, with a reservation set for seven at the renowned Cafe Iruña. I also had us together in Puente La Reina. If we wanted to travel together after that, I would try to book William's agenda.

'Don't forget to tag and leave your pack to be collected in the morning, Jonathan.'

'Europa,' he said. 'That's where we are staying.'

'Yep, you've got it!' When I turned to leave, I could see the disappointment in Jonathan's eyes; he was hoping we'd dine together. But reeling someone in was a delicate process, akin to catching a fish. You had to maintain a gentle tension on the line lest they slip away. Had I allowed us to dine together that evening, his expectations might be fulfilled too soon, the thrill of the chase lost. He could wait until the following night. I excused myself, claiming that I was seeking an early night; keep him interested, with enough space for him to be intrigued.

It was 8:10 PM when my phone buzzed, flagging a call from MI6. I answered cheerfully, 'Good evening, Stephen. You're working late?'

'Some matters can't wait.'

'This sounds serious.'

'It is. We've learned from the National Criminal Intelligence Service that an Albanian Mafia figure, Diego Gavoci, is in Zubiri. According to phone intercepts, Diego is there for William Marshal and what he is carrying. The threat assessment for William Marshal is currently critical.'

'Why would the Albanian Mafia be interested in William Marshal? I know they are ambitious and vicious, but their focus has always been drugs: cocaine, methylamphetamine, heroin. Their side lines are similar: sex trafficking, prostitution and gun-running. Yet, we suspect Marshal is trafficking military secrets. Is the Albanian Mafia entering the world of espionage? If so, that would be a new realm for them.'

'As you say, Claudia, it's highly unusual.'

'Another thing Sir, Diego Gavoci is rarely involved in person. His presence is exceptional.'

'Indeed.'

'Sir, is it possible Gavoci is here to meet with Marshal and not harm him?'

'The intercepts suggest otherwise...' When I did not reply, Stephen continued. 'Do you know where Marshal is concealing the classified information?'

If he is carrying classified information, I thought.

'His daypack I'd suggest; he has it with him all the time.'

'You must get a look inside.'

'Yes, Sir, I will. In the meantime, I would like to attach a tracking device to it, in case he passes the pack to a contact without our knowledge, or if it gets stolen. I've noticed people with Camino lapel pins affixed to their packs. Could we create a miniature tracking device built into one, perhaps a pin with a union jack in combination with the Camino symbol? And Sir, have it delivered to me. I'm confident William would attach it to his pack.'

'A wise precaution, Claudia. Perhaps we should provide one to all members of your walking group, including yourself, of course.'

'Splendid, Stephen. I agree.'

'Good. I'll take care of it and have them delivered to you. We will need a couple of days.'

'Thank you, Sir. Do we have any additional information regarding an imminent attack on William?'

'No, other than we expect it to occur tonight. We know for certain, Claudia, where there's profit involved, Diego Gavoci will be at the centre. Don't underestimate the Albanian Mafia. They will kill entire families while targeting one individual. That's what makes them so feared.'

'That is accurate, Sir. Their ruthlessness is closely tied to the Albanian code of *Besa*, the commitment to keeping promises, within the context of the ancestral code of *Kanun*, granting the right to seek revenge: the principle that blood must be repaid with blood. Unusual as espionage is for them. They might be well-equipped for trafficking classified documents, provided they can acquire them.'

'Precisely, Claudia. Protect William Marshal if you are able but at all costs, don't let what he's carrying fall into their hands. Do we understand each other?'

'It may get messy, Sir.'

'I trust it won't. I'll send you the NCIS profile on Diego Gavoci. Good luck, Claudia.'

The Knights Templar crossed my mind from our earlier conversation. I was about to tell Stephen that if William was hinting at a connection to the Templars; it was probably a ruse. Linking the Templars with the Camino felt like a B-movie plot, far removed from reality. Before I could share my thoughts, Stephen hung up. Moments later, my phone buzzed, signalling an encrypted message from MI6.

***

National Criminal Intelligence Service (NCIS) Profile

Subject Name: Diego Gavoci (Albanian Mafia)

Alias(es): "The Wolf," "D-Money."

Age: 42

Physical Description:

Diego Gavoci is a male of Albanian descent, approximately 6 feet tall, with a muscular build. He has short, dark hair and brown eyes. Gavoci is known to maintain a well-groomed appearance, often dressed in tailored suits and expensive clothing. He has a tattoo on his left forearm—a gang symbol of two side-by-side serpent shaped guns. On the dorsal side of his right hand—near his thumb, is a tattoo of a two-headed eagle (The symbol of being an ethnic Albanian).

Background:

Diego Gavoci is a member of the Albanian Mafia, the Shakja clan from his hometown of Sijak, in west-central Albania. He was born in Albania and moved to London, United Kingdom in 2010. He worked as an enforcer and debt collector. As the clans' criminal activities expanded, he rose through the ranks because of his ruthless nature and cunning intelligence.

Criminal Activities:

Drug Trafficking:

Gavoci is a key figure in the distribution of illicit drugs in London. His network spans across multiple boroughs and involves smuggling narcotics from numerous sources into the city.

Money Laundering:

He uses legitimate businesses as fronts to launder the proceeds from his clan's criminal activities, making it challenging for authorities to trace money back to its illegal origins.

Sex Trafficking:

Gavoci is linked to a surge in the number of trafficking victims brought to the UK. An associate, Luan Plakici was jailed–he offered lucrative jobs in Britain working in the hospitality industry. Instead, the women were treated as prisoners and forced to entertain up to 20 men a day. A 35% increase in human trafficking, with a significant majority hailing from Albania, is tied to Gavoci's dealings.

Arms Smuggling:

While not his primary focus, Gavoci has been associated with arms smuggling.

Associates:

Luan Plakici: Sex trafficker–currently serving time in prison.

Nikolai Vukoja: "The Bear": Gavoci's right-hand man and closest confidant. Vukoja is a ruthless enforcer known for his violent tendencies and loyalty to Gavoci.

Sofia Petrov: "The Serpent": A cunning and manipulative woman who serves as Gavoci's primary liaison with other criminal groups. She specialises in gathering intelligence and handling negotiations.

Modus Operandi:

Gavoci is an extremely calculated individual who rarely gets involved in the actual physical aspects of criminal activities. He prefers to operate from the shadows, delegating tasks to his underlings.

Threat Level:

High. Diego Gavoci poses a significant threat to public safety and the stability of the criminal justice system. His extensive network, financial resources, and ruthless tactics make him a formidable adversary for law enforcement agencies.

***

I studied Diego Gavoci's profile and then closed my eyes. A plan gelled in my mind. I knew that if Marshal was to lead me to his contact, Gavoci had to be stopped without Marshal's knowledge.

Tricky, I thought. *Tricky.*

I took up position in the cramped confines of a hotel cupboard that, when the door was open, had a line of sight to the stairs at the end of the corridor, the only way onto the floor. William Marshal's room was opposite the stairs. Before closing myself in, I placed the ground sensing radar unit, which was part of my deployment kit, out front. It would detect movement in the corridor, allowing me to rest while maintaining vigilance. Six hours later, my watch vibrated, alerting me to movement. Opening my eyes, I noticed there was no light seeping in under the door. The hotel had been plunged into darkness. Activating my night vision goggles, the scene inside my hiding placed transformed into an eerie green. My senses sharpened as I felt Diego Gavoci's presence. Pistol drawn, I cracked open the cupboard door.

Don't take risks, girly. He is a dangerous opponent.

Lowering myself to the ground, I lie flat before continuing, pushing the door ajar. Diego was kneeling at Marshal's room, picking the door lock. With the speed of a wild west gun slinger, a muted thud shattered the silence as Diego fired a silenced shot in my direction. Had I been standing, the outcome would have been different, but in my prone position, the bullet passed harmlessly overhead. A surge of adrenaline rushed through my body and I could taste it on my lips, a sweet nectar fuelling my determination to stop this cold-blooded assassin. Before I could return fire, Diego vanished into the stairwell. I rose from my hiding place and, pushing my back against the hotel wall, began moving down the corridor.

Diego sprung from the stairwell, aiming two shots in my direction.

THUD - THUD.

This time I was ready and retaliated, firing a silenced shot back. He retreated, and I heard him running down the stairs.

He's good.

Diego was fleet footed. By the time I started down the stairs, the front door was closing behind him. If I lost sight of him, he'd slip from my grasp. I jumped the last six stairs, exiting a few seconds behind him out into the cool night air of Zubiri. I saw my target dart into a narrow alley leading to the main road, the N 135 to Pamplona. By the time I reached the N 135, Diego was getting into a matte black BMW M5 parked in front of a pilgrim hostel. He paused and glanced back at me. Under the streetlights, I saw his malevolent grin. He slammed the car door, and the engine roared to life.

You think you've escaped, don't you? Not on my watch you don't.

As Diego drove away, I dashed towards the BMW, scanning both sides of the road for a vehicle I could use. His lack of urgency showed he no longer considered me a threat. I raised my pistol, then lowered it again. Shooting was pointless, but he had to be stopped, otherwise he'd be back tomorrow or the night after or the night after that. I exhaled and slowed to a walk. The street was deserted other than the tail lights on Diego's BMW disappearing into the distance. Fifteen seconds later, headlights appeared from the direction Diego had driven. I contemplated waving down the driver, then hijacking the car. Fortuitously, as it entered town, it pulled into a parking strip, stopping in front of a cafe. The driver popped the boot and, after removing a cardboard box, which I guessed contained fresh vegetables for the business, left the car unattended with its motor running. I seized the chance and stole the vehicle. Gripping the leather-wrapped steering wheel of the sleek Alfa Romeo, I drove off, ready for the high-stakes chase ahead.

At a hundred miles an hour, the countryside unfurled before me; a mesmerizing tapestry bathed in the silver light of the moon. Urdaniz, a small village, lay ahead. Diego's tail lights flickered in the distance and I sped towards them, eager to close the gap before he detected my presence. To my annoyance, the distance between us remained unchanged; he was matching my pace, and the chase was on. The road stretched onwards through the picturesque valley, its winding curves and slopes adding excitement to my pursuit. Correcting for a slide when the Alfa's rear wheels lost traction, I increased my speed. The headlights of the two cars cut through the darkness, illuminating a path before us, two frenzied fireflies darting and swirling through the night.

The villages of Larrasoaña and Zuriain whizzed past, and we were soon on the outskirts of Pamplona. As the ancient city walls loomed, I knew I had to deal with my target, and soon. Speeding through city streets was normal in movies, but it wasn't practical, and the police would be alerted by the chase. Entering Pamplona, I navigated my car through the narrow alleys and winding roads of the old town. The buildings leaned inwards, hindering Diego's progress and my own, except that my familiarity with the city enabled me to close the gap until I was right behind him. We passed iconic landmarks, the Plaza del Castillo a blur of light in the night, the famous Cafe Iruña, where we were to dine the following evening, the grand Pamplona Cathedral, and the ancient Mercaderes street. They all became part of the chase.

'I'll ram him,' I said to nobody but myself.

Diego responded as if he'd heard me and the BMW pulled away. Approaching the Plaza de Toros, Pamplona's historic bullring, I gritted my teeth, eased off the accelerator, pointed my weapon out of the window and took aim at Diego's rear tyre. After a muffled bang, the bullet erupted from the barrel, soaring through the night air before finding its mark. The tyre burst in a dramatic explosion of rubber. Diego's car swerved wildly.

'Good shot, girly,' I congratulated myself.

As if in slow motion, I watched the black BMW collide with a barrier, the car careering into the bullring wall. A thunderous racket filled the air and smoke billowed from the wreckage. Coming to a stop, I whispered, 'He will not have survived the impact.' The words of Stephen came to mind when I said that stopping Diego could get messy. It just had.

He won't be pleased.

Sirens signalled the approach of law enforcement and other emergency services. I couldn't see Diego's condition through the haze of smoke, but it looked dire. The mission seemed accomplished. Selecting a gear, I disappeared into the shadows.

Chapter 7
Pamplona

William Marshal

Waiting in the dimly lit reception area, I glanced at my watch; its hands pointed to six thirty in the morning, the time Claudia told us to meet her.

'Good morning, William. Did you sleep well?' I heard her voice call as she appeared from the nearby stairwell.

Inquiring of one's sleep was a customary greeting, much like, "How are you?" Both demanded a positive response, regardless. I hesitated for a moment, debating how honest I should be. In truth, I hadn't slept well, and I wasn't sure the gruelling walk of the day before was to blame or a disturbance in the night. 'Like a baby,' I replied.

Grinning, Claudia asked, 'Shall we have breakfast first or set off?'

I recalled sharing with Jonathan my rookie mistake of having breakfast rather than putting the miles in before the day became too hot. Had I told Claudia too?

'A full English. Bacon, sausages, fried tomatoes, a couple of fried eggs, baked beans and, of course, black pudding.'

'What, no toast with that?'

'Three slices.'

We both laughed. 'Let's do it, Claudia. Lead on to the first coffee stop of the day.'

I had yet to discover the reason Claudia was undertaking the path of St. James. Unlike Jonathan, who wore his emotions like an open book, she exuded an air of mystique. Or maybe "guarded" was a better choice, a quality I too possessed. I suspected I would need to tread carefully if I were to uncover her motives.

She may be the MI6 agent.

Claudia's plan was to stroll to Larrasoaña for breakfast. 'Instead of passing the village by, when we get there, let's cross the medieval bridge and find a spot to eat,' she suggested. 'The walk to Larrasoaña will only take an hour, or not much more, relatively short by Camino standards.'

The time passed quickly and as we crossed the bridge, a large yellow sign greeted us. Luckily, one symbol displayed was a coffee cup. 'That's our cue,' Claudia declared. Following the directions, we discovered a rustic restaurant at the heart of the village. Inside, a crackling fireplace warmed the dining room, while outside, a terrace beckoned us to be seated.

'Have you walked "The Way" before?' I asked.

'No, this is my first time.'

'Ah, like me. Are you undertaking it as a pilgrimage or simply as a walk?'

Claudia thought for a moment before responding. 'William, that's difficult to answer because it's both. Jonathan will have told you I'm a woman of faith, but I don't seek a religious experience. I'm here for this.' She pointed to the medieval village. 'The rich history, the breathtaking scenery, the crisp freshness of the air, the camaraderie with fellow travellers, the physical exercise and, above all, a chance to reflect. These are crucial for me after some unsettled times. And you, William, what led you to this ancient path?'

'The Pilgrimage is something my wife, Hannah, and I planned to do together. Unfortunately, she passed away before we could embark on this journey. I'm here to honour her memory.'

'Oh, I am sorry, William. I wish I hadn't asked.'

'Not at all, Claudia. It was I who opened the topic.'

'I watched a film called "The Way", starring Martin Sheen. He carried his son's ashes on the pilgrimage. Have you brought Hannah with you?'

I offered a gentle smile, moved by Claudia's interest, yet mindful of her probing nature.

Was she an inquisitor or engaging in casual conversation?

One thing was certain: she was unravelling more about me than I was about her. My mind wavered in the struggle of how to answer, but amidst the questioning, one thought held firm: *It pays to stay close to the truth.* 'Not her ashes. My daughter Samantha, who shared a deep bond with her mother, asked me to carry mementos that held significance for Hannah and Samantha.' I tapped my day pack, as if seeking reassurance from its contents. 'It feels like Hannah is walking alongside me, witnessing the journey she longed to take.'

'That's lovely, but I hope they don't get damaged rolling around in your pack. Mementos are so precious.'

Claudia is cunning. Now I am sure she is prying.

I shook my head. 'There is no risk of that because she put them in a little box. It's a puzzle box, something her mother gave her. When I think about it now, it is like carrying an urn.'

'It's a pity your daughter couldn't do the walk with you.'

'Work commitments. You know how it is. Alas, she is following in her father's footsteps; I wasn't good at taking my holidays. And you, Claudia, are you on leave?'

A smile touched Claudia's lips. 'In between jobs at the moment. Once I'm back in the UK, I'll set about hunting for new opportunities.'

I paused, sensing that if I queried Claudia's line of work, I'd invite the same question. Exchanges like these were of little consequence normally: "Where do you hail from? What keeps you occupied?" were the threads of conventional conversation; I'd always been at ease with them. But with Claudia, an unfamiliar reticence gripped me. Steeling myself, I knew there was no turning back. 'What is your line of work, Claudia?'

'I was a Relocation Consultant.'

'A what?'

'A relocation consultant. I would help people move to an unfamiliar city by taking care of the myriads of things that need to be done.' Claudia grinned. 'Would you like my version or the brochure's version of it?'

I grinned. 'Please, give me the spin. All of it!'

Claudia puffed up her cheeks. 'A relocation consultant is an adept guide for those stepping into unfamiliar cities, orchestrating the intricate symphony of tasks that dance in tandem with moving. The consultant embraces the challenge of unearthing a home to purchase or rent, scouting schools that will nurture the minds of their clients' offspring, securing the family's essential medical contacts ranging from the trusted family doctor to the ever-reliable dentist. Even finding a suitable occupation for the spouse lies within the relocation consultant's purview. They will strive to unravel the labyrinthine process of transitioning to the United Kingdom, a feat that demands the delicate art of alleviating the clients' stress. By doing so, the consultant clears a serene path, permitting clients to channel their energies toward their new vocations and facilitating their swift integration into their novel surroundings.'

'Wow, that is some spin. What kind of person used your services?'

'Among my esteemed clientele were overseas diplomats and distinguished U.S. military personnel stationed in the UK. Either they were affluent, or another benefactor footed the bill.' Claudia took a deep breath before adding, 'What do you think?'

'It sounds a busy occupation.'

'It was a 24/7 role, and I enjoyed it, but I am ready for a change.'

Our omelettes arrived before Claudia could ask about my occupation. Over breakfast, the conversation turned to the day's walk ahead, and whether we'd meet Jonathan on the trail. As Claudia spoke of Jonathan, I noticed a sparkle in her eye. Maybe she was the future Mrs. Swindon? We washed the omelette down with fresh orange juice and coffee before setting off.

Not long after we rejoined the Camino, we met a couple from the UK, Eleanor and Richard, both in their fifties. Eleanor walked while holding onto Richard's arm with one hand and a walking pole in the other, exploring the terrain in front, sweeping the pole back and forth like ground sensing radar. They exuded strength and companionship. We exchanged greetings and learned that Eleanor had lost her sight two years prior and was now blind. We fell into step with them and I wouldn't have dared ask questions about Eleanor's blindness for fear of being insensitive. Claudia was more at ease with Eleanor, who told her that her sight loss began when an illness plunged the world she'd once known into a realm of shadows and finally blackness.

'I used to work as an air traffic controller,' Eleanor explained. 'One ordinary morning, I stepped into the control tower, ready for the day's tasks. As the shift unfolded, an inexplicable illness clawed at me. By midday, it had tightened its grip. I had no choice but to call it quits for the day and head home. Next morning, I woke, my body covered in pustules, inflamed pus-filled sores. Richard took me to Accident and Emergency. A battery of tests showed my systems were shutting down, and I spent the next month in the hospital. I never received a diagnosis, possibly an Autoimmune Disorder was the best they could offer. It was high doses of steroids that eventually switched on my systems, but inflammation in the blood vessels in my eyes caused the rapid vision loss.'

Eleanor's determination transcended her physical challenges. Expressive eyes, unable to perceive the world around her, instead projected wisdom and resilience. Claudia and I were moved by her story and listened keenly as she continued, 'At first, I fell into the depths of depression, but Richard helped me fight back: adversity would not define me. I was determined to find new ways to explore and connect with the world by relying on my other senses. It was me who suggested we walk the Camino. When Richard isn't helping with my footing, I explain the scents, textures, and sounds that paint a vivid picture in my mind. The colours of my new world view.'

Richard's love for Eleanor was clear in how he supported her; life partner, pillar and soul mate. Their synchronicity showed in the way they moved as one, navigating the Camino's path with a spoken, yet unspoken, understanding. The gentle touch of Richard's hand on Eleanor's arm and the way she leaned into his presence said volumes about their partnership, transcending the barriers that might have separated them. Walking together with them, we were inspired by Eleanor and Richard and their mastery of misfortune, their story a testament to the power of love.

After Claudia and I parted ways with the couple, we walked in silence and I wondered if, like me, she pondered if circumstances demanded it, would she act like Richard or fall short. We stopped for a rest, seated on the warm grass.

'Claudia, I'm glad you asked Eleanor about her moving story. She shared it with ease. I probably wouldn't have mentioned her blindness.'

Claudia glanced at me. 'Why is that, William?'

'I wouldn't want to seem intrusive.'

Claudia nodded. 'There's a difference between prying and genuine enquiry. It's as subtle as a whisper in the wind, yet as profound as the depths of an ocean.'

'What do you mean?'

Claudia thought for a moment before she said, 'Imagine you're walking through a quaint village and you encounter a closed door. Prying would be like forcing that door open, disregarding the fact that what's on the other side is not meant for your eyes. Your action is driven by curiosity—now that's nosy. Genuine enquiry is like knocking gently on that closed door, with respect for the boundaries it represents. It's a heartfelt desire to understand, to learn, and to connect. It's about engaging in conversation, asking questions with the intent of enriching your understanding and fostering a meaningful exchange. Genuine enquiry means holding a lantern to illuminate someone's thoughts, rather than shining a glaring spotlight that blinds them. Prying stems from a self-serving curiosity, while enquiry means you possess empathy for your fellow human. When I spoke to Eleanor, had she responded in a way that suggested I was prying, I'd have stopped—but she invited us in.'

After a fifteen-minute break, we continued our walk. The terrain shifted, leading us through shaded forests and rolling hills. Birdsong and the rustle of leaves provided a soothing soundtrack to our journey. Understanding Eleanor's disability, I felt a renewed gratitude for being allowed to view the beauty of this landscape. As we approached Pamplona, the scenery transformed again. The city welcomed us with a blend of history and modern energy. The cobblestone streets led us into the heart of the city, where bustling cafes and shops contrasted with the tranquillity of the Camino. We caught glimpses of the iconic Pamplona Cathedral, its spires thrusting toward the sky. Without checking a map or checking the GPS on her phone, Claudia led us directly to our accommodation. Her face radiated a smile when she spotted Jonathan at a table in front of our hotel. Seeing us approach, Jonathan glanced at his watch and said with a grin, mostly directed at Claudia, 'What kept you?'

Claudia's eyes twinkled as she met Jonathan's gaze and a playful smile curving her lips. She said, 'Jonathan, some of us prefer to savour life's moments, rather than racing through them like a gust of wind.' She paused, her voice dropping to a sultry whisper. 'Why rush when the journey is so captivating?'

Claudia and Jonathan were flirting, and that brought Anna Dupont, the woman I met at the Paris railway station, to my mind. I recalled her departing words, 'Perhaps I will see you on "The Way".' She told me she would start her pilgrimage at Pamplona, where we were at that moment. In vain hope, I scanned around me before giggling at my foolishness. Reality intruded again when Jonathan placed his hand on my shoulder and said, 'Congratulations, William, you've walked well today. Can I buy you a cold beer?'

I am not normally a beer drinker, but after the arduous Camino stage, the prospect of a chilled brew seemed like a gift from the gods. I nodded. 'Make it a pint, please!'

***

Claudia

'Claudia, may I get you a drink?'.

'That's most kind of you, Jonathan, but I'll stick to the water that's on the table.'

I only stayed with William and Jonathan for a short time before excusing myself, saying I was going to check in then freshen up before dinner. 'I'll see you both at the restaurant,' I said as I departed.

***

The Spanish National Intelligence Centre, known as the Nacional de Inteligencia, operated as the dual-purpose guardian of Spain's security interests, at home and abroad. Their reach extended beyond their borders, as evidenced by their contact with MI6 in the wake of Diego Gavoci's demise near the Plaza de Toros. My phone conversation with Stephen Walls, the head of MI6, served as a stark reminder of the complexity that underlay the Spanish-British relationship. In the wake of the Pamplona incident, Stephen Walls poignantly reminded me, while British tourists basked in the allure of Spain's sun-soaked landscapes, the Spanish Government held a more cautious stance toward their British counterparts, a relationship further strained by the repercussions of Brexit and its implications for Gibraltar.

Half in jest, I had suggested that perhaps Britain should consider a return to the European Union, a notion met with Stephen's wry retort, 'They wouldn't take us.'

Stephen, in his recount of the exchange with the Nacional de Inteligencia, told me he'd assured them that the UK bore no responsibility for Diego's fate. He then reminded me again, "Not to let things get messy". Curiously, it wasn't the enigma of Diego that extended our conversation, making me late for dinner, but the rumoured demise of Monya the leader of the most notorious mercenary group in the world and my ex-lover, downed in a suspicious plane crash over Russia after staging a failed coup against the country's military. Although there had been rumours of Monya's death before, this time, both U.S. and UK intelligence officials were suggesting Monya was the subject of an assassination plot, possibly from a bomb on board his private jet.

Monya had made Putin, the strong man, look weak; a perception that had grown since the failed coup attempt. Monya had met with African leaders on the sideline of the Russian-Africa Summit in Saint Petersburg and even become the public face of the Russian support for a coup in Niger; a man who had publicly questioned the rationale behind Putin's war in Ukraine. There was no question–Monya had to go.

'His demise was a warning that challenging Putin is a fool's game,' I said to Stephen.

He agreed, and said, 'General Sergei Surovikin, Commander of the Russian aerospace forces and friend of Monya, was sacked the same day the plane crashed.'

We discussed whether there was enough influence and resources left among Monya's followers for revenge. Stephen did not think so.

'The plane crash may have been staged,' I said. 'Monya could have faked his own death to re-appear to lead a second march on Moscow.'

Stephen disagreed. 'The best intelligence to date is that it's unlikely that the crash was staged.'

Monya and I went our separate ways when I left the Russian Mafia to work for MI6. Yet, when an individual, even one steeped in darkness, with whom you've exchanged intimate moments, departs this world, a tinge of sorrow lingers. It may be fleeting, but the sensation of loss is felt.

Before finishing the conversation with Stephen Walls, I told him about the puzzle box in William's day pack. I expressed my suspicion that, if he carried secrets, they might be concealed in it. I also told him that William didn't know of its contents. Stephen asked if I believed William and I shrugged my shoulders, even though Stephen couldn't see me. From my silence, he deduced I didn't know. Stephen told me that the tracking device and Camino pins I requested would be at the Church of Santiago in Puente La Reina, our destination, after Pamplona.

Finishing the call, I glanced at my watch. It was gone nine o'clock in the evening and I was late. We were lodged close to the southern perimeter of Plaza del Castillo, nestled in the heart of Pamplona. Our designated dinner spot, Cafe Iruña, was a brief stroll to the northern edge of the plaza. When William had said the earliest dinner sitting was nine that evening, I wondered about the wisdom of booking. The Camino Walk was exhausting and our bed beckoned. The next day's trail had a steep climb to the famous Monumento Peregrino on the Alto Del Perdon, or Hill of Forgiveness. To beat the forecast high temperatures, we needed to be walking by six thirty in the morning.

Had William made another rookie mistake, one that we were all part of, or did William have another reason for being at the Cafe Iruña?

I would have to wait and see.

Leaving the hotel, I walked briskly across the Plaza. Nestled amidst a cobbled street, the grand facade of Cafe Iruña shimmered with an aura of elegance. 'William, you have chosen well,' I whispered to myself as I approached. Pausing outside, I admired the tall arched windows adorned with intricate wrought iron grills that offered a glimpse of the world within. Patrons at the charming outdoor seating sipped on their glasses of wine, engrossed in spirited conversations, their laughter harmonizing with the melody of a street musician's guitar. Crossing the threshold, I was transported to a different era, to a place where time had slowed, air steeped in nostalgia. The interior was a symphony of velvet drapes, ornate chandeliers, and rich mahogany woodwork. Dark oak tables bore the marks of countless cups and glasses and the aroma of freshly brewed coffee intertwined with the sweet scent of pastries to create an olfactory embrace. Servers, clad in immaculate white uniforms, moved gracefully among the tables, expertly balancing trays laden with meals that were as much a feast for the eyes as they were for the palate. As I waited to be seated, I took in the rest of the cafe. At its heart was a grand bar, which beckoned with an air of sophistication. Mirrored panels reflected the room's opulence, while bartenders, maestros of their craft, meticulously prepared drinks. The walls whispered tales of celebrated poets, artists, and thinkers who had sought solace within Cafe Iruña's embrace. Ernest Hemingway, the enigmatic American author, was said to have frequented these hallowed halls. The legend went that he had penned fragments of his masterpiece "The Sun Also Rises" within the cafe's confines, his words flowing as effortlessly as the wine from the bar's tap. As I scanned about me, I felt the place was more than just a cafe; it was a repository of dreams, a sanctuary for the weary, and a canvas for the creative.

Above the bustling restaurant's din, I heard Jonathan's voice calling my name. I turned and spotted him and William at a table; they beckoned me to join them with friendly waves. To my surprise, there was another person with them, an older woman, someone I didn't recognise.

Is she the reason William wanted to come here?

The men rose to their feet as I approached, Jonathan hurrying to offer me a chair.

'Thank you, kind Sir,' I acknowledged as Jonathan helped me settle into my dining spot. William, still standing, gestured towards the stranger, 'Claudia, this is my good friend, Anna Dupont, from Paris.'

I quickly assessed her. Anna was a distinguished-looking woman, probably in her mid to late sixties. 'Pleased to make your acquaintance,' I said with a contrived yet genuine smile.

Why are you here, and how long has William known you?

'Are you a fellow Pilgrim?' I asked.'

'Tomorrow is my first day.'

I was about to make an encouraging remark before quizzing her further when my phone buzzed, signalling an incoming SMS message. Believing it might be from MI6, perhaps alerting me of Anna Dupont, I took the unusual step of looking at it while in company. 'Please excuse me for a moment,' I said. After viewing it, I laughed before reading it aloud.

'Hey Mum, I'm stuck at the petrol station and have the wrong debit card. I urgently need $145 sent to my other account if you can BSB: 670899 Account: 1200700.'

Jonathan grinned. 'Obviously, it's a scam. You're too young to have adult children.'

'I am,' I replied in good humour. 'They're a real pest, the scams, I mean, aren't they? Sometimes I get two or three a day and you know that it's only a matter of time before one gets you.'

'It's about to become a lot worse,' William said.

'How so?' I replied.

'Have you heard of WormGPT?'

Jonathan and Anna shook their heads. I pretended to be ignorant, 'No, not WormGPT. I know about ChatGPT. Are they the same thing?'

William was about to speak when a waiter appeared at our table. 'Are you ready to order?'

'Sorry,' William replied, 'We've been talking.'

The server nodded. 'That's fine Sir, I will come back.'

William asked, 'Can we get something to drink?'

'The meal comes with wine and water. You are welcome to order something in addition, beer perhaps.'

William smiled apologetically. 'Oh, I see. Perhaps give us a few more minutes.'

When the server left, William asked if we wanted something other than wine. Jonathan said he wasn't a big drinker of alcohol, to which William replied, 'I thought I recalled you sipping from a wineglass in Roncesvalles and again today.'

'You did, William.' He laughed; 'The Camino seems to have that effect on people, although my beverage was non-alcoholic.'

William nodded, 'With virtually no public toilets along "The Way" and having to use the facilities in the bars, there are only so many coffees a person can consume.'

Jonathan smiled. 'Sparkling water for me.'

William looked at me. 'What about you, Claudia? A beer, perhaps a cocktail?'

In keeping with my guise of being the potential Mrs. Swindon, I also requested water. Luck had been on my side today.

When we arrived at the hotel and Jonathan offered to buy me a drink. Ordinarily I would have asked for wine.

Anna shrugged her shoulders, 'Red wine for me, William. You and I can stagger along the trail together tomorrow.'

That's interesting. It seems Anna Dupont has joined our little walking troupe. I'll need to text Stephen for another pin.

The waiter returned, and we made our choices from the set course menu and ordered our drinks.

When the server left, William continued, 'I was telling you about WormGPT. It is the evil cousin of ChatGPT, artificial intelligence from the depths of the dark web designed for the malicious mass deployment for hacking, spamming and disinformation.'

'It sounds awful,' I said, and Anna agreed.

William nodded. 'It allows bad actors to mimic the real deal in attempts to swindle and deceive people. Claudia, you can say goodbye to a poorly targeted "Hi Mum" scam email or SMS. They're about to get a lot more sophisticated by turning online crooks into computerised chameleons who adeptly target their unsuspecting victims. They will generate voice, video and conversational styles, making it harder to identify scams. Your caller ID will show your daughter is calling and the voice will be identical to hers.'

I knew from my work with MI6 that the cybersecurity community was bracing for a maelstrom of malicious cyberattacks, but not wanting to give my true identity away, held my tongue. Instead, I shook my head in disbelief. 'It's hard enough as it is. Once you could rely on the typo-ridden scam emails.' With humour colouring my voice, I added, 'That's it, no children for me. Sorry, Jonathan.'

Jonathan blushed and ignored my quip before he said. 'It's difficult not to fall victim to the scammers with their use of subterfuge, doctored websites, and calibrated software scripts to persuade someone to give up their personal information. "Social engineering" is what it's called, because it relies on people's typical emotions and behaviours. AI will make it harder to detect phishing scams.'

Anna grimaced. 'In the future, we will all have to be AI and cybercrime experts. I read a story about a scam in the paper today. Had it happened to me, I'd have fallen prey. There was a couple buying a new SUV. The dealer sent them a PDF invoice for payment, but unbeknownst to the purchasers, hackers intercepted the email and altered the car dealer's bank account details. As a result, the payment ended up in the criminals' bank account.'

I shook my head in mock disbelief. 'That's terrible.'

William nodded in agreement. His expression serious, he leaned in towards the centre of the table. 'I've developed something to thwart these cyber criminals.' Our curiosity piqued; we all turned our attention to him. 'I believe I mentioned previously that I used to work for BAE Systems, primarily on military projects...'

I knew that, but this was the first time he'd brought it up with this group.

'...so, I'm kind of an expert.' William leaned in further, as though about to reveal a closely guarded secret. We leaned closer in eager anticipation. 'Businesses will print invoices on something that I've called "paper", which is then delivered to your front door as a "letter", by an organisation I've dubbed "The Postal Service".'

'Nonsense,' Anna retorted, sitting upright in her chair. 'How would postage for mail items to be delivered be paid? It would be far too complicated.'

William grinned and playfully tapped the side of his nose with his index finger. 'Postage stamps. They'll serve as proof that the sender has covered the mailing costs to its destination.'

We all laughed. Jonathan chiming in, 'Brilliant, William, that is absolutely brilliant.'

William, the shy man, was revelling in the attention. 'But wait, there's more!'

'More!' we each repeated in mock unison.

'Yes. I worked on stealth communications for the Royal Navy.'

I knew this was not accurate; Samantha was the one who worked on communications. However, I assumed it was part of the joke he was about to share.

'It was all hush-hush, you understand. With the return of epic showdowns on the high seas and the ever-present threat of nosey adversaries trying to eavesdrop on your salty banter, we at BAE Systems came up with the... "Semaphore"–your go-to ship-to-ship stealthy chit-chat tool. The secret Semaphore relies on sneakily effective, visual signalling tricks, like.' William lowered his voice and whispered. 'Flags and Morse code sent via light shows.' William sat up straight and saluted before adding in a firm and confident voice. 'Be assured, your secrets are safe with Semaphore as it clandestinely weaves a web of secure communication for the Royal Navy.'

I grinned and said, 'Is there an app for that?' A ripple of laughter circled the table. Secretly, I wondered whether William's mention of BAE Systems was a subtle message for Anna, a way of confirming his identity and what he was carrying.

Am I reading too much into his light-hearted banter?

I would need to watch closely our new friend Anna Dupont.

Anna wore a sombre expression, a sign that she was about to be serious. 'Ah, mais oui, letters, like bank branches, are becoming relics of the past, heading down the path of dinosaurs to extinction.'

William nodded, a grin spreading across his face as if he were signalling his intent to lighten the mood again. 'Yeah, next time you see me, I'll be texting my brains out'. His comment elicited a cheerful giggle from Anna. I thought it unusual.

To our surprise, the server returned with a bottle of wine each for William and Anna, plus a bottle of sparkling water for Jonathan and me. When a meal comes with wine, a full bottle is supplied. If one wanted red while the other white—a bottle for each is supplied.

***

With entrées completed, the main course devoured and desserts being served, I discreetly observed my companions engaged in lively conversation. The effortless way they interacted prompted me to reflect on the complexities of human nature and the concealed layers each person carried, akin to hidden compartments within a labyrinthine puzzle. Everyone shielded themselves with their own facade, the persona they projected to the world, self-concealed behind a crafted mask. I wondered if any of my fellow pilgrims were truly who they claimed to be. The person I was sent to watch, William Marshal, the retired physicist, intrigued me the most. A man who was consumed by top-secret projects.

Why would he now betray his country?

The Camino's tranquillity stood in stark contrast to the world of espionage. Yet secrets could fester anywhere, even beneath the warm Spanish sun. An unsettling feeling persisted; something more was afoot. Anna Dupont, the latest addition to our group, who'd crossed paths with William in Paris a few days before. Suspicion gnawed at me.

Is Anna more than a seasoned traveller?

Her demeanour was of sophistication and it didn't align with the profile of a Camino pilgrim.

Is she a foreign agent?

I lacked evidence to support my hunch. Jonathan Swindon? In contrast to the others, he appeared straightforward: 34-year-old on a quest for a life partner, committed to his faith and finding love. I experienced a rare pang of guilt as I watched the handsome American. The possibility of me assuming the role of Mrs. Swindon was a charade.

Sorry, Jonathan.

CHAPTER 8
Bull Run

Claudia

Our quartet departed Pamplona at the crack of dawn, embarking on the journey toward Puente La Reina, a quaint town situated 25 kilometres (15.53 miles) away. 5 kilometres into our trek, we were on the outskirts of Cizur Menor. Nestled southwest of Pamplona, the town was framed by the rivers Arga and Elorz and embraced by the majestic mountains of Peñas de Etxauri and Alto del Perdón our ultimate destination before descending to Puente La Reina.

To my delight, Anna proposed a detour into Cizur Menor. She suggested we explore the town, enjoy a hearty breakfast, and savour a cup of "cafe con leche," coffee with milk, our first of the day. 'Lead on,' William, replied, 'Coffee awaits.'

While the break was undeniably enjoyable, my silent calculations hinted that the deviation had tacked an additional 2 kilometres onto our day's journey. Mentally noting this, I resolved to propose during our evening meal, that we minimise detours—the walk was already arduous enough. A hunch told me that by day's end, Anna and William, being in their sixties, would arrive at the same conclusion.

Our upcoming destination was Zariquiegui, 6 kilometres beyond Cizur Menor. The trail had been steadily ascending and when we spotted the town, our spirits lifted. It was a welcoming spot to rest, refuel, and attend to nature's call. Armed with ham and cheese rolls, plus another cup of coffee, we unburdened ourselves of our day packs and settled on the ground outside the eatery. Other pilgrims, sharing the same path, joined us in an impromptu gathering. Nibbling on our provisions, faces that had become somewhat familiar from our journey since St. Jean surrounded us.

While I already knew the names of a few, formal introductions were exchanged, and camaraderie blossomed during casual conversation. Our walking schedules meant that we'd likely cross paths with these fellow pilgrims again. Friendship was already developing with some of them, and their presence brought me genuine pleasure. And it seemed William and Jonathan felt a similar connection.

The predominant topic of discussion revolved around an American couple not far ahead of us, pushing their soon-to-be-one-year-old son, James, in a pram along the length of the Camino. The name "Baby James" had become a familiar phrase in our conversations, though I had yet to catch sight of them. Alesa, a vibrant American in her late twenties, shared her insights from a previous Camino, telling us that the descent from the summit was rocky, steep, and challenging, seemingly impossible to attempt with a pram.

Chinmay, an Australian man of Indian heritage, was around my age and walking with Federica from Germany and Katerine, fondly known as Kat, from California. Engrossed in Alesa's vivid depiction of the challenging descent, Chinmay, in a surge of determination, rose to his feet, drawing our collective gaze.

'Right,' he snapped. 'I'll catch up with you all in Puente La Reina. I'll attempt to catch up with baby James and offer a hand with their pram, providing the parents an opportunity to manoeuvre down the mountain safely.' Without waiting for any response, he dashed off.

'What a remarkable man,' Anna said. Turning to Federica and Kat, she asked, 'Is he always like that?'

'I don't know,' Kat replied. 'We all met for the first time in Roncesvalles at an Albergue.'

As Kat spoke, I noticed Jonathan's eyes tracing her form. After all, he was in search of the future Mrs. Swindon. Federica and

Kat were both undeniably attractive women and were probably one or two years younger than me. I wasn't eager to compete with them.

Five minutes after Chinmay's departure, Kat suggested to Federica that they should leave. Unlike William, Jonathan, Anna and myself, whose packs had been shipped forward, the two women were shouldering the weight of everything they needed on their backs. With ease, Kat swung her sizeable pack onto her shoulders, prompting Jonathan to inquire, 'How heavy is it?'

'Twenty kilos,' Kat responded.

'Twenty kilos,' Jonathan echoed. 'That's impressive... hey, Kat, with the twenty-kilo pack.' The rhyme elicited smiles from both of them, and it was clear Jonathan liked her. Kat had become a potential threat; someone I might need to eliminate.

Leaving behind the comforting embrace of Zariquiegui, the path ascended through rolling hills adorned with wildflowers, the landscape unfolding like a watercolour painting, each step revealing a panorama of the Spanish countryside. As the ascent continued, the trail transformed into a rocky path, testing the resolve of William, who told us that his feet were hurting. Nevertheless, with each step, I could see his anticipation growing. The summit of Alto del Perdón gradually emerged on the horizon, its iconic metal sculpture of medieval pilgrims leaning into the wind, standing tall against the expansive sky.

Reaching the summit, panoramic views stretched in all directions, the valleys, distant villages, and undulating hills beneath. Surrounded by silhouettes of wind turbines and gazing at the sculpture dedicated to all Camino Del Santiago pilgrims—an elongated metal artwork depicting those on foot and horseback—to my surprise, I experienced a profound connection to the countless souls who'd embarked on this journey before me.

How extraordinary!

I knew that Jonathan's powerful faith would allow me to leverage this experience and guide him towards me by framing the surroundings as a spiritual moment.

Sharing the summit with fellow pilgrims, we waited our turn to photograph the sculpture, ensuring a moment free of other travellers in our images. Posing amidst the symbolic pilgrims, donkeys and horses, our group embarked on an impromptu photo shoot. Taking advantage of the moment, I took a clandestine photo of Anna as she posed within the sculpture, intending to forward it to MI6 later for a background check. I beckoned Jonathan to join me, and together we stood before the sculpture. I read aloud to him the Spanish inscription on it: "donde se cruza el camino del viento con el de las estrellas."

With a feigned quiver in my voice, I said, 'It means "where the path of the wind crosses that of the stars." It is beautiful... The words linger in the air, don't they?'

Jonathan nodded in agreement.

Now, girly. For the manipulation.

'Don't you think that the poetry gives this summit spiritual significance, as if these windswept heights bear a bond between our earthly journey and our heavenly destiny?'

Jonathan nodded, and we shared a moment of contemplation. He said, 'I am in harmony with the inscription. Pilgrimage is not merely a physical challenge; it represents spiritual journey. Before undertaking the pilgrimage, I couldn't envisage how much I would be moved by the trek.'

I had the urge to touch Jonathan's arm, but decided against it. Instead, I remained silent for a moment before saying, 'This is truly a wonderful experience.' Glancing at Jonathan, I realised he wasn't listening; he was scanning those at the summit. He was searching for Kat. Casting my eyes around, I realised Kat and Federica were nowhere to be seen. *They must have begun the descent*, I thought, and I hoped we would not encounter them in Puente La Reina.

The descent from the summit of Alto del Perdón presented a formidable challenge with its ever-changing surfaces. It was a rugged journey, requiring caution and stamina. The steep, unforgiving path unfolded with uneven steps and washouts where erosion had sculpted a precarious dance between stability and peril into the rocky terrain. Jagged loose stones formed a treacherous mosaic, poised to betray the weight of each footfall, putting the ability of even someone as young, strong, and athletic as me to the test.

I pondered how William and Anna, my fellow pilgrims, were coping with the arduous terrain. When I inquired, they both offered a stoic, 'Fine,' though I sensed they were hiding the truth. Anna, having not shipped her luggage, was carrying her pack. If she was speaking the truth, was this evidence of her being a foreign operative? As I gingerly placed my foot on the uneven ground, I realised a misstep would bring an abrupt end to my Camino adventure and my assignment. I chose my footing carefully.

'How on earth did Baby James manage this?' I called out to William and Anna.

William, steadying his balance with one of his walking poles, responded, 'His parents are foolhardy or demand our admiration. I hope that young man... what was his name?'

'Chinmay,' I said.

'Yes, Chinmay. Well, I hope he caught up with them in time. The pusher and baby had to be carried down this. There is no other way.'

Anna added, 'I hope we see Chinmay and the other young ones tonight; they were all delightful, especially Kat with her twenty-kilo pack.' Anna giggled at the rhyme.

I smiled through gritted teeth, 'Yes, that would be lovely.' Women have a sixth sense for rivalry, and I wondered if Anna was upsetting my plan of using Jonathan to stay close to William. *Was this further evidence of her being a foreign operative?*

'I hope so too,' Jonathan added, then remarked, 'Thank goodness it's not raining. This track would be impassable in the wet. Water would cascade down these washouts like a river, making traversing it impossible. I'm tempted to slide down on my bottom as it is.'

Anna smiled. 'Maybe that's how Baby James has done it, bumped all the way down the mountain on his butt.'

The banter distracted us from the arduous trek without diminishing our concentration. In what seemed like an impossibly short time, the trail levelled out and reverted to an easy track. We'd made it.

Walking last in line as we approached Puente La Reina, I observed the others.

The Camino works in mysterious ways.

Although Anna had joined our party only the night before, it was as if she'd been with us all along.

This does not bode well. If there is a spark of interest between Kat and Jonathan, the flame could ignite quickly.

I was more convinced than ever that I would have to take care .of her.

But perhaps flirting with Chinmay might redirect Jonathan's interest back to me? Perhaps doing both was the likely solution. What happened, Claudia, to slowly reeling Jonathan in?

***

William Marshal

Puente La Reina wasn't as I'd imagined it would be. It was more extensive, a town where time seemed to have frozen, preserving the rich fabric of its medieval past. At its core was the eponymous 'Bridge of the Queen,' a masterpiece of Romanesque architecture spanning the Arga River. To my eyes, the bridge, adorned with six majestic arches, wasn't simply a stone structure, more a surviving testament to the town's history. Jonathan told us it bore witness to the footsteps of countless pilgrims embarking on their sacred journey. I noticed Claudia nodding enthusiastically and wondered if her reaction was true or staged for Jonathan's benefit.

Retracing our steps, we found our hotel perched above a busy cafe on the main street, a narrow cobblestone road leading to the famous bridge. There we bade farewell to Anna, who had secured lodgings at an Albergue, agreeing to reconvene for drinks in an hour and a half, time enough to shower and have a nano-nap to recharge.

Alone in my dimly lit room, I fixated on the ornate mirror that adorned the wall, its surface casting a distorted reflection of my surroundings. As my gaze lingered, I contemplated the characters who accompanied me on this walk, and those yet to come. I engaged in a mental chess game, attempting to unravel the identity of the elusive British agent undoubtedly hidden among them.

Deciphering a spy's identity was a formidable challenge, yet a sly smile curled on my lips as I scrutinised the visage staring back at me. In that introspective moment, an unspoken truth emerged. Without a doubt, I was the most astute mind in the room. My confidence in my intellect and cunning dared to surpass that of British Intelligence itself. Over the years, I'd deftly utilised the organisation designed to outwit others, turning their machinations to my advantage. My smile broadened as I mused on the wealth and influence I'd accrued through a labyrinth of clever manoeuvres. My innate ability had allowed me to dance on the razor's edge, navigating a world of crime, shadows and secrets, always one step ahead. I revelled in this game; the grandmaster, orchestrating every move on the chessboard.

The echo of my reference to the Knights Templar for MI6 lingered in my thoughts. It was a calculated truth intertwined with a cunning diversion. A giggle escaped me, stifled immediately as I remembered the potential of eavesdropping devices in my vicinity. A cautious tap to my nose served as a reminder to tread carefully. I pondered. Had any of my companions understood the subtle semaphore clue of Pamplona?

I knew they hadn't.

I was signalling my preference for analogue, rendering phone and computer monitoring futile. When the time came for payment, it would be communicated through the tried and tested methods, pen and paper. Another thought crossed my mind. While working, I maintained a low-key presence on social media because of the sensitive nature of my job. Now that I'm retired, the restrictions have been lifted, allowing me to engage online. I couldn't resist the temptation to share snippets of my Camino's journey, a perfect way of stirring the waters, casting ripples of intrigue in my wake. The semaphore clue and social media posts were perfect contradictions.

Clever, William.

I gazed at my reflection again. Humans, apes, dolphins, and some birds share the ability to recognise themselves in a mirror. It's a test designed to reveal whether a creature comprehends itself as an individual, a skill that implies higher intelligence. I whispered silently, 'I will put Claudia's intellect to the test, for I am convinced that among those around me, she is the MI6 agent.'

The Camino was my escape and also the last chance to indulge myself at the secret service's expense. Once the walk was over, I'd no longer be valuable. A twinge of guilt gnawed at me as I grappled with the shame of betraying Hannah's memory. Throughout my life, I had played the roles of Dr. Jekyll and Mr. Hyde, but I was relieved that she'd never uncovered the truth. Stevenson had eloquently captured the duality of human nature, the notion that within each person exists good and evil. This concept resonated with me as a physicist; in superposition, particles could exist in multiple states simultaneously. Confronting my reflection in the mirror, now unworried by eavesdroppers, I recited, 'Mr. Utterson, the lawyer, was a man of rugged countenance, never illuminated by a smile; cold, scanty, and embarrassed in discourse; backward in sentiment; lean, long, dusty, dreary, and yet somehow lovable.'

***

Claudia

The proprietress of our lodgings, with her broken English, conveyed that our luggage awaited us in the cafe basement. Since the lift could only accommodate two people at a time, Jonathan and William took the first ride down to retrieve their packs. They then ascended to the first floor to reach their rooms. As I waited, my phone buzzed, signalling an incoming text message. The words illuminated on the screen: "Church of Santiago." MI6 was directing me. The pins I had ordered were waiting for me there. I tap my chin.

You have a choice girly: either leave now or gather your belongings and bring them to your room first. Room!

***

The Church stood close to our lodgings, sharing the same cobblestone road. Jonathan would have perceived its weathered walls as a sanctuary exuding an aura of spirituality, whispering tales of pilgrims. Although my perspective was different, I knew we'd encounter many churches, and I needed to be prepared for Jonathan's fascination with each.

What would I say to him when we reached the next church?

A line from Shakespeare's Henry VI immediately sprung to mind. "Now, God be praised, that to believing souls gives light in darkness, comfort in despair." Yes, I mused, Jonathan would fall for that eloquent expression of faith.

As I stepped inside, the subdued lighting demanded that my eyes adjust. The flickering candles and the sunlight streaming through the stained-glass windows cast a warm glow, revealing the beauty of the interior. The space was embellished with elaborate stained-glass windows and weathered wooden pews, evoked memories of other churches I had visited. My gaze fell upon a solitary figure dressed in the attire of a brother seated at the front.

Without turning to acknowledge my presence, he spoke. 'This church was built in the 12th century, reformed and extended in the 15th century with the addition of Gothic-style elements. The portico and the chapter room are from the original Romanesque church, and the altarpiece dates back to the 18th century.'

I nodded. 'The altarpiece takes your breath away.'

Turning, he signalled for me to come closer before inquiring, 'Are you religious, Claudia?'

He used my name with such certainty that it compelled an honest response, though I could have lied, knowing the Bible intimately. 'I consider myself a spiritual person, finding meaning and connection through my personal beliefs and experiences. While I may not strictly adhere to traditional religious practices, I deeply value and explore my spirituality. I hold great respect for the teachings of Christianity.' Not wanting a theological debate, I asked. 'Do you have something for me?'

'Stephen mentioned you are impatient, and he is correct.'

'I apologise, Brother. Is it Brother?'

'Yes. Brother Artōrius. Please, call me Artōrius.'

'I didn't mean to be rude, Brother Artōrius. Accept my apology if I offended you.'

Brother Artōrius adjusted the collar of his worn brown robe and looked at me with a friendly smile. His weathered hands reached for a package beside him on the pew and he presented it to me. As I accepted it, he said, 'There's a stall in the town square that sells Camino trinkets. If your friends inquire, tell them you bought them there.'

'Do they have others?'

'Flags from all over the world?' he enquired.

I nodded.

'Yes. Your friends will find similar pins at the stall.'

'Excellent.' Ready to leave, I turned as a question surfaced in my mind. 'What do you know of the Knights Templar on the Camino?'

'Ah, the Knights Templar on the Camino,' Brother Artōrius muttered, his eyes reflecting the flickering candlelight in the dimly lit space. 'It's a fascinating chapter in history, though I must confess that I'm no expert on the matter. However, I can share what I know.'

He gestured for me to join him on the pew where a leather-bound book lay open. Brother Artōrius ran his fingers over the ancient pages, whispering words of a prayer before gently closing it. Stroking his chin, he said, 'The Knights Templar were a medieval Christian military order formed in the 12th century. Their mission was to protect Christian pilgrims on their journey to the Holy Land during the time of the Crusades. But, when the Holy Land fell, many Templars returned to Europe, and some found themselves on the Camino de Santiago.' Brother Artōrius leaned back, folding his hands. 'Legend has it that the Templars, seeking refuge and a new purpose, established a network of safe houses, hospitals, and even banks along the Camino. They became protectors of pilgrims, ensuring their safety on the road to Santiago de Compostela. The romanticised notion of the Knights Templar on the Camino persists, adding intrigue to pilgrims' journeys.'

I nodded, although he was telling me nothing I didn't know. 'Do you think there's any truth to the tales of hidden Templar treasures along the Camino?'

Brother Artōrius chuckled, 'Ah, the allure of hidden treasures always captures the imagination, doesn't it? While some believe the Templars may have hidden relics or riches along the way, whether this is true remains a mystery. The Camino is a spiritual journey, a path for every pilgrim to discover their own treasures amidst experiences and reflections along the route.' He paused, meeting my gaze. 'Whether it's the history of the Templars or the spiritual quest of the modern pilgrim, the Camino has a way of revealing secrets and lessons to those who walk its ancient path.'

'Thank you, Brother Artōrius. It's always enlightening to learn more about the rich Camino history. One more thing before I leave. What do you know about the Parish Church of Rabanal del Camino?'

I noticed Brothers Artōrius' eyes twitch with a spark of recognition when I mentioned the Church. 'The Parish Church of Rabanal del Camino has great significance for the Camino, especially for those interested in the Templars. This humble church served as a key site for the Knights Templar during their time along the pilgrimage route. Rabanal del Camino was strategically located, making it a natural stop for pilgrims and a crucial point for the Templars to carry out their duties. They established a presence there, using the church as a command post or a place of rest. They ensured the safety of pilgrims and maintained order along the Camino, but some believe that the Templars had a spiritual connection to that location, as if they sensed a significance beyond their earthly duties. As with many aspects of Templar history, the specifics are elusive, shrouded in the mists of time. But Rabanal del Camino remains a place where the Templars' presence echoes, a testimony to their safeguarding role for those who journeyed towards Santiago de Compostela.'

'Safeguarding the pilgrims?'

Brother Artōrius smiled, 'So it would seem, my dear.'

I thanked Brother Artōrius and stood to leave. As I rose, he placed a hand on my arm. 'The Camino holds much waiting to be discovered. As you continue your own journey, may you find inspiration in the footsteps of pilgrims and knights who once trod this sacred path.'

'I have a job to do, Brother and little time for the mystery and speculation that surrounds the Camino.'

'Yes, my dear, but the Camino has a way of touching those who undertake the pilgrimage.' He paused before adding, 'The Templars had a notable castle in Ponferrada too, known as the Castillo de los Templarios. It served as a stronghold and another significant place along the Camino.'

Why did he mention Ponferrada?

***

Back at our lodgings, I freshened up with a shower and a change of clothes before heading down to the bar. There, I found William, Jonathan and Anna waiting for me. William sported the same blue hiking shirt from the previous day, leading me to surmise, that like myself, he was rotating between two sets of clothes, one to wear, the other being washed, or stamped on in my case, while I was showering. I imagined William was doing the same.

Ordering a pint of the local brew, I joined my walking companions at the table. The bar was abuzz with locals, indulging in the pleasures of drinking and enjoying tapas. *Darn!* I castigated myself.

Sloppy, girly, very sloppy.

I was drinking alcohol. My pretence of being a non-drinker was blown. What to do?

Behave as if nothing was out of the ordinary.

'It must be siesta time,' I remarked, observing the proprietor closing the front door. 'I wonder how long they'll be shut? Do we have to leave, or can we stay since we're guests?'

Jonathan surveyed the scene. 'No one else is paying attention. Let's ask,' he suggested, spotting the proprietor nearby, a woman in her fifties and, from her engagement with customers, she seemed a vibrant spirit. Her sun-kissed skin spoke of years spent under the Spanish sun, and her eyes, though weathered by time, sparkled, welcoming patrons like old friends. Dark, wavy hair framed her face, partially hidden by a colourful scarf that danced as she stepped forward. Draped in a flowing, embroidered blouse and a long skirt that swirled around her as she moved, she possessed effortless elegance. Silver jewellery adorned her fingers and wrists and her laughter was melodic, reverberating around the establishment. As the heart and soul of the bar, she commanded the attention of both locals and travellers.

Jonathan raised his hand to catch her attention, asking, 'Do we have to leave?'

She shrugged her shoulders, showing her lack of understanding. Jonathan pointed to the closed front door, and the woman's face lit up with excitement. Placing her hands on her forehead, with index fingers extended, she moved her head in a way that mimicked a bull charging, saying, 'Toro.'

'Bulls?' I questioned, intrigued.

'Si, bulls,' she affirmed, repeating her animated act. She then pointed to an open door on the side of the bar, where people were coming and going. In her broken English, which added to the charm of the place, she explained, gesturing towards the front of the cafe, 'Um. Go lane, see bulls run main street.'

I grinned at my companions. 'Puente la Reina has its own bull run, and we're here for it!' Turning to the proprietor, I exclaimed, 'Ahora.'

'Si,' she replied.

'It's happening now,' I said to my friends.

Sloppy, girly, sloppy, I scolded myself silently for the second time. I had spoken in Spanish and hoped my companions hadn't caught on. This is not like you Claudia! I don't make mistakes and that was the second.

At a neighbouring table, a Spanish man, who had overheard our conversation with the proprietor, turned to us and spoke in flawless English. 'This weekend is our Traditional Fair, but today, Sunday, is the main event with the Bull runs. It takes place right outside. The cobblestone road is blocked at each end, and the bulls run up and down. You must be nimble of foot to get out of the way. Please, you must all come and watch.' Brimming with excitement, he rose to his feet and gestured for us to follow him outside.

He led us to a large gate crafted from steel, its surface bearing a patina of rust, which separated the laneway beside the bar from the cobblestone road out front. The gate's frame was a lattice of horizontal bars, vantage points for onlookers who positioned themselves to view the bull run and the awaiting matadors, mostly young men ranging from their mid-teens to thirties. I hoped the gate was securely affixed to its sturdy hinges.

Turning to face me, our Spanish guide said, 'You should give it a try!'

I laughed. 'It seems more of a bloke thing.'

He nodded as I watched William and Anna jostle for a position on the gate with the other onlookers before I asked, 'When the bulls come, how do the runners get over the gate if the escape route is blocked by spectators?' He shrugged. 'They just do. I hope you enjoy the spectacle.' He didn't bid us goodbye, simply turning to head back to the bar.

Positioned behind William and Anna, I gazed out at the bull run while eavesdropping on their conversation. Their interaction carried a familiarity, a friendship forged by the passage of time. Astonishingly to me, they revealed that they'd met briefly in Paris and then, by chance, again just yesterday in Pamplona. The seamless exchange of banter and the ease of shared silences suggested a stronger bond than was possible after a few days together. As I pondered their attachment, a question floated into my mind.

Had it truly been days since their paths first crossed, or was their rapid friendship a testament to the unique spirit of the Camino?

Here, amidst the journey, it seemed people often experienced instant connections that defied the conventional constraints of time.

'Do you want to, William?' Anna said.

'It's not me, Anna. It's the boys in the street. They want me to climb over and join them.'

'The call of youth, ah!' Anna chuckled. When William didn't respond, she added, 'Go on then, climb over and run with the bulls. You know you want to.'

To my surprise, William smiled excitedly and climbed over the gate to join the other participants in the street.

'Well, I never,' I murmured under my breath as William entered the bull run.

Jonathan and I positioned ourselves among the spectators, each of us vying for a prime spot on the gate. We shouted good-naturedly at him, 'You're mad!' William turned, grinning at us like a Cheshire cat revelling in his mischief. Pointing, I yelled, 'Watch out!'

While William remained oblivious, the enchanting medieval architecture suddenly framed a chaotic scene as the first bull burst into sight. Its powerful hooves clattered against the cobblestones, sending goosebumps down my spine. A tightly packed crowd, all standing shoulder to shoulder along the escape route, collectively held their breath in a moment of shared anticipation. The bull, a magnificent creature with a sleek, muscular form, charged down the narrow streets, its breath billowing out clouds of steam. The confined space created a challenge for both bull and runners. Unfazed, William turned and faced the approaching danger. Everyone involved was assessing the perfect moment to vault the fence, aiming for the thrill of the very last second. As the bull thundered towards William, residents leaned out from their balconies, cheering on the courageous and we erupted into cheers.

'Now!' I called to William, stepping down and back from the gate to give him space to scale it. With a swift agility that belied his age, he pulled himself up as the bull roared by. Once the danger had passed, he jumped back into the narrow street below to await the next encounter.

Returning to my vantage spot, Jonathan said, 'He's daring, isn't he?'

'Yes, he is,' I said, labouring my words.

William beckoned to me. 'Come and join me, Claudia.'

The bull run held no fear for me; my only anxiety was for William's safety. Jonathan's eyes were upon me; he was waiting for my response.

What would the future Mrs. Swindon do?

I considered that Jonathan, being a conservative Christian, likely adhered to traditional gender roles rooted in his interpretation of biblical teachings, where women have primarily responsible for nurturing and supporting the family. Not wanting to appear overly daring and a drinker, I smiled and shook my head. 'Best not be foolhardy.'

William waved to someone standing behind me. Jonathan and I turned in unison to see Kat. I heard William call out, 'What about you, Kat? Will you climb over?'

'I wouldn't miss it for the world,' she shouted back enthusiastically as I moved aside to allow her to climb over the gate.

Jonathan said, 'She's brave, isn't she?'

I pretended not to hear.

'She's brave, isn't she?' he repeated.

'Yes, indeed,' I said through gritted teeth. Now my mistakes tallied three. As things come in threes, I was now clear for the rest of my mission.

'And quite beautiful, don't you think?'

How should I respond to that?

Anna, who was standing on the other side of Jonathan, overheard the conversation and added, 'Yes Jonathan, she's a very attractive woman. Intelligent, witty, and brave too. I will invite her to have dinner with us tonight.'

Well, thank you, Anna! That is all I need.

Jonathan turned his attention to Anna, and they chatted like nervous spouses watching their loved ones engaging in an extreme sport. Cheering erupted from the crowd, signalling a charging bull. When Kat and William mounted the gate, Anna and Jonathan greeted them like conquering heroes. In my luggage, I kept a liquid solution for situations like Kat. Two drops of it in her drink and she'd be bed bound for twenty-four hours. By the time she recovered, we'd be a day's walk away.

Come in to my parlour, said the spider to the fly.

***

The Puente La Reina fair was still in full swing when we retreated to our bar for dinner. The dim lighting, clinking of cutlery and the murmur of conversations created a lively atmosphere. Kat, Jonathan, William, Anna, and I sat around a rustic wooden table. A scent of paella wafted through the air as we indulged in dinner. My friends were blissfully unaware of the unfolding drama. From across the table, I watched Jonathan and Kat and we each listened intently as Jonathan leaned in and asked in a curious tone, 'So, Kat, tell me more about yourself. Where are you from?'

Kat smiled, her eyes reflecting a mix of nostalgia and warmth. 'I'm thirty-two, have a degree in environmental science and originally from California, born and raised. My parents are wonderful people who still attend the local church there. Growing up, we were involved in mission and voluntary work, especially in Mexico and Africa. It was a formative experience and has helped shape my perspective on life.'

'Wow, that's impressive,' Jonathan said.

She's beautiful and religious. I bet Kat is scoring high on the future Mrs. Swindon points.

'Thank you,' Kat said. Have I told you I was a dancer once?'

Is there anything you can't do?

Jonathan's eyes lit up. 'No. This is interesting! Really interesting!'

'Absolutely. I started dancing when I was a child. It became a significant part of my life, and I pursued it professionally, specialising in ballet. I danced in classical pieces like Swan Lake and The Nutcracker. There's something magical about the stage and the discipline it instils.'

Now she's an Anna Pavlova.

Intrigued, Jonathan leaned back, his curiosity piqued. 'That's amazing. What made you shift gears from the world of dance to something like environmental science?'

Kat chuckled, her fingers tracing the rim of her wineglass which held sparkling water.

She has water, when I have wine!

'Life has its twists and turns, doesn't it? After a career as a ballerina, I felt the need for a new challenge. I pursued a degree in environmental science, after which I fell into a job as a white-water rafting guide on outdoor adventures. It was an exhilarating change, being close to nature. Now I'm studying to be a paramedic and hope to work in search and rescue.'

William, who had been listening intently, said, 'That's quite a transition, Kat.'

'Is it?' Anna added. 'It seems to me you have a passion for helping people, and search and rescue is the perfect way to combine your skills and interests. Making a difference when it matters most.'

I observed Jonathan becoming entranced by the richness of Kat's experiences and the layers of her character. Her confidence spoke of the diversity of her life encounters. Her hair, a chestnut cascade, touched with sun-kissed highlights, framed her face adorned with subtle freckles. Almond-shaped eyes, a rich hazel, sparkled with a blend of warmth and determination as she recounted her life's journey. Though once a dancer, her long, slender fingers now gracefully traced patterns on her wineglass, a lingering echo of her past. If we'd met under different circumstances, we would be good friends, but Kat wouldn't be joining us tomorrow. I reached into my trouser pocket, fingers brushing a small vial containing a colourless, odourless liquid, my secret weapon, one that would induce something that appeared to be food poisoning.

The challenge was for me to introduce a dose discreetly into Kat's glass, a vessel she habitually fondled. Seizing the opportunity when William excused himself for the restroom, I moved into his position between Kat and Anna at the table. Displaying one of the Camino pins to the others, I explained that I'd brought one for each of us to wear on our packs. I apologised to Kat, claiming that I hadn't purchased one for her. Taking the bottle of sparkling water from the centre of the table, I asked Kat if she could pass over my glass. With finesse, I uncapped the vial and, as Kat leaned across the table, I took her glass, dripping a few drops of the concoction into her sparkling water as I topped it up.

Concealing the vial again in my pocket, I expressed gratitude as Kat handed me my near empty glass, which I promptly filled, water swirling into the remnants of my wine. Now it was only a matter of time.

As the evening unfolded, the effects of the drug took hold. Kat's vibrant laughter became subdued, and the sparkle in her gaze became distant. The poison worked its magic, clouding her senses and inducing a sense of fatigue. Kat was now becoming an unwitting player in my strategic game. Keeping a watchful eye on my rival, I continued to play my part, engaging in animated conversation with the group while keeping an eye on Jonathan. Sensing the impending shift in Kat's demeanour, I yawned, suggesting that we retire because of the challenging day of walking ahead. The consensus was unanimous; everyone agreed to call it a night. Anna and Kat left the bar together while Jonathan, William, and I ascended the stairs to our rooms. Before going our separate ways, we agreed to leave at seven thirty the following morning.

As I readied myself for bed, my phone abruptly buzzed. The MI6 message advised of a post by William on social media plus his simultaneous text to Anna, telling her of our departure time the following morning. After completing the ritual of brushing my teeth, I inspected William's post, wondering whether there would be a reference to the Knights Templar.

William's Social Media Post

Thrilling evening at Puente la Reina's festival. Bulls, adrenaline, and the Camino magic! Tomorrow, Mañeru awaits with its Knights Templar and Order of St. John history. Onward we go. For all roads to Compostela will be one.

'Is this a cryptic message?' I muttered.

I wouldn't know the connection between the Knights Templar, the Order of St. John, and Mañeru unless I understood it. Tapping the keys on my phone, I sent a message to MI6, asking for Brother Artōrius's help.

Within five minutes, my phone buzzed, signalling a message.

Villa de Mañeru is a place of historical significance that belonged to the Military Order of the Hospital of St. John of Jerusalem. Established by the Knight Templars in 1119 in Jerusalem, following the Crusaders in 1099.

Both the Knights Templar and St. John's are Christian military orders from the Middle Ages. The Knights Templar operated as a monastic order of knights devoted to protecting Christian pilgrims travelling to the Holy Land during the Crusades. Known for their financial activities, they were dissolved in the early 14th century.

Conversely, St. John's, recognised as the Knights Hospitaller, originated as a hospitaller order, dedicated to caring for sick and injured pilgrims. Over time, they transformed into a military order, active in the Crusades. Remarkably, they endure today as the Sovereign Military Order of Malta. The pivotal distinction lies in the Knights Templar's focus on guarding Christian pilgrims, while St. John prioritised their care.

Villa Mañeru and Puente de la Reina emerged as crossroads for pilgrims arriving from Roncesvalles and Somport (Camino Frances), converging with routes from Aragon and Navarre. As the legend goes, "For all roads to Compostela will be one."

Mañeru is a crossroad, my Dear Claudia.

'A crossroad,' I said. 'Crossroads are where paths converge! William is beckoning someone to meet him there.'

CHAPTER 9
Crossroad

Claudia

As we lingered outside our hotel, on the very road that had hosted the thrilling bull run the night before, I secured the Camino pins onto Jonathan and William's daypacks. Turning to Jonathan, I requested that he to do the same for mine. I held onto Anna's pin, eagerly awaiting her arrival. The moment a radiant smile graced William's face, I knew she was approaching. Passing him Anna's pin, I asked him to affix it to her pack. Anna inspected the pins, saying what a wonderful idea it was.

Without uttering a word about Kat, we departed Puente de la Reina, crossing the charming medieval bridge that led us to a delightful level path. Soon, the terrain transformed into an ascent along a steep ravine, offering breathtaking views back over the Rio Arga valley. It was during this climb that we encountered Athira, a 30-year-old Indian woman, navigating the Camino on her own. Carrying a heavy pack and walking with poles like William's, she was struggling with the difficult ascent. On my own, I might not have given her a second thought, but for Jonathan, I donned the compassionate persona of a Camino Pilgrim and asked her to join our team. I told Athira walking with us would prove a welcome distraction from the day's arduous trek. My offer was swiftly endorsed by my companions. Buoyed by their encouragement, Athira agreed to become part of our company. Judging by Jonathan and William's reactions, my display of compassion was received favourably, masking my undercover identity and earning future Mrs. Swindon points.

The ascent levelled off and as the village of Mañeru unfolded before us, William, catching sight of it, said, 'Let's stop there for breakfast.'

In the town square near the church of San Pedro, we settled on a bar with inviting outdoor seating. After placing my order, I discovered William was missing. Scanning the square, I spotted him engaged in a conversation with a Pilgrim, an unfamiliar man of similar age to William.

For a moment I considered joining them but thought better of it, fearing it might raise suspicions. Instead, I watched the stranger.

Around 65 years old, the man bore the weight of experience in the lines etched across his weathered face. A salt-and-pepper beard framed steel-rimmed glasses, and he dressed in layers, a worn sleeveless jacket over his olive-green hiking shirt. His wide-brimmed hat cast a shadow on the creases that criss-crossed his forehead, shielding his face from the morning sun. Durable khaki trousers bearing stains and scuffs, attested to his long journey and well-worn hiking boots were a testament to the miles they'd covered, dusted from the same rocky path we'd traversed. A lightweight daypack rested on his shoulders, rather than the bulkier backpacks carried by other pilgrims, a witness to him shipping his gear forward.

When William returned to our table, I hid my eagerness to ask about his encounter with the stranger. I hoped the others would raise the subject, but, engrossed in their breakfasts, nobody broached the subject. I took a slow sip of my brew and pondered on whether the meeting was suspicious.

Was this the meeting alluded to in the social media post?

My instincts told me there was more to the encounter than met the eye.

Leaving Mañeru as we passed through vineyards and olive trees, I fell in step with Athira, then slowed my pace and called out to the others, 'Wait for us in Cirauqui Plaza.' They waved in acknowledgement as Athira and I fell behind.

Athira's voice resonated with determined assurance as she spoke. 'Claudia, don't wait for me; I'll be fine.'

In response, I offered a reassuring smile and quipped, 'Who's waiting for you? This pace suits me just fine. Being from the UK, we Brits aren't quite accustomed to this heat.' I could sense Athira's lingering doubt, but my words provided comfort.

As we continued our conversation during the walk, my spy instincts kicked in and I assessed the young woman beside me. Athira, a thirty-year-old Indian with recent work experience in Norway, was now on a quest for a PhD placement in Germany. Her frame was stocky, lacking the athletic build often associated with those undertaking a long hike. The visible strain on Athira's face hinted at the difficulty of this endurance walk for her, exacerbated by the weight of her pack containing essentials for the journey. Despite the challenges, her determination shone through with each step. I admired her tenacity. At a height of only 172 centimetres, Athira's resilience was admirable, especially with the substantial load she bore. I felt her journey was physical and metaphorical, every step a testament to her inner strength. Under the scorching sun of the hot day, beads of perspiration glistened on her forehead, proof of her physical exertion. To conquer the Camino mirrored her broader quest for personal and academic achievement. Each step forward was not simply a stride along the path, more a leap towards the next chapter of her life.

'What is that?' I inquired, pointing towards a small stand adorned with an array of food, drinks, plus a few essentials that weary pilgrims might find useful.

Athira reached over, sampling some grapes and grabbing a bottle of water, leaving a generous donation in return. 'It's an honesty system,' she said. 'You don't have to pay, it's sustenance for the weary traveller. I read that kindness stalls date back to medieval days.' Her words carried a sense of appreciation for the age-old tradition, where generosity thrived on the goodwill of those passing through.

I wondered if she was Christian, deeming it unlikely. Concerned that Athira might misconstrue my inquiry, I hesitated for a moment. After careful thought, I phrased my question sensitively, 'What brought you to the Camino? Is it for religious or broader spiritual reasons?'

Athira paused for a moment, a thoughtful expression caressing her face. 'It's more of a personal journey for me. It's about self-discovery and finding a deeper meaning in life. The Camino felt like the right path for that exploration.' As she spoke, her eyes suggested introspection, hinting at the significance the journey held for her.

Brother Artōrius' words echoed in my mind:

'The Camino holds many stories waiting to be discovered. As you continue your own journey, may you find inspiration in the footsteps of both pilgrims and knights who once trod this sacred path.'

Eight kilometres after Mañeru we reached Cirauqui Plaza, a medieval village perched on a hill. Spotting the others waiting for us, they greeted Athira with a smile.

'You've made it, Athira. It's all downhill from here,' Anna said.

Athira responded with a light giggle, then said, 'We're heading to one of the best examples of a Roman Road on the Camino, but I've read that it's tough on the old feet.'

I thought nothing more of the conversation with Athira as we enjoyed our second coffee of the day. It wasn't until the stones of the Roman Road started cutting into the soles of my cross trainers, causing me considerable pain, that I recalled her words. In a whispered realisation to myself, I mused, 'Sometimes it's best not to know what the future holds. Then again, maybe I would have worn hiking boots.' The unexpected challenge served as a reminder that the Camino had its surprises and the journey was as much about adapting to the journey as it was about the destination ahead.

Despite my excellent physical condition, the last few kilometres proved challenging under the relentless heat. I marvelled at my companions' resilience as they pressed on without a single complaint. With Estella tantalizingly visible on the horizon, like a mirage of water in the desert, it stubbornly remained out of reach, teasing our longing with its elusive presence. The lively chatter of the morning dissipated, and a hush settled over us as we trekked in silence. Amid the discomfort of bruised feet, my mind focused on a question.

Why would William choose the Camino as the setting to smuggle stolen secrets? This makes no sense to me.

The trail descended, and the town of Estella gradually revealed its medieval splendour. The Church of San Pedro de la Rúa stood tall, its spires stroking the sky, guiding weary pilgrims to the heart of the historic enclave.

Before we entered the main town, a steep stone bridge appeared, and I noticed that William and Anna practically crawled over it, signalling their exhaustion from the walk. On the other side, a bar with outside tables caught my eye. 'It must be beer o'clock,' I called to my colleagues. William, spotting a vacant table and made a beeline for it, plonking himself down on one of the chairs.

Licking the salt from his parched lips, he apologised. 'Sorry, Claudia, I don't have the energy to move another muscle. Would you mind fetching me a pint?' After a brief pause, he added with a touch of politeness, 'Please.'

Anna, her face tinged with red from the exertion of the walk, settled down beside William. 'Will you make that two?'

'Of course,' I said, while watching William and Anna remove their walking shoes. I'd given up the pretence of not drinking and said, 'I'm having a beer too. Does anyone else want something?' Athira and Jonathan declined my offer, telling me they'd go inside and get their own drinks. Except for Jonathan, we each settled for beer. William and Anna recovered from the vigour of the day's walk remarkably and, within thirty minutes, they seemed relaxed and refreshed. I felt the same.

'Shall we do the walk again?' I asked in a humorous tone.

'No,' came the definitive reply.

The bar was nestled in an ideal location, strategically placed for the stream of fellow pilgrims we'd encountered regularly since St. Jean or crossed paths with once or twice. As they filed into town, waves and brief chats marked our interactions. We had inadvertently become a de facto welcoming committee, greeting conquering heroes upon their arrival.

Atop the stone bridge, I spotted the man, his beard and steel-rimmed glasses unmistakable from the conversation William had engaged in earlier. He began his descent, destined to pass by us. As he drew nearer, his eyes locked onto William's, and a friendly wave ensued. William, recognizing him, gestured for the man to join us. His name was Shaun, and his arrival signalled another round of beers.

Two pints before two thirty in the afternoon was an unknown phenomenon for each of us, and surprisingly, they slipped down without obvious effect other than quenching our thirsts. Shaun didn't stay with us long. He was a retired officer from the Canadian navy, lived on his own, and liked to travel. He shared stories of his long-distance bike rides, but from his demeanour, I could tell he was a solitary person. When his beer was finished, he bid us farewell and left.

As I watched him depart, I realised why William had chosen the Camino; people would enter and leave our lives as we journeyed, sometimes multiple times, making it impossible to spot any foreign agent. 'Poor Kat,' I whispered. 'I overreacted.'

Oh, Claudia, that's so unlike you. Hold on girly, Jonathan was flirting with Kat. Hold your judgement on this one.

The following day, the walk was to Torres del Rio, thirty-two kilometres away, and with temperatures expected to reach the high thirties. Before leaving the bar to find our hotel, we agreed to rendezvous with Athira at the base of the stone bridge at seven thirty in the morning.

***

Our lodging was a contemporary establishment, complete with a restaurant where we convened at eight in the evening for a Pilgrim meal priced at fifteen euros, a sum that covered the delectable dishes plus a bottle of wine per couple. We hadn't long been seated when three English women identified William from our time in Puente La Reina and approached our table with spirited energy. Their smiles animated; they shared the news that they'd captured William's "run with the bulls" on video.

The trio were sisters, Debbie, Jude, and Rachel. Eagerly, they joined us for dinner, transforming the evening into a web of shared tales and laughter, the camaraderie reinforced as we swapped anecdotes, each story adding a layer to the bonds forming among us.

A funny moment unfolded as William and Anna, feeling a tad over full, opted to forego dessert. Regardless, the server arrived with a tempting array of post-dinner delights, asserting with a twinkle in his eye that they'd undoubtedly require energy for the next day's trek. Laughter rippled through the table as they each succumbed. As the night wore on and the clock ticked past ten thirty, we bid adios to everyone, retiring to our rooms with the promise of another day's walk not far away.

Seated in bed, I hastily dialled the MI6 control centre for updates. Once satisfied with the information I received, I viewed William's social media page. To my surprise, he had already made a post:

William's Social Medial Post

The night before the big walk, we had a delightful chicken dinner with three charming English ladies (Sisters). They entertained us with their wonderful humour and shared fascinating stories, from their experiences working with Franciscan nuns to a private tour of Westminster Abbey with the Dean. They truly embodied the spirit of the Camino community. We indulged in a bit too much food and wine, which meant we retired to bed later than planned for our upcoming long day.

I rubbed my chin. 'We didn't eat chicken,' I muttered to myself. 'What's the significance of the chicken?'

Claudia, girly, are you finding meaning where there is none? Perhaps I'm being taken for a fool, and this is another red herring like Mañeru?

This was still early on the walk—mission. Until I knew otherwise, I'd chase every rabbit down its burrow. I was reminded of what Stephen had said. "The realm of espionage is a convoluted dance of contradictions, causing one to question the notion of intelligence itself." I knew I would repeat this many times on this assignment. Redialling the control centre, I inquired if there was

any connection between chickens and our upcoming destinations.
'Leave it with us,' was their reply.

At two thirty that morning, my phone buzzed. The message
read:

> Santo Domingo de la Calzada. A rooster and chicken
> with white feathers are kept alive at the cathedral all
> year round. You will be there in four days.
>
> *Couldn't you have waited until the sun was up?*

CHAPTER 10
The road to Santo Domingo

William's Social Media Post

Our trek from Estella to Torres Del Río spanned a challenging 32 kilometres, consuming a demanding 9 hours and 42,000 steps. Along the way, we shared the path with various companions, relishing both the fantastic company and breathtaking scenery. Despite the enriching experience, the journey proved strenuous, leaving Anna with multiple blisters layered on top of each other. We were thoroughly exhausted upon reaching our hotel. After a refreshing beer and a brief nap, we find ourselves now seated by the pool, where all is well with the world. Tomorrow's walk features a somewhat less demanding 20km, a welcome reprieve before tackling another monstrous stretch.

***

Claudia

I reread William's post, lingering over the words. It solidified my earlier suspicion; there was an unmistakable undertone in his writing suggesting a connection between him and Anna. I had been by Anna's side studying her since Pamplona and concluded she wasn't a threat to William, ruling her out as a foreign spy. The connection was emotional. Chinmay, our companion once more on the winding trail, now loomed as my primary suspect.

My mind revisited Jonathan asking Chinmay about Kat and Jonathan's alert eyes when Chinmay said, 'I'm surprised we didn't see her today.'

I may have overreacted. Regardless, I believed the potion I administered would stop her for two days, but it seemed she was on the move. If I needed to confront Kat again, I was ready. Chinmay gave me the impression that she was pushing ahead at a brisk pace, planning fewer overnight stops than our group. In the unfolding drama, the Camino path would become the judge of her destiny. If she wanted to walk with us, that would represent a threat to the mission.

***

I checked my messages one last time in Torres del Rio. With nothing new in my inbox from MI6, I switched off the bedroom light. The following day promised another early start, and the forecast hinted at a temperature hotter than today's scorching sun.

Athira awaited us outside her Albergue and beneath the soft glow of torchlight, we began our journey. Shortly after departing Torres del Rio, we stumbled upon a monument adorned with stone cairns, another testament to the countless pilgrims passing over the years. Nearby stood a pine tree, its branches festooned with colourful ribbons left behind by those who travelled before us. Athira stroked a ribbon gently. 'It's beautiful knowing that you are part of something larger than yourself.'

Jonathan stood next to Athira and gazed at the ribbons dancing in the breeze, his expression thoughtful. 'It truly is. Each ribbon represents a journey, someone's story, a pilgrimage of its own. It reminds us we're not alone in our journey, that our steps are a part of a grand mosaic of human experience.' In my guise as the future Mrs. Swindon, I open my mouth, intending to interject a religiously significant comment. However, I refrained. This was not the time for deception.

Before ascending the mountain, we traversed a valley where the air was thickened by a relentless hum. Swarms of mosquitoes, unyielding in their pursuit, descended upon us like insatiable predators. The eerie symphony of their incessant buzzing became the soundtrack to our uneasy passage. Our attempts to swat them away proved futile; the persistent pests danced around us; their hunger was palpable in the incessant whine. The air seemed to shimmer with their presence, each tiny winged assailant eager to partake in the feast of exposed skin. Every step became a negotiation with discomfort, the unseen assailants probing for any vulnerable inch of flesh. A cloud of irritation enveloped us as a battle waged on. We pressed forward through the valley, accentuated by sporadic swats to shield ourselves from the onslaught of insatiable mosquitoes. It wasn't until we climbed out of the valley that we were free of them and, if there was a silver lining from the encounter, it was our speedy pace maintained to escape the pests.

After an hour, we strolled into Viana for breakfast. Outside a cafe, perfectly timed to Jonathan's arrival, stood Kat. She wasn't alone, but accompanied by a group of young people, mostly men, some familiar and some strangers. Kat beamed at our approach, warmly hugging each of us. It was hard to miss Jonathan's blush as Kat embraced him, displaying his attraction to her. If Jonathan harboured hopes of having Kat to himself, they were dashed as she enthusiastically engaged in conversation with everyone.

Twenty minutes after our arrival, Kat finished her breakfast and effortlessly strapped her twenty-kilogram pack to her back, bidding goodbye to the group. Before departing, Jonathan said, 'How far are you going today?' Kat shrugged her shoulders and replied, 'I'm not sure. Maybe Logrono, perhaps a little further. Buen Camino.'

'The Camino has spoken,' I whispered to myself.

With Kat's departure, the others, having finished their breakfast, gradually dispersed. As Dale from California prepared to leave, he surprised us all by revealing his age—eighty. 'I feel humbled,' William said.

Next to our breakfast stop was a camping/hiking shop. Anna, who was struggling with blisters, purchased new shoes. When we stopped for our next break on the way to Logrono, she told us that the new footwear had brought relief.

William's Social Media Post

Today, Anna bought sandals to ease the discomfort of her blister struggle. Surprisingly, the expected scorching day eluded us, providing perfect conditions as we ventured into Logroño, arriving with high spirits. Tomorrow brings a formidable 30+km journey to Nájera, complete with some steep climbs, and the temperature is expected to reach around 35°C.

This evening marks our last meal with Athira, our cherished walking companion of the past three days. As we bid adios, our first Camino family draws to a close, and the prospect of parting ways leaves us with a genuine sense of loss. We'll miss her dearly.

Confident that there were no cryptic clues in William's post, I checked the GPS tracking app to see if his day pack was securely in his room—it was. I switched off the light and had drifted into a brief slumber when a message from MI6 jolted me awake. The words on my phone screen delivered a stark message:

There has been an increased level of chatter and activity among the Albanian Mafia. It is unspecific and lacks details regarding time, date, or method. This is troubling, and we recommend a heightened level of concern.

Two thoughts fell into my mind: It was imperative that I stay near William, his safety and the enigma surrounding him demanded my unwavering vigilance. Second, had the Mafia successfully decoded his cryptic post about the chickens? Were they waiting for William at the Church in Santo Domingo de la Calzada?

***

We departed from Logroño under the cover of darkness, following a wide path, making the early part of our journey quite effortless. By the time eight o'clock rolled around and breakfast, we had reached Navarrete, having walked twelve and a half kilometres. The road out of Navarrete was flanked by lush vineyards, and as we passed a charming house, a colourful parrot perched in a cage atop the building greeted us with a cheerful "Buen Camino." It was at nine fifty when we decided to pause for a moment, capturing memories in photographs beside a sign indicating our distance of 593 kilometres from Santiago. Shortly thereafter, we faced a daunting ascent of 750 metres along a path littered with stones as large as coconuts. At the summit, a picturesque rest spot awaited us, offering panoramic views and Navarrete in the distance. As we eased off our day packs and settled on the lush grass, the distinct hum of a drone filled the air. Within close proximity were three individuals, a duo of men and a woman, caught our attention. One man wielded the controls for the airborne device. Upon noticing our curious glances, he beckoned, 'I'm capturing aerial shots. Come have a look.'

They introduced themselves as Cathy, Chuck, and Jean, with Jean skilfully manoeuvring the drone. The aerial footage Jean exhibited on his phone portrayed the Camino from a unique perspective. 'Isn't it even more breathtaking?' he remarked. We all nodded in agreement, captivated by the scene.

The trio exuded warmth, friendliness, and charm, instantly endearing themselves to us. A sense of familiarity lingered in the air, hinting that our paths would cross again. The seamless rapport they established with us left me feeling wary.

Could they possibly be foreign operatives and the drone surveillance equipment?

The remaining walk to Nájera, a town whose name is derived from Arabic, meaning "between cliffs" or "place between the rock," passed without incident with no sign of Mafia or spy activity. We did, however, stop for a chat with Penny from California, who was struggling in the heat, sharing some of our water with her. She was not a threat, was my assessment. To our delight, the guidebook was inaccurate. The route was four kilometres shorter than stated. We had unleashed our Camino legs, covering the twenty-eight kilometres in six hours and thirty minutes. In what was fast becoming a routine, the allure of a welcoming bar enticed us as we entered Nájera. Jonathan and I chose soda water, while William opted for a beer, Anna selecting sangria. Before we could quench our thirst, Alesa, our friend from America, entered town and Anna invited her to join us, setting the stage for additional rounds of drinks. We committed to having dinner with Alesa later that evening before embarking on our quest to locate the hotel. An hour and a half after booking in, William, Anna, Jonathan and I met in the lobby ready to explore the new town.

We hadn't walked far when William exclaimed, 'Look at that!'

In the heart of Nájera, we discovered a medieval monastery, Santa María la Real. 'Wow!' William said. 'It seems to stand as a guardian of history, inviting all who pass to enter... which is us!' he exclaimed.

His enthusiasm was well placed; the stone walls of Santa María la Real rose against the backdrop of the Spanish sky. The monastery was informed by centuries of stories that spoke of its past. We paused at an entrance gate adorned by intricate carvings and symbols before crossing into the heart of the monastery.

Jonathan said in a hushed voice, 'This architectural marvel will unfold its secrets.'

I nodded my agreement.

We entered a courtyard surrounded by cloisters adorned with stone arches. I looked at the information I'd brought up on my phone and said, 'Within its walls, two main sanctuaries await our exploration. The first is the church. Held within its confines is the Royal Mausoleum, a sepulchre of regal importance. The second is the cloister, known as the Cloister of the Knights. Apparently, it will beckon us with an air of mystery and is accessible through the ornate Gate of Charles I. Each is a testament to the architectural expertise of medieval artisans.'

Very poetic. Lead on, Claudia,' Anna said.

The Gate of Charles I greeted us. Its intricate decorations betrayed a grandeur befitting its regal namesake. Above the gate, a colossal coat of arms displayed the double-headed eagle, a tribute to the monarch, symbolising the contributions of Charles I to the construction of the cloister. Inside the cloister was a sight of Renaissance elegance: the Royal Stairs, dating back to the year 1594, with their majestic ascent to the upper levels. These steps, adorned with a hemispherical dome, were a masterpiece of Trompe l'œil (an artistic term for the realistic optical illusion) featuring panels painted with illusions that fooled the senses.

'Impressive!'

My walking companions nodded in unison.

Standing transfixed, my gaze traced the painted motifs. A central figure emerged, a pelican, its presence a narrative within the artistry, though I did not know what that narrative meant. The dome, a celestial crown atop the stairs, cradled the intricate scenes painted on its surface.

Anna, in reverence to her surroundings, whispered, 'The collection speaks of a bygone era.'

'Yes,' I replied and read more from my phone in a soft voice. 'It captures the essence of a king's patronage and devotion to the monastery's construction.'

We ascended the Royal Stairs, where the view from above offered a perspective of the cloister and surrounding landscape. I continued reading, 'The Guard Rail of the Royal Stairs stands as a guardian, its details mirroring the craftsmanship found throughout the building.'

The main chapel stood with its towering spires and stained-glass windows that, as Jonathan eloquently put it, 'Calls for an air of reverence.'

As the afternoon sunlight filtered through the intricate glass, a kaleidoscope of colours illuminated the worn stone floor. Jonathan, sensing a spiritual moment, asked us to stand still. 'Do you feel it?' We each nodded in agreement and to my surprise, I too experienced a sensation. 'The echoes of centuries-old chants linger in the air, transporting us back to a time of devotion and contemplation.'

'Yes,' the others responded, almost as one.

'Yes,' I added, captivated by the blend of history and mystery.

We remained transfixed for over a minute before resuming our exploration of the interior. We discovered ornate chapels and secluded alcoves, each telling a tale of monks and pilgrims who sought comfort within these walls.

Anna tapped my arm. 'The scent of aged wood wafts through the air, doesn't it?'

'Yes,' I said.

'This place is a witness to the relentless passage of time.'

'It is, Anna. It is.'

I took a deep breath, filling my lungs with fresh air as we ventured into the monastery's cloistered gardens. With their tended herbs and medicinal plants, it offered an escape from the intensity of the interior. The sound of a bubbling fountain provided a backdrop, inviting reflection and meditation.

William scanned around him. 'It's like nothing has changed over hundreds of years.'

***

William's Social Media Post

Tomorrow - Nájera to Santo Domingo de la Calzada 22.8km.
While exploring Nájera, we discovered the medieval monastery - truly stunning—a sacred haven. The village itself is charming. At dinner, we were joined by Alesa and we plan to meet up again tomorrow night. The sense of connection among people is truly extraordinary.

'A sacred haven,' I said aloud, the words lingering in the air. Pursed lips, I contemplated for a moment.

What is it?

The answer surfaced as if escaping from my subconscious.

A sanctuary where time slows and the world outside fades away.

Closing my eyes, I allowed the thought to envelop me. Surrendering, I drifted into the embrace of sleep and the elusive promise of such a place.

CHAPTER 11
Santo Domingo

William Marshal

Crafting my nightly post, I repeatedly inserted then erased the name: Cerro de los Templarios–Templar Hill. Although a simple reference to a place we would pass, a puzzle Claudia could effortlessly decipher, a nagging doubt told me I was pushing my luck. What a master-stroke, steering MI6 into joining me on the Camino. However, indulging in misdirection, leading Claudia on a wild goose chase or, as with Santo Domingo, a chicken chase, contradicted the careful game I had always played. I was almost certain Claudia was my protector. Anna and Jonathan seemed unlikely.

Flipping the metaphorical bird at MI6 might offer fleeting satisfaction, but it's counterproductive to my overarching goals.

Leaning back, I considered a different perspective.

Perhaps the Santo Domingo chicken chase is a stroke of genius to lure out Claudia, the presumed MI6 agent, and any other adversaries.

I was trying to justify the folly in my posts.

Tread carefully, William.

I resolved that my daily social media posts would continue, but references to the Knights Templar would surface when they interacted with our activities.

Nah, I want some fun. I am retiring after all.

'When circumstances allow, I'm going to inject creative writing into my accounts, a departure from usual and a shift that will leave the security agency scratching their heads without diverting their attention from safeguarding me.'

I enjoyed a restful night's sleep, perhaps the most refreshing in years, and only stirred when Jonathan's knocks echoed through my door, signalling that the rest of the group awaited my presence. Having prepared the night before, I extended our departure from Nájera by a mere fifteen minutes. As we embarked on our day's journey, my thoughts flitted to what I would pen in my nightly musings. "This morning, we left Nájera and the Monastery of Santa Maria la Real behind." There was a satisfying cadence to the words I was thinking when a flicker of movement in my peripheral vision alerted me. I turned my head, but no one was in sight. The encounter left me feeling unsettled. Anticipating a busy trail ahead, teeming with fellow travellers, I felt a sense of caution creeping in. Opting for care, I chose to stroll beside Claudia, initiating a conversation with her. While there were no overt signs of concern, I recognised the significance of staying alert, particularly considering the value of my belongings.

Moving alongside Claudia, I said. 'I read Nájera means town between the rocks and has Arabic origins.'

Claudia raised her eyebrows and responded, 'Really William, I didn't know that.' Something in her tone implied that this wasn't the case.

'Yes,' I said, and it started a conversation as we trekked onwards.

We traced the well-defined trail, marked by its yellow arrows, winding through the picturesque La Rioja region, a landscape of undulating hills, vineyards, and sprawling fields that created a tranquil backdrop. The path led us uphill along a dirt track, meandering through pine trees and farmland as we advanced toward Azofra, our first opportunity to pause for breakfast and coffee, except that we set our inaugural stop for Cirueña, a hilltop village further along.

We arrived in Cirueña at nine thirty and fate led us to a haven named "Bar Jacobeo," where we surrendered to the pleasures of breakfast. As I savoured the rich aroma rising from my coffee cup, my gaze shifted to Claudia. Her usual attentiveness was nuanced, heightened alertness mirroring my own. I wondered if she had discerned the elusive movements within the morning shadows.

Leaving Cirueña, we traversed the scenic expanse of mainly farmland, passing through harvested wheat fields with stubble and spent sunflower seeds left in the aftermath. The distance to our destination that day, Santo Domingo de la Calzada, seemed excessive even in the ideal conditions. As the sun hung high, casting rays across the countryside, the town emerged on the horizon like a distant promise. Arriving too early to check into our hotel, we sought refuge in a cafe/bar nestled in the town square. From our vantage point, we observed fellow pilgrims trickling in, their weary, determined faces telling of their journeys. Among them was Chinmay, the young Australian man of Indian heritage we'd encountered on our first day and frequently thereafter. Today he joined us for a refreshing beer. There was a subtle wariness in Claudia's demeanour when Chinmay joined us, a sentiment that I didn't share. Having a knack for recognizing those from the underworld, I was certain Chinmay didn't fit the profile, nor did he seem entangled in the espionage games. However, if he were a spy, he was adept at blending in, a skill that eluded Claudia.

****

Easing my daypack off my shoulders, I carefully set it down beside the table. I felt renewed, the afterglow of a refreshing shower at the hotel still lingering. From the cafe where I awaited Jonathan, I had an unhindered view of the Cathedral with the chicken. During the early days of our walk, Jonathan had shared with me his quest to find the future Mrs. Swindon. When Claudia first joined our group, he had pondered whether she could be the one. I spotted

Jonathan approaching across the square and waved for him to join me.

'How are you feeling?'

'William, I'm always amazed at how quickly we recover. After a shower and half an hour's rest, I feel like I haven't completed a big walk today.'

Our conversation turned to the next day's hike to Belorado. When I opened the GPS Camino app on my phone to review the route with him, I was surprised to discover that it couldn't locate my position. Jonathan mentioned the buildings might obstruct the signal, and I nodded in agreement. After some chitchat, our discussion shifted to his quest and Claudia.

'Claudia is a woman of faith, attentive and kind. What do you think of her?' It was an echo of a question he had posed in the early days of our journey.

Discreetly glancing past Jonathan, I watched Claudia slip inside the church. It confirmed my suspicion that she was an MI6 agent and that her interest in Jonathan was a ruse; she lacked any interest in him. Jonathan Swindon was a genuinely amiable man and the burden of concealing the truth from him weighed on me, yet my lips would be sealed.

***

Claudia

The tracking device attached to William's pack pinged, showing his departure from our hotel, his path leading to the Cathedral, a brief stroll from our lodgings. When the signal disappeared, I deduced that he'd entered the church. 'Alright, time to play detective,' I murmured to myself, ready to uncover his intentions.

The weathered cobblestone streets led me to the cathedral. Its Gothic exterior, adorned with pointed arches, flying buttresses, and intricate stone carvings, captivated me. Sculptures and reliefs depicting biblical tales adorned the facade, while statues of saints and angels guarded the entrance. Slipping inside, the scent of aged stone and burning candles tickled my nose. My gaze swept the vast interior, only to find it eerily empty, its echoing halls devoid of life. I'd hoped to blend in with a throng of visiting tourists and I muttered to myself, 'Darn.' I swept the inside again. 'Where could he be?'

Taking cautious steps forward, the echoes of my footsteps were amplified by the emptiness. The soaring vaulted ceilings and stained-glass windows created an unnerving atmosphere. Light filtering through the windows painted rainbows on the stone floor as I moved deeper into the building. I stopped to admire the main altar, a masterpiece of religious art, adorned with intricate carvings, gold leaf, and paintings depicting scenes from the life of Christ. Throughout the cathedral, there were many chapels dedicated to saints with religious figures intended to invite contemplation. In one chapel, an enclosure high on the wall housed a live rooster and hen, cited in William Marshal's social media post.

When MI6 told me of the rooster and chicken with white feathers kept alive at the cathedral, I wondered about their significance. I discovered an ancient tale about a German couple embarking on a pilgrimage to Santiago with their son. Upon reaching Santo Domingo, they sought shelter at an inn where an unforeseen tragedy unravelled. The innkeeper's daughter, smitten with the young man, faced unrequited love. In a vengeful act, she planted a tin jug among the Germans' belongings. As the pilgrims departed, the girl falsely reported a theft, leading to the wrongful capture of the boy, who was then accused of theft and sentenced to hanging.

Undeterred by the injustice, the parents continued their pilgrimage, to return later to witness a miraculous sight. Contrary to expectations, their son remained hanging, but miraculously was alive. Legend holds that the young man credited Santo Domingo for aiding his survival, while others insisted it was the fervent prayers of his parents seeking a saint's intervention to keep their son alive by holding him from below.

Upon learning of this extraordinary tale, the parents rushed to the mayor to share the news of the miraculous event. Met with scepticism, the mayor assured them that their son was as alive as the roasted rooster and hen he was about to consume. In a mystical twist, as he prepared to feast on the birds, their feathers returned and the rooster and hen came back to life. This fantastical event gave rise to a famous saying: "Santo Domingo de la Calzada, where the chicken sang after being roasted." Ever since, the cathedral has kept live chickens in commemoration of this extraordinary event. The lively duo seemed blissfully unaware of their historic significance. The spectacle made me smile; a place where the sacred and the whimsical coexisted.

I scanned the cathedral for William.

This is wrong!

The church was a tourist attraction, and I felt uneasy that I was still alone. I bit my lip and glanced around when a piece of wood fell and splintered next to me. Instinctively, I dropped to the ground, seeking refuge behind a weathered pew. The scent of gun smoke hung in the air, mingling with the wax of burning candles. A quiet determination surged through my veins as I realised I was being targeted, targeted by a silenced weapon. The cathedral, which should have been a sanctuary, was being transformed into a battleground, but I was unarmed and dare not move. My eyes darted around the dimly lit space, trying to discern any sign of my unseen assailant.

Where are you?

The silence amplified the sound of my heartbeat. Unarmed, I speedily assessed my options. The pew, once a haven, now became a refuge. I made a decision to inch along its length, craving the shelter of the shadows, hoping it would shield me from the unseen danger. Before my plan could unfold, the pew erupted in a hailstorm of splinters and debris around me.

Darn it, I'm pinned down. I will have to make a run for it before the assailant discerns my vulnerability and moves in for the kill. Buying time is crucial now!

To divert the assailant's attention, I pulled out my phone and keyed in the phrase "Gun Shot" to Google. A feeble plan I knew, but under the pressing circumstances, it was the only idea that came to mind. With a glance around, I turned up the volume and hit play, and the sound of a gunshot echoed through the cathedral. The effect was immediate, the stillness shattered by the artificial noise. It was a reckless gamble, relying on the assailant's instincts to react. I braced myself for a swift escape as my heart pounded in my chest.

Poised to make a run for safety, the creaking of a large door broke the silence, followed by the cadence of approaching footsteps. Haunting Gregorian chant, like a spectral mist, reverberated through the medieval cathedral, ethereal notes weaving through the towering arches and lingering in the lofty heights of the stone sanctuary.

I remained concealed; my senses heightened by the soundtrack that now filled the space. A custodian of the church, a figure cloaked in holy orders, came into view as footsteps drew nearer. An unexpected twist, an ally, perhaps, or merely good fortune. Regardless, he arrived at a moment crucial for my escape.

The assailant's opportunity had evaporated as the strains of the Gregorian chant continued. I stood from my hiding place and a shiver ran down my spine. I am not religious but, at that moment, I felt shrouded in the cloak of a higher power; the cathedral conspiring to shield me from harm. As I readied myself to depart the church, my gaze lingered on the monk draped in his habit, the hood concealing his face. Then I had a flicker of recognition... was this Artōrius, my MI6 contact from Puente La Reina? I dare not confirm my suspicions, so I gave a respectful nod of my head as I left.

***

William Marshal

I took a contemplative sip of my beer and chose not to respond to Jonathan's query about Claudia. 'Jonathan, my friend, I was happily married for many years until Hannah's passing, yet matters of the heart remain elusive to me. I'd say that love has a way of surprising you when you least expect it, like a gentle breeze catching you off guard. While searching for it, you might walk right past without realizing. Love has its own pace. Savour the Camino family and journey, and let love find itself. You have time, dear friend.'

'William, sanguine advice, and I agree with your sentiment,' Jonathan replied with a broad smile. 'Kat with her twenty-kilo pack has Mrs. Swindon potential, though!' We both laughed and, as Jonathan continued speaking, my gaze drifted past him to the church entrance, where I had expected to see a flurry of tourists. My unease grew when none appeared after Claudia entered. I was about to suggest to Jonathan that we explore the cathedral, when I noticed a monk pause at the entrance and enter. A few minutes later, Claudia emerged and a tide of relief washed over me.

Reaching for my daypack, I rose from my chair and waved in her direction. I said to Jonathan, 'I can see Claudia. Come on, let's go and meet her.'

William's Social Media Post

This afternoon, we embarked on an exploration of Santo Domingo de la Calzada. Whether it was marvelling at the famous chickens, ascending the steps to discover the Cathedral roof, or reaching the pinnacle of the bell tower in the town square, a haze of fatigue descended upon us. Seeking respite, we withdrew to our room to immerse ourselves in the local culture and partake in the customary siesta. Now rejuvenated, we are getting ready to rendezvous with Alesa, our friend from America, for dinner. Our journey continues tomorrow as we set out on foot towards Belorado.

CHAPTER 12
Our Family

Jonathan Swindon

Today marked our parting with Alesa, a delightful companion who had shared our journey over the past few days. Along the Camino, people come and go, like fleeting whispers in the wind. Perhaps that's why the connections forged here are so intense; they remind us that life is transient, and those we hold dear may be gone tomorrow. It's a poignant metaphor urging us to cherish every moment and every person while they're still with us.

Setting out for Belorado, the path ran alongside the main road, lacking inspiration, but it led us onwards. Its surface was a challenge, reminiscent of walking on a pebble-strewn beach, harsh and painful on our feet. Recalling William's words from the previous day, "To savour the journey itself," I looked upon today's seemingly mundane path as a necessary journey that enhances the uniqueness of other days.

With four villages to traverse on our way to Belorado, we decided not to burden ourselves with supplies, expecting opportunities for sustenance along the way. It wasn't until Villamayor del Rio that we stumbled upon our first respite, a coffee oasis. To my delight, we reunited with a group of young people, as William and Anna called them. We'd encountered them regularly, including our friend Kat with her 20-kilogram pack. She was a woman of natural presence. Her poise and charisma radiated effortlessly, drawing people towards her like moths to a flame.

Over a late breakfast, as temperatures soared towards 30 degrees Celsius, we discussed our journey to San Juan de Ortega the next day, a trek of twenty-eight kilometres with a formidable 1,150-meter climb towards the end. Aware of the challenges awaiting us, Kat decided to extend her walk of that day by avoiding

Belorado. While I'd have liked her company at our evening's dinner, I concealed my disappointment, acknowledging the wisdom in her choice. The group of boys she walked with opted for an alternative, planning an early, "very early," start for the following day.

The stretch from Villamayor del Rio to Belorado was a mere four kilometres and, as had become our tradition, we located a bar near the trail to welcome our fellow pilgrims upon their arrival. Anna, with her magnetic presence, had a way of drawing people towards us. Before long, Canadians we'd met previously, Cathy, Chuck and Jean, people of William and Anna's age, joined us at the table. Taking the opportunity, Anna asked if they would like to join us for dinner. They accepted, and I hoped over the meal, Jean would share more of his drone footage.

Observing Anna and William engaged in conversation with our fellow Camino travellers, a remark Kat had made to them resurfaced in my mind. "You two are like my Camino parents." It might sound peculiar for a thirty-four-year-old to acknowledge, but the sentiment resonated with me and caused me to think of my own family.

The Swindon family called the town of Harmonyville their home, a picturesque enclave nestled in the landscapes of Oklahoma, a place where modest abodes lined the streets, each with its own character, stories echoing within their walls. Our residence was a two-storey house with a white picket fence that spoke of simpler times. Its facade, painted in a warm hue of cream, exuded a sense of comfort and belonging. A well-tended garden framed the front yard, adorned with vibrant flowers that mirrored our family's tight-knit bonds and love for simplicity.

My father, Richard, was a respected mechanic in Harmonyville, known for his skilful hands that could breathe life into the most worn-out of engines. The garage next to our home buzzed with the hum of tools and the aroma of motor oil, a smell I loved as a child, a testament to my father's unwavering dedication to his craft. My mother, Margaret, had gracefully balanced the roles of home-maker and part-time librarian at the local Public Library. Her nurturing and love for literature infused our home with intellectual curiosity. Sunday nights were sacred to us, a time when our family gathered around the sturdy oak table for a roast dinner. The smell of savoury herbs and spices would waft through the air as dad carved succulent slices of meat, setting the stage for laughter, shared stories, and the comforting embrace of familial bonds. Though not fervently devout, my parent's commitment to the Catholic faith was interwoven into the fabric of our family.

In the Swindon household, my siblings had flanked me. My older brother, Thomas, chose the rhythmic beat of the corporate world, orchestrating success with every keystroke on his computer. Meanwhile, my younger sister, Emily, met a fate that forever altered our family's narrative. A palpable emptiness enveloped the dining table following Emily's passing. Cancer had slipped into our lives, casting a shadow over our once-vibrant family. Emily, a spirited soul, had valiantly fought the illness, leaving an indelible mark on our hearts. In my mind's eye, I still see her bedroom, adorned with remnants of youthful exuberance, which bore witness to the strength she displayed during her battle, and when she lost the battle, it left an unfulfillable void in the Swindon home. The Sunday roast dinners, once vibrant with life, became a bittersweet reminder of the chair that now stood empty.

Emily's departure prompted me to question the beliefs of my upbringing and shrouded me in grief. At the crossroads, where I veered away from the well-trodden path of Catholicism, I felt I'd lost my way. Yet God had other plans for me, steering me to embrace the evangelical Christian faith. It provided purpose and a compass for the journey ahead, a comforting guide when the nightmares which began haunting my dreams after Emily's passing threatened to consume me.

Graduating secondary school, I attended Oral Roberts University, a private evangelical institution, to study business. Oral Roberts became more than a place of learning for me; it became a crucible of transformation. My alma mater sculpted not only my intellect but also the faith that guides my every step.

Perhaps it's the lingering influence of my Catholic upbringing that steered me towards the Camino de Santiago. I can't be certain, but I found myself irresistibly drawn to its ancient cobbled paths, not merely to trace the dusty footprints of pilgrims past but also in search of the elusive presence of the future Mrs. Swindon. To me, this sacred pilgrimage wasn't only a journey of spirituality; it's a path where the destinies of kindred souls weave together. Despite William's cautionary words about finding love, the rhythmic tap of my boots against the age-old stones resonated with the beat of my hopeful heart. The Camino, a passage of faith, trials, and tribulations, unfolded as the backdrop to unearth the missing piece of my life's puzzle. Whether I encounter the future Mrs. Swindon or not, I am grateful that God has blessed me with wonderful companions, like Anna Dupont, on this transformative quest.

As I watch Anna talk with ease with Cathy, Chuck and Jean, I imagine her story. Anna Dupont, our enigmatic fellow pilgrim on this journey, is a captivating presence that defies a simple description. Her age remains a mystery, a detail she has chosen not to disclose, though I estimate her to be in her mid-sixties. She possesses a timeless grace, an ageless quality that adds to her persona. She has a rare gift, making people feel at ease, a talent that has endeared her to all who tread alongside us on "The Way." Her French heritage is present in the soft lilt of her voice, an accent that enhances her words, as though her presence carries the fragrance of lavender fields and the echoes of Parisian streets. I would not describe her as charismatic, yet she exudes a magnetic warmth that draws people to her. Genuine kindness radiates and there is subtle wisdom embedded in her every glance or smile. She has an unspoken depth to her, a reservoir of experiences that begs to be explored. I learned Anna has journeyed through the shadows of loss, saying goodbye to a husband with whom she enjoyed a long and blissful marriage. Of course, this strikes a chord with me, as I have experienced grief. William, too, walks in the shadow of loss. As I contemplate the enigma that is Anna Dupont, I wonder about the chapters of her life story that remain unwritten. A curiosity pervades my thoughts, a yearning to understand the woman behind the warmth. My eyes fall on William and I listen as he and Jean talk of the Knights Templar. Jean, a man in his sixties like William, says he is going to write a book about the Camino, weaving a story about the Templar into its pages.

William Marshal, my companion and a person I now call a friend, reveals himself to me in layers. Unlike the puzzling Claudia and Anna, William isn't shrouded in mystery, yet he is a complex character in his own right. Warm and engaging, yet he carries an air of someone who appreciates his own company. His ease with our fellow travellers seems to hinge on the presence of Anna Dupont by his side. Without her, I suspect William might find the social intricacies of the Camino difficult.

In the confines of his daypack, William guards a cherished memory, that of his late wife, Hannah, who walks the path with him in spirit. It's a touching reminder of his enduring connection to a love that transcends the physical world. Beneath the warmth and intellect that William exudes, I occasionally catch glimpses of a more intricate game at play. I can't put my finger on it, but there's a sense that our travelling group might be part of a larger game that William is playing. I see it also with Claudia.

To the casual observer, Anna and William appear as a couple. I wonder if Hannah, William's late wife, played a role similar to Anna. An enabler who oiled the wheels of social interaction. I contemplate the complexities that lie beneath the surface of our shared pilgrimage.

Claudia, at first glance, embodies everything a man like me could desire. Attentive, kind, sensitive, warm, and undeniably beautiful, she possesses a grace that extends beyond physical appearance. When she listens, it is to understand, and her knowledge of the Bible and the Christian faith only deepens the connection we share. We align in beliefs and values, like kindred spirits navigating the Camino together. Yet, beneath this veneer, there's more to Claudia, layers that remain unspoken, facets of herself deliberately concealed.

Walking beside Claudia on the Camino, I have noticed that she glides effortlessly across the terrain with the stealth of a hunter. One night, from my hotel room door, I watched Claudia walking down the corridor. If one closed one's eyes, her presence would evaporate as if the world around her was undisturbed.

Claudia is physically strong, and with her by my side, I feel safe. Was she a divine gift, an appointed protector sent by God for our group, our guardian angel? Claudia is undeniably an angel, her beauty captivating, perhaps with wings discernible to the heart even if unseen by the eyes. My yearning to love her is strong, but a voice within cautions me. She is not the future Mrs. Swindon; a sentiment that William attempted to convey.

Claudia is like Anna Dupont in her ease of people, effortlessly engaging in conversations with strangers. Despite her serene demeanour, I sense, like the rest of us, she carries a burden, venturing on the Camino in pursuit of answers to questions that remain unspoken.

My thoughts shift back to our group when I hear Claudia say my name. 'Jonathan, would you read a book about the Camino centred on a Knights Templar mystery?'

I took a moment to ponder before responding, 'Is it a historical tale or a contemporary one?'

Jean, the prospective author of the Camino story, chimed in, 'It will be set in the present, and readers will have to solve Templar clues that unfold as the characters walk the trail.'

Nodding in agreement, I said, 'Sure, I would read that. There is no shortage of material here.'

'Well then, Jean,' Claudia said, 'it seems you're onto a winning formula and have sold four books already.'

Chuck added, 'Make that six, Jean. Cathy and I eagerly await it.'

***

After a delightful evening meal, I bid farewell to my companions, who were still engrossed in conversation, and embarked on a solitary stroll back to our hotel. Unintentionally taking a wrong turn, I stood before the imposing entrance to the Church of Santa Maria. Positioned against the hillside, its structure of weathered stones bore witness to centuries of shifting seasons and the ebb and flow of community life in Belorado.

In the dwindling light, the church's exterior revealed a timeless elegance. I expected it to be locked, inaccessible at that time of the evening, but an irresistible force drew me to the massive wooden doors, worn smooth by the hands of visitors throughout the ages. To my astonishment, the opening was ajar. Crossing the threshold, I spotted three naves and four chapels, bathed in the fading crimson of sunlight filtering through the time-stained windows. Sturdy columns, survivors of the ages, framed the interior, unveiling a trove of artistic treasures narrating biblical stories that transported me back to the Catholic faith of my youth. The church's beauty was undeniable, yet the dimly lit interior cast eerie shadows, sending a shiver down my spine as memories of haunting nightmares resurfaced. I jumped as the entrance door banged shut, jolting me from my thoughts. 'Is someone there?'

'Oh, hello there,' said a friendly voice. 'Don't worry, I always check to see if we have visitors before locking the doors for the night.'

An elderly man wearing religious attire, features concealed beneath a hood, emerged from the shadows. Gesturing towards the grand altarpiece, he said, 'A magnificent Baroque masterpiece, dating back to the late 17th or early 18th century.' A momentary pause lingered before he continued, 'It commands attention with its intricate detailing and ornate craftsmanship, a visual spectacle recounting the devotion woven into the fabric of these walls.' Our eyes met, and he remarked, 'It reminds you of your youth.' Taken aback by the unexpected connection, I was left momentarily speechless. Before I could gather my thoughts, he gestured for me to follow, sharing his wealth of knowledge as we navigated through the sacred space. 'This chapel is dedicated to La Inmaculada,' he pointed out. 'Note the carved figure, a testament to immaculate artistry, representing purity and grace.' Moving on to another corner, he halted once more. 'And here, the chapel dedicated to Saint James the Apostle. The altarpiece encapsulates the very essence of religious fervour. If you stand still, Jonathan, you may hear the echoed prayers of pilgrimages that have transpired in his name.'

I shivered as I pondered the familiarity in his words. Hesitating, I finally spoke. 'You seem to know who I am. May I inquire about your name?'

'I go by the name Artōrius.'

'Have we crossed paths before?'

'I doubt it, my child.'

His response left me puzzled. 'If we haven't met, how do you know who I am?'

Artōrius chuckled. 'While I was in town earlier today, I overheard one of your friends addressing you by that name. I have an excellent memory.'

It was a plausible explanation. 'Artōrius, there's something else you mentioned to me. I can't recall your exact words, but we were examining some carvings, you remarked. They reminded me of my youth. How did you come to that conclusion?'

Artōrius smiled, his expression wise and knowing. 'I noticed you cross yourself.'

His words perplexed me. 'I haven't done that in years.'

Artōrius nodded sagely. 'Exactly. Your manner spoke of your infrequency, a telltale sign of a lapsed Catholic. That's how I deduced the carvings stirred memories of your devout youth.'

Before I could respond, he said, 'Before the last light leaves us, it's time to lock the church for the night.'

As we approached the overpowering wooden doors, Artōrius uttered something that disturbed me. 'You seem uncomfortable in the dark. Is that because of your nightmares?'

His knowledge of my dreams left me bewildered.

How did he know?

I wanted to respond, but words eluded me. From beneath his religious attire, Artōrius produced a set of ancient keys that dangled from a circular key ring. He extended them for me to see, each key a testament to the church's rich history. Crafted from weathered iron, the keys bore the marks of countless years, their surfaces etched with the passage of time. Ornate patterns and intricate designs adorned their shafts, and my imagination conjured images of the many hands and stories intertwined with these artefacts.

'Come,' Artōrius said. As we approached the doors, the keys clinked softly and echoed through the silent church.

He presented the keys for me to take and I accepted his offer. My eyes were drawn to them and I explored their details with my hands. Each key bore a unique design, some long and imposing with irregular teeth, reminiscent of the tides of time, while others were short and stubby, their simplicity contrasting with their importance. The collective weight of the keys, both physical and metaphorical, hung heavily in my grasp. A surge of pride enveloped me as Artōrius entrusted me with the nightly ritual of securing the holy space.

'Which key?'

Artōrius pointed. I selected the key. Its intricate teeth fitted the lock with a satisfying click.

With the door now secure, I passed the keys back to Artōrius. As he took them, he stared at me as he said, 'You see, Jonathan, the path of faith is not always an easy one. Deeply religious individuals grapple with their own fears and doubts. Dreams, especially nightmares, are a battleground for the soul.'

I furrowed my brow, acknowledging the undeniable truth. 'But why the devil? Why do I dream of such a malevolent figure?'

Artōrius replaced the keys, then clasped his hands thoughtfully. 'The devil, in a way, becomes a symbol. A symbol of the challenges and temptations we face on our spiritual journey. When our subconscious grapples with faith, it sometimes conjures up the devil as a metaphor for our struggles, a reminder that the path to righteousness is not always a smooth one.' I nodded slowly, attempting to absorb Artōrius's words. 'So, these nightmares, they're not a sign of weakness or lack of faith?'

Artōrius smiled gently. 'No, my child. They're a testament to the strength of your convictions. Confronting the devil in your dreams is akin to facing your inner demons. It's a way for your spirit to overcome the challenges that life throws at you. Embrace those dreams, for they are a part of the journey towards true faith.'

I closed my eyes, absorbing Artōrius's wisdom. My nightmares had begun with Emily's death, and I pondered on its significance. When I opened my eyes, I was alone; Artōrius had vanished.

Was Artōrius a dream?

CHAPTER 14
Transcendent Change

Claudia

My day unfolded in unexpected ways. The guidebook prepared us for a challenging ascent to Alto de la Pedraja, perched nearly 1200 metres above sea level. Anticipating a scorching day, we embarked before the break of dawn, bidding farewell to Belorado under a cloudless sky, a brilliant full moon illuminating our path, allowing us to trek without the aid of headlamps. As we ventured on and dawn broke, the vast expanse revealed uninterrupted vistas stretching from the eastern to the western horizon. As if scripted by some unseen hand, magic then enveloped us as a cosmic spectacle unfolded with the ethereal dance of the moonset and the emergence of the sun on the horizon. Nature's canvas painted a breathtaking masterpiece before our eyes. Astronomy isn't my forte, but I comprehended the rarity of this event, owing to the intricate choreography of the Earth, moon, and sun. We stood transfixed as Anna suggested a name for the occasion: "Selenehelion." It was a sight to behold, which played out in William's social media post. Initially, it took me by surprise, straying from his typical style. However, upon reflection, memories of Cathy and Chuck conversing with him during dinner flooded back. The couple had shared their mutual passion for literature and poetry, with William seeking Cathy's thoughts. It became apparent that the eloquence of William's words, beautifully portraying the splendour of our morning experience, bore the unmistakable imprint of the Canadian couple's influence.

William's Social Media Post

> As the moon gracefully descends, casting its silver glow upon the world, the anticipation of a new day unfolds. The sky undergoes a subtle transformation, shifting from the deep hues of night to the soft palette of dawn. In this magical transition, nature seems to hold its breath, and a profound sense of serenity envelops the surroundings. As the first light emerges on the horizon, one can almost hear the whispers of a poem by Rumi: 'The morning wind spreads its fresh smell. We must get up and take that in, that wind that lets us live. Breathe before it's gone. It's a time when the celestial dance of night and day creates a fleeting yet enchanting spectacle, leaving an indelible mark on the canvas of memory.'
>
> Let's not forget to look back and appreciate the beauty we've left behind.

Having traversed the globe, I couldn't recall encountering such a spectacle. William's post, penned during our customary post-walk ale, stirred inquisitiveness in me that led to me sending a text to an astronomer friend. I shared her response with the group.

> Observing both the moonset and sunrise simultaneously is not an everyday occurrence, making it a relatively rare and special event. The timing of witnessing both celestial events aligns when the moon is on the western horizon and the sun is rising on the eastern horizon. This unique convergence is influenced by factors such as the specific geographical location, time of year, and the relative positions of the sun and moon in the sky.
>
> The rarity adds to the enchantment of the experience, making it a memorable and awe-inspiring moment for those fortunate enough to witness the simultaneous moonset and sunrise.

Yet, the unexpected didn't end with our witnessing the celestial event. As the others walked ahead that morning, Jonathan and I lingered at the Monumento de los Caidos, a poignant symbol of Spain's unhealed memories from its civil war. This memorial marked the shallow graves of those summarily executed during a dark chapter in Spain's history, marking a sombre testament to the nation's collective wounds. In reverence, we'd bowed our heads before turning to continue our journey.

We had taken a few steps when Jonathan asked, 'Claudia, do you believe in angels?'

Surprised and unsure of how to respond, I grappled with the question. Posing as a devout Christian, my instinct urged me to answer in the affirmative. Surprisingly, as a person of little faith, I astonished myself by replying sincerely in the affirmative.

'Absolutely, Jonathan. I believe in the heavenly beings that watch over us, guiding and protecting us on our journey. Angels are messengers of God, their presence felt at unexpected moments. Don't you think so?'

'Claudia, do you think a fallen angel can seek redemption?'

I sensed the direction of Jonathan's probing questions and it sent a shiver down my spine. He was about to broach the subject of whether I sought atonement on "The Way." Normally, queries like these wouldn't have unsettled my conscience, but the celestial encounter earlier in the morning had stirred a sense of something greater in me. At that moment, I scrutinised my past and contemplated the meaning of life.

My path to the intelligence services hadn't been a noble calling to serve Britain; rather, circumstances in my underworld life compelled me to switch sides. In my tenure with MI6, I'd engaged in deception, manipulation, and murder, all deemed necessary to protect the realm. Prior to serving King and country, my motivations were a twisted blend of schadenfreude and financial gain. That I wasn't a nice person hadn't troubled me until today. Normally, the convergence of the setting moon and rising sun would not breach my emotional defences, but the transformative experience of walking the Camino was affecting me.

I had paused for a moment and gazed at Jonathan, contemplating his question, the man ignorant of the impact it was having on me. Finally, with a smile and a reassuring tone, I said, 'In the eyes of God, renewal is always an option. A fallen angel seeking grace is rather like our own pilgrimage, recognizing our mistakes, embracing change, and moving towards the light of forgiveness. Redemption is a path available to all who seek it.'

Jonathan nodded and exhaled before asking, 'Are you seeking something from the Camino?'

I stared at Jonathan; my expression unreadable. 'The Camino is a journey of discovery for me. Like us all, I've grappled with demons and seek comfort in the embrace of change. Life's twists and turns have led me here, hoping to find peace and renewal. The pilgrimage teaches us that redemption is a universal path available to all who earnestly seek it.' I paused, my eyes flickering with vulnerability. 'We each carry burdens and the Camino offers a chance to lighten the load and emerge anew.'

I observed Jonathan, contemplating my words. Unexpectedly, again, for this day held surprises, what I had shared with him was the unvarnished truth.

Claudia, why do you presume his thoughts are centred on you? It's entirely plausible that he is speaking about any member of our walking group. Or perhaps he's directing his words towards your inner voice instead.

That evening, we ate with Cathy, Chuck, and Jean, who'd become regular companions on "The Way." As they bid us farewell, I realised I hadn't sought an MI6 background check on them—an omission if my role as William's guardian angel was to be fulfilled.

As they prepared to leave, I called out, 'Wait, can we have a group photo?'

'That would be great,' replied Cathy with a smile.

Just as we were making plans for the photo, the cafe owner approached to clear our table. Cathy politely asked if he could take a picture of us all. Graciously agreeing, he accepted my phone, a gesture that was repeated for Chuck and Jean. When Jonathan told us he wanted a photo too, I assured him I'd share one with our group.

***

Before I tuned off my light for the night, my phone beeped with an incoming message from headquarters. It read...

Subject:

Background Checks on Chuck, Cathy, and Jean

Agent: Claudia

Following your request, we have conducted thorough background checks on the individuals you mentioned: Charles Fredric Walters (Chuck), Catherine Mary Walters (Cathy), and Jean Bernard.

Dr Charles Fredric Walters (Chuck):

- Age: 62.
- Place of birth: Ontario, Canada.
- Occupation: Chief Medical Officer British Columbia Public Health.
- Marital Status: Married to Catherine Mary Walters.
- No known association with security services.

156

- No criminal record.

- Interests: Poetry, language, wilderness canoeing, and hiking.

Catherine Mary Walters (Cathy):

- Age: 62.

- Place of Birth: Newfoundland, Canada.

- Occupation: ICU nurse.

- Marital Status: Married to Charles Fredric Walters (Chuck).

- No known association with security services.

- No criminal record.

- Interests: Poetry, music, wilderness canoeing and hiking.

Jean Bernard:

- Age: 69.

- Place of Birth: Saskatoon, Canada.

- Occupation: Retired IT professional.

- Immigration Status: Immigrated to Norway in 2020.

- Marital Status: Married to Ingrid Olsen (2021)–Ingrid Olsen is a Norwegian Citizen.

- No known association with security services.

- No criminal record.

- Interests: Woodwork and wood turning.

In summary, all three individuals, Chuck, Cathy, and Jean, have no known connections to security services. Their backgrounds appear to be consistent with their stated occupations and interests.

The security evaluation hardly surprised me. However, Jean, with his tale of crafting a contemporary book, delving into the mysterious world of the Knights Templar along the Camino, piqued my curiosity. I expected him to have a place on the MI6's radar. Yet Jean was leaving the Camino the following day, making his way back to Norway. Any connection to William, or being a foreign operative, appeared highly improbable.

I checked my tracking app, which confirmed that all of our party, their day packs at least, were in their rooms.

CHAPTER 15
The Meseta

William's Social Media Post

Our Camino journey pressed on as we ventured toward Burgos. The trail gracefully unfolded, revealing a picturesque Spanish landscape winding its way through quaint villages and serene countryside.

Reaching Atapuerca, the trail took an arduous turn, ascending steeply with a surface that mimicked a rugged goat track. The strain on our feet was horrible, but making the summit brought us face-to-face with the high wooden Cruz de Matagrande–Cross of Matagrande, standing at an elevation of 1082 metres. It was a potent symbol of faith and challenge and marked a significant point in our pilgrimage.

As we neared Burgos, the scenery underwent a seamless transition, presenting a harmonious blend of rolling hills and expansive fields before giving way to the suburbs. The city itself unfolded, crowned by a breathtaking Gothic cathedral that served as a gratifying endpoint for this leg of our journey and where we all attended a Pilgrim's Mass.

Some of our pilgrim friends are having a well-deserved rest day in Burgos, while we press on. There's a unique sensation of knowing that while our friends pause, we forge ahead into the unknown. Uncertainty lingers about the unfamiliar faces and stories awaiting us on Meseta, and I wonder whose footsteps will intersect with ours in the days ahead.

Today, during the journey, we remember to look up.

***

Anna Dupont

I hadn't slept well, waking up nine times through the night according to my app. Waiting for my alarm to sound, to signal our early start from Burgos, I reread words from William's post.

> I wonder whose footsteps will intersect with ours in
> the days ahead.

His writing wasn't what I expected. When I first encountered William in Paris, I pegged him as a private individual inclined to solitude, awkward in social situations, typical characteristics of an intelligent person and, as I suspected, someone possibly on the spectrum. On the Camino, he'd effortlessly connected with the people we encountered. In his latest social media update, he'd expressed sorrow at parting ways with the strangers we'd encountered and his anticipation of fresh faces on our journey.

I emerged from my hotel room, joining the others at six that morning. The early hour gifted us a serene stroll past the cathedral, bathed in the glow of streetlights. Leaving the city was easier; the route was more clearly marked than when we entered. Soon, we were on the Meseta, starting a steady ascent to its pinnacle. At the top, the vastness of the landscape unfurled, a boundless expanse of flat plains extending in each direction. I'd read that this heart of Spain nestled between the historic cities of Burgos and León was a defining section of the Camino de Santiago, a challenging 180-kilometre journey. The Meseta is known for its climatic extremes. In the summer sun it's a relentless adversary, the flat, shadeless fields unbearable in the scorching haze, a test of resilience. Winter brings a fresh challenge, a biting cold that chills to the bone. Despite entering the Meseta in early October, the lingering summer temperatures demanded our early departure. The section is often bypassed by pilgrims, but I was grateful we chose otherwise. Long stages unfolding beneath expansive heavens was what I needed.

An excellent breakfast at Tardajos marked our halfway point to the overnight stop in Hornillos del Camino. Temperatures were contrary to our expectations and remained moderate, allowing us to linger over a second cafe con leche without worry. As we approached the village of Rabé de las Calzadas, home to 200 souls, vibrant wall murals adorned with bible verses, delighting Jonathan and Claudia. Our conversations veered toward the moving Pilgrim's service we'd attended in Burgos Cathedral. Our faith, though traversing different roads, intricately wove our group together.

Leaving Rabé de las Calzadas, the rhythm of our steps momentarily gave way to the steady clip-clop of hooves as pilgrims on horseback passed us by. Claudia, usually fearless, surprised me with a confession as she observed the riders. 'Walking seems a more sensible way to travel. Those four-legged monsters are huge!' I agreed as her words lingered in my thoughts.

Claudia, once seemingly unflinching, had undergone a transformation since the journey began. Her affable nature had become more genuine, no longer a facade, including her relationship with Jonathan. Their interactions were now comfortable, no longer trying to impress each other. What was clear was Claudia's deep affection for William. They conversed effortlessly and in moments when he stumbled on the path, Claudia was there to prevent him from falling. William perhaps saw his daughter Samantha mirrored in Claudia, and I felt Claudia viewed herself as his protector.

We spotted our destination around ten thirty that morning, a welcome sight, but there was still a considerable walk ahead of us. The downhill descent was steep, but the path, unlike previous occasions, was sound. As we made our way down, William struck up a conversation with an Irishman named Seamus, a fitting name for someone we'd meet on the Camino. We all enjoyed his company. Upon reaching Hornillos del Camino, we discovered a traditional town square, complete with a bar situated across the road. Seamus joined us for a lengthy conversation before continuing his trek.

Having chosen not to take a rest day in Burgos like many of our friends, we found ourselves in the company of a new group of pilgrims. A man named Rob, roughly our age, William and myself, and hailing from Melbourne, Australia, gathered people around him, like Claire, Isaac and Miria. He started a friendly conversation with us. While waiting to check into our accommodation, much to my delight, the renowned couple we'd heard about strolled into town: Ian, Catherine, and their one-year-old baby, James. This was the trio that our young friend Chinmay had assisted during the challenging descent from Alto de Perdon, our first day out of Pamplona. Claudia, our resident photographer, eager to document our encounters on the trail, brought us together for a spontaneous photo shoot.

On top of meeting the baby, James, a double delight awaited us today. Our hotel offered a timely service: washing and drying clothes for a mere five euros, a welcome release from my usual routine of stomping on laundry in the shower and hanging it in the room to dry overnight. The second treat unfolded as we explored the village. We stumbled upon a bar that promised a two-course dinner, complete with wine and live music, all for fifteen euros. Unable to resist such a tempting offer, we promptly booked our reservation. Returning later that evening, we were sat at a spacious table along with two newfound Camino companions, Adriana and Jody. I looked forward to convivial conversation over our meal. As the dinner was served, the evening's entertainment started. The hours flew by and we were the last to leave the bar after relishing a fabulous evening of good food, wine and live music. Back in my hotel room, I eagerly awaited William's nightly social media post, confident that he would eloquently chronicle the second treat of the day.

William's Social Media Post

Whenever the bearded man had sung, Claudia and William had exchanged glances, whispering to each other the name of the piece and the opera it hailed from. While I expected such knowledge from William, Claudia's familiarity with operatic music surprised me, given her age. Her depth of understanding continues to astonish me and, as we approach Foncebadón, I wonder what offering she might choose to leave at La Cruz de Ferro. Did she like me, carry a stone?

I glanced at William's post once again, just as I had done the day before. Social media platforms, once havens for light-hearted and feel-good content like William's, had transformed. They have moved from spaces of casual interaction to arenas of activism. In this era, people turned to online platforms for their news consumption, inadvertently subjecting themselves to a barrage of disinformation and manipulation. The absence of balance and news verification, inherent in respected media, makes these spaces fertile ground for those wishing to cause mischief to thrive. Despite feeling the pull to disconnect from social media, I'd clung to it, and was finding joy in William's posts. He was capturing our shared journey perfectly and bringing happiness amidst the digital noise.

***

Claudia

Alone in the solitude of my hotel room, I immersed myself in William's nightly post. Just as I was revisiting our evening, my thoughts were abruptly shattered by the buzz of my phone, signalling an incoming message from MI6. The SMS was brief:

Ruins of San Antón.

'Well, that's not helpful,' I muttered to myself, making the shift from the enchanting world of opera to the stark reality of my clandestine mission.

***

Anna Dupont

The day's walk, from Hornillos del Camino to Castrojeriz was a pleasant twenty-one kilometres and with mild temperatures forecast, we set out early at six in the morning. There's a shared appreciation among us for strolling in the dark, especially witnessing Meseta sunrises. By eight, our breakfast destination came into view. Tucked away in a Meseta fold, Hontanas lay off a minor road, a hidden gem known mostly to pilgrims. The parish church, presided over by a tall tower, was the first thing to catch our attention as we entered the town. Claudia told us that it was dedicated to the Immaculate Conception and had a rich history. I wondered how she knew.

'Originally,' Claudia said, 'it was constructed in Gothic style during the 14th century. It underwent later refurbishments in neoclassical fashion.' She looked at Jonathan and said, 'Did you know the interior harbours a baroque altarpiece by Fernando de la Peña, along with a copper processional cross dating back to the 13th century?' She pointed to another building. 'See, beside the church is the Palacio del Prelado Burgalés, believed to be the remains of the palace of a prelate from Burgos, the ancient lord of the town.'

Jonathan shook his head in disbelief. 'How do you know all this stuff?'

Claudia giggled, then held up her phone. 'Because I can read.'

'Right, for that,' Jonathan declared with a mischievous glint in his eyes, 'I vote Claudia buys everyone breakfast. All those in favour?'

I raised my hand and beside me, William followed suit.

Jonathan's grin widened. 'The tribe has spoken.'

Momentary perplexity crossed Jonathan's face. After a brief pause, he raised an eyebrow and said, 'Claudia, haven't you played this trick on us before, reading from your phone?'

'I can't remember.'

Jonathan wiggled a finger at Claudia. 'You're lucky to get away with buying only one breakfast.'

'Would it help if I told you that legend has it that the Virgin Mary appeared to a resident of Hontanas?'

Jonathan nodded thoughtfully. 'No, but that is interesting.'

Near to where we were standing, an Albergue caught our attention. It had undergone recent modernization, offering meals to weary travellers. Entering, we found it catered to walkers of all preferences, with shared dormitories and private rooms adorned with plush white towels. We found a spot at a table alongside Rob, the friendly Australian we'd encountered the day before, who boasted of a walking speed of 7kph. After he left, we lingered over a second cup of coffee and had the pleasure of meeting Tara from the USA. Claudia had her phone out again, capturing the moments as she took photographs of us with our newfound friends. In my quest to remain elusive, I tried to avoid having my photo taken by offering to be the photographer, but this was now proving difficult.

Leaving Hontanas, we passed a weathered building adorned with a painted reminder that Santiago was still a formidable 457 kilometres away. I inhaled, a surge of pride bubbling up even as my troublesome feet sought assurance as to whether I could endure the remaining journey. Each evening, since our pilgrimage began, William had diligently applied rock tape from Claudia's first aid kit to tend to my blistered feet, which were also swollen. Despite my age, I considered myself fit and believed that I could tackle the distances.

I had heard about pilgrims enduring swollen feet from trekking long distances daily. Yet, the realisation hit me belatedly as I rushed to meet William in Pamplona. The shoes I had on were still new, and my "match fitness" for extended walking was not quite up to par. The consequences of my inadequate preparation now loomed ominously ahead.

Rested and having enjoyed a hearty breakfast, we ventured out once more, the expansive sky above painting an azure canvas. 'Where else in the world would you rather be?' I muttered to myself. On one side, the Meseta rose majestically, while on the other, the land had been ploughed, a promise of future crops.

About six kilometres beyond Hontanas, the ruins of the Convent de San Antón and pilgrim hospital emerged on the horizon, its archway spanning the road.

Claudia, leading our group, came to a sudden halt. 'Hey, guys, do you mind waiting a couple of minutes before heading to the old convent? I need to rush ahead; there's nobody around, and I'm absolutely desperate for the loo. I should be able to find somewhere private amidst the ruins.'

My heart went out to Claudia. The Camino was devoid of public lavatories and, when bars or restaurants were scarce, finding a discreet spot was the only option. This challenge was worse on the Meseta, with its vast, open spaces.

***

Claudia

Approaching the Ruins of San Antón, I felt the chill of a bead of sweat running down my back. Not knowing what to expect, I pulled my pistol from its hiding place in my daypack and tucked it into my trousers, concealing it with my shirt as my heart quickened. Ducking behind the remnants of a stone wall, I readied myself. The ruins loomed ahead, their ancient stones holding secrets and perhaps danger. The serene Camino was now my battlefield. My senses alert, the wind carried whispers of a hidden threat as I approached the archway leading into the ruins. Seeing no one about, I drew my weapon, a familiar weight in my hand, my senses heightened. The monastery was eerily silent, devoid of the usual pilgrim chatter.

Is this part of someone's master plan?

As I stepped through the arch, I perceived shadows on the crumbling walls. I scanned for any sign of danger. MI6 wanted me here, and I was about to find out the reason.

A barely audible sound reached me, masked by the rustling leaves and distant echoes of pilgrims. I crept toward it, my training kicking in. In a concealed alcove, I spotted the outline of a figure. Readying myself in defence, I cautiously approached to discover Artōrius waiting. Pointing to my weapon, he said, 'Is that anyway to greet a friend?'

I shook my head apologetically. 'Sorry, I wasn't told what to expect.' Putting my weapon away in my backpack, I said, 'Which begs the question, why not? Why wasn't I told you would be here?'

Artōrius smiled, 'The usual, the secured service has been compromised. Well, they are not sure, so while they discover the source of the breach, a cryptic message had to do.'

I glanced over my shoulder to check the coast was still clear and that my friends hadn't entered the monastery ruins. 'Couldn't it have waited for Castrojeriz?'

Artōrius shook his head. 'No. Stephen Walls told me that you must be informed immediately.'

'Sounds serious.'

Artōrius shrugged his shoulders, 'Maybe, maybe not. Time will tell. It's about Anna Dupont, she's not known.'

'That's not a surprising revelation. As far as I can determine, she's a nice person walking the Camino, who probably has the hots for William, which is why she made the split-second decision to join us in Pamplona. I doubt she has come in contact with the authorities or has a social media presence.'

Artōrius shook his head. 'That's not what Stephen is saying. She's not known! Period!'

I was confused. 'Are you suggesting that she's entirely unknown?'

'Precisely, Claudia. Which is why Stephen told me to warn you.'

'Who is she?'

'That, Claudia, is a question I will leave to you. I can hear the chatter of your friends approaching and our time together is over.'

I turned but couldn't see them. 'We still have some time,' I said, but Artōrius had vanished.

I walked back out to where the others were. The ruins of the monastery and pilgrim hospital, a once-grand medieval ecclesiastic structure, were no longer menacing to me. Anna Dupont occupied my mind and my fingers brushed against the vial nestled in my pocket. I pondered whether she should meet the same fate as had Kat. As Anna and William leisurely made their way together, engrossed in chatter, the notion of harming Anna crossed my mind fleetingly. Yet the reasoning that William would tend to her should she become unwell quelled the thought momentarily. Regardless, with William's appointment looming at Rabanal del Camino, any delays would be unwelcome for him; he would have no choice but to depart. The stakes were too high for me to gamble with. Until I unravelled the enigma surrounding Anna Dupont's true identity, I had to remove her, discreetly, from our midst without raising eyebrows or hindering our journey.

Waiting for everyone to join me, I stood beside the information board, which told of the convent's history. As they arrived, I read the inscription to them.

'Ruins of San Anton Convent 14th Century. The convent was founded in 1146 under the patronage of King Alfonso VII. Former main Preceptory of the Antonian monks in Spain. This order was dedicated to the care of pilgrims and to cure those who suffered from the "Fire of San Anton", a disease that spread during the Middle Ages. They helped pilgrims and were conferred with the Cross of Tau as a sign of protection against evil on the way. Once the order had disappeared in 1787, some of its possessions were consigned to the collegiate church while the rest, because of the effects of the Ecclesiastical Confiscations of Mendizábal in 1835, passed into private hands. Since 2002 a pilgrims' shelter has been in operation here. The entrance to this convent was protected by an elevated 16th century arch. A magnificent gothic facade is still standing as well as the impressive ogival windows of the church's apse. The baroque altarpiece is preserved in the church of San Juan Bautista.'

Jonathan said, 'What were the ecclesiastical confiscations of Mendizábal?'

'I'll tell, provided it doesn't cost me another breakfast.'

'That sounds fair.'

'Do you want the short or long answer?'

'Short,' my walking companions said in unison.

'A set of decrees that resulted in the expropriation and privatisation of monastic properties in Spain.'

William pursed his lips. 'Perhaps a little more information would be interesting.'

I smiled, pleased at the request. 'A series of measures undertaken by Juan Álvarez Mendizábal, a Spanish liberal politician, in the 19th century. Mendizábal served as the finance minister under Queen Isabella II. In 1836, he initiated a set of radical reforms aimed at reducing the power and wealth of the Catholic Church in Spain. Mendizábal's confiscations targeted the vast landholdings and properties owned by the Church...' I was interrupted when Jonathan coughed. 'Yes?' I enquired.

He grinned, 'This may cost you another breakfast.'

'Most unfair. The tribe did ask... Now where was I? The primary objectives were to secularize these assets, transfer them to the state, and use the proceeds to alleviate Spain's financial crisis. The measures included the disentailment of Church lands and the suppression of monasteries and convents. The ecclesiastical confiscations of Mendizábal had significant implications for the power dynamics in Spain. They contributed to the ongoing process of desamortización, or disentailment, which aimed to modernize the economy and reduce the influence of the nobility and the Church. The reforms, however, sparked considerable controversy and opposition from conservative factions in Spain, particularly those aligned with the Church.'

William nodded. 'Understanding the history and context adds significance.' His gaze swept across the surroundings. 'The ruins are eerie yet beautiful. This deserves a spot among my cherished moments along the Camino, I'd say.'

'Shall we get a picture?' I said, pointing to a spot in front of a stark depiction of Christ crucified.

Anna produced her phone and said, 'I'll take and share it.'

I hadn't noticed Anna's reluctance to appear in our photos until now.

Photos taken, 'Onward and upward,' Jonathan said as he led us out of the ruins to continue our journey. Another three and a half kilometres later, we arrived in Castrojeriz, where we planned to spend the night. Locating our hotel, we noticed a sign out front that read "Hotel Closed," presumably for the siesta.

'It must be beer o'clock,' William said.

'And lunchtime,' Jonathan added.

Across from the closed hotel, we spotted a bar with outdoor seating. After enjoying a meal and a couple of drinks, I volunteered to check out our accommodation. When I investigated, it was clear the hotel was closed indefinitely.

This is not good.

I returned to share my findings. Anna shifted uncomfortably in her seat. 'I'm not concerned about finding a place to sleep, but we all had our luggage shipped to the hotel. Where are our things?'

'Where on the Camino indeed?' said Jonathan.

William shrugged. 'What do we do now?'

Jonathan mimicked William's gesture and echoed his words, 'Yes, what do we do now?'

Anna stood. 'Men, Claudia. They'd prefer to freeze and starve to death before asking for help. Come on Claudia, we'll ask the owner of the bar about the hotel.'

I didn't want to reveal that I could speak Spanish, so I turned to Anna and said, 'Do you have Google Translate on your phone?'

'We'll figure something out, Claudia.'

Inside the bustling bar, our presence caught the attention of a woman hurrying about, attending to customers. Anna said, 'Do you speak English?' The woman understood the question but signalled a negative response. 'French?' Anna tried again. Once more, the woman shook her head. Swiftly, Anna jotted something on her phone and displayed it to the lady. In response, the woman retrieved her phone from her pocket, typed a message, and showed it to Anna.

'It's closed for the winter,' Anna said.

The woman exchanged another message with Anna and displayed it for her to see. Anna nodded affirmatively. Turning to me, she said, 'She asked if we had a booking, and I said we did.'

I overheard the lady mutter, 'Esto está mal,' which I recognised meant, 'This is bad.' The hotel had failed to honour our booking, much to her displeasure.

'What's her name?' I inquired of Anna.

Anna promptly typed the question into her phone. The lady smiled and responded, 'Olga. My bar.' Anna pointed to herself, saying, 'Anna,' and then gestured towards me, adding, 'Claudia.'

I gauged Olga to be in her mid-fifties, a robust woman who commanded attention. Her chestnut hair, interlaced with strands of silver, was neatly tied into a practical bun, with a few rebellious wisps around her face. Adorned in a vibrant apron, reflective of her personality, she wore around her neck a gold locket shaped like a heart, an unassuming accessory hinting at a rich personal history. I wondered; what experiences had shaped her kindness towards strangers and if the gold heart was part of that story.

The local Civil Guard were enjoying their lunch outside the cafe. With a quick gesture, Olga signalled for us to follow her as she strutted over to where they were seated. Eavesdropping on their conversation, I learnt that they, too, were dissatisfied with the hotel and were eager to lend a hand.

'Excuse me,' Anna interjected, holding her phone up for Olga and the Guardia to see.

Olga's expression hardened, and I overheard her saying, 'Their luggage was sent to the hotel, and now they don't have it.'

A member of the Guardia responded promptly, 'We'll need to assist them in locating it.'

Under my breath, I murmured, 'This kind of help would never happen in Britain.'

In the distance, a woman's voice called out, growing louder with every step she took towards us. 'I'm searching for a William and Anna. I've got your luggage.'

William raised his hand, and the woman made her way over to our table. Olga, Anna and I gathered around as the woman explained that she managed the local Municipal Albergue. When the luggage transport company discovered that our hotel was closed, they had entrusted our belongings to her care. She repeated the story in Spanish for Olga's benefit. Inquiring about vacancies at the Municipal, Olga was met with a disappointed shake of the woman's head.

Turning to us, the woman said, 'Sorry we have no vacancies at the Municipal.'

Undeterred, Olga assured the lady that she would secure accommodation for us. After dialling a number, she engaged in conversation with a receptionist inquiring about rooms for us. After a pause, Olga's expression brightened. 'Eso es excelente.'

Turning to the proprietor of the Municipal, Olga asked her to inform Anna that she had found a place for us all to stay. With a nod, Olga handed her phone to Anna as the hotel receptionist spoke English. Once the booking was confirmed, we followed the Municipal lady to the Albergue to retrieve our belongings and then Olga's son drove us to our lodgings.

***

With my feet luxuriating in the foot pool and a glass of chilled white wine in hand, I was secretly pleased our original hotel had closed for winter. Olga's son had dropped us off at the secure entrance of the Quinta San Francisco Hotel. After confirming our guest status through the intercom, the gates unlocked, welcoming us into this unexpected haven. As I took a sip of my drink, I marvelled at our luck. Who would have imagined that nestled within the quaint village of Castrojeriz, we would find such a beautiful place, a seamless fusion of classic and modern design, offering a sanctuary of comfort and tranquillity?

After a day of walking, a rendezvous with Artōrius and the saga of lost luggage and closed hotel, our refuge emerged as a perfect haven for weary travellers. Our hotel took its name from the 14th-century Convent of San Francisco whose ancient ruins were in the grounds of the hotel. Quinta San Francisco invited me to immerse myself in a blend of history and contemporary comfort. Our rooms boasted austere yet modern décor, with the warm embrace of oak wood panelling creating an atmosphere of peace and calm - or so the establishment's brochure promised. After our more modest lodgings, this hotel commitment to guest comfort was exemplary in every detail, from the quality of beds to the softness of monogrammed sheets and towels, plus the invigorating showers. I was at home.

Before indulging in the foot pool, I'd strolled through the grounds and visited the remnants of the Convent of San Francisco, it's an historical charm adding to the picturesque setting among flowerbeds and orchards, I stumbled upon a vegetable garden where the chef was hand picking ingredients for the evening meal. We'd booked a table at the hotel restaurant, "La Bodega," known for its set-course menu that celebrated seasonal products and local Castilian cuisine. Dinner promised to be something special.

In this wonderful setting, I almost forgot about the mysterious Anna Dupont and the need to neutralize her without compromising my mission. With a sigh, I drained my glass; and allowed the Quinta San Francisco Hotel to weave its enchantment, a refuge that exceeded mere respite. It was a blissful escape. As the water shimmered, I hummed a tune from The Sound of Music: 'How do you solve a problem like Anna Dupont? It can wait until tomorrow.' I chuckled, swept away by the beauty of the moment. 'Ah, this water is beautiful.'

Returning to my room, I took a moment to freshen up and ponder my attire for the evening's dinner. As I entered the La Bodega restaurant, a sense of pleasant surprise washed over me as I noticed a unifying theme among us all. Each person had taken care to don their most elegant garments. Jonathan, clad in his suit, exuded a striking aura of handsomeness among the gathered company.

Over pre-dinner drinks, we had a delightful conversation with David and Ros, fellow guests and pilgrims.

Dinner unfolded sublimely, the meal and wine an improvement on what we'd previously enjoyed. Despite the cost, the change of the hotel had been a serendipitous blessing. That evening, we deviated from the norm of our journey, dining with our own troupe, without the company of other pilgrims. The lively conversation that circled our table was constant, with our banter revolving around the notorious steep climb out of Castrojeriz to Alto de Mostelares at 900 metres, as well as the scarcity of dining options en route to Fromista, twenty-five kilometres away. After dinner, we ventured to a supermarket to stock up on provisions for the journey ahead. Filling his shopping basket, Jonathan looked quite at home in his suit.

It wasn't until I was preparing for bed that I realised how engrossed I'd been in preparations for the next day. I'd not yet devised a plan to remove Anna from our walking group. Reminiscing the delightful foot pool, I whispered to myself, 'Anna Dupont can wait.' Taking my phone, I moved to view what William had written about the day. I logged into his social media page.

William's Social Media Post

As we I strolled along the path from Hornillos to Castrojeriz, my mind envisioned crafting tales about the ever-changing landscape and the places we passed.

The village of Hontanas seemed like a backdrop fit for a Hollywood Medieval blockbuster, and the ruins of San Anton convent whispered of a setting perfect for a spy mystery yet, instead of narrating these picturesque scenes, I share the heart-warming story of the kindness, bestowed upon us by the people of Castrojeriz, especially a gracious lady, Olga, who owned the bar where we sought refuge while waiting for our hotel to open—only to discover the hotel was closed for the winter....

I smiled when I read on...

Claudia is in her element. Here we are, basking in the unexpected luxury of a 4-star hotel, a transformed monastery that surpasses all expectations.

A small part of me can't help but wonder, did Claudia orchestrate this all along... ha-ha. They even have a special pool for weary walkers to soak their feet.

Tomorrow, we resume our more modest "Way". A long distance awaits.

CHAPTER 16
The Meseta Continues

Claudia

The day marked an early start for our twenty-six-kilometre journey to Fromista. As we left Castrojeriz, the trail merged with a meticulously restored section of a Roman road, originally constructed to offer a safe passage across the marshy Odrilla valley. A kilometre beyond, a wooden footbridge spanned the Rio Odrilla, marking the prelude to a challenging ascent up to the Alto de Mostelares, where Anna directed our attention to the remnants of ancient Roman mines that once yielded mica. A climb like the one we faced in Castrojeriz might have appeared daunting a week prior, but the winding path swiftly propelled us to an elevation of 900 metres. As we crested the peak, a surge of euphoria washed over us, marking another triumph on our pilgrimage. At the summit was a monument erected by fellow pilgrims and we took a well-deserved break in a rest area, savouring an expansive view that stretched back towards the township of Castrojeriz.

The climb guided us back to the Meseta, which unfurled like an expansive canvas of limitless horizons. Reinvigorated, we continued our journey toward Puente de Itero, Itero de la Vega, and Boadilla del Camino. As far as the eye could see, we were alone in the expanse of the Meseta. Suddenly, in awe, William stopped, spun around and shouted, 'This is magical!'

I had to agree with him.

Progressing along the elevated Meseta, we eventually descended steeply into Itero de la Vega. Choosing to forgo a coffee break, we pressed on with a relatively flat and straightforward stretch ahead. An hour and a half later, we gazed up at the "Rollo of Justice," a decorated jurisdictional column crowned by a Gothic spire. It dominated the town square of Boadilla del Camino, next to the parish church of Santa Maria. Unanimously, we agreed we'd earned our first cafe con leche of the day, which morphed into two.

The stroll from Boadilla del Camino to Fromista, our overnight destination, emerged as one of my cherished segments of the journey. The path traced a scenic route along a welcome shaded tree line, hugging the tranquil Canal de Castilla. Upon arriving in Fromista, we indulged in cool drinks under a marquee at a local bar, observing our fellow pilgrims as they gradually joined the gathering.

Tara, whom we'd shared a coffee break with back in Hontanas, took a seat at our table for a while. Although I'd sent a picture I'd taken of her to MI6, I was yet to receive a background check. As she spoke, I listened attentively, making mental notes. She told us; she worked for the Roman Catholic Church, specifically the diocese of St. Louis. From her description of her work, she was clearly a passionate devotee of Catholicism. Tara also shared her talent as a skilled piano player. Despite the pending background check, I found it hard to perceive Tara as a threat; she seemed genuine and benign but I was aware of the need to address the situation of Anna Dupont.

After settling into our hotel, indulging in refreshing showers and tending to our laundry, I joined the others for an exploration of the village. I'd read about the cultural treasures in town, including churches like San Pedro and Santa María, along with the hermitage of Santiago and its revered image of the Virgen del Otero. However, for me, Fromista's most interesting gem was the Church of San Martín, a genuine work of art. Founded in 1035, the temple distinguished itself with the simplicity of its lines and the harmony between architecture and an array of decorations. Despite my temptation to offer a commentary on the places we visited, I refrained, harbouring a mild fear of having to foot the bill for everyone's dinner.

During our dinner, Tara joined our table, and her company was convivial. Before dessert was served, my phone buzzed with a message from Stephen Walls.

Please call.

'My friends, will you excuse me?' I said. 'Despite the wonderful accommodation of last night, I didn't sleep well. I need an early night.'

'You're not having dessert?' Jonathan inquired.

From his tone, I sensed his disappointment that I was retiring early. I resolved to give him more attention the following day. Chuckling, I said, 'Surprising, isn't it? I hope it's not a glimpse of what's coming. Maybe I should start exercising more.' Everyone giggled.

Alone in my room, I felt the need to procrastinate before contacting the office. I read William's daily social media post. It made me smile. 'So true,' I whispered to myself.

William's Social Media Post

On the Meseta, with no one in sight ahead or behind us as far as the eye could discern, Anna and I delved into conversations about how the Camino continues to metamorphose. Since departing from Burgos, the camaraderie of those we'd grown to cherish now exists as a mere memory, and our troupe journeys onward in solitude.

The terrain unfolds into picturesque farmland, embellished with a charming tree-lined canal. Amid this serene backdrop, we reflect on the swift pace at which life can evolve.

The Meseta, with its solitude, and ever-changing landscapes, serves as a metaphor for the ebb and flow of our personal journey. We traverse not only physical terrain but also the transformative currents of the Camino, where each step uncovers a new revelation, and the beauty of change is as constant as our footprints on this sacred path.

Having absorbed the post, I pondered on the people we'd shared the path with: Athira, Jean, Chuck and Cathy, Shaun, Alesa, Athira, Rob; Ian, Catherine, and their one-year-old baby James, Chinmay, Jack, Federica and Kat. While I hadn't cherished their company in the same way William described, their absence left a void. I revisited the message on my phone, a simple yet urgent "please call." 'If I have to,' I said aloud.

I picked up my phone but hesitated before placing it back down. Opting for my map, I studied the next day's route, revealing an alternative path to Villalcázar de Sirga that traced alongside the river. The thought of the scenic journey brought another smile to my face.

I will suggest we go that way.

Gathering determination, I lifted the phone once more and dialled MI6.

'Good evening, Claudia,' Stephen said.

'Sir.'

'I apologise, Claudia, for the lack of communication. It was a necessary precaution, as you would understand. Artōrius assures me he shared our concern about Anna Dupont with you. What did you make of the information?'

'Sir, it was more a matter of what I inferred from the lack of information. I can think of many reasons someone might adopt a secret identity, including the extremes of witness protection or operating as a foreign agent. It would help, Sir, if you could disclose the scenario.'

'Indeed, Claudia. We are continuing our inquiries. We've uncovered some early images of her; however, the assessment is they are deep fakes, created by artificial intelligence through deep learning, capable of generating fake images or videos of real people. At the moment, we are none the wiser. You should assume her to be hostile until we confirm otherwise. What action have you taken to protect William Marshal?'

'For now, Sir, I'm maintaining my vigilance. Anna and William have formed a close bond and if I am to remove her from our group, it must be executed with care to avoid jeopardizing the mission.'

'Do you perceive her as a threat?' Stephen inquired.

I hesitated, weighing my response. In truth, I didn't. After a brief pause, I replied, 'Stephen, I approach everyone with caution. It's second nature to me.'

The ensuing silence showed Stephen's scepticism. He was concerned I was "going native," or, as it's termed in our profession, experiencing "deep cover syndrome." The phenomenon occurs when an undercover operative becomes emotionally or psychologically entangled with the group they are investigating, leading to a potential division of loyalty between the law enforcement agency and the infiltrated group. Stephen was apprehensive about my ability to carry out the mission.

'Claudia, are you sure you're not becoming too absorbed in walking the Camino?'

Avoiding Stephen's question, I said, 'Are you pessimistic this evening, Sir? There is an unusual weight in your voice' I heard Stephen exhale heavily.

'Claudia, when I joined MI6, the West was revelling in the end-of-history theory, celebrating the final triumph of liberal democracy. The notion of lasting peace in the Middle East, anchored in a two-state solution, seemed plausible then. It was conceivable that Russia would develop into a Western ally, and in China, political liberalization was expected to accompany economic liberalization. Globalization would bring substantial improvements in living standards and mitigate geopolitical tensions through the interconnectivity of international trade. A new information-based economy promised increased productivity and the potential end of boom-and-bust cycles. Progress appeared inevitable. Instead, we find ourselves at the end of progress.'

'This morning, I woke up to reports of fresh attacks on British and U.S. shipping in the Red Sea by Iranian-backed rebels, escalating tensions in the Middle East. There are growing calls in the U.S. Congress and from conservatives in the House of Commons for a more robust response. Moments like these can entangle us in another disastrous war, precisely what Russia and China desire.'

I started to respond, but Stephen continued before I could utter a word.

'All-out war hasn't erupted, Claudia, partly because no aggressor nation has given us sufficient cause. Neither the UK nor the U.S., nor our combined treaty allies, has faced a kinetic attack by a nation-state. We've witnessed cyberattacks, economic manoeuvres, and grey zone jostling, but no direct kinetic assault. Our response must be measured, as we're aware the gravest danger lies on the horizon. The post-war period is over; the pre-war world has arrived. In no more than five years' time, we might find ourselves entangled in multiple theatres involving Russia, China, Iran, and North Korea. Each of these autocracies has escalated military pressure on its neighbours: Russia's invasion of Ukraine, Iran igniting a ring of fire with proxy forces surrounding Israel, nuclear-armed North Korea abandoning its reunification policy in favour of conquest with a barrage of ballistic missiles, and China incrementally increasing territorial and political pressure across a broad spectrum of nations. I fear that the demands for U.S. and British power could be overwhelming. We must avoid entanglements to conserve UK resources and prepare for the gravest of potential crises, a war against China. Such a conflict would divert U.S. resources from Europe, embolden Russia, and likely lead to a direct confrontation between the UK and the Kremlin.'

'I'm not being pessimistic, Claudia. Defeatism is not an option. Never in British history has the role of MI6 been more crucial. We find ourselves in a sombre era when the phrase "security through strength" is truer than ever. If William Marshal is selling UK military secrets and there's a nest of spies within our defence industry, we must eradicate the threat. You must ensure whatever William Marshal is carrying does not fall into the wrong hands; simultaneously, we—by which I mean you—must uncover his contacts. Descend every burrow and root them out.' There was a pause before Stephen snapped, 'I do not want a repeat of the cold war Russian spy bungles on my watch. I'm sure that I make myself clear, Claudia?

Stephen's words had their desired effect, to sharpen my focus; I was now honed to achieve my mission. 'Crystal clear, Sir.'

'Good, I'm pleased to hear that.'

'Have you discovered what William Marshal has hidden inside the puzzle box?'

'No, not yet, Sir. He keeps it inside his daypack, which is always with him.' A sudden thought crossed my mind.

Did he bring the daypack to dinner this evening?

I couldn't recall. I chastised myself, *Sloppy Claudia, very sloppy.*

'Sorry Claudia, I missed that. Did you say something?'

'No, Stephen, simply musing.'

'Okay... We've also continued our inquiries into why the Albanian Mafia was interested in William Marshal and uncovered a link to Iran, which makes more sense. Iran's Ministry of Intelligence and Security has been enlisting criminal gangs and their networks to carry out assassinations and kidnappings across numerous jurisdictions. They've recruited members from the Hells Angels Outlaw Motorcycle Group and leaders in the Albanian Mafia, specifically Diego Gavoci, the person you encountered in Zubiri. Our assumption that the Albanian Mafia was entering the world of espionage is false; Diego Gavoci was just a hired thug working for Iran. We've intercepted intelligence chatter suggesting that another attempt will be made on Marshal in León, probably to grab what he is carrying.'

'When foreign regimes resort to using underworld thugs, it makes my life a lot easier.'

'How so, Claudia?'

'Thugs need to look intimidating, tattoos, threatening insignias and the like, so they stand out and even more so on the Camino. If Iran has engaged criminal gangs, they won't be difficult to spot among the pilgrims.'

'That may be true Claudia, but don't let Anna Dupont's benign looks lower your guard.'

'Be assured, Stephen, I won't.'

With the phone call to Stephen Walls concluded, I checked my tracking app to locate William's daypack. It was in his room, two doors away from mine. Despite a fleeting temptation to break in and inspect its contents, I dismissed the idea. If William had become lax about leaving his bag unattended, my priority was to caution him about the risk of theft - especially before we approached León.

***

We had opted for a later start for our stroll from Fromista to Carrion de les Condes, covering a leisurely twenty kilometres. After approximately thirty-five minutes of walking, we arrived at the village of Población de Campos, intending to take the alternative path I'd recommended, that traced the river to Villalcázar de Sirga for a delayed breakfast. Lost in thoughts about Anna Dupont, I missed the turn, and we had to backtrack. Recrossing the bridge, we spotted the track running alongside the river. Following the route, it wasn't long before we heard approaching steps from behind. Kat, with her hefty twenty-kilo pack, greeted us with a radiant smile and a wave.

'Hi, Kat,' Jonathan called out.

'Gee, it's lovely to see you guys,' Kat responded and, after some casual banter, Kat told us she was also opting for the scenic river route but had plans to push on past Carrion de los Condes, implying that she would walk at a brisk pace.

Recalling the delicate condition of Anna's feet, I pondered.

That's how I can handle Ms. Anna Dupont by pushing her limits, setting a blistering pace while walking with Kat.

I found the idea so satisfying that I had to bite my lip to stop grinning. My scheme held some irony, considering during my last encounter with Kat, I poisoned her. She'd now unknowingly play a role as my accomplice.

As Kat set off, I fell in beside her and struck up a conversation. I increased my pace, forcing her to quicken hers. As we gained speed, a smile spread across her face; she clearly welcomed the company, as long as it didn't impede her progress.

Jonathan joined us to form a trio, walking side by side across the track, Kat in the middle. I heard the rhythmic sound of William's walking poles contacting with the ground behind me; he was planning to join our group, and wherever William went, Anna was sure to follow.

Villalcázar de Sirga and breakfast awaited us ten kilometres ahead. I hoped that the brisk hour and a half walk on the challenging terrain would take a toll on Anna's feet, deterring her from continuing.

'Do you enjoy walking alone?' Jonathan asked Kat.

'On the Camino, I have the best of all worlds,' she replied. 'Sometimes, I'm alone, which is wonderful, but at other times, like now, I walk with my Camino family, which is also delightful. And occasionally, I stroll with people I've met at the Albergue, like Chinmay, Federica and Jack Rabbit, which I find enjoyable too. I like time on my own. It allows me to reflect and think about my place in the world. What I'm really looking forward to is meeting my father, who's flying in from the States to walk the last 100 kilometres with me. How cool is that?'

As we followed the river path, Jonathan and Kat chattered happily beside me. Their laughter blended with the murmur of the water accompanying our steps. Looking up, a clear blue sky stretched endlessly above, creating a picturesque canvas that painted the landscape with vibrant colours. The sunlight filtered through the leaves, casting a dappled pattern on the trail as we walked alongside the water. My eyes caught glimpses of wildflowers lining the path, delicate petals nodding in agreement with the breeze. The rhythmic rustle of the leaves above was nature's symphony, accompanied by the dance of sunlight shimmering on the water's surface. Dragonflies flitted about, iridescent wings adding flashes of colour to the natural masterpiece, the distant calls of birds a soundtrack to our journey. For a moment, the mission receded as the beauty of my surroundings enveloped me. I felt connected to the world like never before.

It's as if the landscape holds secrets, whispering tales of the majestic beauty we often miss.

A twinge of guilt tugged at my conscience. On this blissful path, my mission meant that I had to prevent Anna from completing the Camino. My duties as a spy for His Majesty's service often affected others; it was inevitable.

I heard Jonathan say to Kat. 'I doubt my father has the physical ability to undertake the walk, even the last hundred kilometres. Your dad must be fit, and his feet tough.'

Jonathan's story, intertwined with the profound loss of his sister, made it highly unlikely that he would extend an invitation to his father to accompany him on the journey. But, perhaps the transformative power of the Camino had reshaped his feeling and he should? Completing the final hundred kilometres together with his father could be a healing experience.

Kat responded with a sigh. 'I hope so, Jonathan. When I invited him to join me, I didn't consider his abilities or condition. I've always seen my father as a superhero, someone who could conquer anything. Walking the Camino has given me a newfound appreciation of the challenges of walking day after day, even for someone of my age. I hope he'll be okay. I think he will be.' She was quiet for a moment before saying, 'As children, we always view our parents as if they're indestructible. Why is that?'

I saw Jonathan gaze into the distance as he weaved through his memories. Slowly, he said, 'I think, Kat, we see them as the pillars of our world, their strength a source of comfort and security.' He paused... 'Then, as we grow, we notice their humanity and their vulnerabilities. It's a shift from the idealised image of superheroes to an understanding of the complexities that make them human, like us. Perhaps we can come to appreciate them in a different light.'

'Should I have considered his abilities before inviting him to join me, do you think?'

'No, not at all. I'm sure your father sees the invitation as a wonderful gift, to spend time with his daughter, and that's special in its own right. What about you, Claudia? Would your father come if you invited him?'

I pondered the question, crafting the version of the truth I wished to reveal. I considered:

You know, my relationship with my father is... complex. There are wounds that time alone can't heal. As a child, I was kidnapped and endured unimaginable horrors. Max and Olivia, two MI6 agents, stumbled upon my image online and rescued me from a life of darkness. They brought me back to my family, but it didn't go as well as I'd hoped. Finding my place became a struggle, eventually leading me down a path that ...

No, I would not share this truth, not with anyone.

After a moment of hesitation, I said, 'Oh, inviting my father? It's an intriguing thought. He's quite set in his ways, always busy with work and such. I doubt he'd find the time for the journey.' Wanting to move the attention off me, I called to William, who was walking behind me. 'William, would you invite your daughter to walk the last hundred kilometres of the Camino?'

'I suppose I shared some similarities with your father, Claudia, always busy. You know that song, "Cats in the Cradle"? It's the story of a father who never has enough time for his son. Later, the son grows up to be just like him, making the father proud—except that his son has no time for him. If you were to ask my daughter, she'd say. "I would love to, Dad, if only I had the time."'

'Does that make you sad?' Kat inquired.

I focused my attention, eager to hear William's response.

'Do I carry regrets? That's a tough question. I've never been one to cling to regrets. In the moment, we simply follow what we believe is necessary. Would I have liked my relationship with Samantha to have been like the one she had with my wife, Hannah? I didn't think about it when Hannah was alive and now it's too late.'

'Maybe' Kat said. 'If Samantha is like me and my friends, then fathers will hold a special place in their hearts. You should ask. She can only say no.'

William was quiet for a moment before adding, 'It probably sounds cowardly, but I prefer not to know.'

That was a brave answer, I thought.

We walked in silence for a time until my spy senses kicked in. During our journey, Anna had kept silent about her family and Kat's question presented an opportunity to delve into Anna's history. I trusted my instincts to discern if she was being truthful.

'Would you invite your children to join you for the final hundred kilometres, Anna?'

Anna was silent for a moment.

CHAPTER 17
Anna Dupont

Anna Dupont

Listening to the conversation unfold, I knew inevitably, one of them would ask me.

What would I say when my time came?

I wasn't always Anna Dupont. I came into this world as Claire Peis, taking my first breath in the tranquil village of Hohenberg, nestled amid the picturesque landscapes of Bavaria, Germany, a village of cobblestone streets and timber-framed houses, a place that would set the stage for my formative years.

My father, Klaus Peis, worked as a carpenter, crafting intricate wooden pieces that adorned homes throughout the village. Ingrid Peis, my mother, was a seamstress known for creating embroidered garments, a skill she passed on to me. I recall our household filled with the scent of freshly cut wood and the rhythmic hum of a sewing machine, a sanctuary for my siblings and I. Hohenberg was a tight-knit community and played a pivotal role in shaping my values. The Peis family attended the local Lutheran church, where traditions were upheld and the echoes of hymns filled the air on Sundays. My early years were marked by the celebration of local festivals, where the community gathered to share in the joy of traditional music, dance, and hearty Bavarian cuisine.

I attended the local village school, a charming institution nestled amidst rolling hills. The school was where children laughed as they learned about German history, literature, and mathematics. It was here that my enquiring mind and love of storytelling blossomed; it set the stage for a pursuit of the arts. Despite the challenges of post-war Germany, our family thrived, and I embraced my family and cultural roots. I had happy memories but, little did I know, that the quaint village of Hohenberg would become a distant memory and circumstances would lead me far from the comfort of my German home.

My rebellious spirit manifested itself early in the form of bold fashion and life choices, unconventional hairstyles, and an unapologetic embrace of art, literature, and music that challenged the status quo. I adored the work of avant-garde artists, devoured literature that explored human complexities and danced to rock and roll, a music that echoed the heartbeat of a generation yearning for change. Gatherings and impromptu discussions with my peers informed my concept of a new world. The aroma of freshly rolled cigarettes, strumming of guitars, and passionate debates about politics and philosophy filled the air. Armed with a desire for self-expression and a thirst for knowledge, I became a central figure in bohemian circles. My conservative upbringing clashed with my newfound ideals, leading to tensions within the Peis household. The once disciplined girl of Bavarian traditions now challenged the foundations of their world. I pushed against boundaries, yet remained connected to my family, torn between the allure of a better world and the love I held for the people who shaped my life.

In the late 1970s, fuelled by a need to break free from the constraints of my upbringing, I embarked on a journey to the vibrant and pulsating heart of cultural expression of the time, Berlin. I remember the city as a melting pot of creativity and progressive ideals; it offered me the sanctuary I sought for my artistic aspirations. In the eclectic neighbourhoods and pulsating nightlife, I immersed myself in the avant-garde art of Berlin. I'd traded the tranquillity of Hohenberg for the graffiti-laden streets of the German capital, where every corner yelled of artistic rebellion. Here, I honed my craft, experimented with new media and forged connections with fellow creatives, who shared my passion for pushing the edges of artistic expression.

Amidst the canvases and studios, my quest guided me into the embrace of a charismatic man, an artist and political activist destined to revolutionize the world, or so I thought. Entranced, I fell in love. His aggression caught me off guard and I dismissed it as a fluke. His apologies were accompanied by gifts that lulled me into a deceptive sense of security. Captivated by the fervour of our collaborative artistic endeavours, I unwittingly became enmeshed in a tempestuous relationship that gradually diminished my own sense of identity. The liberated bohemian romance metamorphosed into a gilded cage, trapping me within the confines of a violent liaison and continual emotional strife. As the years unfolded, I ignored and then faced the harsh reality of an abusive relationship, my art tainted by dark shadows of control and manipulation. In my late forties, the indomitable spirit that had fuelled my rebellious youth resurfaced. I made the courageous decision to leave everything behind. I severed my ties and fled to a village in the south of France where, among the vineyards and lavender fields, I hoped to rebuild my life.

Walking beside the river with my Camino friends, memories flood my mind of the day I first arrived in Bellefontaine-sur-Lierre. The village greeted me with its charming fountain at the centre, waters speaking tales of centuries past. The gentle flow of the Lierre river wound through the cobblestoned streets, weaving a magical tale of tranquillity and enchantment. I remember the warmth of the southern sun as it caressed my cheeks, the scent of lavender dancing in the air and knew here my soul could be soothed. I knew I'd made a good decision and stood at the threshold of renewal, determined to carve out a new life in that place. My eyes had been drawn to a weathered and forgotten building tucked away in a corner of the village square. A faded "For Rent" sign hung in its window, an invitation waiting to be answered. Running my hand along the stone wall, I listened: the building was calling to me, whispering, "Enchanting Pages." My destiny was within those walls and

Enchanting Pages would be a bookshop, my home, and a sanctuary for bibliophiles and dreamers alike.

The man's name was Monsieur Dubois, in his seventies, with a gentle demeanour that belied the weight of years upon his shoulders. He was stout, evidence of a life well-lived with a few too many indulgences along the way. His eyes were warm and spoke of the kindness and wisdom of a lifetime. When I first met Monsieur Dubois, he greeted me with a cautious smile, his weathered face lined with traces of laughter and sorrow. Despite his initial reservation, I sensed a glimmer of curiosity when I outlined my vision for transforming his run-down building into the bookshop, Enchanting Pages. With patience and persuasion, I had explained my idea, offering to breathe life into the vacant space in exchange for a temporary reprieve from rent. He had given me an audience, his expression thoughtful as he balanced the pros and cons. It was clear that the building held sentimental value for him, a relic of bygone days steeped in nostalgia.

A village wary of outsiders echoed the plight of many small places in rural France, requiring fresh faces for its continued existence. Monsieur Dubois recognised this need and after much deliberation, he had relented, swayed by my enthusiasm and determination. He offered me eight months of rent-free occupancy, on the condition that I undertook transforming the site into the bookshop of my dreams. To my surprise, he offered to lend a hand with the renovations, eager to see his beloved building brought back to life.

We embarked on the journey together with Monsieur Dubois, more than simply the owner of a run-down building; he became a partner in my endeavour, a steadfast ally in the face of many challenges and setbacks. With his guidance and support, Enchanting Pages took shape. Each stroke of paint and every nail hammered into place, a testament to our shared vision. In Monsieur

Dubois, I had found a kind man and not only a landlord but also a friend who believed in my vision. We worked side by side, breathing new life into an old building. Years later, I remain profoundly grateful to Monsieur Dubois and the opportunity he bestowed upon me. I kept my tumultuous past hidden from him and he refrained from prying. Bellefontaine-sur-Lierre symbolised a fresh start, with Monsieur Dubois serving as my guiding light through the uncertainties of my journey.

Furnishing the shop was an adventure too and luck had been on my side when I learned that a municipal library, undergoing renovations some forty kilometres away, was discarding its old shelves and furniture. With the help of a local man with a truck, a friend of Monsieur Dubois, I transported the treasures to my shop, each piece carrying its own unique story, adding to the charm of my newfound haven.

The locals of Bellefontaine-sur-Lierre had been drawn to my project. With my elegant looks and genuine charm of those years, I was able to elicit their support and help. Whether it was lending a hand with painting or offering words of encouragement, the villagers embraced my endeavour with open arms, eager to see Enchanting Pages come to life. The building had been transformed under my care and I'd chosen sympathetic colours for the walls that complemented the golden sunsets that bathed the village each evening. Soft rugs adorned the wooden floors, inviting patrons to lose themselves in the world of words. Cozy armchairs nestled in corners, perfect for curling up with a good book and a steaming cup of coffee. Being an artist, I added my personal touch to the interior. Alongside the shelves of books were my paintings, each a reflection of the beauty surrounding us, the rolling vineyards and fields of lavender.

I started modestly, with a curated selection of used books, serving freshly brewed coffee to travellers and locals alike. But

Enchanting Pages quickly became more than just a bookstore, more a sanctuary where people could come for company or to immerse themselves in the world of literature. As my finances improved, I'd expanded my offerings, introducing new works and hosting author readings and book clubs. With each passing day, Enchanting Pages grew in reputation and charm, a testament to the power of perseverance and the magic of storytelling. And as I watched the villagers flock to my shop, their smiles reflecting the joy and wonder found within its walls, I had finally found the peace and purpose I had searched for.

What is making the Camino journey inspiring for me is the people I'm encountering along the way, individuals like William, Jonathan, and Claudia, who were becoming dear to my heart; I cherished them deeply. Connections like those also made Enchanting Pages extraordinary. One memory I have is of Sophie, a young woman excited to become a writer. On a rainy afternoon, she stumbled upon my bookshop, and our chance encounter blossomed. Over weeks, I became her mentor and confidante, offering guidance and encouragement. Eventually, Sophie found inspiration amidst the shelves of Enchanting Pages and embarked on her own literary journey. I saw her name grace the pages of a newspaper, heralding her victory in a prestigious literary award. It was a moment to savour.

I also remember fondly Jacques, a retired literature professor whose love for classic novels rivalled the authors themselves. He wove through the aisles of my bookshop, a regular whose presence infused the air with intellectual fervour. With each visit, Jacques ignited lively discussions on authors and literary movements, his vast knowledge a magnet for curious minds. Then there was Pierre, our local historian, whose anecdotes breathed life into the pages of forgotten times, and Isabella, a retiree whose heart beat to the rhythm of romance novels. Yet amidst the many patrons, it was

Henri, who left the biggest mark on my life. As time passed, a bond of trust blossomed between us, forged through shared confidences and unspoken understanding. Sensing the echoes of my own enigmatic past, Henri revealed his own tale cautiously, like fragile pages from a forbidden manuscript. He was a person aged by years of service in the shadows, a retired operative of the Service de documentation extérieure et de contre-espionnage (SDECE). Behind his weathered face was a wealth of experience, his past shrouded in secrecy. When the shadows of my past emerged, threatening to engulf me in their darkness, Henri emerged as my unlikely saviour. With the precision of a master strategist, he crafted a meticulous plan, my lifeline to freedom.

The day my violent ex-partner darkened the threshold of my bookshop remains etched in my memory like a jagged scar. It was then that I turned to Henri, the only beacon of hope in my storm-tossed world. With quiet determination, he marshalled his connections, summoning the clandestine forces of his past to orchestrate my escape. Forged documents materialised, a shield against the prying eyes of the man who sought to drag me back into the abyss. Henri's brilliance came to the fore as he deployed diversionary tactics, weaving a web of deception to confound my pursuer and ensure Claire Peis disappeared into the shadows. Under his guidance, I shed my former self like a snake shedding its skin, emerging anew as Anna Dupont. Every aspect of this persona was crafted by Henri, a suit of armour to shield me from a threat that lingered in the remnants of a long-forgotten life.

In the chaos of my departure, one regret lingers like a haunting refrain: Monsieur Dubois, the gentle soul who owned my building and who gave me my new life in Bellefontaine-sur-Lierre, was abandoned without a farewell. His absence in my life is an agonising reminder of the sacrifices made in the name of survival, a silent tribute to the cost of freedom.

As Anna Dupont, I moved to the ancient streets of Paris, the City of Lights. The bustling metropolis, with its grand boulevards and iconic landmarks, provided the perfect backdrop for my clandestine rebirth. Here, anonymity cloaked me like a veil, granting me the freedom to craft a new existence untouched by the shadows that haunted me. In my quest for normality, I found employment in a library nestled within the heart of a secluded side street. Surrounded by towering shelves of books, I felt pangs of nostalgia for the bookstore I'd left behind and the companionship it once offered.

To my surprise, I discovered an affinity for the burgeoning world of IT. As technology surged forward, I embraced the digital frontier with a fervour born of necessity. With each keystroke, I honed my skills, transforming myself into a proficient navigator of the digital realm. In this developing landscape, technology became my ally, offering me a means to traverse the complexities of the modern world while remaining veiled in anonymity. It was a source of unexpected empowerment.

Why I felt compelled to approach William, the lost soul at the Paris railway station, remains a mystery to me. Perhaps it was a fleeting impulse sparked by empathy, or a subconscious yearning for connection in the midst of my solitude. Whatever the reason, it propelled me to act on instinct, setting into motion a chain of events I could never have anticipated.

Now, as I walk the river path towards Villalcázar de Sirga, despite the ache in my feet and the weariness that weighs upon my limbs, I find beauty in the simplicity of this pilgrimage and the connections forged along the way. I am reminded that sometimes the truest adventures begin with a single step.

My heart is heavy with the burden of my secret. In keeping my past hidden, I've woven a web of lies: my false identity, a tale of a marriage and a husband's untimely demise. That innocuous fib feels like a weight I'm forced to carry. How could I confess to William that I'd been untruthful? Is there any path back from deception between friends, or have I irreparably damaged trust? I was trapped. My lies would continue because there was no way out of them.

'Anna, will you invite your children to join you in the final hundred?' I heard Claudia ask.

'Thank you for the suggestion, Claudia. It's a beautiful idea to have my children join. However, I hope to walk the final one hundred kilometres with Jonathan, William, and you. Our journey together has been meaningful and I would like to see it through to the end with the companionship of my new friends.'

I almost wept at the sound of my own words, which were a mix of truth and lies.

***

Claudia

A flicker of satisfaction filled me as Anna responded to my question. Her words betrayed none of the intricate web of secrets I was determined to unravel. She maintained the facade of camaraderie while her life remains a mystery. She was polite in her answer, yet the detachment in her tone piqued my curiosity. Emphasising the significance of our shared experiences on the Camino was deliberate, an effort to deflect attention from herself. I had to remain vigilant, discovering her deception and why she deceives. Beneath her composed exterior lies a labyrinth of hidden truths waiting to be uncovered. Had I the time, I'd unravel the enigma that is Anna Dupont, but I don't have that luxury. I would break her this day. I extended my stride, quickening the pace, and to my satisfaction, Kat fell into step beside me.

Arriving at our breakfast spot, Villalcázar de Sirga, around nine thirty that morning, we settled into a cafe overlooking the grand Templar church of Santa Maria la Virgen Blanca. Amidst the company of Kat and fellow pilgrims like Chinmay, whose demeanour always lifted our spirits, we enjoyed our meal. I glanced at Anna. She remained stoic, but her discomfort was obvious as she massaged her swollen feet.

Job done, girly.

Anna noticed me scrutinising her and teased me by saying, 'Come on, Claudia, in thirty words or fewer, tell us about Villalcázar de Sirga.'

Chinmay, intrigued, chimed in, 'Do you know about this place?'

Anna giggled and said, 'I say this in the nicest way possible, but Claudia is a walking oracle. Not only is she an absolute delight to walk with, but she's also incredibly knowledgeable.'

Chinmay rubbed his chin, saying, 'Really?'

With a playful glint, I shot Chinmay a look. 'Seriously? You doubt my status as a well-read woman?'

Were I not part of an undercover mission pretending to court Jonathan, I would have fancied Chinmay. Before he could answer, I waved my arms dismissively. 'I enjoy learning about our surroundings, okay?'

Chinmay, relieved to be off the hook, said. 'Go on, in thirty words or fewer, tell me about Villalcázar de Sirga.'

'Nah.'

'Please.'

'Okay Chinmay. Villalcázar de Sirga, originally known as Villasirga, gains prominence through its Templar connection highlighted by King Alfonso X the Wise's inclusion of twelve poems dedicated to the Virgin of Santa María la Blanca, housed in the church.' I pointed to the building opposite us. 'The Templars commissioned the construction of this church on which all the activity of this town revolves in the 14th century. The town's significance grew because of its association with "The Way of Saint James," the Virgin's miracles, and theories suggesting its strategic location of the church by the Templar was not coincidental. Despite changing hands between religious orders and lordships after the Templars' demise in 1312, Villalcázar de Sirga retained its importance, cementing its place in history. Telluric forces, magnetic fields, Templars, miracles and pilgrims. All of these words are closely linked to Villalcázar de Sirga.'

'I didn't know this was a Templar church,' William said.

I was surprised William didn't know, but kept my thoughts to myself, offering a nonchalant shrug. 'The Templar influence is pervasive.'

I was surprised for a second time when Chinmay said, 'It's here... Um, on the spring equinox, if you are in the exact point when a ray of sun reaches some statue, it reveals the place where the Templars hid their formidable treasure.'

'We should look inside,' William said.

Chinmay shook his head. 'It doesn't open until eleven.'

I grinned, 'No treasure then. Not today anyway.'

Kat rose to her feet, offering a slight bow of the head. 'Thanks for your wonderful company. I'll be on my way.'

Chinmay and the other people who had joined our table also stood, bidding us farewell. As they walked away, Chinmay paused, then turned back, calling out, 'Message me when you reach Carrion de los Condes, we'll catch up for a drink.' Although he was talking to all of us, his words were aimed at Anna.

'Could it be that Chinmay and Anna are working together?' I pondered, before dismissing the notion as absurd. One thing was clear: Chinmay wasn't an underworld figure or Hells Angel. I prided myself on being an excellent judge of character.

Although Anna is my target, I harbour reservations about her being a threat. I question MI6's assessment of the situation.

***

Anna Dupont

After bidding farewell to Kat and the others, we lingered over another coffee before resuming our journey. When we rose, a pain shot through my right foot, but I concealed it from the group. Midway to our destination, we encountered Tara. Using the guise of offering her company, I slowed my pace and told the others to continue without me. 'I'll catch up with you in town,' I assured them. Unfortunately, the pain in my foot worsened and by the time Tara and I reached Carrion de los Condes, I was limping noticeably. As we entered the town, we strolled past the Monasterio de Santa Clara, reputedly a resting place for St. Francis during his pilgrimage on the Camino de Santiago. Tara wished to pray, so I left her there and continued alone. Locating William and the rest proved effortless; they lounged outside a bar, enjoying drinks and our picnic lunch in the shade.

'Are you okay?' William asked, seeing me limping.

I grimaced as I glanced down at my throbbing feet. 'It's my feet,' I admitted, forcing a smile to reassure my companions, though inside I felt a gnawing worry. 'They're painful. I think today's pace has taken its toll. Hopefully, it's nothing some drugs won't fix.'

Deep down, I knew it wasn't simply a matter of popping a few pills. I needed rest, and maybe more than that. I took refuge in the shade with the others, biding my time until I could check into our accommodation. But the shadow of doubt lingered, the possibility of not being able to continue the walk a real concern. The fear echoed relentlessly in my mind.

The Hostel la Corte stood as a central hub, nestled in a prime location. My room had a pleasant ambiance, its door opening onto a courtyard, the ideal spot to rest my weary feet. My tranquillity evaporated when Chinmay's message flashed across my screen, beckoning us to join him. Rallying the others, we found ourselves in the company of Chinmay, Jack Rabbit, and Alex from the USA, a new acquaintance, and other familiar ones, Kat and Clara. The energy crackled with anticipation as the young pilgrims unveiled their plan to depart under the moon's silver glow and camp in the wilderness. Their enthusiasm was infectious, conversation lively and, for a moment, I was transported back to my youth, brimming with a similar passion and zest. I hoped they would tread carefully in life and love and not stumble as I had.

Observing William and Jack engage in conversation as if they had been friends for a lifetime, I realised that amidst the journey on the Camino, the notion of a generation gap felt entirely archaic. Here, all individuals are on an equal footing. Jack, a burly Irishman working as a carpenter, carried a massive pack that he effortlessly whisked along the trail at an impressive speed, earning him the nickname "Jack Rabbit." He was one of those rare souls that leave a lasting impression on anyone fortunate enough to encounter them. Despite his quiet demeanour, Jack exuded a charismatic aura, blending a reserved nature with wisdom far beyond his years.

In San Juan de Ortega, William shared only cryptic hints about his conversation with Jack, yet it was clear their exchange had a deeply affected him. The nuances of their discussion, shrouded in mystery, seemed to have stirred something profound within William, hinting at a connection that was more than mere words.

Checking his watch, Jonathan assumed the role of the resident sage, regaling us with tales of the famed singing nuns of Carrion de los Condes. According to him, like clockwork, these nuns graced the Albergue Santa Maria with their performances every afternoon. Intrigued by the promise of music, we bid adios to the younger pilgrims and embarked on a quest to find the Albergue.

Although my journey along the Camino was driven more by opportunity than religious fervour, I was enchanted by the nuns' performance. Devoted to their art, their voices filled the air with harmonies that transcended language barriers. Their spirit was inclusive too, inviting pilgrims to join in songs that celebrated the diversity of the nations represented on the Camino. Despite an invitation to attend a Pilgrim Mass at the adjacent church, our dinner reservation at the hotel's restaurant held us to other plans. The nuns left an indelible positive mark on my Camino experience, a beacon of hospitality along "The Way". I was, however, taken aback by Claudia's unexpected singing along to the Spanish songs. I discreetly noted this observation, reminded once again that each of us carries our own secrets as we traverse the path.

It was eight thirty that evening when we were seated for dinner. Entrée was a lamb and potato soup followed by lamb ribs and salad. I could not even contemplate the dessert. An additional thrill was the unexpected sight of our youthful companions passing the restaurant window, silhouetted against the backdrop of the illuminated church. They waved goodbye gleefully. I felt truly valued.

Having bid everyone a good night, I retired to my room. Plonking myself on the corner of the bed, I rubbed my throbbing feet, the day's strain obvious in their swollen contours. A tear welled up in the corner of my eye. The next day, it was possible that I would be forced to give in. I took out my phone to text William, letting him know about my dilemma, but changed my mind.

Come on Anna, you can do one more day. You know you can.

CHAPTER 18
Templars Treasure

Claudia

The walk had been pleasant, and Kat's companionship added a touch of joy. A pang of remorse nagged at me; the brisk pace had undoubtedly taken its toll on Anna's feet. My mission demanded I keep her at arm's length from William until her true identity was revealed. There was no other choice, but it did not sit easily with me.

As I lay on the bed, I scrolled through to view William's daily social media post, looking for clues.

William's Social Media Post

Yesterday, I shared the experience of embarking on our journey alone, but today, companionship graced our path from Fromista to Carrion de los Condes.

Our tale unfolds with the rhythmic sound of footsteps hastening behind us along the river path. Kat, shouldering her famous 20-kilogram pack and determined to conquer 31 kilometres before the mercury touched 30 degrees Celsius, catches up. She eases her pace, joining us for a 10 kilometre stretch from Población to Villalcázar, where we pause for a shared breakfast.

Kat proved to be delightful company. Her journey to the Camino was inspired by a book by Paulo Coelho "The Pilgrimage." She produced a copy and invited me to select a random page and pen a few words, which she reveals will be a future discovery upon her return home.

The Camino is awash with remarkable stories, and today, Kat added another layer of richness to our pilgrimage. The Camino is the chicken that lays the golden egg.

I read the last sentence aloud. 'The Camino is the chicken that lays the golden egg.' The phrase struck a chord, albeit a perplexing one. While familiar with the idiom "killing the goose that lays the golden eggs," symbolizing the folly of destroying a valuable resource out of greed, and the classic Aesop's fable "The Goose that Laid the Golden Eggs," the reference to a chicken puzzled me. I furrowed my brow as my fingers absently scratched my head.

'A nod to the Knights Templar perhaps,' I mused. 'What is William up to?'

I thought about reaching out to MI6 for help, but reconsidered. William knew we read his posts, so I'd ask him.

The following morning, I found Anna waiting outside the hotel with my other companions; her presence took me by surprise. Despite her discomfort, she was ready for another day on the trail. 'She's a fighter,' I muttered to myself, knowing the pain she must be enduring.

'Claudia, do you have any ibuprofen?' she asked, her voice strained.

'Yes... Are you alright?'

'My right sneaker is killing my foot. The foot is swollen, and the pain is unbearable.'

'Anna, are you sure you should continue? Our first stop today is seventeen kilometres away. Once you leave the city, you'll be committed.'

'I have to, Claudia. Walking the Camino has been a lifelong dream and I can't give up now.'

'Are you sure?' Jonathan and William asked in unison.

Anna nodded.

I gave Anna two pain killers. 'You could rest today and walk with us again tomorrow.'

She shook her head resolutely.

You are a brave woman, and I salute your courage. However, if you pose a threat, today marks the final chapter of your story.

We walked in silence for what felt like ages and I imagined Anna praying to God to lift her pain. After an hour and a half, I spotted twinkling lights ahead along the trail, soon followed by the welcoming sight of chairs and tables, accompanied by the soft strains of music. A young man was operating a makeshift cafe, serving up coffees, food, and even free orange juice, all accompanied by a genuine smile. Anna collapsed into a chair, desperate to relieve the strain on her feet. The concern on William's and Jonathan's faces was unmistakable, mirroring my worry for her well-being; although mine was partly contrived.

'Hey, Claudia,' Anna said, her voice betraying her distress. 'Do you have anything stronger than ibuprofen in that magical first aid kit of yours?'

I paused, torn between my desire to assist her and my ulterior motive of preventing her from completing the walk. William had used my first aid kit, so lying was out of the question. 'I have some Prednisolone. It's an anti-inflammatory that could also give you a boost in energy. But it's not recommended to take it along with ibuprofen.'

Anna waved off my concerns with a dismissive gesture. 'I'll grab you a coffee and some breakfast. Just get me those pills.'

'Anna,' William said, his voice displaying his caring nature. 'My shoes are larger than yours. We could swap. It might help ease the pain of your swollen feet.'

Anna shook her head. 'You can't walk in my smaller shoes. It would be madness. You'd end up like me.'

'Let's give it a go. Besides, I like sandals, particularly pink ones; they'll go with my complexion.' He fluttered his eyes.

'Thank you, William, but I'm sure I'll manage with Claudia's drugs.' Anna stood. 'I'll get the coffees. Do you want one too, Jonathan?'

'Yep. I'll come with you,' Jonathan replied, rising from his seat.

As Anna and Jonathan strolled towards the counter, Anna called over her shoulder, 'I'll bring breakfast back as well. A trade for the drugs.'

William rubbed his face, his despair evident by the furrowed lines of his brow. 'I can't imagine what it must be like for Anna, walking in so much agony.'

I nodded. 'The drugs will help ease the pain, but her right foot is badly swollen; it might be a grave injury; she may need to call it quits.'

'She's a tenacious woman, Claudia, so I hope not on both accounts, the injury and stopping.' William's voice betrayed his admiration of Anna.

I nodded again and then changed the topic. 'I was reading your social media post last night and was wondering about the reference to the goose that lays the golden egg.'

William smiled as he corrected me. 'Chicken, Claudia. It was the chicken that lays the golden egg, a reference to Terradillos de los Templarios, the first village we reach tomorrow. A former stronghold of the Knights Templar, as the name implies.'

'I'm all ears.'

'Forgive my story telling if it's clunky. Are you sure you want to know?'

'You know I do.'

'Okay. In the annals of history, Claudia,' William said, his tone dripping with intrigue, 'King Alfonso VIII of Castile donated the village to the Order of the Temple in 1191. The name of Terradillos is derived from its brick and adobe houses and translates to "place of small earthen roofs or terraces". During the 12th century, the village had a pilgrims' hospital dedicated to San Juan, now a haunting echo of its former glory. As you probably know, the Templars' mission was to protect the holy places and, as part of the itinerary of "The Way of Saint James," they oversaw guarding the pilgrims' centre. The village once housed two churches: the vanished church of San Esteban and the current church of San Pedro, which now extends its hospitality to weary travellers, adorned with a 17th-century altarpiece and a 13th-century crucifix. And now Claudia, for the tale that captivates all who hear it. Terradillos is also linked to the legend of the chicken that lays the golden eggs. According to lore, the parish priest of the church of San Esteban would journey to Santiago each year with a golden egg. But when the offering fell short, the chapter of Santiago de Compostela demanded the hen that provided the treasures. To thwart their efforts, the Templars buried the famed chicken in the Alto de Torbosillo.' With a mischievous grin, William added, 'We'll catch sight of the hill tomorrow if we look to the right. Did you bring a shovel?'

'I'll check in my backpack,' I said, grinning.

When Jonathan and Anna returned with our coffee and breakfasts, I shared William's tale of Terradillos with the others. As I finished, the astute Anna posed the obvious question. 'Is the story of the chicken that laid the golden egg from Terradillos de los

Templarios linked to the fable of the goose that laid the golden egg?'

William was so excited by Anna's question that he clapped his hands, inadvertently spilling his brew. Hastily, I reached for a paper napkin to soak up the mess and William thanked me.

After taking a sip from his cup, William said, 'I'm so glad you asked, Anna. The story of the chicken that laid the golden egg from Terradillos de los Templarios does share similarities with the fable of the goose that laid the golden egg. Clearly, both stories revolve around a miraculous bird laying valuable eggs, triggering greed, which results in the loss of the source of wealth. But they are distinct stories within a different context. The fable of the goose is a popular moral tale that dates back to ancient times and has been passed down through many cultures. It teaches a lesson about the dangers of greed and the importance of appreciating what one already has. The legend of the chicken is different—it is specifically local and connected to a history that includes the village and the Knights Templar. The story emerged from the folklore surrounding the Templars and their link to the Camino de Santiago pilgrimage route. It does share similarities with the fable of the goose, but you should not see it that way. It is uniquely, rooted in the history of Terradillos de los Templarios.'

Jonathan leaned back in his chair, his expression contemplative. 'I wonder,' he mused aloud, capturing the attention of everyone at the table. 'Is the story of the chicken telling us that Terradillos, perhaps on Alto de Torbosillo, is where the Knights Templar buried their treasure, the gold?'

He looked at each of us, one after the other and, when we remained silent, he continued, his voice barely a whisper. 'The Templars possessed significant wealth. Tales of hidden treasure have fuelled speculation and inspired treasure hunters for centuries.'

Anna scratched her head. 'I remember Chinmay telling us yesterday that the secret of the Templar treasure was to be found in the church in Villalcázar de Sirga. It makes you wonder, how many hidden treasures did they have?'

I tapped on my nose. 'The answer to that, my friends, is easy. How many do you want them to have?' My response made us laugh. The possibility of uncovering a centuries-old mystery was preposterous.

'Right,' William said, story time is over. 'It's time to hit the road.'

As we stood, the story of the chicken and the templar treasure faded as we shifted our focus to the ongoing journey. With our backpacks slung over our shoulders and our laces tight; except for Anna, who loosened the straps on her sandals to ease the pain, we set off once more.

The rest of our walk to Calzadilla de la Cueza, which was to have been our first stop, was uneventful. Arriving, we took the opportunity of another coffee and obligatory toilet break. As we left the cafe for the last leg of the journey into Ledigos, I noticed Anna grimace and a part of me hoped that today would be her last. Our accommodation, attached to a bustling restaurant cafe, awaited us at the far end of Ledigos. When we arrived, Anna collapsed into a chair at a cafe table, her face pale. Swiftly shedding her footwear, she examined her feet with a mixture of frustration and resignation. A familiar face, a young woman we'd encountered a few times on the trail, approached and joined us. To my dismay, she produced a canister of Tiger Balm cream and handed it to Anna, encouraging her to rub it into her feet. Meanwhile, William returned from the bar with our drinks and a glass of ice for Anna to use on her swollen foot. The others rallied around Anna, offering encouragement to persuade her to continue walking the following day, as did I, while secretly wishing otherwise.

William kicked off his shoes and placed them in front of Anna. 'Please, try them; if they're not to your liking, I won't mention them again.'

Anna slipped her socks back on before trying the shoes. Standing, she took a few tentative steps, her expression transforming into one of surprise. 'Wow,' she exclaimed, 'The wider toe box makes a difference, so much less pressure on my foot. There's pain, but it's an improvement. Thank you, William. I'll take up your offer.' She flashed a mischievous grin before adding, 'Good luck with my sandals.'

My efforts to distance Anna from our group were faltering, and my fondness for her was growing. While I had entertained this notion previously, I silently reiterated it. *Maybe MI6's suspicions were unfounded.*

***

As the day neared its end, I reminded myself to contact Stephen later. I wanted to check if there had been any advancements in uncovering Anna's mysterious background. In addition, I eagerly awaited news on the alleged threat targeting William once we reached León.

Alone in my room, I picked up my phone to call headquarters, then changed my mind and read William's daily post.

William's Social Media Post

Pilgrims of the Camino offer a flood of advice - from toe socks to walking poles. It's a saga. Yet, amid the comedic chaos of walkers wobbling into cafes like characters from the Ministry of Silly Walks, we've uncovered a vital truth. Forget sore feet; it's the lack of public toilets (none), and the long distance between cafes on "The Way" that leaves pilgrims mastering the art of the super bladder. So, amidst the laughter, let this

Reading William's post made me giggle, for what he described was accurate: I'd squatted in many undignified places. Lounging on the bed, I mused aloud. 'I'll give Stephen a call tomorrow night. If anything urgent arises, he'll contact me. In the meantime, I'll remain vigilant and keep my senses sharp for anything suspicious.'

***

We left Ledigos before the break of dawn, merging into a steady stream of pilgrims embarking on the day's journey. Among them was Jim, an Englishman who appeared uncertain about the path ahead. Sensing his need for company, Anna slowed our pace, allowing him to join our group. I was sure the leisurely speed would be a relief for Anna's foot, too.

As we approached Terradillos, the darkness still enveloped us, shrouding the Templar church in mystery. Trying the door, I discovered it was locked. Anna said, 'No searching for clues to the treasure here, today.'

Jonathan said, with mock disappointment, 'Well, there goes my retirement plan. Looks like I'll have to find a job when I return home.'

With a grin, I interjected, 'Unless you stumble upon a wealthy future Mrs. Swindon on "The Way."'

William strode over and stood before a metal sculpture of a Knights Templar, a sentinel at the entrance of the church. The beam of our headlamp illuminated its intricate surface. We photographed the sculpture before proceeding along a path flanked by poplar trees towards our breakfast stop at San Nicolas del Real Camino. While my companions engaged in conversation, my thoughts returned to the sculpture. Enthused by William's daily writing, inspired by

Chuck and Cathy's shared love for poetry, I found myself composing a social media post in my thoughts, a practice I was not accustomed to.

In the heart of Terradillos de los Templarios, where time and legend intertwine, stands a sentinel forged from history and imagination. The moonlight, like a silvery veil, drapes over the ancient cobblestones, casting elongated shadows around the enigmatic figure. The knight's armour is an intricate fusion of antiquity and innovation. Plates of burnished metal encase the body, but upon closer inspection, one discovers an unexpected twist: interlocking gears, cogs, and rivets. It's as if the blacksmiths of old conspired with clockmakers from a distant future. The helm is a masterpiece—a visor adorned with delicate filigree, revealing only the knight's resolute eyes. These eyes, deep and unyielding, hold secrets etched across centuries. Clutched in a gauntleted hand, the sword gleams like a sliver of moonlight itself. Its blade bears ancient runes, whispered incantations that bind the knight to duty. The shield, emblazoned with the emblem of the Knights Templar—a crimson cross against a field of midnight blue—reflects the knight's unwavering faith and commitment.

The sentinel stands tall, feet planted firmly on the grassy earth. A guardian of forgotten oaths, it gazes beyond the horizon, as if awaiting a signal—an echo from a brotherhood long disbanded. Its posture exudes both strength and weariness. Battle-worn but unyielding, the knight's shoulders bear the weight of forgotten quests and lost comrades.

The buzzing sensation in my pocket snapped me out of my reverie, pulling me back into the present. I slowed my pace, allowing my walking companions to move ahead while I discreetly checked my phone. It was an encrypted message from Stephen Walls.

> We have uncovered a connection between Anna Dupont, formerly known as Claire Peis, and the Direction générale de la Sécurité extérieure (DGSE), formerly known as the Service de documentation extérieure et de contre-espionnage (SDECE)

The DGSE, France's equivalent of Britain's MI6 and America's CIA, was not an entity to be taken lightly. I continued reading.

> Remove her from the walking group. It is a priority. I will contact you tonight.

I read Stephen's message again; short of extreme measures, like poisoning Anna Dupont or pushing her off a cliff, neither of which I would consider, I'd already exhausted all reasonable options to dissuade her from continuing. Her being a foreign agent explained Anna's unwavering determination. She was a professional.

Even with Anna's injured foot, we maintained a brisk pace along the path, eventually catching up to David and Ros, the English couple we'd encountered at Quinta San Francisco. Arriving at our breakfast stop, a cafe in San Nicolas del Real Camino, William placed his backpack next to his chair while he, Jonathan, Anna, David and Ros went inside to order food and café con leches for each of us. Seizing the opportunity, I discreetly examined the contents of William's pack. Nestled within was the puzzle box, wrapped in a towel to prevent him from discomfort during his walk. Other than light refreshments, a spare pair of socks, and a sun hat, there wasn't much inside. With a sense of urgency, I unwrapped the box, but my attempts to open it were met with frustration. In desperation, I snapped a photograph before re-wrapping it and returning it to its original position in the backpack. I had barely finished replacing the pack when William and the others emerged from the cafe. Satisfied that my actions had gone unnoticed, I welcomed them back.

As we enjoyed our breakfast, I was again struck by Anna's magnetism, effortlessly pulling people into conversation with us. Among the familiar faces who briefly joined our table were Sean, Clare, Isaac, and Miriam. Then came two newcomers, Ana and Ian, who told us they were all the way from the Sunshine Coast in Australia. Pretending to be captivated, I seized the opportunity to have Ana and Ian pose for a photograph alongside William, Jonathan, and Anna. They were not to know that this snapshot would find its way into the hands of MI6.

Were Ana and Ian known to the intelligence community?

With Anna's charisma, identifying collaborators had become a daunting task. Now, knowing that Anna was connected to DGSE, I thought Anna's connections ran deeper than I'd suspected. Even if I removed her from our group, those connections would remain, through fellow pilgrims, "seemingly" enjoying the camaraderie of the Camino de Santiago. Of all the people we'd met, I was most suspicious of Chinmay. He was in regular contact with Anna and told her he would meet us in León. It seemed León was shaping up as a pivotal place on the journey.

Where's Chinmay's security check? I must ask Stephen about it.

When we were alone again and our coffee cups were empty, William said it was time to be moving on. Jonathan grinned as he stood. 'Do you know what today is?'

William, Anna and I looked at each other before each shaking our heads.

'Just short of Sahagun, we'll cross the official halfway mark.'

'Really!' William said. 'It's all going to be over too quickly.'

I pondered whether Anna shared the sentiment. Despite her foot injury, she acknowledged William's remark with a nod and echoed his words, 'It's all going to be over too quickly.

We walked in near silence for the next six kilometres, each lost in our own thoughts, until our eyes caught sight of the midpoint marker near the 12th century Ermita del Puente site. Ermita del Puente, just beyond the medieval bridge spanning the Valderaduey River, had once been a pilgrim hospice and burial ground. Flanking the Camino were two magnificent sculptures: one of Alphonse VI the Brave (1065-1109), revered as the Promoter and Protector of "The Way of St. James," and on the other side, Bernardo de Seriedad, an Abbot esteemed as one of the founding figures of Sahagun. William captured a photo of Jonathan and myself standing between the towering statues and I returned the favour for Anna and William. Despite my mission, I felt a sense of accomplishment as we crossed into the second half of the journey.

Entering Sahagun, a vibrant wall mural caught our attention. Jonathan mentioned it depicted characters from the film "The Way." I confessed my ignorance of the movie, much to the amusement of the others. Teasing, they reminded me of my fondness for National Geographic-style descriptions of the places we had visited and Anna said, 'You've never heard of "The Way". Oh Claudia, what are we going to do with you?'

They each giggled. Pretending to be perplexed, I said, 'Was it on the BBC?'

Just short of our hotel, Anna sighted a sign offering massages. 'Sorry guys, I've got to try something to ease my pain.' William pointed to a cafe a little further on as he said, 'Take as long as you need. We will wait for you there.'

Three quarters of an hour later, Anna emerged and joined us at our table.

Jonathan asked, 'How did it go?'

'When I took my shoes off and rolled up my hiking trousers, the Masseur said, "Mamma Mia!" He was concerned about my calf. He sold me some cooling lotion.'

William said, 'How are you feeling now?'

'A lot better, though it's still painful. Shall we find where to collect our "half way" certificate?'

While I nodded, I said, 'Are you sure you're up to it?' Inside, I was thinking,

One more day, Anna Dupont. If you don't give up by then, I will have to resort to the potion in my pocket.

Finding where to obtain our certificates proved a challenge, a blessing for me, the extra walking adding to Anna's discomfort. After asking in a few places, we were finally directed to Santuario de la Virgen Peregrina, originally a Franciscan convent founded around 1257. The sanctuary rested on a hill on the outskirts of the town. The entry fee included the certificate, more a letter stating that we had passed through Sahagun rather than a halfway certificate, but I kept my observations to myself since my friends didn't know I could read Spanish. On the way back into town, we stopped at a local restaurant, selecting a range of tapas for a late lunch, before booking into our hotel.

Not wanting to give Anna time to recuperate, after a freshen up and washing my clothes, I sent a text message to the others suggesting that we meet in ten minutes for an afternoon drink. We strolled into the centre of town, finding a bar where we sat for a while, chatting with two new people, Lorraine and Phil, from California. Their story was inspiring.

Phil had a slender figure standing tall at over 183 centimetres. He possessed a quiet yet commanding presence with gentle features betraying a lifetime of wisdom rather than his seventy years, a face etched by wrinkles that spoke of his experience. His words carried the weight of knowledge and authority. Lorraine seemed a decade younger, though she was not. Standing at 175 centimetres, she was slight but sprightly, exuding an energy that belied her age. Like her husband, she had a quiet demeanour, but her presence held its own authority.

Lorraine told us she was walking the Camino for her 70th birthday and Phil added that when they finished the trail, they would return to war-torn Ukraine to continue their humanitarian work leading a charity helping displaced citizens. The couple had our attention.

With inquisitive questioning by William, Phil shared their story. Born to parents of the hotel industry, Phil's early years were defined by constant movement caused by the transient nature of his family's lifestyle. His mother toiled as a cleaner while his heavy drinking father worked as a cook, often struggling to maintain his family unit. Growing up amidst the hustle and bustle of pubs where he had helped out since he was old enough to wipe a table, Phil told us he'd developed a sense of duty and a desire to serve, something woven into his fabric.

In his childhood, he'd been a loner, the result of an itinerant upbringing, leaving him disconnected from his peers. He recalled an incident in fifth grade when he found himself summoned to the headmaster's office, facing a panel comprising a psychology education specialist, the headmaster and his classroom teacher. The discussion started with his academic progress, but his mind had wandered. He'd been fascinated with space exploration and the problem of carrying enough fuel for propulsion. Nuclear war had been high probability at the time and he suggested to the panel using controlled nuclear explosions as a motor for deep space missions. They were shocked, immortalised by the psychologist uttering an expletive. Phil's parents sought stability for their children after this incident, putting an end to their nomadic lifestyle.

Witnessing the struggles of his parents, Phil vowed to carve out a different path than that of his parents for himself, one defined by sobriety. Always fascinated by learning, he pursued higher education with a voracious appetite for knowledge, earning a Bachelor of Science, a Master's in Engineering, and eventually a Doctor of Divinity, reflecting his interests and commitment to understanding the world from every perspective.

Phil's career path led him to disaster relief, first with the United Nations and later through a charity he established, rooted in the principles of his faith. Through this, Phil and Lorraine sought out displaced communities affected by catastrophic events, like the 2004 Indian Ocean tsunami and the 2018 Sulawesi earthquake and tsunami. Approximately 230,000 lives were lost in the 2004 disaster and hundreds of thousands were displaced. In 2018, more than 4,340 people died with over 200,000 displaced because of earthquakes and the resulting tsunami.

Lorraine told us she and Phil married at age twenty-five and raised three children together. When their youngest child left home, they seized an opportunity through their church to establish the charity, channelling their freedom and resources into making a difference to the lives they touched. 'There are now around 3.7 million persons displaced internally within Ukraine,' Lorraine said.

Phil added, 'Hopes of pushing Russia back to its legal boarders are being eclipsed by a focus on survival. Russia captures by destruction. There's been widespread torture and murder of Ukrainian civilians. Rape, kidnapping and murder have been utilised in Russian-occupied territory to subdue citizens. We feel compelled to act.'

Later, when our group was alone, Jonathan said he'd been moved by Lorraine and Phil's story and their dedication to helping others. 'It is a testament to the influence that an individual can wield to shape the world.'

Together, Phil and Lorraine formed a formidable pair, their years of shared experiences plain for anyone to see. I refrained from taking a photo of them as I didn't need MI6 to tell me they posed no risk.

It was Sunday, so the bar closed early and when we left to return to our hotel, Anna was limping.

Not long now, I thought.

On the way back, Anna said. 'I don't think I can go out again today. Do you mind if we find somewhere to eat for an early dinner?'

'Sure,' William said, 'Except it's quite difficult to find anywhere to eat early in Spain, plus it's Sunday.'

To my satisfaction, the search for a place to eat added a couple of extra kilometres to our day, placing more pressure on Anna's foot. The only place we could find was the cafe where we'd waited while Anna had her massage. The sight of identical menus displayed on sandwich boards outside many cafes/bars along this stretch of the Camino had always given us cause to pause. We harboured a suspicion that the meals were pre-packaged and sourced from a central distributor, rather than freshly prepared on-site. So, we'd always opted to dine elsewhere. This days circumstances left us with no alternative but to accept the menu. Settling into our seats, and having placed our order, our concerns were confirmed. The server returned too soon, placing before us what appeared to be hastily arranged plates of pasta. The meals lacked the finesse of a freshly prepared dish, with clumps of pasta sticking together. A quick exchange of glances confirmed our shared suspicion: this meal had likely been tipped unceremoniously from a plastic container, heated in the microwave and transferred to our plates. Resigned, we each sampled the lacklustre fare before us. The pasta was tepid, sauce thin and unremarkable.

Anna raised an eyebrow, poking at her plate with a fork, expression a mixture of disappointment and amusement. 'I guess presentation isn't their strong suit.'

William, always the optimist, attempted to salvage the situation, suggesting a sprinkle of grated cheese from the meagre condiment selection provided. 'Maybe this will help,' he offered with a hopeful smile, though the dubious look on his face betrayed his uncertainty.

Jonathan, ever the realist, summed up our collective assessment with a grimace. 'Definitely not cooked on site, but it's memorable, for all the wrong reasons.'

I glanced around the cafe, half-expecting the server to return with the familiar bottle of wine we'd grown accustomed to receiving during our meals. A glass or two would surely have improved the uninspiring flavours of our meal. Yet even that small comfort was not forthcoming.

To add insult to injury, the exorbitant price tag attached to our meal left us feeling aggrieved. We resisted a shake of our heads in disbelief as we forked over our hard-earned euros for what amounted to little more than cafeteria food. The only bright side was that, by the time we returned to our hotel, Anna's limp was more pronounced.

Alone in my room, awaiting the call from Stephen Walls, I read William's social media post.

William's Social Media Post

🚶💥 What a day on the Camino! 😊 Today's stroll to Sahagun turned out to be quite the adventure! Last night, Anna's feet were giving her trouble, but she powered through and swapped shoes with me this morning. A foot massage in Sahagun provided some much-needed relief, although now I'm feeling the discomfort too! 😄 Along the way, we indulged in breaks, including a search for the legendary Knights Templar Chicken rumoured to lay golden eggs (spoiler alert: we're now jet-setting home in style ✈️). Our breakfast stop turned into a heart-warming chat with fellow travellers, adding to the magic of the journey. 😌 Sahagun marks our halfway point, certified by a visit to the Santuario de la Virgen Peregrino church. With Anna wearing my shoes and shorter treks ahead, we're hopeful her feet will bounce back before the longer days. Onward we go! 💪

The post, embellished with a variety of emojis, seemed strange to me, particularly as it deviated from William's typical style. I stroked my chin thoughtfully. 'There's a twist here. There has to be!'

***

We had a treat this morning, savouring a hotel breakfast before heading towards El Burgo Ranero. As my companions relished what they claimed was 'delicious toast,' my mind was consumed with frustration and disappointment. Recalling Stephen Walls' familiar refrain from the previous night, 'The realm of espionage is a convoluted dance of contradictions, causing one to question the very notion of intelligence itself.'

I had been resolute in my belief in Anna Dupont's innocence. However, MI6's insistence on her removal from our group had cast doubt on my judgment. As a seasoned agent, I prided myself on my ability to discern threats accurately.

'Are you alright?' William's question jolted me from my thoughts.

'Oh, lost in thought,' I replied with a strained smile. 'Daydreaming...off with the fairies, I suppose.'

But inwardly, I couldn't shake off the weight of regret. I should have trusted my instincts and now I am worried about the consequences I had inflicted on Anna Dupont. I'd been relentless in my efforts to break Anna and distance her from our walking companions, accepting that MI6's intelligence was accurate.

Stephen had revealed, 'Anna is a woman named Claire Peis. She isn't affiliated with the French spy agency; instead, a retired operative from the SDECE assisted Claire Peis in adopting the persona of Anna Dupont to flee a violent domestic situation.'

I was disappointed in MI6, but I knew I couldn't dwell on the past—move on was my motto. I had a mission to complete and would not let emotion cloud my judgment.

Darn. In my disappointment however, I forgot to inquire about Chinmay.

I observed Anna across the table, her fingers wrapped around a cup of coffee and wearing William's shoes, and I felt I needed to say something to make amends, though I knew it would never be uttered. 'Perhaps a chance would materialise to do something nice for her,' I whispered. Kat and Anna had been collateral damage, and they were unlikely to be the last.

As we left Sahagún behind, our journey through the old town took us beneath the weathered stones of the Arch of Saint Benedick, remains of the Abbey of San Benito de Sahagun, and across the Rio Cea via the sturdy embrace of the Puente del Canto, known affectionately as the "bridge of songs". Stepping off its ancient span, we were enveloped by a canopy of trees. Anna pointed out that these trees were purported to have sprung from the spears of Charlemagne's troops, known as the Legend of the Flowering Lances, a tale of verdant growth that supposedly unfolded in a single night. Though I knew that this legendary poplar grove was the setting for an episode chronicled in the Turpin Chronicle, I held my tongue and instead urged Anna to spin her yarn.

Her voice carried a love of storytelling as she began recounting the legend, her tone engaging. 'The tale speaks of a clash between Emperor Charlemagne and the Muslim Aigoland. For three gruelling days, the battlefield echoed with the clash of swords and the cries of men, as the Muslim army swelled with each passing hour.' As she wove the narrative, Anna described how on the fateful third night, Charlemagne's weary troops drove their lances into the earth, seeking respite from the relentless turmoil. With the dawn's light, they awoke to a miraculous sight: their weapons, once instruments of war, were now bark and leaves, an eerie portent of martyrdom.

'The soldiers, undeterred by the ominous signs, pressed on into battle,' Anna continued, her voice trembling as the tragedy unfolded. 'But the fighting was fierce, and the losses staggering. Among the fallen were those whose lances had transformed in the night; their lives claimed by the cruel hand of fate. Amid the chaos, hope emerged as four Italian Marquises arrived to bolster Charlemagne's forces. With renewed vigour, they turned the tide of battle, driving Aigoland and his troops into retreat, their pride wounded by the unexpected reinforcement.'

'And so it was,' Anna concluded, her eyes lingering on the gnarled branches overhead, 'that after the bloodshed had ceased, the roots of those fateful lances once again stirred to life, birthing the grove of Poplars through which we now tread, a testament to the sacrifices of those who came before us.'

Anna's rendition of the legend flowed like poetry. Her words had been a blend of passion and knowledge, drawing us into the tale as if we were characters in the story she'd told. In contrast, my delivery was matter-of-fact, lacking the vibrant flair that Anna infused into her storytelling. I allowed a smile to drift across my face as I reflected on my tendency towards clinical recounting. My tale would have told of the legendary poplar grove as the site of the episode written in chapter eight of the fourth book of the 12th century Codex Calixtinus, known as the Turpin chronicle.

Why did some people find my historical narratives dull. Perhaps I needed to take a page from Anna's book and inject a bit more life into my retelling?

'Don't laugh,' Jonathan said, 'But who was Charlemagne?'

Anna's lips curved into a gentle smile as she turned to face Jonathan, her eyes alight with the spark of knowledge. 'Charlemagne was far more than a person from the pages of history. He was a towering figure of the medieval world, a king whose name resonates through time.' Glancing at me, Anna inquired, 'Can you help, Claudia?'

I gently shook my head. 'I'm your student, Anna.'

With the graceful bow of her head, Anna continued, her words painting a portrait of the legendary ruler. 'Born Charles the Great, he ascended to the throne of the Franks in 768 AD and through a series of military campaigns and political manoeuvring, he forged the Carolingian Empire, stretching from modern-day France to parts of Germany and Italy. But Charlemagne's legacy extends far beyond conquest. He was a patron of learning and culture, spearheading a revival of scholarship known as the

Carolingian Renaissance. Under his rule, centres of learning flourished, and he himself was a patron of scholars, including the renowned Alcuin of York.'

Anna's enthusiasm for the subject was infectious, her eyes gleaming with wonder. 'In 800 AD, Charlemagne was crowned Emperor of the Romans by Pope Leo III, a pivot in European history, laying the foundation for the Holy Roman Empire.'

'So, you see, Jonathan, Charlemagne was not just a king or an emperor, he was a visionary leader whose legacy continues to shape our understanding of the medieval world to this day.'

Jonathan said, 'Thank you Anna. Our American history is so recent in comparison. Travel expands the mind and we leave a little wiser.'

Continuing along the path for another four kilometres, we arrived at Calzada del Coto. Here, the route split in two: the Real Camino Francés and la Calzada de los Peregrinos. Opting for the former, we walked to Bercianos del Real Camino for a much-needed coffee break. As the others enjoyed their refreshments, William's social media post troubled me, keeping me on guard as I scanned around for anything unusual. Two coffees later, with nothing other than good company in the vicinity, I wondered if I'd read too much into William's emojis.

Jonathan announced, 'We should push on to our overnight stop at El Burgo Ranero'

I noticed Anna grimace. I asked how her feet were holding up. 'Not good,' she replied.

Anna limped the last few kilometres into El Burgo Ranero, her steps faltering with each stride. Finally, she collapsed into a weathered chair outside a cafe, exhaustion etched across her face. With trembling hands, she unlaced William's shoes and let out a sigh of relief as she slipped them off her swollen feet. The shoes had helped her, but when she raised her right foot, the extent of the swelling was clear.

'I'm so sorry,' I whispered to myself. I offered to buy everyone a drink and went inside the cafe to order. When the owner brought our refreshments, his eyes fell upon Anna's injured foot and without a word, he disappeared briefly, returning with a bag of ice to offer relief.

Where we'd stopped was a pretty resting place. Rows of terracotta-coloured buildings lined the thoroughfare, facades weathered by time and the sun, a sun which hung low in the sky, casting long golden shadows across the street. On the pavement was a chalk drawing of hopscotch, left behind after the children played.

Sipping our drinks, we observed an older man pedalling toward us on a well-used bicycle, its once vibrant paint chipped and rusted. He halted before us, a solitary figure clad in a worn brown fleece jacket and faded trousers, his polished black shoes contrasting. The sun's rays caught his face, exaggerating the lines etched by years of living, like a well-read novel. In accented English, he introduced himself as Father Calieo, the Catholic priest of El Burgo Ranero. His weathered hands, bearing the marks of countless bestowed blessings, rested gently on the handlebars of a relic passed down through generations of parish priests. Gesturing down the street, he pointed toward the church.

From his trouser pocket, Father Calieo retrieved folded bits of paper inscribed with English Bible readings, which he explained were meant for pilgrims. Handing one to each of us, he bid us farewell before riding away. Curious, we unfolded the papers to discover the messages he had imparted.

Mine bore the words, '"Trust in the Lord with all your heart and lean not on your own understanding; in all your ways submit to him, and he will make your paths straight. Proverbs 3:5-6.'" I said.

Anna shared hers next, '"For I know the plans I have for you," declares the Lord, "plans to prosper you and not to harm you, plans to give you hope and a future. Jeremiah 29:11.'"

Jonathan pondered his passage before stating, '"Blessed is the one who perseveres under trial because, having stood the test, that person will receive the crown of life that the Lord has promised to those who love him. James 1:12.'"

As William unfolded his paper, a moment of apparent confusion flashed across his face before he chuckled softly. '"Or Who will descend into the abyss? Romans 10:7,'" he read aloud, his expression a mixture of amusement and contemplation.

'How extraordinary to be gifted such treasures.' Anna remarked, her tone tinged with intrigue.

Jonathan nodded. 'What a remarkable experience. I feel truly blessed.'

Anna's comment made me curious. I had been vigilant, searching for anything out of the ordinary. Could this be it? Was the priest the anomaly I was seeking, the reason William's reading was distinct? Was there a message veiled in the words? I would speak with Artōrius; he would know the meaning of the passage.

Not long after Father Calieo bid us farewell, Phil and Lorraine strolled through El Burgo Ranero, en route to Reliegos. They joined us at our table. Conversation swiftly shifted to Ukraine, their next destination after the Camino, and the stalled aid package in the American Congress. President Volodymyr Zelensky's dire warning from the previous night's news echoed in our minds: the looming threat of escalating casualties, both civilian and military, unless the promised military aid reached the front lines without delay.

I relished the rapid-fire exchange of thoughts within our group. When major issues like COVID or the conflict in Ukraine dominate the headlines, the widespread media coverage inundates the general population with a constant stream of information. It's during times like these that the average person often transforms into an "Armchair Expert". As we conversed, I noticed the illusion of understanding that enveloped us, a sense of false mastery over complex topics, fuelled by our reliance on media coverage. Yet, amidst our chatter, Phil's words resonated. 'The war in Ukraine leaves the world a more perilous place,' he said, his voice tinged with concern. 'Russia's invasion serves as a stark reminder that naked aggression is not relegated to history. Under Putin's leadership, Russia poses a persistent and immediate threat. Ukraine's downfall could usher in an era of even greater instability, or worse, embolden more dangerous forces. And let's not forget China, viewed by many as an increasingly assertive player on the global stage. The dynamics of great power rivalry could be catastrophic for mankind and its civilisation.'

Anna nodded before sharing her thoughts. 'I rarely advocate for increased military spending, but in Ukraine's case, they're left with little choice but to defend themselves or face assimilation into Russia.'

'I hail from the United States,' said Jonathan. 'Our country is deeply divided on whether we continue military and economic help for Ukraine.'

Lorraine nodded, before adding, 'Our charity focuses on aiding the displaced, a consequence of conflict. We prefer to leave the politics to others, focusing instead on providing tangible help to those in need.'

When Phil and Lorraine bid us farewell, Anna dropped a bombshell: she'd made the hard choice to halt her journey along the Camino. Despite her ongoing struggle with foot problems, her decision blind-sided us all.

'Don't withdraw just yet,' I said, feeling a hypocrite 'Let's check into our hotel, and you can rest with your feet elevated. Tomorrow, take a taxi to Mansilla de las Mulas and give yourself a day of respite, then reassess tomorrow evening. I understand your agony, but give it one more day before ending your pilgrimage.'

We've travelled too great a distance together for you to give up now.

My thoughts were coalescing into words, but I caught myself just in time. Anna wasn't "Giving Up". It would have been an awful thing to say.

I wouldn't let Anna quit. She'd had shown remarkable fortitude in the face of adversity, manufactured by me.

'One more day,' William said. 'Please do as Claudia suggests. Take a taxi tomorrow and then gauge how you feel.'

'Absolutely,' Jonathan chimed in. 'Give yourself a day to rest, then assess how your feet are holding up.'

Anna stayed silent.

'We're putting pressure on you, I understand,' William said. 'But it's because we want you to continue with us.'

Anna let out a heavy breath before she said, 'Okay. Where should I meet you tomorrow in Mansilla de las Mulas?' We each searched for a meeting point using our smartphones. We settled on Plaza del Pozo, in the heart of the old town.

***

Our lodging was half a kilometre away from El Burgo Ranero, a hotel at a sprawling service centre along the main highway, a far cry from the charming settings we'd grown accustomed to. While the others rested, I ventured back to El Burgo Ranero, exploring a different facet of the town and stumbling upon a traditional hotel we hadn't noticed before. Consulting the "Wise Pilgrim App," I learned that the hotel's restaurant boasted an ambiance akin to Grandma's living room, with meals prepared by Grandma herself. Later that evening, we gathered there for dinner, and it proved to be a positive experience and there was a bonus: Anna managed the walk without too much difficulty.

Later, back at the hotel, I read William's nightly post before contacting Steven Walls.

William's Social Media Post

For those acquainted with Father Brown, the British period detective from a television series, picture meeting Father Calieo today. He's the parish priest of El Burgo Ranero, pedalling around on his bicycle, warmly greeting and blessing pilgrims passing through his town—a delightful scene straight out of the early 1950s.

I reviewed the post again. There was nothing suspicious about it.

***

'Good evening, Stephen,' I said when he picked up his phone.

'Claudia. As always, it's nice to hear from you. How is the walk progressing?'

'It's progressing. Any further intel on what will happen when we arrive in León?' I asked.

'No. Unfortunately, the chatter has gone quiet.'

'Chinmay, Sir. I'm still waiting for his background and security check.'

'I will look into it.'

'Thank you, Stephen. And what about the puzzle box?'

'Not as yet, Claudia. We still haven't discovered how to open it. Any developments on your side?'

'You would have seen William's unusual social media post, the one punctuated by emojis?'

'Indeed.'

'Today, we had an interesting experience when a priest gave us each a Bible reading.'

'That wouldn't be out of the ordinary on the Camino.'

'No, Stephen, in itself, it's not. But it was William's passage that caught my eye. It was unusual compared to the ones given to Jonathan, Anna, and myself. I thought Artōrius might make sense of it.'

'You think it's a coded message?'

'I do, Sir. I do indeed.'

Chapter 20
León

Anna Dupont

Waking up this morning on the Camino, a sense of loneliness crept in for the first time. I knew it was too early for a taxi, and my companions had already started their walk to Mansilla. I was on my own. With time to spare; I pondered the shape of my life upon returning to Paris. Since assuming my new identity, solitude had been my constant companion, and I had grown accustomed to its embrace. I reflected on the camaraderie I once shared with friends in my previous life as the bookshop owner, conversations flowing, meals savoured, experiences shared. My new life was security, though "safe" might paint a more accurate picture, yet it felt shallow. At my stage of life, the thought of forming fresh bonds appeared daunting. The Camino felt like a mirror, revealing the emptiness within me without providing a clear path to fulfillment.

Seated by the window, I watched the traffic whizzing past on the motorway and thought about the elusive nature of love. I'd been ensnared by the charms of a man who proved to be as cruel as he was captivating. The years that followed were a blur of survival, escaping his control, reclaiming my autonomy piece by piece. It seemed I'd never truly known love.

Love? The word echoed in my mind. It was often portrayed in stories as a sweeping force, a whirlwind of passion and desire, carrying victims off their feet and into the throes of ecstasy. I'd tasted such intensity moments when time stood still, the world falling away, leaving me yearning for more. Love, the feverish rush of a stolen kiss beneath the moonlit sky, the electric thrill of fingertips tracing patterns on heated skin and the primal hunger of lust. Love, a symphony of sensations, a crescendo of longing and fulfilment. A feeling that leaves you intoxicated with desire, craving the heady rush of its embrace.

My reflections led to memories of our attic apartment in Berlin, a cramped space, stuffed with the clutter of our artistic pursuits; we lived and loved, our fervour bordering on madness. The attic, with its sloping ceilings and sunlight streaming in through dusty windows, was our sanctuary from the outside world. Boldly coloured canvases leaned against every surface and the pungent scent of turpentine hung in the air, mingling often with the aroma of our bodies intertwined in passion, a wild dance, fuelled by our intense connection and our turbulent relationship. Bruises marred my skin from his violence, yet raw energy passed between us when we coupled. Amidst the chaos of our lives, we sought refuge in each other's arms. I remember the soft glow of candlelight casting enchanting shadows across the exposed beams overhead, heightening the sense of seduction that enveloped us like a warm embrace. Our kisses were desperate and hungry, each touch a silent plea for reassurance in the face of uncertainty. In those stolen moments of passion, I transcended the pain and turmoil of my existence, losing myself in the raw, unbridled intensity of our connection.

In that attic apartment, surrounded by the remnants of my artistic pursuits, I believed I had discovered love, despite its tumultuous and passionate nature. Yet, it wasn't until love had shattered my trust in its very essence that I recognise that there was more. There are the practical facets of love, the everyday gestures that knit two souls together in quiet companionship. The comforting familiarity of a partner's touch, the simple act of knowing precisely how each prefers their morning tea. There are shared moments of laughter over breakfast and shared tears in the stillness of night, instances of vulnerability and strength intertwined.

With a sigh, I said aloud. 'I yearn for an enduring connection, one anchored in mutual respect and understanding. For someone to stand beside me through life's storms, offering unwavering support in times of need. I crave the bonds of friendship like those I am finding along "The Way" of the Camino, bonds that are more than fleeting passion and that will endure the test of time.' Looking at my feet, a tear silently traced my cheek 'Going home isn't possible. I'm not ready to leave William, Claudia, and Jonathan.' A thought struck me. 'I think I'm in love with William. Does he feel the same way?' Another tear joined the growing cascade as I remember the lies I'd told. 'Will William understand or am I destined to be alone?'

Picking up my phone, I keyed in the taxi number I'd seen plastered on a weathered sign while wandering through the winding streets of El Burgo Ranero. Within minutes, Hugo pulled up in his sleek Tesla, ready to convey me to Mansilla. As we cruised along the road, tracing the path of the Camino, I kept a keen eye out for my crew. Spotting William, Clauda, and Jonathan ahead, I urged Hugo to slow down, and he tooted the car's horn. The trio, making swift progress without me, waved back, and I felt a tinge of sadness at my isolation.

Covering a mere nineteen kilometres, my journey by car to the heart of Mansilla de las Mulas was swift, albeit at the expense of 27.00 euros, a small price to pay. The town centre was eerily quiet, hardly anything stirring. To pass the time until my companions arrived, I sought refuge in a cafe, where I indulged in another cup of coffee and read about the town. As I sat, I observed a nearby market being set up and hoped that it would provide a distraction for me. When the market opened, I meandered through its stalls, taking in the sights and sounds. I was drawn to a display of colourful T-shirts and I picked out one to replace the worn garment I'd been wearing throughout my journey. Soon, a

WhatsApp message from William alerted me to their arrival. Since it was too early to check into our accommodation, we chose a caffeine fix before a stroll through the market. Claudia picked up some apples. She said, 'They'll be a welcome addition to our journey snacks.'

Jonathan was keen to explore the ancient city walls. Nervous though I was about my feet, I joined them. Claudia, I think to distract me from the pain, started sharing titbits of the town's history as we walked.

'Mansilla de las Mulas sits on the banks of the river Esla, its ancestral origins shrouded in mystery.'

'Mystery,' I said. 'That sounds fascinating.'

'Long ago, this village stood as a crossroads in the ancient Asturica region, near the city of Lancia. When the Romans arrived in the 70s, they christened it Mansilla, erecting a formidable military stronghold and encircling it with sturdy walls.'

Claudia paused, assessing whether we were interested before continuing. 'In the middle of the 6th century, the Goths seized control, to be followed by the Arabs. King Alfonso I, a devout Catholic, reclaimed the town in 753. Subsequently, it suffered the ravages of Almanzor's raids in 996. Yet it was Alfonso V the Noble who oversaw its restoration, though it wasn't until the reign of Fernando II, in 1181, that Mansilla de las Mulas truly flourished, granted a charter to encourage settlement and marking the beginning of its illustrious history as a significant border town between the kingdoms of León and Castile.'

Jonathan raised his hand playfully, mimicking a classroom setting. 'Yes?' Claudia responded, adopting a mock authoritative tone.

'Yesterday it was Charlemagne. Now I ask, what were Almanzor's raids?'

'You're not alone, Jonathan,' I said. 'I'm curious too.'

From her expression, I sensed Claudia believed I already knew the answer and was supporting Jonathan.

'To be honest, Jonathan,' Claudia said. 'I was clueless myself until I resorted to some web searching to pass the time before I went to sleep last night. Almanzor's raids were a series of devastating attacks led by Almanzor, the de facto ruler of Muslim Al-Andalus in the 10th century. He launched these raids primarily against Christian territories in the Iberian Peninsula, including towns, cities, and religious sites. Almanzor's objective was to expand Muslim influence and weaken Christian resistance. These raids inflicted widespread destruction, pillaging, and loss of life, leaving a lasting impact on the affected regions.'

'Thank you,' Jonathan said, and mused for a moment before saying, 'Claudia, there's joy in delving into the history of these places, like peeling back layers of time, adding to the richness of my pilgrimage. As I have already said, coming from the United States, where history is comparatively recent, I hadn't appreciated that each town we encounter has its own intricate story that echoes through time. It's thanks to you, Claudia, by sharing your stories and insights, that I'm gaining a newfound reverence for this journey. I always hoped for a spiritual experience on the Camino, but I never imagined it would be a cultural odyssey too.'

Claudia playfully nudged Jonathan in the ribs, before saying, 'And I thought that you only joined us on the Camino in search of the elusive Mrs. Swindon.'

'No fighting children,' William said with a smile.

I was about to tease Jonathan as well about the future Mrs. Swindon, but my train of thought was derailed by the buzzing of my phone. 'Guess what? Cathy and Chuck have rolled into town. They ask if we'd care to join them for dinner tonight?'

William's eyebrows lifted in interest. 'Sounds splendid, Anna. Any idea where?'

Quickly typing out a response to Cathy, I awaited her reply. Moments later, her message arrived. 'She suggests finding something nearby to where we're staying and letting them know.'

Our lodging was a spacious four-bedroom house. As we made our way there, a restaurant caught our eye a few doors down. After freshening up, we booked a table at the restaurant and had a drink before heading out to explore. My friends kept their pace slow, but walking was difficult for me; though I did not complain and I was pleased when we returned to the restaurant. Before we knew it, we were engaged in conversation with other patrons until, to our delight, Cathy and Chuck appeared.

Cathy and Chuck were delightful company, and conversation flowed easily around our table. Following dinner, Claudia asked about my plans for the following day. With a sigh, I revealed my plan to catch the bus to León, hoping that, with a couple more days of rest, my feet would be up for rejoining the walk.'

Claudia emptied her wineglass. 'León is only nineteen kilometres away. How about we start early and race Anna's bus? We could arrive by ten and spend the day together exploring León.'

William and Jonathan were comfortable with Claudia's suggestion.

***

Claudia

After bidding good night to Cathy and Chuck, we left the restaurant and headed back. William and Anna walked side by side, while Jonathan and I strolled together. Upon arriving at the house, Jonathan and I chatted as we climbed the stairs, exchanging wishes for pleasant dreams before retiring to our adjacent rooms. As my door clicked shut, a tug of desire pulsed through me. A period of abstinence forced upon me by the demands of my profession heightened my urge, a hunger unsatisfied for too long. Lying on my bed, an image of Jonathan Swindon lingered in my mind, like a tantalising whisper on the breeze. He was a prop for my mission, however there was something about him that drew me in, something I couldn't quite put into words. Maybe it was the warmth of his smile or the kindness in his eyes, but whatever it was, tonight it had ignited a spark within me that was difficult to ignore. As much as I longed for his touch, I knew the reality of our situation all too well—Jonathan was a devout evangelical Christian with principles that guided his beliefs. Sex before marriage would be foreign to him, a line he probably wouldn't cross. Desire burned within me, aching to be released. I imagined his lips on mine, his hands exploring my body, but I was a woman of control, someone who knew how to keep her desires in check. MI6 required discipline and I would not let my emotions get the better of me, not when so much was at stake. I rubbed my chin in thought.

Why do Christians, like Jonathan, abstain from sex before marriage? Is it relevant in their thirties?

'Sure,' I said, aloud. 'I can understand the rationale for teenagers. It's about maturity, responsibility, and avoiding potential consequences like unwanted pregnancies or emotional turmoil. But what about adults who have lived life, experienced relationships and can make informed decisions? It feels somewhat outdated.

Shouldn't we have the freedom to explore our desires and build connections without a lingering expectation of purity?'

With a heavy sigh, I pushed aside my longing, forcing myself to focus on the task at hand. I would continue to play the potential future Mrs. Swindon to maintain my cover and guard my heart against the allure of forbidden passion. To distract myself from thoughts of Jonathan, I reached for my phone and dialled Steven Walls.

'Good evening, Sir.'

'Claudia,' he replied tersely.

'We arrive in León tomorrow and I was wondering if there are updates on the threat to William?'

'No,' came Stephen's sharp response, which surprised me.

'Is something bothering you, Stephen?'

'Sorry, Claudia, you've caught me at an inopportune moment. I'm annoyed. Germany has leaked British Military secrets to Russia. Accidentally, so I'm told. Accidentally!'

'Oh dear.'

'Oh dear indeed. Believe it or not, Russian media intercepted a conversation involving Lieutenant General Ingo Gerhartz, the head of the Luftwaffe, and other air force officials. During this discussion, Gerhartz disclosed sensitive information regarding the delivery of Storm Shadow missiles to Ukraine by us and the French. The breach occurred because Gerhartz was using off-the-shelf, unsecured video conferencing software instead of an encrypted line. Off-the-shelf software, Claudia! He made a Zoom call, or something similar. I mean, what was the man thinking? Gerhartz spoke of British troops being "on the ground" in Ukraine, which is highly classified and not intended for public knowledge. Putin has repeatedly threatened to use nuclear weapons if NATO put troops into Ukraine. The Kremlin has accused Britain of serious provocation. Oh, and he told the Russians how we transport our missiles in Ukraine, "In Ridgeback armoured vehicles."'"

'That is an embarrassment for Germany.'

'Yes, Claudia, especially as not all of our NATO allies are aware of our troops' presence in Ukraine. Any hope of Germany sending the Taurus missiles is all but over. This breach could have far-reaching consequences.'

'Are you telling me that the German officers discussed sending the Taurus missile?'

'They did, Claudia. Ukraine's interest in acquiring the Taurus lies in their stealth. They're less susceptible to detection, plus they boast a range of up to 500 kilometres. Having them would significantly bolster Ukraine's leverage, particularly in the Black Sea and elsewhere. A recent statement by the German Chancellor, emphasised that German soldiers are to remain unlinked to targets within the missile system's reach. The leaked conversation revealed, there is talk of Ukrainian troops receiving training on German soil before being returned to Ukraine, where British forces would then take over because Britain is already handling satellite data on behalf of France, crucial for Ukraine to program missiles.' Stephen took a deep breath. 'Imagine exposing that British forces would take over because we are already doing it for the French. Unbelievable!... The fact that the recording of this conversation ended up on Russian television is embarrassing, to say the least. It is totally unacceptable. All of this is unacceptable!'

'Yes, Stephen. Very unacceptable. If the recording hasn't been tampered with, it further highlights the dangers of lax security, underscoring the importance of safeguarding sensitive information in diplomatic and military communications.'

'Yes, yes, Claudia... Not all is well in the NATO alliance as we shift to a war economy. We could do without this.' Stephen paused for a moment. 'These are worrying times. Russia's expansionist ambitions will not stop in Ukraine. The UK and Europe need years to improve our military capabilities.' Stephen inhaled before he said, 'Enough of that. You now have my undivided attention. Is there anything I can assist you with?'

'Chinmay?'

'Ah, yes. The man isn't on our radar. Chinmay is an Australian living in Manchester on a Youth Mobility Visa. He builds websites, good ones, so I'm told. We don't see him as a threat.'

'Thank you, Stephen... We are in León tomorrow, so I was hoping MI6 might have information that could aid in protecting the sensitive data William Marshal possesses.'

Stephen let out a sardonic laugh. 'Losing the plans for our future AUKUS submarine, if that is what he has, would be more than just embarrassing. I'll see what I can do. Meanwhile, Artōrius is awaiting your arrival in León.'

'That's good news, Stephen. Where should I expect to meet him?'

'He'll find you, Claudia. One more thing. I don't want a repeat of Pamplona.'

***

William, Jonathan and I rose early, determined to reach León shortly after Anna's arrival. All went to plan and by ten o'clock we were in Cathedral Square, our meeting place. My heart sank at the sight of Anna's distress. She was clearly in pain, her feet causing her considerable discomfort. Despite having travel insurance and being ready to cover the costs, she had been turned away by a doctor. The local hospital had also refused to treat her, citing her non-EU citizenship. Anna recounted how the local tourist information centre had directed her to a nearby physiotherapist. She had secured an appointment for five thirty that afternoon. As Anna recounted her story, I felt sad knowing I'd caused her suffering.

Looking about the square, I asked, 'Coffee, anyone?'

Anna gestured with a wave of her hand towards the many cafes nearby. 'There are lots of choices.'

'There are,' William agreed. 'How about we opt for the closest one?'

As we settled into our seats around the outside table at the cafe, the vibration of my phone in my pocket signalled an incoming SMS. The message was from Artōrius and read:

Meet me in the Cathedral.

That isn't very specific, I thought. As if Artōrius had read my mind, a new SMS appeared. It read:

Now.

What about William? I have to watch out for him.

Another SMS popped up on my phone:

William is safe - for the time being.

How does he do that? Okay, girly. Slip away to the church without the others joining me. How? Hey, one moment, this is the Camino, right?

'Hey, guys,' I said, addressing my companions. 'Do you mind if I have some private reflection time in the Cathedral while you enjoy your coffees? Twenty or thirty minutes should be enough.'

'That's a delightful idea,' Jonathan said as I rose to leave.

Anna was staring at her phone, a smile playing on her lips. 'Chinmay wants to join us for dinner tonight.'

Walking towards the church, I called back, 'I'll look forward to Chinmay's company.'

****

Stepping through the grand entrance of León Cathedral, the beauty of the ancient structure was unmistakable. It wasn't as striking as Burgos Cathedral, but it was still imposing, the stained-glass windows a spectacle of light to behold, painted the interior with a mosaic of colours, casting a mystical aura over the vast space. Rows of towering columns pointed towards the heavens; their weathered surfaces bearing witness to centuries of history. Amidst the hushed whispers of tourists and the soft echoes of their footsteps, my eyes scanned the crowd, searching for Brother Artōrius and his worn brown robe. There was something truly magnificent about medieval architecture, a striking grandeur that modern building failed to achieve. Looking, the cathedral seemed to consume me in its antiquity, every corner hiding secrets and stories from the past. Near the altar, bathed in a golden glow, was Brother Artōrius, standing tall, his humble attire a contrast to the opulence surrounding him. His gaze met mine as I approached and calm washed over me, amplified by his presence. Inside the church, where time stood still, there was comfort in meeting him.

Was it the strength of faith embodied by Brother Artōrius that had this effect?

He gestured towards a pew, and we sat together.

'I find these spaces moving, Brother Artōrius, even though I don't share in your faith.'

He turned towards me; the light filtering through stained glass, casting coloured patterns across his face. 'A Cathedral is not only a structure of stone and mortar. It is a repository of the lives that have passed through its halls, prayers whispered within its walls and the dreams woven into its fabric.' He gestured towards the soaring arches and statues that adorned the Cathedral's interior. 'The convergence of history and faith is how the cathedral finds its power to captivate us. Even those who do not share our beliefs find inspiration in the art and architecture, where historical significance and cultural heritage speak to us all. These grand structures of opulence with their chequered pasts reflect the spirit of human creativity in people of all beliefs and backgrounds.'

'There is truth in that, Brother Artōrius.'

'Yes, Claudia.' Artōrius clasped his hands together. 'Last time we met, I told you that the Camino is a spiritual journey, a path for each pilgrim to discover their own treasures. Has that proved true for you?'

Scanning about me, pondering for a moment before replying, I met Artōrius's gaze. 'I'm not ready to answer that question yet.'

Artōrius nodded thoughtfully. 'You were curious about the passage from Romans 10:7 given to William, "Or Who will descend into the abyss?"'

I nodded.

'This verse is part of a larger discourse by the apostle Paul, where he discusses the righteousness that comes through faith in Jesus Christ. In this passage, Paul is quoting from the Old Testament, specifically Deuteronomy 30:13, which speaks of the word of God being near and accessible to us. Now, when Paul references "the abyss", he's not speaking of a physical chasm or depth, but rather it's a metaphorical representation of separation from God, a state of spiritual darkness or despair. The question posed here is rhetorical, emphasizing that we don't need to search high and low, or descend into some unreachable depths, to find God or to understand His message. Instead, Paul is highlighting the accessibility of God's word and the simplicity of salvation through faith. The passage continues to affirm that the message of faith is already near us, in our hearts and on our lips, waiting to be acknowledged and embraced.'

'In essence Claudia, this verse serves as a reminder that the path to righteousness and salvation isn't a journey into the unknown, but a recognition of the divine presence that surrounds us, always within reach for those who seek it.' Artōrius, gave me a wry grin, 'A message meant for you too, perhaps?'

'Maybe,' I said as I shifted my gaze to him, anticipation clear in my expression. 'Do you see a coded message within the biblical passage? One doesn't jump out at me.'

'Perhaps you're looking in the wrong place.'

'What are you suggesting?'

'I suggest nothing. I offer only an observation.'

'You know what it means, don't you?' When Artōrius remained silent, I pressed further. 'Answer me this then, is there something to find in the Bible text given to William?'

Artōrius's grin widened. 'For you or William?'

'Brother Artōrius, please, I don't have time for games. We are on the same side, are we not?'

'You perceive correctly that he was handed a message, but what it means, I cannot say. If neither of us can understand it, I return to my earlier observation; perhaps you are looking in the wrong place?'

You're a wily old man.

I kept the thought to myself, saying instead. 'There is wisdom in your words, Artōrius. I will sleep on it.'

'As will I, Claudia. On another matter, Stephen wanted you to know that a thug has been dispatched to steal William's day pack. He will arrive this afternoon.'

'Does this thug have a name?'

'Yes, it's Ryan Pearson, a member of an outlaw motorcycle gang.'

'Charming.'

'He won't prove too difficult to spot. Now, if you will excuse me, Claudia, I have to leave you.'

I nodded my acknowledgment as Artōrius stood to leave. A thought crossed my mind, but when I turned to ask him a question, to my surprise, he had disappeared. Scanning the cathedral, I found no trace of him; he had vanished, as if into thin air.

How do you do that?

***

The warm evening breeze carried the scent of freshly made pizza and the melodic strains of Spanish guitar music as we settled into our seats at a tiny restaurant nestled in the heart of León, a stone's throw from the Cathedral. The outdoor seating area spilled out onto the cobblestone square, wooden tables and chairs scattered beneath colourful umbrellas, a cozy atmosphere providing a vantage point to admire the architecture that surrounded us.

Chinmay, a ball of energy, engaged each of us in vibrant conversation. Despite being closer in age to Jonathan and me, it was clear he held a special place for Anna and William. They asked to have their photo taken together.

We learned that Chinmay and some of his travel companions had taken a rest day in León. His friends had departed earlier that day, but Chinmay had opted to stay behind for another night, intending to tackle a couple of big walking days to catch up with them.

'Well, if I could drag myself out of bed early enough, I might catch them,' Chinmay chuckled. 'But I must confess, I'm not an early riser. I'm one of those types who prefers to roll over and go back to sleep.'

'Why not walk out with us in the morning?' I suggested. 'We can be your motivation.'

'Sounds like a plan. Maybe it's motivation that I need.'

'It's settled then. We'll meet you at six thirty in the morning on the bridge crossing the river Bernesga, near Plaza San Marcos. It's a perfect starting point for our journey.'

Chinmay grinned, excitement in his eyes. 'Count me in. I'll be there, bright and early—hopefully!'

I smiled, knowing there was only a remote chance that he'd be there.

The aroma of pizza wafted across our table and Jonathan said, 'That smell makes my mouth water and stomach rumble in anticipation.'

'Let's order, shall we?' Anna said.

Despite the hustle and bustle of the square, and my alertness keeping a watchful eye out for any signs of trouble, there was an undeniable sense of tranquillity that enveloped our table. We were savouring each other's company, engaging in lively conversation and relishing the food, drink and charming surroundings. I briefly pushed my mission to the back of my mind, letting my concerns fade away momentarily, replaced by contentment and peace. It was a reminder of the beauty and joy to be found in life's simplest pleasures, something, because of my work, I frequently overlooked.

I gazed at León Cathedral and marvelled at the architectural structure that had stood the test of time. It loomed as a silent guardian of the city. Its imposing spires, adorned with intricate carvings and statues that told stories of centuries past, reach towards the heavens. The setting sun cast golden rays upon the Cathedral, making it come alive, its stone facade glowing with an ethereal beauty.

My enduring fascination with the history of ancient structures likely explained why I found such joy in traversing the Camino. However, there was something extra about the León Cathedral. Perhaps it was the way the light danced off its stained-glass windows, painting colourful patterns on the old stone walls. Or maybe it was the sense of awe that washes over you when you stand in its shadow. Maybe it was the company of my companions or a combination of everything. That evening, when I should have been watching, my attention was drawn back to the Cathedral. The spotlights illuminating it made me smile. Long shadows crossed the square with pockets of darkness where anything could hide. Brother

Artōrius's words hit me: "A Cathedral is not merely a structure of stone and mortar."

Concentrate, Claudia

Brother Artōrius's warning of Ryan Pearson rekindled in my mind. I scanned the crowd, searching for signs of trouble. With the bustling activity of tourists and locals, it's hard to tell from where the threat would come, but come it would.

I think I see him! A strong, tattooed man in a dark shirt, blending into the shadows, scanning the square as if searching for something.

He's a predator stalking its prey, his eyes darting around the square, searching for William.

I can't afford to let my friends catch wind of my unease, so I summon a smile and join the conversation. Yet, my senses remain alert, fixed on the figure I suspect to be Ryan Pearson. He lurked in the crowd, his intentions veiled, poised for the right moment to make his move.

Chinmay takes a bite of his pizza, his eyes widening in delight. 'Man, this is some good stuff! I didn't expect Spanish pizza to be this amazing.'

I chuckled, relishing the cheesy goodness of my slice. 'Spain never fails to impress with its cuisine,' I remarked, earning a nod of agreement with William. My gaze wandered back to the Cathedral. 'And the view here is breathtaking. I could spend all night soaking it in.' Cursing silently, I realised I'd let my guard down for a mere moment, and now the tattooed man had vanished.

Damn!

MI6's cautionary words come to mind as I scan the crowd again, feigning captivation by the Cathedral's illumination.

As my gaze flickered, I noticed movement as a figure took a seat at a nearby table.

It's him.

He was all muscle, rippling beneath his black shirt, but it wasn't his physical presence that seized my attention. The tapestry of tattoos that adorned his arms each narrated its own tale: fierce dragons, delicate flowers, they cascaded from shoulders to wrists, an exhibition to demand being noticed. His predator eyes swept our table as I struggled to maintain my composure, trying to conceal my unease from my friends.

With darkness fully descended, the Cathedral became more breathtaking under the spotlights. Anna penetrated my consciousness as she said, 'Look at the Cathedral, Claudia, isn't beautiful.'

I tore my attention away from Ryan Pearson for a fleeting moment, during which he seized the opportunity. With swift precision, he snatched William's pack from the back of his chair before vanishing into the crowd.

'Hey! My backpack!' William shouted, leaping to his feet in shock.

'Damn!' I muttered. With adrenaline surging, I told everyone to stay put as I gave chase through the winding streets of León. It was a perfect evening to be out, so the streets teemed with people enjoying the city, making it difficult for me to keep track of Ryan Pearson as he manoeuvred through the crowd. The sounds of the city faded into the background as my focus narrowed solely on catching up to him, my breath coming in ragged gasps as I pushed my legs to their limit, legs fatigued from the day's walk. Rounding a corner, I spotted Ryan Pearson, who quickened his pace as I closed in on him.

Come on girly, you can run faster than this

Abruptly, Ryan Pearson veered off the main street and ducked into a narrow alleyway, fleetingly vanishing from sight.

'Where are you going now?' I puffed, my heart pounding.

Following suit, I navigated the labyrinthine maze of alleys and side streets.

He's planned his getaway and knows exactly where he is. Damn!

I rounded a corner and spotted him, and then his motorbike waiting at the end of the alley, its engine idling as Ryan Pearson raced towards it. My breath caught in my throat as I realised what was about to happen. Ryan Pearson wasn't acting alone. Why on earth had I assumed he would be?

When Pearson reached the motorbike, a figure dressed in dark leathers turned to greet him. Her face was obscured by the helmet, from which blond hair cascaded to her shoulders. Without a word, backpack in hand, Ryan Pearson jumped on behind his accomplice. She revved the engine, ready to escape, but I wasn't about to let them escape that easily. With a last burst of speed, I lunged forward, my hand outstretched in a desperate attempt to grab the backpack. Frustrated, I watched helplessly as the bike raced off. Ryan Pearson giving me the bird as he disappeared into the night, a roar echoing through the alleyway. They narrowly missed a young woman parking her scooter.

I clenched my fists in frustration, my mind racing, contemplating what I could have done differently. If only I had been faster, if only I had anticipated their escape plan. The post mortem could wait. Scanning the darkened alley, my eyes took in the young woman and her motor scooter.

It will do.

With swift determination, I closed the distance between me and the unsuspecting woman, grabbing hold of the handlebars of her scooter. The young woman turned to me in surprise, her eyes widening as she realised what was happening.

'Sorry Love,' I said.

Before she could speak, I mounted the scooter, fingers deftly finding the ignition as I fired up the engine. The scooter's whine drowned out her protests as I peeled away from the curb, adrenaline kicking me into action. With a twist of the throttle, I shot off, wind whipping my face, hair streaming behind like a wedding veil. Through the streets of León in Spain, I gave chase, my eyes fixed on the road ahead. The nimble scooter responded to my every command, weaving through the labyrinth of streets. Every corner, every twist and turn brought me closer to Ryan Pearson and his accomplice. The thrill of pursuit fuelled me, propelling me forward with unwavering focus.

They will not escape.

The streets melted away as I sped through the city, alleyways and main roads reverberating with the roar of my engine. Whizzing by time-worn stone structures, I found myself captivated by their fronts aglow in the dancing light of street lamps.

Keep your eyes on the road, Claudia.

The motorbike I pursued looped back toward our origin, and once more, the towering spires of the Cathedral caught my eye. Navigating the labyrinthine alleys of the ancient town posed a formidable obstacle, with twisting pathways and sharp turns pushing my reflexes to the limit as I closed the gap on the faster bike up ahead. Pedestrians scattered in Ryan Pearson's wake; their shouts of alarm drowned out by the roar of his engine as the accomplice's motorbike careened up onto the footpath to avoid the congestion of the streets. Swerving, I avoided a group of tourists as

I followed suit. Closing in, I was gaining the upper hand until I heard the unmistakable sound of sirens behind me. Glancing back, I saw the flashing blue and red lights of police vehicles in hot pursuit. I cursed. I wasn't the only one chasing after the criminals.

Damn! Stephen will be far from pleased if the police catch me.

'Not now,' I yelled. 'Not when I'm so close to the goal.' With the police hot on my tail, my options were dwindling.

Come on girly!

I gritted my teeth and pushed the scooter to its limits, weaving through traffic with renewed urgency as I outmanoeuvred the thieves and the police. But the streets were crowded, and each turn led to frustration. When Ryan Pearson surged ahead, I knew that time was running out. With one last burst of speed, I rushed ahead, determined to catch up to before they disappeared into the night. The motorbike ahead cut a sharp corner, missing a lamppost by inches. My heart pounded as I followed suit, eyes fixed on the backpack clutched in Ryan's hand. As they careered around the corner, disaster struck for them, but good fortune for me. The backpack snagged on the pole, causing it to rip free of Pearson's grasp. With a thud, it fell to the ground, skidding across the pavement.

In that second, everything slowed down in my mind. The backpack was abandoned on the ground, a prize out of reach. There was no time to hesitate. With the police hot on my heels, I veered towards the bag, hand darting out to snatch up the fallen backpack as I rode past. It thudded against my chest as I scooped it up, its weight a reminder of the stakes. I turned down a narrow alley, away from Ryan Pearson and, with renewed determination, gunned the scooter and sped off, racing to escape the grasp of the law. Sirens wailed behind me—I had to act swiftly to shake off the police.

Glancing over my shoulder, I spotted a dirt path leading off the main road snaking down towards the Bernesga River. Without hesitation, I veered off the road and onto the path, the two-wheeler bouncing and jolting beneath me. The path grew steeper as I descended the embankment, branches of overhanging trees brushing against my shoulders as I pushed into the treacherous terrain. Finally, I reached the edge of the Bernesga River, its waters shimmering in the moonlight as they flowed lazily downstream. The river was flanked by lush greenery, tall trees swaying gently in the breeze and wildflowers blooming along the water's edge. The air was thick with the scent of earth and foliage, a respite from the chaos of the city streets.

With the police hot on my trail, I couldn't stay by the riverbank for long. I scanned the surroundings. Ahead, I spotted a cluster of trees, their dense foliage perfect to conceal the motor scooter. I abandoned it and slipped into the shadows, melting into the darkness, and watched the police cars speed past, lights flashing as they searched for a sign of their elusive quarry. When the coast was clear, I emerged from the shadows and joined the throng of people walking along the riverbank, blending into the crowd.

'Well done, girly,' I whispered to myself.

Taking my phone from my pocket, I rang William and told him I had his pack.

'You're amazing, Claudia,' he replied.

'I will be back in fifteen minutes. I hope you haven't eaten all the pizza.'

'We are working on it,' he giggled.

On the walk back to the restaurant, I seized the opportunity to inspect and attempt to open the puzzle box. For the second time, I cradled the wooden box in my hands, its surface gleaming in the city lights, its dimensions no larger than a jewellery box, embellished with elaborate carvings that adorned every surface. My fingers traced the edges, searching for seams or hidden compartments, but to no avail. Its secrets remained hidden by a design that eluded my ability.

You're an intelligent woman, Claudia. Surely this shouldn't be an obstacle.

Contemplating the enigmatic artifact, I pondered its origins. The intricate workmanship suggested a bygone era, transforming it from a mere puzzle box into a testament to the artistry of its creators. Carefully placing it on the surface, I meticulously photographed every detailed facet, planning to transmit the images to MI6 for further scrutiny. Satisfied with the task, I secured the box back within the confines of William's backpack.

Back at the restaurant, I held out the backpack. 'Hey, William, look what I found.'

Taking it from me, William asked, 'Is everything still there?'

I shrugged my shoulders, my expression conveying little.

Anna opened her mouth to speak but William chimed in, 'Now then Claudia, as our resident historian, what can you tell us about the history of this wonderful city?'

It was a tactic to divert attention away from the puzzle box, a tactic I supported. 'Will my answer cost me breakfast?'

'Perhaps,' William said.

Anna looked perplexed. 'Are we not going to ask Claudia about the chase?'

I waved my hand dismissively. 'It was nothing... You wanted to hear about León. If it's not to cost me breakfast, I'd better make it entertaining. But before I do,' I glanced around the table at the empty plates, 'did you save me any pizza?'

Jonathan shook his head, his grin widening. 'We saw the way you sprinted after that thief, with all the hallmarks of an Olympic athlete. Eating pizza didn't seem fitting for you, so we helped you out, eating it all.'

'Really?' As I was about to continue, a server approached the table with a steaming pizza in hand. Placing it in front of me, he said, 'Señorita Claudia. Tengo para ti nuestra especial Mediterránea, Pizza–Miss Claudia, I have for you our special Mediterranean Pizza.' My friends erupted in laughter.

How would Anna narrate this tale, and in poetic form, how might Chuck eloquently render it? This task is within my grasp.

I took a piece before I started speaking in a hushed voice, 'Gather round, my friends, and let me regale you with the riveting tale of León, Spain.'

'Nice start,' Jonathan said.

I took another bite of pizza. 'This city,' I gestured, my eyes tracing the Cathedral square, 'Nestled amidst the rugged Castilian hills, harbours secrets etched in stone, whispered by the winds that sweep through its narrow streets. Within these ancient walls is a story written in blood and fire.'

Chinmay grinned. 'If this is how you'll tell stories to our children, you'll frighten them.'

I chuckled, rolling my eyes. 'Oh, Chinmay, my storytelling is meant to enchant, not frighten. What's a tale without a thrill? I'm a woman of thrills!' I flashed him a mischievous grin and smiled when he blushed.

'Returning to my hushed voice, I said, 'Founded in the shadow of empire, León emerged as the military encampment of the Legio VI Victrix around 29 BC. The soil beneath our feet bore witness to the tramp of disciplined Roman soldiers, their crimson banners fluttering against the vast Spanish sky. But it was the Legio VII Gemina, the "twin seventh legion," that etched its legacy into the bedrock of León. Their definitive settlement in 74 AD transformed this outpost into more than just a garrison—it became a hub of commerce and culture.'

'Gold, my friends, flowed like liquid sunlight through León's veins. The glittering bounty of Las Médulas, those ancient mines nearby, fuelled trade caravans that wound their way across Iberia. Merchants haggled in the bustling markets, their voices echoing off the stone facades. And yet, beneath this mercantile veneer, a deeper current pulsed. There was a spiritual heartbeat. For León was a city of faith, where the Catholic faithful knelt in prayer, undisturbed even when the Arian Visigothic king, Liuvigild, swept through like a tempest in 540.'

'But fate is a fickle mistress...'

'Like you,' Jonathan interjected.

I fluttered my eyes at Chinmay and Jonathan. 'Are you boys flirting with me?'

They looked at each other, shaking their heads.

Pretending to be disappointed, I said, 'Oh, never mind then.' After a pause, I continued. 'In 717, the Moors descended upon León, their scimitars flashing in the sun. The city fell, its walls breached, its people scattered like autumn leaves. Yet hope clung stubbornly to the stones. León, resilient and unyielding, was among the first to rise from the ashes during the Reconquista. It clasped hands with the Kingdom of Asturias in 742, forging a pact that would echo through the centuries.'

'And then came the pivotal year of 910—the dawn of León's golden age. The city ascended, crowned as the capital of the Kingdom of León. Here, scholars unfurled scrolls, poets dipped quills into ink pots, and craftsmen chiselled their dreams into alabaster. Under the wise gaze of King Alfonso VI, León became a beacon—a forge where intellect and art danced in a harmonious frenzy.'

'Danced in a harmonious frenzy.' Anna repeated. 'I like that.'

'Why thank you,' I said. I took another bite of my dinner. 'The air hummed with possibility. Philosophers debated under the arches of the San Isidoro Basilica, their words like fireflies illuminating the night. Painters adorned the cathedral's walls with frescoes that whispered of celestial realms. And the troubadours? Ah, they serenaded moonlit courtyards, their verses echoing through time. León was a symphony of creativity, each note resonating across Europe.'

'Yet, as with all great cities, León's story bore scars. Wars raged, courtly intrigues spun their silken webs, and the Leónese monarchy extended its dominion southward. Amidst the turmoil, the city blossomed—a centre of culture and learning. Its streets echoed with the footsteps of visionaries; its plazas hosted debates that shook civilisation. Monuments rose—a testament to resilience. The Casa Botines, the Palacio de los Guzmanes, and the Royal Collegiate of Saint Isidore—each a brushstroke on the canvas of time.'

'So, my friends, as we sit here eating pizza, let us remember León not merely as a city but as a living chronicle—a saga of blood and fire, of wisdom and wonder. For within these ancient walls, the heart of Spain beats, echoing the footsteps of kings, poets and dreamers.'

I leaned into the table, gesturing the others to join me. 'And perhaps, just perhaps, if you listen closely, you'll hear the whispers, the echoes of León's past being carried on the wind, urging us to write our own chapter in this timeless tale.'

Jonathan clapped. 'Exquisite Claudia, truly exquisite. What a day. I'll certainly have plenty to write about in my post tonight.'

William said, his tone polite yet firm, 'If you don't mind, Jonathan, could you kindly leave out the theft of my backpack? It would detract from the Camino experience.'

Jonathan nodded.

***

In my hotel room, I opened my phone to check William's nightly post but closed it again, choosing sleep instead. I was exhausted.

Chapter 21
Road to Astorga

Anna Dupont

Reluctantly and mindful of the toll it would take on my weary feet, I made the tough choice to forgo walking the Camino again today. As I lie in bed, a twinge of longing gnawed at me, knowing that my companions had set out for Villadangos del Páramo without me. Resolving to make the most of the situation, I rose at seven thirty that morning and reached out to William via SMS, inquiring whether Chinmay had met them at the bridge. His response came swiftly:

We waited fifteen minutes before leaving without him.

I chuckled at the predictability of Chinmay.

Emerging from the hotel into the still-dark morning at eight, I journeyed alone through the city streets in search of the bus station, feeling secure as I navigated the quiet avenues early in the day. Along the way, I stumbled upon a bar where I took breakfast before resuming my quest. Luck was on my side as a kind local, with his basic English skills, guided me to the right bus stop. He outlined the procedure: priority boarding for those with pre-booked tickets, any remaining seats available for spontaneous travellers like myself. Again, fortune favoured me and I secured passage on the bus bound for my destination.

The route William, Claudia and Jonathan were walking that day ran parallel to the bus route and when I caught sight of them, I was surprised at the distance they'd covered in such a brief time. Seeing William striding out in front, walking poles in hand and wearing his backpack, I remembered the previous evening when he'd briefly showed us the Puzzle box. Claudia had mentioned that the box contained memories of his late wife, Hannah. I respected his privacy, but part of me longed for him to open up those memories and share them with me. Yet I had not shared my truth with him.

I nearly missed my stop, but a glance at our itinerary pointed out the correct village. Stepping out of the bus, I began to doubt myself. I consulted my Camino app and Google Maps, as I was puzzled by the derelict structures occupying the spot where our hotel was supposed to be. After wandering aimlessly for a while, I headed to the nearby truck stop cafe to wait by the side of the Camino for my friends to arrive.

After ordering my second coffee of the morning, I settled into a seat by the window, intent on keeping watch. I wrapped my fingers around the warm mug, its comforting heat seeping into my palms. My eyelids grew heavy, and I succumbed to their weight, allowing them to close. I was soon in the corner of a chapel, surrounded by the scent of incense and the melody of a man singing at the altar, his voice echoing against the stone walls.

'Hello, Anna,' a gentle voice said. Startled, I turned to find an aged person clad in priest robes sharing the pew with me.

'Hello, Father. You called me by my name. Do I know you?'

He shook his head, then gestured towards a small name tag that hung on my pack.

'You see well, Father.'

He replied with a warm smile 'So I have been told, my child.' After a brief pause, he added, 'I am known as Father Andrius.'

'Ah, Father Andrius. Hello.'

'Anna, my child, is something troubling you?'

I dropped my head into my hands, then glanced up, eyes searching his face for answers. 'Father Andrius, I've been carrying a burden, a secret that weighs heavily on my heart. I fear I've deceived someone I care about, and I don't know if I can ever make it right.'

Father Andrius, his expression one of understanding, gently said, 'Tell me, Anna, what troubles your soul?'

Taking a deep breath, I recounted my story and the web of lies I'd woven to shield myself from a past I wished to forget. I spoke of my encounter with William in France and then on the Camino and my blossoming feelings for him, plus the fear that my deception would shatter any chance of trust between us.

Father Andrius listened, his wise eyes reflecting the flickering candlelight. 'My dear Anna, the journey of truth is a winding path fraught with twists and turns. But remember that not all untruths are born of deceit.'

Furrowing my brow, I was puzzled by his words. 'What do you mean, Father?'

Father Andrius offered a gentle smile 'It's not the words we speak but their intentions. Context, consequences and ethical principles are involved. There is a difference between deceiving for selfish reasons and bending the truth to shield someone from harm or protect oneself from pain. The heart knows the difference.'

'Are there instances in the Bible where deception is justified?'

'That is a troublesome question, my child. The story of the Hebrew midwives in Exodus 1:17–21 is often cited as an example of deception being portrayed in a positive light in the Bible. In this passage, Pharaoh commands the Hebrew midwives, Shiphrah and Puah, to kill all Hebrew baby boys at birth. However, the midwives disobey Pharaoh's orders and allow the boys to live. When Pharaoh questions them about why they haven't carried out his command, the midwives respond with a deceptive explanation, saying that Hebrew women give birth quickly and deliver their babies before the midwives arrive. However, my child, it is worth noting that while this passage depicts the midwives' deception in a positive light; it does not explicitly endorse deception as a moral principle. Instead, it serves as a caution about the complexity of morality.'

My shoulders sagged. 'Thank you, Father. You've given me much to ponder.'

'Remember, Anna, the truth has a peculiar manner of coming to light in due course. Place your trust in the path ahead and have faith that sincerity, blended with kindness, will guide you.'

Overwhelmed by doubt, I pleaded, 'Father, please advise me. Should I disclose the truth to William, tell him my true identity and my history?'

With a gentle tone, he responded, 'My dear Anna, honesty is a virtue intertwined with intricacies. While truth is potent, we must handle it with prudence and wisdom.'

'If I continue to hide the truth from William, can our relationship ever be built on trust?'

Father Andrius placed a comforting hand on my shoulder, his gaze steady. 'Trust is not solely built on the foundation of words, Anna. It is nurtured through actions, sincerity, and the depth of one's character. Truth and trust are not yours to wield.'

The sound of a car horn outside jolted me out of my slumber, my hands still around the cup, steam swirling from its contents. I had drifted into sleep. Outside the window, I spotted my friends in the distance. I took my coffee outside to greet them, but they seemed unsure if they'd arrived in Villadangos del Páramo.

'Are we here already?' William said, sounding surprised. 'I thought we had a couple of kilometres to go.' As they made their way over, I noticed them surveying the surroundings, taken aback by our location.

'According to my map, the old town is a couple of kilometres further yet,' I pointed out. 'Hopefully, it's a little more inspiring.'

Jonathan glanced at the truck stop and said, 'That shouldn't be difficult. We probably should have chosen somewhere a little further along or taken the scenic route via Villar de Mazarife. With not much to see, this could be a long day.'

Claudia touched Jonathan's arm as she pointed up the road. 'The old town may be filled with wonders. Besides, if we'd taken the alternative path, Anna wouldn't have been able to meet us. We're a team, after all.'

Jonathan grinned at Claudia, then at me. 'Now you've told me that, Villadangos del Paramo will be a paradise! We didn't stop for breakfast, so I suggest we walk up to the old town and eat, but only if your feet are up to it, Anna. Otherwise, the truck stop is looking like a hatted restaurant.'

We all shared a laugh at Jonathan's joke.

'It's the pounding all day that hurts my feet. A stroll to town and back shouldn't be a problem.'

***

The town appeared tired, devoid of activity and lacking attractions. Jonathan's prediction rang true; it would be a drawn-out day. Eventually, we discovered a small panadería along the Camino trail, its outdoor tables beckoning us to a late breakfast that stretched into lunch. We whiled away the hours playing with stray cats and scrolling through our social media feeds, time dragging by.

With plenty of time still to kill, we ventured back into the heart of the town, where we stumbled upon a restaurant that had opened its doors to a bustling crowd of customers. Opting for drinks, we lingered before eventually making our way out of town, retracing our steps towards the truck stop in search of our elusive hotel.

Near the truck stop was a building that bore the semblance of a hotel. We stepped through its entrance into a deserted reception area; the silence echoing around us. Our calls for attention went unanswered, adding to the eerie atmosphere. Peering behind the unattended counter, we spotted our luggage, confirming that we'd arrived at the correct destination. Four-room keys were waiting on the reception desk, presumably ours.

Despite the emptiness, the hotel exuded a modern charm. Shrugging, Claudia said, 'It's strange, isn't it? Let's explore before finding our rooms.'

We found a tastefully decorated dining area and inviting lounges. Everything was in place for a lively establishment, yet there wasn't a soul in sight. Jonathan remarked that other Pilgrims had swiftly realised that Villadangos del Paramo was a poor spot to while away a day and moved on.

***

Seated on the comfortable bed of my room, it was difficult to ignore the persistent throbbing in my swollen foot. 'Just one more day,' I said, musing on the daunting twenty-nine kilometres journey to Astorga. I opted to take the bus again and grant myself another rest day, but I felt a pang of guilt at the decision. Were it not for me, my friends would have lingered in León before embarking on today's twenty-one-kilometre trek. They'd have arrived in the afternoon with less time to fill.

Only a few days ago, covering twenty-one kilometres would have seemed like an impossible feat. Now, having already achieved hundreds of kilometres, the distance no longer seemed a burden.

Even Claudia, already in good shape, had improved her endurance. They now had what athletes referred to as "match fitness." I wondered how I would feel when I rejoined them. It was impossible to deny that I was a hindrance to their progress. My friends intended to tackle the challenging route from Hospital de Órbigo, over the hills, a daunting 900-meter climb, and would travel at their best pace. Their goal: to reach Astorga by mid-morning to ensure I wouldn't be waiting long for them. If they arrive before morning tea, it would be an astonishing achievement. I reassured myself that in Astorga, they'd discover a plethora of sights to fill their time. Nestled at the crossroads of the Camino de Santiago pilgrim route and the Roman Silver Road, Astorga boasted a medieval walled Old Town and the renowned Episcopal Palace, a masterpiece by Gaudi housing the esteemed Los Caminos Museum and a majestic Gothic Cathedral. And for Claudia, a fellow connoisseur of fine cuisine like me, an array of eateries promising to satiate her discerning palate.

***

William Marshal

I went down to the hotel lobby promptly at five twenty-five in the morning, finding it deserted except for Claudia, who offered a wave of acknowledgment as I approached. 'I believe,' she said, 'Our group were the only residents last night.'

'Seems that way,' I replied with a nod.

Claudia glanced at her watch with a hint of impatience. 'Where's Jonathan? We've got a big day ahead of us if we're going to beat Anna to Astorga.'

'I didn't realise we were racing against the bus,' Jonathan quipped as he descended the stairs.

I pretended to be shocked, shaking my head with a hint of amusement. 'Racing the bus is all fun and games for you young ones, but spare a thought for your elders. The last thing I need is to end up with injured feet like poor Anna. Besides, you two obviously need adult supervision.'

Ignoring my jest, Claudia turned and asked, 'Are you both ready?'

'Absolutely,' Jonathan and I replied in unison.

Claudia smiled. 'Then let's get going. Breakfast awaits us in Hospital de Orbigo, at a charming eatery just beyond the 200-meter-long, 13th-century stone bridge. At least, that's what my internet search tells me.'

Curious, I inquired, 'How far is that?'

'A short leg this morning, only fourteen kilometres.'

'A short leg!' I replied.

'Yes, William, but it's our best chance for a coffee until close to Astorga.'

Jonathan chimed in, 'I'm surprised you're allowing us a stop at all if we're going to beat the bus.'

'It's a big day, Jonathan,' Claudia replied, her tone serious. 'We need to pace ourselves if we're going to cover the distance swiftly.'

I raised my walking poles. 'Fourteen kilometres before the first stop, it is then. Let's go!'

The Camino trail before us was narrow but relatively flat, making it easy going. Striding briskly in single file, my mind wandered to my upcoming rendezvous in Rabanal del Camino in two days' time and the Bible reading Father Elias had given me. The passage demanded swift action.

I grappled with conflicting emotions as I walked. I knew I should depart for England once the exchange was completed, yet a compulsion urged me to see the Camino journey through to its end. Departing prematurely would render the entire pilgrimage futile; remaining would risk everything, a paradox that weighed heavily on my mind as the kilometres slipped away beneath my feet. I barely paid attention as we made our way into the town of Hospital de Orbigo, until Claudia's voice crashed into my thoughts.

'Here it is,' she said, and we halted at the edge of the medieval stone bridge, its ancient arches standing proud despite being constructed in the 13th century. 'It's as breathtaking as the pictures,' Claudia said, her eyes scanning the structure. 'And it comes with a romantic story.'

Jonathan's curiosity was piqued. 'Now you've got my attention. How does romance intertwine with a stone bridge?'

Claudia began, a hint of excitement in her voice. 'Well, I am glad you asked, Jonathan. According to tradition, one of the most renowned events in history occurred right here in 1434.'

'1434,' I repeated.

Claudia nodded. 'In 1434, the medieval knight, Don Suero de Quinones, found himself spurned by a woman he loved. In response, he organised a jousting tournament, challenging all men of equal rank to a duel that would determine whether they could cross this very bridge. His aim was to defend his honour and prove his worthiness.' Claudia paused before adding with a smile, 'As all men should.'

Jonathan and I remained silent.

Seeing we were not taking the bait, she continued. 'The tournament was a solemn affair, lasting nearly a month. Don Suero claimed to have broken over 300 lances, emerging victorious against all who dared to challenge him while also safeguarding the bridge. Afterwards, he made a pilgrimage to Santiago to express his gratitude for the honour bestowed upon him. However, in 1468, Don Suero de Quinones met his demise at the hands of Gutierre de Quijada, a knight he had defeated in the legendary joust of 1434.'

'To this day, the town celebrates the Fiesta of Passo Honrosso at the beginning of June, commemorating the event. During the festival weekend, residents of Hospital de Órbigo don medieval attire, transforming the streets into scenes from the 15th century. Knights brandish swords and shields, monks and peasants roam the streets, and maidens don elegant velvet dresses.'

Jonathan grinned. 'I could see you in velvet dress, maiden Claudia.'

It was Claudia's turn to ignore the comment, and she continued, without batting an eyelid. 'Among the festivities, a jousting tournament takes place in the town's arena and a medieval market offers a glimpse of the past.'

'That would be worth attending,' I said. 'I wish Anna was here to see the bridge. It is spectacular, although a little lacking in flowing water.'

Claudia shrugged her shoulders. 'They built a dam, William.'

I nodded. 'As they do, Claudia. As they do.'

We'd been walking for over two hours, however Claudia planned only a brief break, so, after a quick coffee and croissant, she promptly had us back on the trail. Despite our reluctance to leave Anna alone in Astorga for too long, as we exited the village, we veered right towards Villares, opting for the longer but more attractive route. We journeyed across the countryside, passing through Villares de Órbigo and Santibáñez, gradually ascending 900 metres to the ancient stone cross of Santo Toribio, a towering structure adorned with carvings, reflecting the significance of the pilgrimage. From there, we were rewarded with a panoramic view overlooking the valley towards Astorga.

I sighed. 'I wish Anna could see this, the cross and the view.'

Claudia nodded and peering towards the cross she said, 'It's known as the Holy Cross of Santo Toribio and holds a significant place in the history and tradition of the Camino. It's steeped in legend and lore, origins shrouded in mystery, but it is believed to date back several centuries, possibly to the medieval period. An enduring legend is the connection to Saint Toribio of Liébana, a revered saint who lived in the 6th century. According to tradition, Saint Toribio played a key role in promoting devotion to the cross. It is told that he travelled to the Holy Land and brought back a fragment of the True Cross, which was later enshrined in a monastery in Liébana, near the Camino route. Pilgrims travelling along the Camino de Santiago would often stop at the Cruceiro Santo Toribio to pay homage to Saint Toribio and seek his intercession for a safe and successful journey. Over the centuries, the cross has become a cherished symbol of the pilgrimage experience, which is why I wanted us, but mainly you, Jonathan, to journey this way. What you're witnessing is an important symbol of faith along "The Way."'

As I observed Claudia talking to Jonathan. I thought of her interaction with Anna. I'd noticed a shift in her manner. At the start of our journey, Claudia was purely professional, actions calculated to maintain her cover as an MI6 agent. As we neared Astorga, her facade was softening, showing genuine care for her companions.

'Thank you, that was interesting.' Jonathan said.

Claudia's professed religious beliefs had initially seemed an elaborate ruse, designed to ingratiate herself with Jonathan. As we approached the last leg of our journey, I wondered if there was more to her faith than met the eye. Perhaps, like each of us, she was touched by the spiritual nature of the Camino, finding meaning amidst the history and the companionship of others.

In Claudia, I could see echoes of my turmoil as I pondered what would transpire as we reached Rabanal del Camino. The pilgrimage had built a connection to her and our destinies were intertwined in ways we each had yet to understand.

Claudia gestured for us to follow her to the stone cross. Placing her hand upon the ancient structure, she asked us to close our eyes. For a moment, we stood in silence, absorbing the history in the air. As if in response to our emotions, a breeze brushed our faces.

Claudia said, 'Can you sense those who have walked this path before us?'

I felt a tingling sensation followed by a lump forming in my throat. I tried to speak, but found myself unable to form words. Tears welled in my eyes as I nodded.

***

Claudia

I glanced at my watch and felt contented as I noted the time: precisely eleven. With a smile, I composed a text message to Anna, informing her of our whereabouts in the Cathedral square, near the Palacio de Gaudi. Almost immediately, her reply came through.

> Unbelievable. I arrived 30 minutes ago. See you all soon. You are wonderful friends.

I showed Anna's response to the others and from their reactions, I sensed the shared pride in our accomplishment. We'd covered the distance in a mere five hours, including breakfast and a stop for morning tea, plus capturing photos at the Cruceiro Santo Toribio. My eagerness to ensure Anna wasn't alone for long was driven by my guilt when I set a brisk pace while walking with Kat, causing Anna's foot problems. Time was slipping away for me to make amends. If MI6's intelligence proved correct, the next day, when we reached Rabanal del Camino, was when William would be apprehended with his contact as they exchanged British military secrets. My covert mission would then end, and MI6 would want my prompt return home. In the absence of William and myself, Anna and Jonathan would have to navigate the last of the Camino on their own.

Anna greeted us with warm hugs as we met. 'How are those feet?' I asked.

She held up a packet of paracetamol and ibuprofen for us to see. 'I'm determined to walk with you all tomorrow.'

'That's great news,' William and Jonathan said in unison.

I pointed to the Palacio de Gaudi. 'Are we going to explore?'

Anna smiled, 'Yes, but not until we've had a coffee. You guys have earned a rest.'

'Have you found anywhere nice?' William asked.

Anna shook her head. 'I haven't had a chance yet, William. As I found the pharmacy, Claudia messaged me to tell me you'd arrived. You must have sprinted.'

Jonathan placed his hand on my shoulder. 'Young Claudia here whipped us along.'

Ignoring Jonathan, I said, 'Coffee sounds great.'

Anna nodded. 'Excellent. We'll be spoiled for choice but, judging by the crowds, finding a seat might be tricky.'

***

After coffee and a welcome toilet break, we queued to purchase our tickets. Having been in many churches along "The Way", I was looking forward to seeing a unique form of architecture and I wasn't disappointed. The moment we stepped through the portico, the grandeur of Palacio de Gaudi unfolded. The enormous voussoirs of the flared arches greeted us, a striking contrast to the sturdy support of the building.

Moving through the interior, we whispered as we marvelled at the Greek cross plan inscribed within the square layout. The gable roof, adorned with slate and bordered by a continuous granite balustrade, added to the structure and we imagined the chimneys designed by Gaudi, forming an ensemble with three angels poised atop the roof, though regrettably unseen.

Reaching the spiral staircase, I said, 'Up or down?'

Jonathan rubbed his chin before pointing down. We descended to the basement to enter an open space devoid of room divisions, originally intended for the Diocesan Archive and Epigraphic Museum. Today, it housed a collection of epigraphic, numismatic, and lapidary treasures. The sight of the unique catenary arch, surrounded by a pit providing light and ventilation, left us all in awe of Gaudi's ingenuity.

Ascending to the lower level, we encountered a richly decorated interior that contrasted with the modest exterior. The Mudejar style vaults were of glazed ceramics while the starry capitals and stained-glass windows exuded elegance and refinement.

Venturing to the first floor, we explored the bishop's domain, with its central space surrounded by numerous chambers. The repetition of glazed ceramics along the ribbed vaults added to the splendour. We admired the Chapel, Throne Room, and Gala Dining Room, each intricate, reminiscent of Sainte Chapelle in Paris.

Finally reaching the second floor, we encountered a simpler loft-like space crafted by architect Ricardo Garcia Guereta. Though lacking in decoration, the floor boasted two balconies serving as a choir for the chapel, offering a retreat amidst the opulence below.

We agreed to explore the building separately but, in reality, William and Anna went off together, and I left with Jonathan.

We descended back to the bishop's domain, where Jonathan stopped, scanned around and said, 'We have seen some magnificent churches and cathedrals walking the Camino de Santiago, each one filled with stunning stained-glass windows, intricate altarpieces and rich history. Being here reminds me of Gaudi's Sagrada Família in Barcelona. That church.' he breathed out heavily, searching for the right word. 'Touched me on a deeper level.'

'What do you mean?' I asked.

'It was... um, more spiritual.'

'Really. The cathedrals of León and Burgos, and the churches in almost every town we've past, are centuries old and filled with so much history and devotion.'

'I know, Claudia, I know. And they were breathtaking but sometimes, almost too much so, with their elaborate gold altarpieces and like. When I stepped into the Sagrada Família, I was transported to another world. It wasn't about the grandeur of the architecture or the beauty of the artwork, but something more profound. The Sagrada Família was never meant to be a place of religion. It was built to tell the story of the sacred family—maybe that's it?'

'Really, Jonathan. I didn't know that.'

'Yes, every element of the Sagrada Família was designed to tell a story. Visiting was like experiencing the Bible in stone and light. Did you know that the central towers are dedicated to Jesus

Christ and the Virgin Mary? The four towers, known as the towers of the Evangelists, at the corners of the central square, are each dedicated to the Gospel writers, Matthew, Mark, Luke, and John, who chronicled Jesus' life. And then there are the facades, each representing different aspects of Jesus' life and teachings. To me, the Sagrada Família is not only a building, it's an immersive journey through spirituality, an expression of religious symbolism, the Bible made of stone. For me, that's what sets it apart from the churches we've visited along the Camino.'

Pausing to contemplate Jonathan's words, I grasped his viewpoint, though it didn't align with my own. After a moment of reflection to organise my thoughts, it was clear there are two divergent approaches to showcasing reverence, both leaning towards extravagance. Preferring to sidestep an intellectual debate, I remarked, 'The medieval structures we've come across along the Camino embody the reverence of their era, whereas the Sagrada Família presents a modern interpretation.'

Jonathan nodded; he was acknowledging my different perspective, while not necessarily agreeing with me.

I hesitated, considering my next words carefully. 'When you return to the United States, Jonathan, do you want to become a pastor of an evangelical church?'

Jonathan hesitated before replying. 'No. There was a time when I thought that was my path, but not anymore.'

'What led to this change of heart?'

Jonathan evaded answering the question. 'It's not one thing.'

Sensing his reluctance, I steered the conversation elsewhere and gestured towards our surroundings instead. 'Gaudi's work is truly remarkable.'

***

After settling into our hotel and taking an hour to freshen up, we met up and swung by a nearby supermarket to stock up on supplies for the following day's walk. Afterwards, we rendezvoused with Chinmay at the hotel's restaurant for a drink, securing a reservation for dinner at eight thirty that evening.

Even though Chinmay was a constant presence on our Camino journey, we had never asked him why he wanted to walk "The Way." It was his former teacher from Australia, during his final year of school, who had recommended he undertake the Camino. Now living and working in Manchester, that suggestion had suddenly resurfaced in Chinmay's mind. Instead of procrastinating, he travelled to France and began the pilgrimage. We never questioned why his teacher had suggested such a journey, but from the way Chinmay spoke about the walk and his eagerness to share the experience with his mentor, it was obvious that the Camino was profoundly impactful for him.

It was delightful to catch up with Chinmay, after which we opted for a stroll along the city walls. As we meandered, we stumbled upon a vibrant plaza where, to our surprise, we encountered Clare and Isaac, accompanied by several other fellow travellers we'd met along our journey. They were engrossed in pizza and drinks and, upon spotting us; they waved and asked us to join them. We happily lingered, relishing the ambiance, camaraderie, and spirited conversations until it was time to leave for dinner. And what an extraordinary dinner it turned out to be; a standout moment of our Camino journey so far, with flavours and dishes that exceeded our high expectations. Savouring every bite, I retired to my room, utterly content.

Slipping off my shoes, I sank into the comfort of my bed. Dinner had added to the exhaustion of an already long day, wonderful though it was. With everything set to come to a head the following day, I went online to read William's post. It hadn't appeared, not surprising given our recent retirement for the night. I made myself a cup of tea before checking again. Finally, the post popped up on my screen:

William's Social Media Post

Today's journey took us to Astorga, a city brimming with a medieval allure that we were eager to explore. With an early start before dawn and favourable weather conditions, we found ourselves greeted by the city's enchanting charm after five and a half hours of walking.

The highlight of our visit was undoubtedly the Gaudi-designed Episcopal Palace, a true architectural masterpiece. The man was a genius.

We had a lovely dinner in the vibrant restaurant attached to our hotel. Tomorrow, Anna rejoins us as we walk to Rabanal del Camino, a town of pure Templar origins, on our way to Foncebadón. Then in two days' time, the famous The Castillo de los Templarios en Ponferrada and the "Book of Kells" (9th century), awaits.

Note: The weather has taken a turn, with heavy rain forecasted for the foreseeable future.

Before I could finish reading it for a second time, Stephen from MI6 was already on the line. 'What's your take on William's post?' he inquired urgently.

'I'm just going through it now, Stephen,' I replied, as I tried to decipher the cryptic message.

'Claudia, we've assumed the handover will take place in the parish church in Rabanal del Camino. But now, with this mention of the whole town being Knights Templar, I wonder if he is hinting at something else.'

'One thing is for certain, Stephen. Whatever William is trying to convey, it's not meant for us to understand.'

'We have our surveillance equipment in place at the parish church and people ready to apprehend him and his contact inside. If the handover happens outside of the church, we must not lose what he's been carrying. Not under any circumstances, Claudia. Do I make myself clear?'

'Yes, Stephen. And if nothing happens tomorrow?'

'You're the agent on the ground, Claudia.'

'My suspicion, Sir, is that William has moved the handover to Ponferrada.'

'You might be onto something, but what clues led you to this conclusion?'

'He alluded to it in his social media post. There was a line that caught my attention: "Then in two days' time, the famous The Castillo de los Templarios en Ponferrada and the "Book of Kells"." The book is on display in the first room of the Templum Libri exhibition. I think that the handover will be there.'

'Why would he move it, Claudia?'

'Walking as a group and with Anna's return, there'll be no chance to slip away when we reach Rabanal del Camino. It's only a village we are passing through. Ponferrada offers an overnight stop and affords him time.'

'Ah, yes. That seems plausible.'

'Thank you, Sir. Do we have any leads on William's contact?'

Frustration tinged his voice as Stephen replied, 'No, Claudia. That information continues to elude us.'

Chapter 22
Knights Templar

William Marshal

Anna's radiant smile greeted us in the hotel lobby as we gathered for our trek to Foncebadón, a challenging ascent of 1400 metres. 'I'm on the road again,' she exclaimed with infectious enthusiasm.

We were all thrilled to have her back, but for me, it was an especially joyful reunion. When I initially planned this journey, the idea of meeting Anna or the others in our small troupe hadn't even crossed my mind.

We trudged through drizzling rain, me in my raincoat and the others under Ponchos, toward Murias de Rechivaldo, our planned breakfast stop. I contemplated the twists and turns the journey had taken. My original plan had been meticulously crafted: transport the goods along the Camino de Santiago route, rendezvousing at the Knights Templar Church in Rabanal del Camino. Fate had a way of unravelling the threads of the "best-laid plans of mice and men." Walking with Anna and the rest of our group had been an unexpected deviation from my plan. Through my years of experience, I'd learned that plans were always a guide, not meant to be rigid; they needed to cater for ever-shifting currents. The handover was now to occur in Ponferrada. This simple change spoke volumes of my ability to bend with the winds, the hallmark of a true master.

The Albergue in Murias de Rechivaldo served excellent coffee and while eating breakfast, it wasn't long before we were joined by other pilgrims, including Chinmay. Eager to get back on the road, we were among the first to depart, greeted by a break in the rain and better walking conditions. Our goal: to conquer the steep ascent to Foncebadón before the weather took a turn for the worse.

The path from Murias de Rechivaldo to Rabanal del Camino was a steady climb that paralleled the road, with a bustling stream of pilgrims stretching out ahead of us. As we walked, taxis zipped past, shuttling weary travellers who'd underestimated the challenges of the Camino after joining in Astorga.

'Woo hoo!' Jonathan exclaimed as we passed a marker showing that only 246.6 kilometres remain until we reached Santiago.

As the clock struck 11:00 AM, our group reached Rabanal del Camino, prompting us to opt for an early lunch break. As others joined us at the lunch table, I felt reassured by my decision to change the rendezvous point – there was no opportunity for me to slip away. The closest I came to the church was as we strolled past it, a fleeting moment that brought a smile to my face as I envisioned the surveillance MI6 had likely established, only to witness me innocently walking by.

Departing town, Anna spotted a young girl with a small owl on her arm. Curious, Anna trailed after the girl into a nearby bar, requesting permission to photograph her and her companion. The girl introduced herself as Lusha and told us that the owl was called Luna. Her proud parents were happy for their daughter and Luna to have their photographs taken.

The path from Rabanal del Camino to Foncebadón was five and a half kilometres. As we gained elevation after leaving Rabanal, the terrain became more rugged, with rocky outcrops and dense forests lining the trail. The ascent towards Foncebadón didn't test our endurance as we'd feared, but I was concerned for Anna's feet. If she was experiencing pain, she didn't complain. As we climbed, we were treated to a wonderful vista of surrounding valleys and distant peaks. In the last stretch of our journey, fatigue weighed heavily upon us. Yet, as we reached the crest of the last hill, a palpable sense of triumph washed over us. Before our eyes lay Foncebadón, nestled atop a rugged hillside. This highest village along the Camino was a spectacle to behold. The once-desolate ghost town now pulsating with life, reborn from the ashes of its past.

Turning to admire the breathtaking view, Anna remarked, 'Simply stunning, absolutely beautiful.' Her sentiment resonated with all of us, and we collectively marvelled at the sight. As we took in the surroundings, our gaze landed on our accommodation situated to the left—it was a sight to behold. 'It looks good,' Jonathan said. Prior to checking in, we took a leisurely stroll along the cobblestone street that meandered through clusters of ancient stone houses that bore witness to centuries gone by. At the centre of Foncebadón stood the venerable church, a tribute to the town's patron saint, Santa Maria Magdalena. Claudia eloquently described the church as a symbol of the village's deep-rooted religious legacy.

Surrounding the village was the rugged beauty of the Spanish countryside. Rolling hills blanketed with lush greenery stretch as far as the eye can see, while towering peaks loomed majestically in the distance. The air was crisp and invigorating, carrying a faint scent of pine and wildflowers. Foncebadón seemed warm and welcoming.

Our accommodation was to our liking, it was a delight. Downstairs was a bustling bar, dining room, an outdoor area with a view, and a supermarket equipped with everything needed for a pilgrimage walk. For a small fee, we could have our clothes washed and dried, which we did before heading to the dining room where we met our Canadian friend, Sean. He was staying at a nearby Albergue. When Sean left, we took another walk around town, where we chanced upon Isaac, perched like a leprechaun on a brick wall, jotting in his journal. He told us, he'd walked to the top of the mountain and back so that he could see the La Cruz de Ferro in the daylight. Our group would pass it in the dark, as it remained dark until nine in the morning.

Nestled atop a mound of stones, the La Cruz de Ferro, known as the Iron Cross, marks the highest point on the Camino. It is a simple, powerful symbol which commands reverence from pilgrims who approach it. Its exact origins remain mysterious. Some legend has it that the Celts used it in pre-Christian times for unknown rituals. Others suggest that the La Cruz de Ferro can be traced back to the time of the Roman Empire, where it once served as a boundary marker. The most popular legend attributes its creation to the Apostle James. Over the centuries, it has become a sacred site along the Camino. Pilgrims place stones at its base. Every stone represents a burden, a fear, a hope, or a prayer–a manifestation of the struggles we each face on our journey through life. La Cruz de Ferro is a symbol of hope, redemption, and the power of the human spirit to transcend adversity. I wondered whether my companions carried a stone on the journey and if they intended to place it at the cross the following day.

Leaving Isaac behind, we made our way back to the hotel. Claudia and Jonathan disappeared into their rooms, while Anna and I opted for a glass of wine, settling outside to enjoy the view of the landscape spread out before us.

After a moment of quiet contemplation, I broke the silence. 'You know Anna, sometimes I feel like life is slipping away from me, like sand through my fingers.'

Anna nodded; her eyes fixed on the horizon. 'I know what you mean, William. It's like we're nearing the end of a spool of thread, racing against the approaching years. When we were younger, we never dwelled on the end. Now, it's impossible to ignore.'

I sighed; the weight of regret is heavy on my shoulders. I need to share the truth, but only some of it. 'I spent too much time away from home, chasing after things that now seem insignificant. My wife... she deserved better. And my daughter, well, I can't say I've been the father she needed.'

'Life has a way of unfolding in unexpected ways, William. I've had an interesting life but I haven't escaped pain. My own battles have left scars that nobody sees.'

'I'm sorry, Anna. I had no idea.'

She offered a sad smile. 'There's a lot we don't share on the Camino, but somehow, walking these ancient paths feels like we've opened our souls to each other.'

I took a sip of my wine, the taste mingling with the weight of our conversation. 'So, what do you plan to do when you return home? I keep thinking about all the time I've wasted, all the moments I could have cherished more.'

Anna considered the question for a moment, her eyes distant, as if lost in a reverie. 'I suppose I'll continue living as I always have, finding pleasure in the simple joys of life. Maybe I'll finally write that book I've been putting off for years. What about you?'

I shook my head, a sense of uncertainty clouding my thoughts. 'I don't know. This walk has made me realise that I... we must make the most of the time we have left.'

Anna smiled softly; her gaze filled with understanding. 'Yes, embrace life and all moments of it.'

'You told me you'd continue living as you always have. If there were no barriers, what would you do?'

'If money was no concern, do you mean?'

'Yes, if money is a barrier for you.'

Anna leaned back in her chair, a glimmer of excitement in her eyes. 'William, I'd have a quaint and quirky bookshop in a small French or English village. It wouldn't matter if the bookshop made money because it would be a gathering place. That's what I've loved about the Camino. We gather with people.'

'A book shop. That would be lovely.'

'Idealistic, you mean?'

'Not at all, Anna.' I paused, contemplating, before asking, 'Would you want to travel?'

'Travel would be lovely but I would yearn to return to my bookshop, a place where I am surrounded by people and friends, because relationships are all that matter, in the end.'

I took another sip from my glass, the warmth of the wine soothing. 'Are you ever lonely, living on your own?'

'Sometimes,' Anna confessed with a wistful sigh, 'The Camino, in a sense, feels unreal because you're constantly surrounded by people. Returning to an empty apartment will be a challenge at first. But eventually, it'll become the new normal again. What about you, William? Being on your own now that Hannah has passed must be difficult.'

'It is definitely not good for me and I know I must make connections.'

'An online dating site, perhaps?'

I hesitated, but before I could respond, the sounds of Claudia and Jonathan approaching interrupted our conversation.

'It must be close to dinnertime,' Jonathan said as he settled at our table.

The meal lived up to the charm of the location and the dessert, cheesecake with berries on top, was delightful. When we finished our meal, we checked the following day's weather on our phones. The forecast was ominous, fog and heavy rain. With a twenty-nine kilometre walk ahead of us, we unanimously agreed on an early night.

Alone within my room, I penned my nightly social media post, this time devoid of any hidden message.

> Undeterred by her foot injury, Anna is back, unwilling to miss a moment more of this incredible journey.
>
> The walk from Astorga to Foncebadón unfolded through the breathtaking countryside, offering a stark contrast to the bustling roads of the past week. The crisp air, rustling leaves, and the symphony of nature created a tranquil atmosphere.
>
> Our destination, Foncebadón, stands at 1,400m and the 28km walk from Astorga proved to be a rewarding challenge. The climb, while not as daunting as the guidebook suggested, still gave a genuine sense of accomplishment.
>
> Tomorrow we will pass the Puerto Irago Cruz de Ferro—a humbling monument. Here, pilgrims place a stone at the base of a cross, symbolizing the act of unburdening oneself by leaving something behind.

***

Leaving our hotel, we found ourselves enveloped in thick fog, the damp chill seeping through our layers as we outfitted ourselves in wet weather gear, preparing for the journey to Ponferrada. Guided by a gradual ascent, we ventured towards the haunting misty silhouette of Puerto Irago Cruz de Ferro, which loomed in the cloak of darkness. When we reached the monument, a solemn silence settled over us. Alone in the eeriness, I watched as each of my companions approached the iron cross. Anna tenderly placed a stone at its base, a gesture of reverence. Whether Claudia and Jonathan followed suit in placing a stone, I couldn't say, nor did I feel compelled to inquire. The ritual of Puerto Irago Cruz de Ferro was deeply personal, a communion between each pilgrim and their journey.

It was my turn. As I approached the Puerto Irago Cruz de Ferro, a myriad of thoughts swirled within me, each vying for my attention. The weight of my dual existence, the dichotomy of my loyalty to the UK and my entanglement in a life of crime, pressed heavily upon my conscience, something that was new since Hannah's passing. With each step closer to the towering iron cross, the gravity of my past and present sins pulled me back. Standing before the cross was similar to the Catholic act of confession, my faith, the tradition of baring one's soul before God, of seeking absolution for one's transgressions.

Is this simple gesture of placing a stone at the foot of the cross, akin to laying bare my sins before a higher power? Will it offer me redemption and if it does, is that right?

I wished that we'd seen the cross after Ponferrada and the exchange. I was surprised when my hand trembled as I reach into my pocket to retrieve a small stone, its smooth surface unreadable, like the unexpected emotions raging within me. As I place it at the base of the cross, I cannot shake off the nagging doubt that creeps into my mind.

Can it truly be this easy? Can a single act erase the stains of my past and grant me absolution?

'I'm sorry, Hannah,' I whispered and turned away. The weight of what I carry to Ponferrada cannot be atoned this easily, I know this in my heart. Joining the others, I wonder whether Anna will take me into her confidence to share the burden she's left behind.

We continued on in the cold, dark, rain and mist until a glow in the distance caught our eye. As we approached, a food truck materialised from the gloom, a small building to one side housing tables, chairs, and an open fire. We were in Manjarin.

'Unbelievable,' Jonathan said. 'Coffee and a fire. Who dares to say, God is not true? This is a miracle.'

Earlier than expected, we enjoyed coffee and an impromptu breakfast while warming our hands next to the fire. We stayed longer than we should have, ordering a further round of drinks, delaying venturing out into the cold and rain. When we finally left the shelter, prompted by fellow pilgrims seeking the warmth and dry we'd enjoyed, the sun was rising and the mist clearing, giving us panoramic views of the pink and blue sunrise.

The rain cleared and the walk across the plateau opened up a vista, causing Jonathan to say, 'Life can't get any better than this.'

His reflection was tempered as we walked past a memorial to a person his age who'd died during the walk. Soon, we topped the next peak and descended, dropping from 1500m above sea level to El Acebo, where we paused for another coffee. The weather closed in again, unleashing a deluge of bucketing rain, complicating our descent to Molinaseca. The path, already treacherous with rocks and rubble, became slick and uncertain, each step akin to walking on ice. One wrong move would cause an injury, rendering us unable to proceed. Moments like these proved the worth of my walking poles, providing stability and support amidst the challenge. After what felt like a long and endless perilous trek, feet soaked through, we stumbled onto the road to Molinaseca. With each step, the weight of exhaustion clung to us like the rain-soaked clothes we wore. Anna, undeterred by fatigue, reached for her phone and sent a message to Chuck and Cathy, fellow pilgrims and now good friends, she knew were already in Molinaseca, asking if we could meet. They swiftly replied, asking us to meet them at the hotel for lunch.

Entering Molinaseca, our path led us across the medieval bridge crossing the Meruelo river. Under normal circumstances, we'd have paused, capturing photographs of the seven - arched landmark to engage in discussions about its origins, likely dating back to Roman times. Claudia, with her penchant for history, would have regaled us with tales of how, with subsequent modifications, the bridge reflected Romanesque architecture. Today was different. Our usual fascination with history was overshadowed by the pressing need to reach Chuck and Cathy's hotel near the bridge. We were driven by a primal instinct to seek refuge from the unforgiving elements and find rest.

When we entered the restaurant attached to their lodging, I noticed a glimmer of moisture in Anna's eyes as she caught sight of them, plus another Camino companion, Alesa. Her expression spoke a silent narrative of relief that the harrowing journey from Foncebadón was finally over. Tears threatened to spill over when we exchanged heartfelt hugs and there was a collective sigh of relief as we shed our drenched outer layers. Jonathan, Claudia, Anna, and I, still wearing our sodden shoes, gratefully sank into the empty chairs surrounding their table, ready to savour their companionship and the promise of a hot meal.

'Tough?' Chuck inquired; voice edged with concern.

I nodded, my expression a silent confirmation of the challenges we'd faced. I breathed out heavily before saying, 'Yep, tough. Brutal and dangerous, in fact.'

Surrounded by the comfort of friends and the warmth of the restaurant, our spirits soared. Our relief was amplified because of what we'd endured during the day's trek. The arduous journey from Foncebadón soon faded, overshadowed by the camaraderie and joy of our reunion. Lunch was a humble affair: slices of jamon (dry-cured ham), golden-fried eggs, crispy chips, and frothy beer (a couple of pints). Yet, each morsel felt like an indulgence. Chuck shared a tale that elicited sympathy and amusement. He recounted how the nail on his big toe turned black and eventually fell off before reaching Molinaseca the day prior. With a collective understanding of the toll the journey exacted on our bodies, Chuck and Cathy told us they would to take another day of rest before resuming their Camino pilgrimage. We promised to meet them in Santiago in front of the Cathedral, even if it was in the pouring rain. Alesa's voice proposed a cheery toast, and we raised our glasses, 'To friendship and food.'

Glancing at my watch, I reluctantly interjected, 'I hate to be the bearer of bad news, but we have another seven kilometres to cover to reach Ponferrada. It's time we gather our resolve and face the rain to conquer the last leg of our journey.' Unspoken was my hidden agenda; I had a clandestine meeting planned in Ponferrada, though I now wished that I hadn't. Once we checked into our hotel and everyone dispersed to freshen up, my plan was to slip away unnoticed and return without them noticing I was missing.

As I rose to depart, an impulse seized me, and I turned to Chuck, beckoning for a parting gift for the journey ahead, a poem to linger in my thoughts. Chuck, with a thoughtful nod, delved into the depths of his mind, sifting through memories for something truly extraordinary. And then, with an eloquence that dripped from his every word, he began:

> 'Go placidly amid the noise and the haste, and remember what peace there may be in silence. As far as possible, without surrender, be on good terms with all persons.

Speak your truth quietly and clearly; and listen to others, even to the dull and the ignorant; they too have their story.

Avoid loud and aggressive persons; they are vexatious to the spirit. If you compare yourself with others, you may become vain or bitter, for always there will be greater and lesser persons than yourself.

Enjoy your achievements as well as your plans. Keep interested in your own career, however humble; it is a real possession in the changing fortunes of time...'

Chuck is a master.

With heartfelt farewells, Alesa accompanied us to the outskirts of the town, enveloping us in warm embraces and well-wishes as we embarked on the next leg of our journey. 'Be careful,' she said to me, noticing my limp. I held up my walking poles and with a smile said, 'This old man has two walking sticks. I will be fine.'

The trek to Ponferrada was a soggy affair, each step accompanied by a relentless downpour. Relief washed away the discomfort as we finally crossed into the city limits where a sign showed us the way to our hotel, our bed for the night after a gruelling nine-hour journey from Foncebadón. Stepping into the hotel lobby, exhaustion mingled with accomplishment, Jonathan told the receptionist how grateful we were to find the hotel after the gruelling journey. She smiled in understanding as she handed us our room keys. With our luggage in tow, we dispersed, each heading to our respective rooms, agreeing to meet back in the lobby an hour and a half later when we'd visit the Templar Castle.

The Templar Castle was across the road from where we were staying the night. I had ample time to freshen up and attend to my tasks before rejoining the group. I pondered whether Claudia would be summoned back to Britain after my rendezvous or if she'd continue the walk.

***

Claudia

Stepping into my room, the familiar buzz of my phone alerted me to a new message. Glancing at the screen, I noted the coordinates of the MI6 surveillance van, *C. Gily Carrasco, 7*, near the Radio Museum. Accompanying the location was an invitation for me to join them. I checked the tracking app for William's backpack; he remained in his room. Calculating the timing, I realised the handover would probably occur within the hour and a half window before our scheduled rendezvous in the lobby. Rubbing my forehead wearily, I weighed my options. A hot shower would be a welcome reprieve after the gruelling walk, but time was of the essence if I intended to slip out unnoticed before William ventured to the castle.

Rapping lightly on the side door of the sleek black van, it swung open with a soft whir, granting me access. Stepping inside, I was greeted by the operation controller Ria, a familiar face from previous assignments. Beside her stood her colleague Nevil, whose determined demeanour betrayed him as a seasoned professional. The van interior was dominated by surveillance equipment, with two large digital screens displaying live footage from MI6 operatives on the ground. Ria directed me to a vacant seat positioned for a good view. Ria and Nevil sat on either side of me and, no sooner had I settled in, than my tracking app pinged, alerting me to William Marshal's movements.

'Here we go,' I said.

Ria acknowledged with a nod, her attention already shifting to her task. Speaking into the microphone in front of her, she alerted her team. 'We have eyes on him,' came the reply through the speaker system. Simultaneously, live footage of William lit up on one monitor, as an agent started following him.

With his day pack slung over his shoulders and walking poles in hand, William walked along the street, limping noticeably, his gait betraying his urgency. He crossed the road towards the castle entrance. After procuring a ticket, he proceeded to the entrance. The MI6 agent tailing him paused to avoid arousing William Marshal's suspicion. William disappeared across the drawbridge over the moat and into the fortress. Inside, another agent awaited, ready to pick up the surveillance.

Over the speaker system, an agent reported, 'We've conducted a thorough sweep of the surroundings, and it appears that William Marshal is not under surveillance by any foreign party.'

'It seems,' I said, 'Whoever William Marshal is to meet is already inside the castle walls.'

Moments later, the next agent accepted tracking duties, and we observed William as he approached the New Palace housing the revered Templum Libri and the Book of Kells.

Ria turned to me; her eyes focussed. 'We've cameras and listening devices within the Templum Libri. They'll provide a live feed and audio as events unfold. Nevil, bring them up for us, please.'

Nevil nodded, tapping icons to bring the feeds online. We watched as William stepped into the room. Amidst the exhibits, he appeared engrossed, a lone figure amidst the historical riches. Soon, a man of similar age approached from behind, presence unnoticed until he placed a hand on William's shoulder. A smile passed between them before they exchanged greetings.

'Hello, Sir William,' the man greeted warmly.

'Lewis,' William responded.

Lewis glanced around before leaning in, voice low. 'Do you have it?'

William unslung his backpack and reached inside, retrieving the puzzle box. He held it out for Lewis to inspect.

Ria rapped her fist against the control bench. 'Got them.' Pressing the button on her microphone, she snapped instructions. 'Wait until the targets exchange item, then make the arrest discreetly, as we've planned.'

William's booming voice was clear through the speakers in the van.

'Here it is,' he said, passing the puzzle box to Lewis.

As Lewis' fingers wrapped around the puzzle box, I observed a woman approach Lewis. After displaying her credentials, she introduced herself, her voice dripping with officialdom. 'Good afternoon. I am Evelyn Sterling, a representative of His Majesty's Secret Intelligence Service, MI6. I need you to cooperate fully. Any resistance or attempt to flee will be met with resistance. We suspect your involvement in obtaining protected information under the espionage provision of the National Security Bill. Please come with me, Sir.'

A look of confusion swept across Lewis' face as Evelyn retrieved the puzzle box from Lewis and handed it to a colleague before slipping her arm into his, guiding him away. To a casual observer, their departure appeared nothing more than a couple strolling arm in arm.

Simultaneously, a similar scene unfolded with William, as he too found himself confronted by MI6 agents executing their meticulously planned operation.

Ria told me that MI6 had secured a four-bedroom house a stone's throw from the castle, where William and Lewis would be taken for interrogation. We could watch the proceeding on the screens. The men were ushered into separate rooms, William in the kitchen and Lewis in the dining room, each with a table in the middle, a seat flanking either side. The men were searched and, when William's pockets were emptied on to the table, they revealed four admittance tickets to the Templar Castle, his hotel key, a small wallet which housed some cash and his driver's licence.

William is clever. Clever indeed!

William was the first to face questioning. Despite the gravity of the situation, he maintained his composure, vehemently denying any involvement in wrongdoing. His laughter rang out when the interrogator said the puzzle box concealed state secrets. Pressed to open the box, William's expression turned rueful as he confessed his ignorance. Following a set of instructions laid out on the desk before him, the agent conducting the interrogation deftly manipulated the intricate mechanisms of the box until its lip slid open with a whisper. With a gentle tilt, he emptied its contents onto the table, revealing nothing more than the cherished mementos of William's deceased wife, Hannah. The interrogator's expression tightened. Retrieving a file from his desk, he extracted a copy of the Knights Templar coded message that had been discovered on William's computer and handed it to him. William scrutinised the document for a moment before shaking his head, sighing wearily, and saying. 'Ask Lewis.'

'We will,' the agent assured him. 'But why don't you tell me first?'

William locked eyes with the agent, a spark of defiance mingled with disdain in his gaze. 'The answer lies within my name, though I remain very much alive. The agent looked puzzled. So, with a huff, William continued. 'Lewis is my brother-in-law, Hannah's kin, and a respected anthropologist. The Templar code has been a familial pastime since Hannah and I wed. Sir William

Marshal, my namesake and a figure of British lore, was posthumously honoured as a Knight Templar. His resting place is Temple Church in London, where his effigy stands. Lewis, always one for jest, dubbed me "Sir William," prompting Hannah and I to exchange Christmas and birthday greetings written in Templar code, often with cryptic undertones. Following Hannah's passing and Samantha's declaration of not continuing the family line, the ancestral puzzle box passes to Lewis' elder daughter. In adherence to tradition, I sent him a cryptic Templar message. Logically, the exchange should occur in a locale associated with the Knights Templar, thus Ponferrada's Templar castle seemed fitting. I was giving it to him when we were apprehended.'

The agent rubbed his temples, grappling with the conundrum confronting him.

Lifting my focus from the interview for a moment, I turned to those in the van, the penny dropping. 'William Marshal has outsmarted us all.'

Ria looked confused. 'What's going on?'

'I don't know yet, but I think William Marshal has played us.'

'Who's this knight, Sir William Marshal?' Ria said.

I searched using my phone, reading my findings to her. 'The fourth son of a minor noble, William Marshal (c 1146–1219) rose to become one of the most admired knights in English history. In his early years, he fought in tournaments where hundreds or even thousands of fighters would engage in melee-style mock battles. He rose to stardom, travelling from tournament to tournament and got rich on the prizes he won.'

'He served five English kings, and married the heiress Isabel de Clare, becoming one of the richest men in the country. William helped in the negotiations between King John and his Barons that led to the signing of the Magna Carta in 1215. When King John died in 1216, making nine-year-old Henry III king, William became Regent of England. Although he was about seventy by then, he led the young king's army to victory over French forces and rebellious barons the following year.'

I looked at Ria. 'William Marshal is a famous name in British history.' I exhaled as a realisation struck. Artōrius would have made the connection between our suspect and the Knight Templar, William Marshal.

Why hadn't he shared this information with me?

The omission irritated me. Determined to address the issue, I made a silent vow to confront Artōrius the next time our paths crossed, and with Artōrius, one could never predict when that might be. The man lurked in the shadows, never far from the action.

Ria pointed at the other monitor. 'Marshal's accomplice, Lewis, seems nervous.'

'I'm sure he is. Being arrested is not what Lewis expected when he agreed to play William's game. Okay then, I'm out of here.'

Ria's confusion was evident when she said, 'Aren't you going to wait until they interview Lewis?'

'There's no point. Our William Marshal has outsmarted us. Let William go so he doesn't miss his meeting with our Camino group. Keep a hold of Lewis until you confirm his identity, although I know he is who William Marshal claims him to be. Their rendezvous in Ponferrada is a part of a Templar game the family plays. Lewis is likely innocent in all of this.'

Ria nodded as she posed another question. 'You suspect Marshal is up to something?'

I nodded, although inside I was smiling.

I liked a worthy opponent.

'Ria, I know he is. What that may be, I don't yet know. Please inform Stephen that I will call him tonight.'

***

I waited patiently in the hotel lobby for our group to arrive. Soon enough, Anna and Jonathan joined me and we engaged in light conversation while we awaited William. Anna was surprised when he walked through the front door.

'Where have you been?' she said with a mixture of curiosity and concern.

William held up admission tickets to the castle, offering an explanation with a smile. 'After our long day, I figured the last thing you would want was to wait in line.' He handed out the tickets.

Anna's face lit up with gratitude. 'Oh, Monsieur William, you are a thoughtful man.'

Returning her smile, William's gaze flickered with a hint of unease, though he quickly masked it. I made a mental note to inquire about it later. His response carried a warmth that belied the unease he felt. 'You haven't called me Monsieur since we met in Paris.'

'Such an act of kindness deserves the nicest of formalities.'

William responded with a gracious nod. 'Why thank you, Madam.'

Anna's eyes drifted to the walking poles William held, her concern clear in her voice as she inquired, 'How is your leg?'

'It's much improved with the rest. I might use only one stick for our tour of the Templar Castle. Give me a moment while I take the spare to my room.'

***

Jonathan Swindon

Standing before the formidable walls of the Templar Castle, I felt a shiver of awe. As I entered through the gate alongside my friends, I felt transported back in time to an era when the Knights Templar reigned supreme. Claudia's voice drifted over the other visitors recounting the castle's rich history. 'Founded in the 12th century, it stood not only as a fortress but also as a testament to the power and influence of the enigmatic order. Nestled amidst the picturesque hills of Castile and León, its strategic location made it a vital outpost along the Camino de Santiago.'

Inside the castle's walls, echoes of centuries past reverberated. I wandered through its labyrinthine corridors, my imagination running wild with visions of armoured knights and clandestine meetings. The Templars, with their iconic white mantles adorned with the crimson cross, had once called this place home, dedicating themselves to protecting pilgrims like myself and the quest for divine purpose.

As we prepared to depart, Claudia shared a darker aspect of the castle's history. 'With the dissolution of the Templar order in the 14th century came a tumultuous period for the fortress, as it passed into the hands of numerous noble families, each leaving their mark upon its storied walls. Enduring sieges, reconstructions, and transformations over the centuries, the castle bore witness to the shifting tides of power throughout the ages.'

Back in my room after a long and eventful day, I reflected on my journey along the Camino. Earlier today, at Cruz de Ferro, I chose not to add a stone to the mound. Though I had carried one at the start of my journey, meeting Artōrius changed my perspective, leading me to discard it. As I logged into my social media, I felt compelled to share this revelation with those following my pilgrimage.

***

Claudia

Exhausted, I collapsed onto the bed, the events of the day swirling in my mind like a tempest. It was difficult to comprehend the whirlwind of experiences packed into a single day. The gruelling trek from Foncebadón, the heartwarming lunch in Molinaseca with Alesa, Chuck, and Cathy, plus the arrest and subsequent release of my walking companion, William Marshal.

Fingers trembling with fatigue, I reached for my phone, intending to call Stephen Walls. But at the last moment, I hesitated. Instead, I opted to distract myself by scrolling through William's social media posts. However, as I hovered over his profile, a pang of anger seized me and I searched for Jonathan's updates instead.

Jonathan's Social Media Post

Amidst the ancient stones of Cruz de Ferro, where the weight of pilgrims' journeys converges, I stand with empty pockets, contemplating the symbolic ritual that unfolds around me. Many carry memories, each a polished stone of remorse, releasing them onto the mound in a profound act of unburdening. The collective weight lifts, a testament to the transformative power of the Camino.

I chose not to add to the mound. My mistakes and regrets are myriad, yet they have sculpted the person standing here before the Cruz de Ferro. How fortunate I am to share this moment with friends by my side. As Carlos Costaneda wisely said, "We either make ourselves miserable or we make ourselves strong. The amount of work is the same." In this sacred space, the echoes of the past become stepping stones toward strength, not stones added to the mound.

'Jonathan,' I said aloud, a smile tugging at the corners of my lips. 'Your words are truly moving, and you'll make someone a wonderful Mr. Swindon.'

My phone abruptly rang, and to no one's surprise, it was my boss on the line.

'Good evening, Sir.'

'I'll get straight to the point, Claudia. What went wrong today?'

'William was not smuggling British secrets hidden in the puzzle box and the references to the Knights Templar were a ruse.'

'That was not my question, Claudia.'

'No, Sir, it was not. We've been played.'

'Indeed. Ria informed me of your suspicions regarding William Marshal's activities.'

'Yes, Stephen. William's presence on the Camino would not ordinarily have garnered the attention of the underworld. Somewhere, someone knows more than we do. He has, or more likely, *had* something in his possession.'

'You believe a handover has taken place?'

'No doubt at all, Stephen. How he managed it right under our gaze, I don't yet know. What he carried; I also don't know, although I doubt it was plans to our next generation submarines. During the initial stages of our journey, prior to the Camino's transformative effect on him, William displayed a mischievousness. I am convinced he hinted at his intentions, assured that we'd struggle to decipher them. I will work it out!'

'What do you propose, Claudia?'

'I continue the Camino', I said without hesitation.

Surprise coloured Stephen's voice as he echoed, 'You continue the Camino?'

'Yes, Sir. By the time we reach Santiago, I will know what he was up to.'

'I trust your judgment, Claudia, although I intend to withdraw our team from Spain. You will be on your own.'

'I understand, Sir. I will need access to the footage from today.'

'You expect to find something?'

'I don't know Stephen, but something is niggling at me.'

'I see. We will also go over footage from this end.'

Shifting gears, I said, 'Have you determined how the Security Service communications were compromised?'

'Indeed, we have, Claudia, but it was not our own communication systems. We discovered Chinese tracking devices embedded in the electronics of Downing Street and our own vehicles.'

'Electronic Trojan horse!'

'Yes, Claudia. The Internet of Things makes use of an interactive component called a "Cellular IoT module" or CIM. These are currently used in all electric vehicles, and also in smart energy metres, some cameras, speaker and heating systems and even doorbells. The essence of CIMs is that they collect numerous types of data depending on the equipment they're installed in. They share it with other components in an internet-connected network from which they can receive data. Unless disabled, CIMs are continuously connected to their manufacturers, ostensibly for remote repairs and updates. The risk from CIMs is clear, and the ones in our vehicles were used for tracking. The Chinese government is weaponizing these and other electronic products and no one is immune.'

'Civil society will be the first victim of cyber warfare.'

'Indeed, Claudia.' There was a momentary lull in the conversation before Stephen continued. 'I will leave William Marshal in your hands, but I expect regular updates.' He concluded the call.

Chapter 23
O'Cebreiro

Claudia

Our current destination was Villafranca del Bierzo, a mere twenty-four kilometres away. Despite William's brush with the British Security Service and his release, he didn't seem suspicious of me and my covert operation with MI6. But I suspected he knew. With Jonathan and Anna unaware of the events of Ponferrada, the walk started, much like any other day. Fortunately, the weather was an improvement, and the terrain was less challenging than the previous day's ordeal. As we departed Ponferrada, Anna's radiance hinted at a respite from her recent reliance on painkillers. I hoped her foot troubles were behind her, though I feared that by day's end she'd reach for those familiar pills again.

The route wound its way along country roads, meandering through traditional towns and villages. Our first pit stop was for breakfast in Columbrianos, a welcome departure from the usual pastries. I indulged in British toast and marmalade and, enjoying a second cup of coffee, marvelled at how swiftly the challenges of the prior day's trek had faded from memory, replaced by our moderate walk, by Camino standards. After a brief exploration of Columbrianos, we resumed the pilgrimage, William and I taking the lead ahead of Anna and Jonathan.

When I was certain we'd distanced ourselves from the others, I broached a delicate subject with William. 'Yesterday, when Anna addressed you as Monsieur William, I noticed unease in your demeanour. Why did it unsettle you?' He hesitated in discomfort so I added, offering him an exit, 'It's okay if you'd rather not discuss it.'

William nodded slightly and said, 'You've a keen eye, Claudia. It's likely no secret that I've grown fond of Anna as our

Camino experience has unfolded.' He paused, his expression troubled. 'Anna was a complete stranger when our paths first crossed in Paris. She addressed me formally at first, normal in the French language, of course, as Monsieur William. I recollect her English was... somewhat broken, far from the fluency she's shown since joining us in Pamplona. It's unsettled me and I wonder if Anna is who she claims to be.'

William is acting like the pot calling the kettle black.

Suppressing a smile, I maintained a serious expression. 'William, we all harbour secrets and Anna will be no exception. Perhaps the woman you encountered in Paris wasn't authentic, but the one who walks among us now is.'

His expression reflecting a mix of apprehension and curiosity, William said, 'Should I confront her?'

'If Anna were to ask you to divulge your secrets, would you?'

William chewed his lip, betraying his inner turmoil. 'A tricky question. Some things are best left unsaid, don't you think?'

I nodded. 'William, you have the answer to your question.'

He regarded me intently. 'Do you know her story?'

'If I did, William, it wouldn't be mine to share.'

His next question caught me off guard. 'Do you know my story?'

After a moment that I hoped he hadn't noticed, I shook my head. 'Not yet.'

'That is an interesting response, Claudia. It implies that you will.'

I offered a fading smile. 'The Camino continues to surprise. It has a way of revealing much about each of us, things we wouldn't ordinarily share openly. As the miles pass by, the onion layers that cocoon us are peeled away. Some of Anna's layers have already been shed and I doubt that you or I will be exceptions.'

'Why is that, Claudia?'

Taking a moment to ponder my reply, I was keenly conscious of the intricate web of secrets enveloping us. It felt like the opportune moment to confront him, to reveal that I was aware of his facade and that his hidden truths were no longer secure. 'Because, William, on the Camino, the journey isn't just about the physical miles we cover. It's a journey of self-discovery, of shedding pretences and revealing truths. And sometimes, those truths are revealed even if we want to keep them hidden.' I let my gaze meet his. 'We're all bound to unravel a bit on this path. It's a matter of time.'

William gazed into the distance, before saying, 'It's just time, is all. I could buy anything, but I couldn't buy time.'

An intriguing response. But has he grasped my underlying message? Perhaps he is sending me a message.

Anna's yelling broke the silence that had descended on us. 'Wait up! You're leaving us behind.'

We entered Villafranca del Bierzo at precisely twelve forty-five that afternoon, our strides weary yet determined after conquering a brief arduous ascent. With check-in time still some time away, we sought refuge in a local bar, eager to lunch and appease our grumbling stomachs. Though Anna maintained her usual composure, her silence betrayed the battle she was having with her ailing foot. When our fellow pilgrims, Ian and Ana from the Sunshine Coast in Australia, pulled up chairs beside us, Anna's customary chattiness was missing.

After enjoying our meal, a bowl of steaming pasta accompanied by freshly baked bread, we bid farewell to Ian and Ana. They departed to their own destinations and, with the afternoon sun casting long shadows, we made our way to the hotel. Anna, her discomfort palpable, hastened to her room, no doubt seeking comfort by elevating her foot. I hoped the simple walk the following day to Vega de Valcarce would allow her to recover before the strenuous climb to O'Cebreiro.

From the window of my room, I looked out at the commanding presence of a castle across the road. Researching it on my phone, I discovered, it was constructed in 1515 atop the remnants of an earlier bastion and bore witness to the tumultuous epochs of conquest and conflict. Once the domain of Don Pedro Alvarez de Toledo, the second Marquess of Villafranca, it bore assaults from both English and French forces during the turbulence of the Independence War in 1809, 1815, and 1819. Today, its walls are under the stewardship of the Marquess of Villafranca.

Should I share my discovery with the others? Perhaps not, unless they ask.

Before reconvening with the group for dinner, I ventured on a solitary stroll, hoping to chance upon Artōrius amidst the cobblestone streets. Instead, I met Chinmay, who confided in me about the persistent ache in his leg, linked to past ACL surgery. His struggles mirrored Anna's ordeal; a reminder of the physical toll the Camino exacted on pilgrims. When the others joined me, Anna expressed a hope to encounter Chinmay, but he'd already retreated to his Albergue.

Over dinner, a pall hung over us all. Anna's subdued demeanour cast doubt upon her ability to complete the trek. The events of the prior day in Ponferrada continued to gnaw at me. I was angry at being outmanoeuvred by William, attesting to his cunning.

A day on and I'm none the wiser.

Despite my begrudging admiration for William's intellect, his sombre mood puzzled me. He should be jubilant after besting MI6, yet his demeanour was tempered, hinting at a complexity that eluded my grasp. His cryptic remark about time lingered, like one of his Templar clues waiting to be unravelled.

A veiled confession perhaps, or a reflection of his own turmoil?

Jonathan's despondency was more straightforward. He was feeling the weight bearing down upon us, Anna's injury, William's incongruence, and my own unresolved frustrations.

***

Leaving Villafranca del Bierzo shrouded in darkness, we were surprised by the charms awaiting discovery. There was far more to the town than we'd seen the day before. Navigating its silent streets and crossing a solitary bridge, we finally broke free from its confines, stepping onto the trail ahead. To our surprise, we were not alone in our early departure; the distant glimmer of headlamps hinted at the presence of fellow travellers also making an early start. I imagined they were making for O'Cebreiro by day's end.

Most of our journey unfolded along lengthy secondary roads, accompanied by the constant hum of a bustling freeway looming close, often above us. Our path traced the course of the Rio Valcarce faithfully.

En route to Vega de Valcarce, we adhered to the tradition of halting at the first bar for breakfast, which led us to the village of Trabadelo. Here, we encountered Ian and Ana, with whom we'd lunched the previous day. They'd stayed in the Albergue next to the bar and were departing as we arrived, their sights set on O'Cebreiro, our destination for the following night. As we seated ourselves to order breakfast, Sean entered, our friend from Canada. He stayed briefly before continuing on his own journey towards O'Cebreiro. With only eight kilometres remaining of our day's trek, we indulged in a second cup of coffee, each of us silently yearning to follow the same path as our friends. The sombre atmosphere lingering from yesterday cast a shadow over us, the constant rain and overcast conditions not helping either.

Our spirits found a reprieve as we passed through the village of La Portela de Valcarce. Seeking refuge from the relentless rain, we stepped into the sanctuary of the Catholic church, Iglesia de San Juan Bautista. Inside, the air was heavy with the scent of incense and the echoes of centuries past. A young man, a fellow pilgrim on the Camino, his heavy pack resting against a pew, stood reverently before the altar. His resonant voice echoed around the ancient church as he sang a haunting hymn. Goosebumps prickled our skin as we savoured the beauty of his melody. The warmth of his voice seemed to shield us from the chill of the weather outside, a cocoon of sound and emotion. It was a Camino moment so typical that it felt scripted.

Anna looked unsettled, so I asked, 'What is it?'

'I'm overwhelmed by a moment of déjà vu, as if I've experienced this moment before, though that's impossible. Isn't it?'

'Is there something you remember about this place?

'No, only encountering someone... it was an elderly priest, I think. But I recall this beautiful hymn.'

Has Artōrius found his way into Anna's dreams?

I gave a knowing nod.

When the pilgrim's voice fell silent, he turned towards us, his eyes meeting mine. A sense of familiarity crept over me, though I couldn't pinpoint ever meeting the man before. Yet, an uncanny resemblance tugged at my memory, hinting at a past encounter with someone remarkably similar. His gaze spoke of wisdom beyond his years and when he smiled, his eyes, illuminated by flickering candlelight, reflected back the warmth of Brother Artōrius in Puente La Reina, but the face was much younger by half a century. The voice resembled the one I'd heard mouthing the Gregorian chant in Santo Domingo de la Calzada, where I'd faced danger. Anna and I had both felt something within these walls.

'That was beautiful,' Jonathan said, breaking the spell.

The man offered a bow of his head, another gesture reminiscent of Brother Artōrius, before turning back to face the altar.

Leaving the church, Jonathan said, altering the mood, 'That young man evoked images of ancient warriors and knights of old in me. In another era, I could easily imagine him clad in the armour of a Templar knight. His presence commanded respect, though he didn't speak.'

William nodded in agreement; his expression was thoughtful. 'He didn't need to speak.'

Anna, her curiosity piqued, hesitated as if considering turning back. 'Did it really happen? I need to go back and check.'

William touched her arm, his gaze steady. 'Some things are best left unknown.'

It seemed each of us had been touched by something that we couldn't explain.

Resuming our journey to Vega de Valcarce, the memory of the haunting melody and the enigmatic figure lingered in our minds, casting a subtle veil over the dreary landscape. Despite the incessant patter of raindrops against our coats, we were lost in contemplation, our thoughts drifting back to the encounter in the church.

Thirty minutes later, we arrived at our destination: a small village nestled beneath the towering expanse of a freeway that soared overhead like a modern-day colossus. The cobbled street was from an earlier time and we were transported back in time to an era long past.

With the clock ticking just past eleven fifteen in the morning, it was too early to check into our accommodation. Seeking refuge from the torrent of rain, we found shelter in a nearby bar, settling at a table before ordering hot coffee to ward off the lingering cold. As we sipped our drinks, we exchanged greetings with fellow pilgrims who sought shelter from the weather before continuing on their journey. The rain showed no sign of abating, casting a veil over the village streets. With the prospect of a long wait until check-in time, we had hot soup for lunch, hoping to thaw our chilled bones and warm our spirits.

At one in the afternoon, we made our way over the bridge, crossing the river, a tributary of the Rio Valcarce, to our Pension where we checked into our rooms. Mine was rustic with a cozy ambiance that promised a comfortable retreat. Before parting ways to freshen up and unwind, we unanimously agreed that the rain made exploring the village less appealing. I volunteered to take on finding a suitable place for dinner, though I felt apprehensive. In the town, the options for dining seemed sparse, leaving me uncertain about what culinary delights awaited us. I hoped for something special to revive our spirits, even if only for a short time.

***

Returning to our lodgings after dinner, I waited patiently for half an hour before checking William's social media post. A smile crept across my face as I read his words, finding resonance with my own sentiments about our evening's escapade.

William's Social Media Post

Searching for dinner in the quaint village where we're lodging for the night, we expected a pilgrim's meal - a generous three courses, but a standard formula. Serendipitously, Claudia came across a charming restaurant in town. The experience was outstanding—the host was warm and hospitable, the local wine was exquisite, the food was abundant and delectable, and the conversation with fellow guests was delightful. Surprisingly, the bill was even less than what we'd pay for a pub meal back home in the UK. Another best night ever on the Camino. Five stars.

The day's walk hadn't been strenuous, and nor was it the following day, so I was not ready to retire for the night. Instead, I logged into MI6 to review the footage from Ponferrada. Watching it several times, I zoomed in on a critical moment: the window of opportunity for William to pass on whatever he was carrying lay between his disappearance across the drawbridge over the moat and the surveillance agents picking him up on the inside. William remained out of sight for over a minute. If the transfer had occurred during that interval, the recipient must have exercised caution, choosing to delay their departure from the castle until a safer moment. Unfortunately, the surveillance footage offered no glimpse of their identity or subsequent movements. Yet, as I pored over the footage, something nagged at me, like a whisper of unease that refused to be ignored. *What is concealed within the shadows of the footage, waiting to be unearthed?*

'It will come to me,' I said to myself. 'It will come to me.'

***

With the day's journey spanning only 13.2 kilometres, albeit uphill, we allowed ourselves the luxury of a leisurely morning, indulging in a well-deserved lie-in, followed by a hearty breakfast at our cozy accommodation. The rhythmic patter of rain against the windows served as a reminder of the inclement weather outside, urging us to don our full wet weather gear and a desire to delay our departure. We lingered over a second cup of coffee, savouring the camaraderie that comes with shared moments on the Camino.

Setting out, the terrain was manageable at first, with the path winding along the road. Yet, as we ventured further from Herrerias, our journey underwent a dramatic shift. Directed onto a steep path ascending towards O'Cebreiro, we became enveloped by the dense canopy of ancient chestnut trees, their branches heavy, as we walked on a carpet of fallen leaves and nuts. Emerging from the shelter of the chestnuts, we were greeted by the full force of nature's fury, a relentless barrage of gusting winds, biting cold, and rain cascading down the hillside. It saturated the earth beneath our feet and seeped into our footwear with chilling efficiency, reminding us of our vulnerability. Persisting despite faltering determination, we battled the elements conspiring against us. Struggling, we stumbled upon the village of La Faba, where a lone bar owner was preparing to open for the day. With gratitude, we sought refuge within its embrace, escaping the deluge to find comfort in the company of fellow pilgrims seeking respite from the storm. The next stretch of our ascent towards Laguna de Castilla was meant to follow a road, but we were met with a neglected farm track, its surface uneven and weather-beaten. Undeterred by the unexpected detour, we pressed on, resolved to conquer the challenges ahead. The rain was so persistent that we sought refuge again, this time in a bustling bar along the way. Another round of steaming coffees offered a reprieve from the weather. Once more we ventured out and despite the relentless downpour and the unyielding assault of the weather on our senses, our spirits remained buoyant as we approached the last stretch into O'Cebreiro.

Upon arrival, the village emerged from the mist like a ghostly apparition, shrouded in a thick veil of fog. Our entrance was marked by the presence of a striking, life-sized bronze statue of a woman perched atop a stone wall. Poised with her legs delicately crossed at the ankles and hands serenely placed in her lap, her gaze was fixed upon the rugged expanse of the Galician landscape. Despite bearing the weathered patina of time, the statue exuded an enduring charm, its once-shimmering bronze surface transformed into a captivating shade of green that only added to its mystique.

William draped his arm around the figure and turned to me with a request, 'Claudia, will you take my picture?'

I chuckled. 'Sure William, though on a sunny day, the view behind the statue would be better. Do you realise you look like a drowned rat?'

William's response was immediate, punctuated by a good-natured pat on the statue's shoulder. 'Yes, but a happy rat.' Turning to the statue, he addressed it with genuine curiosity. 'Will you tell me about her, Claudia?'

I shrugged. 'You assume that I'll know.' To my surprise, Jonathan and Anna burst into laughter, their voices melding in unison. 'You've researched everything for today's trek. Of course you'll know!'

'It won't cost me a breakfast, will it?'

William shook his head. 'I'd almost forgotten about that. It seems such a long time ago, but then again, it's as if it was only yesterday.'

With William's photograph stored on my phone, I suggested, 'With check-in hours away, let's find somewhere dry. Then I'll regale you all with the fascinating tale of the bronze statue that graces the landscape near O'Cebreiro, a place steeped in history and mystique along the Camino de Santiago.'

Jonathan grinned. 'Claudia, you're becoming a wonderful storyteller.'

Finding sanctuary in a nearby bar, we ordered bowls of soup to ward off the chill and revive our weary bodies.

'Before Claudia tells us about my green lady, would anyone like a glass of red to go with your soup? And Jonathan, another coffee perhaps?' William's offer carried genuine hospitality and with a spring in his step, he rose from his chair to fulfil our requests. As he moved effortlessly across the room to fetch our drinks, something dawned on me. In Ponferrada, William had a noticeable limp. Yet here in the heart of O'Cebreiro, he moved with the agility of a man half his age

Was William's limp in Ponferrada a facade, a ploy to confuse the watchful eyes of MI6 to facilitate his clandestine exchange?

The pieces of the puzzle were falling into place, consolidating in my mind. The answers I sought lay within the video footage from Ponferrada. I now knew where to concentrate my attention.

'Are you alright?' William inquired, catching my distant expression as he carefully set my wineglass before me.

'Absolutely,' I replied with a grin. 'Lost in thought or in this case, captivated by a pilgrim woman statue.'

Once everyone had their drinks, I raised my glass and proposed a toast. 'To O'Cebreiro. A place of miracles. Are you ready for the story?' My friends nodded in unison.

'The statue was brought to life by a talented sculptor named Miguel Couto. It portrays a female wanderer, her gaze fixed upon the vast undulating landscape–when it's not foggy.' I took a sip from my glass. 'This isn't just any pilgrim statue, for it subverts tradition in several ways. Unlike most contemporary pilgrim statues, which predominantly depict male figures, this one, as you know, is of a woman, representing the countless female pilgrims who have embarked on the journey.'

'Like you and I, Claudia,' Anna said.

'Like you and I, Anna. The bronze surface has undergone a transformation. Exposure to the elements has given it a green patina and this colour change isn't accidental; it's been deliberately accelerated to protect the statue from corrosion.'

Jonathan set down his spoon, his curiosity piqued. 'Is it really old?'

I paused, considering his question. 'I don't know for certain. The statue appears relatively recent in Camino terms, but my research tells that Miguel Couto was a sculptor born in 1864 in Rio de Janeiro, Brazil. But that doesn't quite add up.'

Anna smiled. 'You have the right name, Claudia. Miguel Couto is indeed the artist behind this work, but not the one born in Rio de Janeiro. The sculptor responsible for this masterpiece was born in Malpica, in 1971. He's a Galician artist who specialises in crafting bronze sculptures in his foundry in A Coruña.'

With surprise in my eyes, I said, 'Thank you, Anna. Do you know of Miguel Couto's works?'

Anna nodded. 'In a previous life, I was a bit of an artist myself.'

William grinned in astonishment. 'An artist! How wonderful! I would love to know about that.'

Anna's expression suggested her willingness to explain, but she redirected the conversation. 'Knowing something about an object's history gives it more meaning, fostering a connection.' After a brief pause, she added, 'I've made this observation before, I think.'

Jonathan shrugged. 'It may have been me, but it doesn't matter. History adds a layer of understanding.' He paused, taking another sip of his soup before turning his attention back to me. 'Claudia, you called O'Cebreiro a place of miracles. Are you going to share that with us as well?'

I shook my head gently. 'No, I wouldn't want to bore you. But if you're interested, search for Juan Santín and the Santa María la Real church. Legend has it that 700 years ago, during mass, bread and wine miraculously transformed into flesh and blood. The Miracle of the Holy Grail, it's quite an intriguing tale, part of the mystique that surrounds the Camino Francés. The Virgin Mary statue in the church is said to have turned her head to witness this holy spectacle, forever linking her presence to the miracle.'

As I finished my soup and savoured my wine, my attention drifted to William and Anna. With each step along the path to Santiago, their bond had deepened. A part of me wanted to warn Anna to resist becoming attached. I was nearing a breakthrough in uncovering William's illegal activities, and once I did, he'd face justice with a lengthy jail sentence.

After the soup, Jonathan proposed heading to the bar connected to our lodging, an idea born of the hope that they might accommodate an early check-in for us. Regrettably, upon inquiring, we were informed that check-in time was strictly set at three in the afternoon, no exceptions made for earlier arrivals. Disappointed, we realised there was still an hour and a half to pass before we could settle into our rooms. With the rain showing no signs of relenting, we made ourselves comfortable and ordered more wine, along with a plate of local sausage, cured meat, and bread to share. Jonathan declined, not feeling well.

Concerned, I asked, 'Nothing serious, I hope?'

'No, no. The cold got to me today, that's all. I'll have an early night. I may even skip dinner.'

The meats were too rich and fatty for us. William, Anna, and I exchanged glances; the meal wasn't to our taste.

Shortly before three in the afternoon, the landlady made her way to our table, kindly notifying us that our rooms were now available for check-in. As we began our preparations to disperse, I casually mentioned my intention to attend the Pilgrim's Mass at the Santuario de Santa María a Real later that evening at six. I had assumed that Jonathan could not join me because of his illness, but it came as a surprise when both William and Anna politely declined the invitation as well.

After a refreshing shower and ensuring that all my daily tasks were completed, especially washing my clothes ready for the next day's journey to Triacastela, and recharging my electronic devices, I allowed myself the luxury of a brief thirty-minute nap. I left my lodgings promptly at five thirty, intent on securing a seat towards the rear of the church. To my astonishment, I found it already filling with pilgrims, but I found a place at the back.

I have a fondness for old architecture and Santuario de Santa María a Real was no exception, its fabric offering a window into history and faith. The walls were fashioned from stone, designed in the pre-Romanesque style. Along the length of the nave, a succession of curved archways guided my eyes towards the altar, now bathed in soft light. Above the altar, a prominent crucifix hung on the stone wall, a solemn and comforting sight. Wooden pews, worn smooth by worshippers, flanked the central aisle, above which wooden ceiling beams traversed the length of the church, connecting earth to heaven with their strength.

Startled by the unexpected but familiar voice of Artōrius, I turned to find him occupying the space next to me. 'Hello, Claudia.'

Suppressing my surprise, I responded casually, 'I was hoping you'd be here.'

'I'm pleased, Claudia. I noticed you admiring the building.'

'Yes Artōrius. Although it has undergone restoration, it is believed to be the oldest church on "The Way of St. James". Built in 813 AD, I read, to serve pilgrims who climbed the pass.'

Artōrius nodded, 'So it is said... This village was originally a Celtic settlement. O'Cebreiro roots connect it to a time long before the Camino became a well-trodden pilgrimage route.'

'That surprises me, Artōrius. I believed archaeologists maintain that nothing referring to the Celts is found in the records for this region.'

Artōrius let out a soft chuckle. 'You're quite the scholar, Claudia. The concept of Celtic ancestry is a complex one, but I'm confident in its truth.' He glanced around the church before continuing. 'This sanctuary once served as a haven for pilgrims, offering comfort and aid to weary travellers on their spiritual journey. As time passed, it developed into a Benedictine priory, playing a role in spiritual guidance and practical support.'

His voice taking on a reverent tone, Artōrius said. 'If you close your eyes, you will hear the whispers of prayers from centuries past. You'll feel devotion permeating these walls.'

I closed my eyes, but all I could discern were the sounds of the present. It wasn't until Artōrius lightly touched my arm that everything changed. In that instant, the veil between past and present dissolved, and I was immersed in the chorus of whispered prayers. As I reopened my eyes, the world around me was unchanged, as if the experience had been a fleeting dream.

'Takes your breath away, doesn't it?'

I nodded my agreement.

'Unfortunately, Claudia, the church, fell victim to fire during the War of Independence, resulting in the loss of valuable documentation and historical artefacts.'

Artōrius pointed, 'The sanctuary's structure of thick slate masonry walls has three naves with barrel-vaulted apses and a bell tower, distinctive in this region. Legend has it that on foggy days, monks would toll the bell to guide pilgrims. In the apse to the right lies the Chapel of the Miracle, where medieval treasures like the chalice and paten involved in the miracle are venerated, alongside relics gifted by the Catholic Monarchs during their pilgrimage. Adjacent are the sepulchres of the key figures of the Miracle. To the left of the High Altar lies the Chapel of San Benito, honouring the founding monks of the church, with the sepulchres of the former parish priest and advocate of the French Way, Don Elías Valiña Sampedro resting at its feet.'

'Ah, the man of the iconic yellow arrows.'

'So, it would seem, Claudia. It is said that in 1984 he put in motion a mission to rescue, clean, and mark the trails along Camino, starting in Roncesvalles, in the Pyrenees. Legend has it that Don Elías drove across the whole north of Spain in his Citroën GS, packed with yellow paint, painting arrows leading to Santiago. And the rest, as they say, is history, because here we are.'

The church hushed as the priest entered. We all rose to our feet, and I leaned towards Artōrius, my voice barely audible above the silence. 'I need to talk to you before you leave.'

Artōrius inclined his head, his eyes betraying a knowing smile. 'I thought as much, which is why I'm here.'

Though I didn't adhere to any faith, I couldn't deny the priest's skill in setting the mood for the traditional communion mass. His sermon, peppered with English remarks, resonated with many in attendance. After the service, he called upon the pilgrims to stay behind for a special blessing. Motioning for us to join him in the sanctuary, he distributed small polished stones adorned with a simple yellow arrow. As I accepted mine, I wondered how many among us were familiar with the legend of Don Elias.

When the congregation dispersed and the echoes of the service faded, I sought Artōrius once more. Rubbing my chin thoughtfully, I broached the topic that had been weighing on my mind. 'Why didn't you tell me that William Marshal was the name of a Knight Templar?'

'Would it have changed anything?'

'Yes,' I said.

A smile played at the corners of his lips. 'In what way, my dear?'

'I would have realised that the code found on his computer and his social media posts about the Templars were all part of his intricate facade.'

'I see.' After a moment of silence, Artōrius added, 'But deep down, you already knew, didn't you?'

'What do you mean?'

'You had your suspicions long before embarking on this mission. Remember what you said to Stephen Walls before setting out: "The old Knights Templar cipher code is a far cry from the level of encryption either William Marshal or Samantha is capable of. His use of it and the ease with which you found it raise questions. Is he playing with us, and why the Templar? Could Marshal be guaranteeing that we are tasked with ensuring his safety during the pilgrimage? After all, the Knights Templar held a similar responsibility on the Camino." It seems, Claudia, you had already unravelled a piece of the puzzle back in Britain.'

The memory of my conversation with Stephen Walls flashed through my mind, and I wondered how Artōrius could recall it so precisely when he hadn't been present. Pushing the thought aside, I said, 'No, what I said to Stephen was a superstition. It's only now that I understand William Marshal deliberately drew the attention of the security services and I've been by his side as his protector on the Camino, fulfilling what he desired. I saved him, first in Zubiri and then in León.'

Artōrius nodded solemnly. 'You were his Knight Templar!'

I glanced at Artōrius, frustration simmering beneath the surface. 'What I don't understand is what he was doing and what I was protecting.'

There was a brief pause before Artōrius responded, his tone measured. 'What has William told you?'

'Artōrius!' I retorted, exasperation creeping into my voice. 'If you know something, just tell me. I don't have time for these games!'

Artōrius replied softly, 'I'm afraid, my dear Claudia, I can only assist you in uncovering the answer. I counsel you to challenge your prism.'

'Artōrius! Enough of this!'

'I don't possess the knowledge, even though you may wish I did.'

I regarded the enigmatic old monk sceptically. He seemed as shrouded in mystery as any of the legends and fables we'd encountered along the Camino de Santiago. If this were centuries ago, I would not have been shocked to discover the garb of a Templar Knight concealed beneath his weathered brown robe. Though I kept my musings to myself, I had the feeling that he could discern the thoughts.

I sighed, resigned to the monk's ways. 'Brother Artōrius, William Marshal has softened as we journeyed. At first, he exuded arrogance, a man convinced of his intellectual superiority in any gathering. I suspect that's why he played with us, confident in his abilities. I glimpsed that aspect of him again in Astorga, though it seems he has returned to his more recent demeanour. The explanation for how he transported the goods lies in Astorga, I am sure of it.'

Artōrius replied cryptically, 'Then the answers you seek lie within those moments.'

I nodded. Determined to avoid another cryptic response, I carefully chose my words. 'When I last inquired, you mentioned that neither of us can understand it. I wonder, Artōrius, have you given more thought to the Bible reading William was given?'

He chuckled softly. 'If the answer isn't within the reading, then what remains?'

'The chapter and verse.'

'So, it would seem, Claudia.'

A sudden commotion from the sanctuary of the church drew my attention. Spotting a large raven, I exclaimed, 'How did you get in?' But when I turned back to Artōrius, I found myself alone. He had again vanished without a trace.

He has a habit of doing that.

After the encounter with Artōrius, I expected to feel frustrated, but I felt buoyed, knowing I was on the verge of unravelling the mystery. I hurried back to my lodgings.

Despite the absence of any clues in William's daily social media posts following the events of Astorga, I found myself drawn to read them.

Williams Social Media Post

Our ascent to O'Cebreiro was a chilly, wet, and windy journey, battling gusts of up to 35 km/h. The steep terrain had transformed into a makeshift stream and the frigid water made us keenly aware of the minimal protection footwear provides. We navigated the ascent with caution, climbing with baby steps. Unfortunately, the breathtaking views hoped for were obscured by fog

Shifting my focus from William's post, I reviewed the footage from Astorga. I stopped and said aloud, 'It is a truth we hold dear. We often reminisce fondly about the challenges we have overcome.'

***

Jonathan Swindon

Glancing at my watch, I saw I'd been asleep for over four hours. Sitting up in bed, a wave of relief washed over me. I was finally free from whatever had been plaguing my stomach. With the help of the afternoon nap, I was starting to feel like myself again. However, a pang of disappointment hit me when I checked the time once more and realised that I'd missed the Pilgrim's Mass. I guessed that the church would be locked, but I put on my warm clothing and wet weather gear anyway and ventured out to check.

To my surprise, the church door stood unlocked and the interior lit, though I appeared to be the sole occupant. Stepping inside, I gravitated towards the left chamber, where I saw a baptismal font crafted from a single piece of stone, a size that hinted at a tradition of immersion baptisms. Next to the font, a crucifix hung on the wall, its design unfamiliar to me. Approaching it with a hopeful curiosity, I wished for some accompanying explanation to shed light on its significance. Despite my belief that I was alone,

I wasn't startled when a vaguely familiar voice spoke from behind me.

'The San Damiano Crucifix is a replica of a twelfth-century icon. It doesn't depict the body of a lifeless corpse, rather the eternal and incorruptible essence of God Himself, the source of life and the beacon of hope for resurrection. In this depiction, the Saviour gazes directly at us with eyes of compassion, exuding a regal, triumphant strength. He appears not as a victim hanging on the Cross, but as a divine figure supporting it, standing in His full stature. Rather than being contorted by the agony of nails, His hands are spread serenely, conveying supplication and blessing. Unlike the crude portrayal of crucifixion's brutality, this one embodies the nobility of eternal life.'

Turning around, I saw Brother Artōrius. 'The Crucifix... It's quite beautiful.'

'It is,' he replied with a bow of his head. Meeting my gaze, Artōrius continued, 'You're not surprised by my presence, Jonathan.'

I shook my head. 'No, Brother. From time to time, I've glimpsed you along our journey, never too far, but never too close. I sensed your watchful eye over my progress, and I recall your words. "The path to righteousness is not always an easy one." I felt as though you were sent to guide me on this journey.'

Artōrius chuckled softly. 'You've found your own way. I've merely been an observer.' He paused for a moment before adding, 'I'm glad your nightmares have stopped, though there was nothing to fear.'

His remark caught me off guard, prompting me to raise an eyebrow. 'How do you know?'

'The weariness of sleepless nights is not easily concealed. Yet here I see a man refreshed, despite the rigours of the Camino.'

'You are perceptive, Brother,' I said, though awe lingered in me, hinting at a deeper authority at play.

'Jonathan, today holds special significance for you. Would you kneel with me before the altar to pray?'

Tears welled within me at his words. 'Yes, I would like that. Today marks the anniversary of Emily's passing, my sister. How did you know?'

Artōrius didn't answer, instead he motioned for me to follow him, and we returned to the main church. As we walked towards the front, he said, 'I had no knowledge of your sister Jonathan, but one day, I would be honoured if you shared her story with me. I only surmised that for someone to brave today's inhospitable conditions, it must bear great spiritual significance.'

Kneeling before the altar, I felt Artōrius's light touch on my arm as he spoke:

'Oratio pro anima defunctae Emily.'

'Omnipotens Deus, qui in tua misericordia sperantium animas semper in vita et morte custodis, te humiliter deprecamur pro anima sororis nostrae Emily, quae de hoc mundo migravit. Concede ei, quaesumus, requiem aeternam et lucem perpetuam. Per Dominum nostrum Iesum Christum, Filium tuum, qui tecum vivit et regnat in unitate Spiritus Sancti, Deus, per omnia saecula saeculorum. Amen.'

Though Latin was unfamiliar to me, I understood his words with clarity:

'Prayer for the departed soul of Emily.'

'Almighty God, who in your mercy always watches over the souls of those who hope in you, both in life and in death, we humbly pray to you for the soul of our sister Emily, who has departed from this world. Grant her, we beseech you, eternal rest and perpetual light. Through our Lord Jesus Christ, your Son, who lives and reigns with you in the unity of the Holy Spirit, one God, forever and ever. Amen.'

'Amen,' I repeated.

We rose to our feet, and I knew it was time for me to take my leave. Walking down the aisle alongside Artōrius, he surprised me with his question.

'Have you discovered the future Mrs. Swindon during your journey?'

I couldn't recall ever mentioning my quest to Artōrius. Chuckling, I gestured to imply that finding the future Mrs. Swindon was not a priority for me anymore. I said, 'It no longer seems important.'

He nodded knowingly. 'Then, Jonathan, my son, you are ready.' After a brief pause, Brother Artōrius held out his hand and said, 'I have something for you, Jonathan.' It was a stone adorned with the recognisable yellow arrow of the Camino. As I turned the stone over in my hand, a wave of familiarity washed over me. It resembled the one I had once carried for the Cruz de Ferro, the same one I had cast aside.

Chapter 24
Sarria awaits

Claudia

Nestled in the snug confines of our lodgings at Casa Simon in Triacastela, it's hard to fathom the trials of the day we've just weathered. It began in the comfort of our hotel, with a modest breakfast of coffee, toast, and butter—no jam or marmalade to sweeten the morning. Out the window, the darkness betrayed the storm raging, rain lashing against the glass in a furious whirl propelled by relentless winds. Anna proposed another round of coffee before facing the elements, but William stood firm, insisting we don our wet weather gear and confront the challenges head-on. Anna muttered something about a taxi, but aside from me, no one acknowledged her remark. Or if they did, they remained silent.

Our trail of the current day left O'Cebreiro with a hopeful beginning, its sturdy path and ample shelter providing relief from the biting winds and showing kindness to our feet. Skipping past the first village of Linares, we ventured across the plateau toward Alto San Roque. As we neared the forest's edge, a deafening roar filled the air like a thunderous rumble of a jet engine. Not an aeroplane. This was the wind, lurking in ambush. Emerging from our refuge, we were nearly swept off our feet and rain slashed through the air, stinging our faces. Every step was a battle against the elements. Atop the summit, where breathtaking vistas usually unfolded, that day presented only a desolate, isolating stretch before me. Shivering from the cold, I felt as if crossing a forsaken wasteland—bleak and unforgiving.

This is challenging.

William's voice cut through the howling gale and I glanced at him, puzzled. 'I want to come back,' he said. 'Imagine how different this would be under gentler conditions, like a sunny day, clouds parted and views stretching into the distance. It would seem a paradise, not Hades as it is now.'

'I'm not seeing it,' I shouted, my words diminished by the roar of the elements.

'The air would be crisp and invigorating,' he continued, undeterred, 'the landscape bathed in golden sunlight and mountains standing proud against a clear blue sky.'

I chortled, though it sounded guttural as my teeth chattered in the cold. 'I'm still not seeing it, William.'

We stopped for coffee at Alto do Poio, as much an opportunity to shelter as the desire for caffeine. After half an hour, we ventured back out to start our descent from the highest point. Our next stop was at Biduedo, where we were greeted with bowls of hot Galician soup, another respite from the conditions outside. A broth of potatoes, carrots, and turnips in a flavourful stock, it warmed us from within, the ultimate comfort food for the conditions. As we relished our meal, we watched other tired travellers also seeking shelter from the relentless elements. Jonathan gestured towards a group of Asian hikers; their thin ponchos were inadequate against the drenching rain. They were soaked through to the core.

'They're lucky the conditions didn't kill them,' Jonathan said.

'It's freezing up there and with the biting wind, they're fortunate they didn't succumb to hypothermia,' I whispered.

Anna chimed in, hoping that they'd abandon the trek for the day and opt for a taxi instead. From our table, we couldn't overhear their conversation, but judging by the exhaustion etched on their faces, it seemed unlikely that they'd continue their journey on foot that day.

'Are we ready?' William said, casting a glance around. We each nodded, Anna adding, 'Okay then, let's do it.'

Jonathan looked out the window, his voice taking on a rhythmic cadence.

'Let the rain kiss you,

Let the rain beat upon your head with silver liquid drops,

Let the rain sing you a lullaby,

The rain makes still pools on the sidewalk,

The rain makes running pools in the gutter,

The rain plays a little sleep-song on our roof at night.'

He paused for a moment, a grin spreading across his face, before adding, 'And I love the rain. It's by Langston Hughes, a renowned American poet.'

Jonathan, who knew? You continue to surprise. Is this Cathy and Chuck's influence again?

We made good progress, arriving in Triacastela too early to check into our accommodation, Pension Casa Simón, a tastefully refurbished old house. While we whiled away the time in a nearby bar, William ventured out in search of rainproof pants. He returned with a grin stretching from ear to ear. Not only had he secured his trousers, but he'd also noticed the owner of the Pension, Simón, seated by a crackling fire through the window. William had mustered the courage to ask if they might check in early and Simon had agreed.

At the Pension, soaked and bedraggled from the day's walk, we were greeted warmly by Simón and he offered us slippers for our chilled feet, placing our sodden shoes in front of the fire to dry. Taking our raincoats, he hung them up under the stairs to drip dry. For a mere twelve euros, Simon offered to wash and dry our laundry—an offer too generous to resist. With gratitude, we each retreated to our respective rooms for a rejuvenating, hot shower, leaving our laundry outside for Simón to collect.

Returning to the lounge, I found Simón tending to the roaring fire. As I made myself comfortable in an armchair, he gestured towards a bottle of red wine on the sideboard. 'It's two euros a glass,' he said. 'We operate an honesty system here. Let me know how many glasses you've had and I'll add it to your account tomorrow.'

Grinning, I said, 'Simón, you can't enjoy an open fire without a glass of red to accompany it.' As I made a move, he motioned for me to stay seated and poured me a glass of wine, filling the glass to the brim, a gesture of hospitality that warmed me as much as the fire. As I savoured my tipple, two guests arrived at the Pension, Patrick and Jo, a couple around William and Anna's age, hailing from a village near Oxford, England. Simón welcomed them with the same enthusiasm he'd shown us, helping them shed their raincoats and placing their soggy shoes by the fire alongside ours. Once settled into the comfortable seats, they proved to be lively conversationalists, their presence adding to the warmth of the room. When Anna, William, and Jonathan joined us, the atmosphere became more animated. Patrick and Jo were surprised when Anna told them she knew of Horton-cum-Studley, where the couple lived, from a fiction book called "Claudia"—my namesake. As we engaged in lively conversation, Simón inquired about our dinner plans. Without missing a beat, we agreed to find a restaurant for dinner, expecting Simón to offer a recommendation, which he did. What none of us expected was his next move. He surprised us by braving the rain to go and personally reserve a table for us, a gesture of hospitality that left us feeling touched.

While the restaurant Simón suggested was pleasant, it was the company and conversation that made the evening special. As we shared stories and laughter, the adversities of the day's challenging walk faded into the background, replaced by the camaraderie that's a feature of the Camino.

Alone in my room at Pension Casa Simón, I reached for my phone, intending to read William's daily post. At the last moment, I changed my mind and opted to read Jonathan's instead:

Jonathan's Social Media Post

What an adventure! The descent from O'Cebreiro felt like a scene from a movie or a chapter from a book. With almost zero visibility at the summit, the wind howled, driving the heavy rain sideways, hitting our faces with such intensity that it felt like our cheeks were being sandblasted. As we descended, we occasionally found shelter from the wind, but its presence was unmistakable, echoing like a jet fighter overhead. As the altitude lessened, the visibility improved, revealing other pilgrims walking along the trail ahead.

The trail meandered through small villages on its way to Triacastela. During our first coffee stop, an hour into the descent, some wisely opted for a taxi because of the relentless rain. Undeterred, we pressed on for another two hours before pausing for hot soup, where other Pilgrims opted for a taxi. Recharged, we ventured back into the elements. Just when we felt like conquering heroes, walkers' years senior to us breezed past, as if on a delightful Sunday stroll, shouting "Buen Camino" into the wind.

Now, at our sensational accommodation, a fire warms our souls, clothes, and shoes. My friends sip red wine and we swap stories with fellow travellers. The audacious descent seems like a lifetime ago. The enduring spirit of the Camino is truly remarkable. I am blessed to walk this path.

'Well written,' I said aloud as my phone beeped, the caller ID displaying Stephen Wall's' name, signalling that the MI6 boss was seeking an update. Taking a moment to deliberate, I declined the call. Instead, I opted to send him a text message, explaining that I was currently in the company of others and promising to call him the following evening.

Despite being fully clothed, exhaustion weighed heavily upon me as I sank onto the bed and rested my head on the pillow before drifting off into a deep and much-needed sleep.

***

This day marked the beginning of our journey to Sarria, the last leg of our Camino, signalling just 100 kilometres left to Santiago. Inside, the fire crackled and as we poured ourselves coffee; we were greeted with toasted ham sandwiches crowned with fried eggs, alongside refreshing orange juice. Departing our accommodation proved a challenge. With trepidation, we donned our rain gear and stepped outside. Taking the first tentative steps, we cast one last glance back at our sanctuary. Anna confessed to feeling the prickling of tears, a sentiment shared by us all.

Originally, our plan had been to follow the route via Samos, intending to visit the monastery of San Xian de Samos nestled on the banks of the river Sarriá. The Benedictine monastery, dating back to the 12th century, had a harmonious blend of architectural styles, ranging from Romanesque to Gothic, Renaissance, and Baroque. It was a sight not to be missed. When we reached the trail junction, buffeted by the relentless rain and wind, we opted for the direct route to Sarria, prioritising warmth and dryness over exploration.

To my astonishment, as we made the steep ascent out of Triacastela to Alto do Riocabo, I noticed William walking without his poles. 'William!' I called out. He turned to face me. 'You've forgotten your poles.'

'No, Claudia, I didn't forget them. I left them at the Pension. Simon told me he was sure he could gift them to someone.'

Surprised, I said. 'You don't want them anymore?'

'Well, the rugged climbs are behind us now, they've served their purpose well.'

I nodded, though it took a moment for his words to register. "They had served their purpose," he had said. His limp, the makeshift use of his poles as walking aids in Astorga—all made sense now.

What William smuggled wasn't concealed inside the puzzle box. No, it was hidden within the poles.

I resolved to seize a moment of privacy at our first coffee break to send a message to MI6. I planned to ask them to compare the walking poles William took into the Templar Castle at Astorga to the ones he left behind at Pension Casa Simón. Our journey was far from over. The truth was slowly revealing itself, one step at a time.

Roughly twelve kilometres out of Triacastela brought us to the village of Pintin, where we halted for a much-needed coffee break. Upon returning from the restroom, having sent my message to headquarters, I was delighted to find Patrick and Jo seated at a nearby table. We exchanged greetings and engaged in some small talk, although the conversation flowed less freely than the night before. The impending return of rain and wind weighed heavily, casting a sombre shadow. Eventually, Patrick and Jo bid us farewell, eager to continue their journey ahead of us. We lingered, opting for a second cup of coffee.

I peered at William over the rim of my cup, the steam from my brew swirling around me. My mind raced with questions.

What were you hiding inside the poles? Plans for the next generation of submarines? No, I can't imagine you as a traitor to your country.

The pieces of the puzzle came together in my mind as I recalled snippets of conversations with William and what Stephen Walls had said. According to the MI6 chief, William had quipped, *I'm a high-end gigolo* during a discussion about his finances. In Pamplona, he told Anna, *Next time you see me, I'll be texting my brains out.* And finally, during our walk to Villafranca del Bierzo, he'd uttered, *It's just time is all. I could buy anything, but I couldn't buy time.* It dawned on me that William's playful banter was not mere quirks, but calculated phrases. They were all lines from a film, "The Mule" starring Clint Eastwood and carried a hidden message. With apparent arrogance, William had been sending a message to the security services, and to me, suggesting he was a "mule." I took another sip of my drink. Artōrius's words echoed in my mind, urging me to shift perspective. Realisation struck:

This isn't espionage. William isn't trafficking national secrets. He worked for organised crime. That's why the rival gangs made attempts on his life.

I scratched my head. It seemed improbable that he was transporting drugs; perhaps something more valuable, like diamonds, or in this modern age, something entangled in the web of cybercrime, a computer chip, perhaps. On the Camino, William had crafted the illusion of being a turncoat to secure MI6's protection. During his tenure at BAE Systems, he'd always been under surveillance, a perfect cover for smuggling contraband. The puzzle was coalescing, and I had to restrain myself from shaking my head in disbelief lest William notice. Before briefing Stephen

Walls, I would await MI6's report on the walking poles to confirm my suspicions.

Leaving Pintin behind, I had a spring in my step as we continued our journey, our path guided by the iconic yellow arrows, the traditional markers of the Camino. The trail wound along a rolling country road, making our walk easy. As we neared Aguiada, a welcome sight greeted us. The rain eased, and the sun made a cameo appearance, peeking out from behind the dark clouds. Glancing skyward, William licked his finger and playfully held it up to the wind. We collectively concurred that the worst of the day's weather was probably behind us. With a sense of relief, we stowed away our wet weather gear, anticipating clearer skies ahead.

Approaching Sarria, the landscape underwent a subtle transformation, becoming more rugged as we ascended and descended gentle slopes. Eventually, the silhouette of Sarria emerged on the horizon, a beacon of progress on our journey. It took some time to reach the edge of town, where we stopped to capture the moment, posing beneath the sign bearing the town's name.

The road leading into Sarria guided us past a Pilgrim's Office, prompting us to halt and have our Camino passports stamped, a ritual marking progress on the journey. Outside, as we stowed our passports in our backpacks, William's voice cut through the air with a note of celebration.

'This is it, the final stage before Santiago. To commemorate our achievement in making it this far, let's dine at Sarria's finest restaurant—on me, with champagne to accompany our meal. Apologies, Jonathan.'

Jonathan responded with a grin, 'Sparkling water pairs perfectly with any meal, my friend.'

Turning to me, William said, 'Claudia, you're a woman of exquisite taste. I trust you to choose the perfect restaurant for our celebration.'

Smiling, I said, 'I'm sure I can find something exuberantly expensive.' Yet, as the words left my lips, something nagged at me. If William had served as a courier - a mule - for organised crime for years, how had he received payment without raising red flags with security services? The solution appeared to be hidden within the Bible passage William received in El Burgo Ranero; I was convinced that those verses held the secret instructions for compensating him for this mission.

***

After checking in at our Sarria accommodation, I told everyone that I'd text them later with my dining choice for the evening and the meeting time in the foyer. Alone in my room, I followed my arrival routine, preparing to shower and launder the clothes worn during the day. As I stepped into the bathroom, my phone buzzed. Pausing, I debated whether to continue with my shower or retrieve the phone from the bed. Opting for the latter, I checked the message. It was from MI6, responding to the query of earlier:

> Walking Poles: They appeared identical. However, under scrutiny, they were different. Marshal did not leave the castle with the poles he entered with.

Slapping my thigh triumphantly, I exclaimed aloud, 'I knew I was right!' I tossed the phone back down on the bed, deciding to ring Stephen Walls once I had freshened up.

Hanging my freshly laundered shirt over the shower door and draping my underwear across the arm of the lone chair in the room, I dressed and reached for my phone. With a swift search, I typed in

"The finest restaurants in Sarria." Almost instantly, the results materialised:

- Restaurante Cinza e Lume
- Restaurante Mar de Plata
- O Rest
- Parrillada O Recuncho
- Mesón O Tapas
- Matias Locanda Italiana
- A Valiña

Surveying my options, I muttered, 'Eeny, Meeny, Miny, Moe.' Opting to begin with O Rest, my hopes deflated as I discovered it was fully booked for the evening. Next in line was A Valiña, only to face the same disappointing outcome. Upon dialling Mesón O Tapas, I was met with the news that because of the impending big foot race in the morning, where hundreds of competitors would sprint from Sarria to Santiago along the Camino, with a twenty-four-hour cutoff to finish, I'd be fortunate to secure a dining spot anywhere.

'Very disappointing,' I muttered aloud.

I rang the reception at our hotel and inquired if they could accommodate our group. 'Certainly,' came the response. I promptly reserved a table for eight thirty that evening, the restaurant's opening time.

Although William didn't voice disappointment, dining at the hotel lacked the pizazz of the restaurant he'd wanted, no candlelight casting a warm glow, no aroma of Spanish cuisine wafting through the air, no gentle murmurs of fellow diners creating an atmosphere of intimacy. It felt like the other places we had eaten along "The Way." Despite this, William ordered a bottle of French Champagne and sparkling water for Jonathan. We filled our flutes and toasted the beginning of the last leg of our journey.

'To friends,' he said.

'To friends,' we repeated.

Like so many evenings spent together on the Camino, conversation flowed easily. Across the room, a couple resembling William and Anna in age caught Anna's attention. I watched as her gaze lingered on them. The man radiated a sense of refinement, his shimmering silver hair catching the light in a way that hinted at a lifetime of wisdom and rich experience. By his side sat a woman with mischievous eyes that sparkled, her infectious laughter ringing out and filling the room with lively energy. A smile tickled Anna's lip. Sensing my gaze, Anna turned to me and said, 'Do you ever look at people and wonder what their story is?'

Upon hearing Anna's question, William leaned in to reply. 'I do. In that couple—yes, they are indeed a couple, there's something wild. Their story mirrors the secrets we each harbour.'

As William spoke of secrets, I noticed the bond between him and Anna and it made me feel like an intruder. Their relationship had been developing along the trail, and this moment marked the transition from friendship to something deeper, perhaps. Now knowing that William wasn't a traitor and that his journey was probably his final stint as a mule for organised crime, I no longer felt an urgency to warn Anna.

'Jonathan,' I said, 'I need to stretch my legs before bed. Would you mind accompanying me?'

'Sure,' he replied. Rising from the table, Jonathan and I bid William and Anna a good night.

***

Anna Dupont

Lost in thought about William's comment about hidden secrets, I missed Claudia and Jonathan bidding us goodnight.

Do William's words imply something deeper? Did he know I had secrets hidden in my past? Did he suspect that Anna Dupont wasn't my real name?

I'd engaged in deception, but it wasn't unethical. I believed in conducting oneself with integrity, especially in relationships. Trust formed the bedrock of any bond, at least in my convictions.

I mulled over the idea of confiding in him before redirecting my attention to the couple we'd been observing. 'They seem to be adventurers,' I said. 'They embody the spirit of exploration, delving into the unknown.'

William nodded. 'Did they know each other before they started on this adventure?'

'No, I don't believe so,' I said. 'There's a freshness to them, a glimmer in their eyes that speaks of a newfound connection. They set out on their individual paths, only for them to cross unexpectedly. Two souls, converging on shared treasure.'

'Ah, tales of treasure and riches. Were they seeking gold, diamonds, and fame?'

I shook my head. 'No, the treasure they sought was knowledge and understanding. It wasn't something they could each find in solitude. Together, well, that changed everything.'

After a momentary pause, William nodded thoughtfully. 'I see, their journey is not simply about the physical trek; more a journey of self-discovery. Each step brings them closer to their destination and an understanding of themselves and each other. The secrets they carry within, the experiences that shaped them, are hidden treasures waiting to be unearthed.'

'Should all our secrets be unearthed?'

William took a moment, his expression reflective as he weighed his words. 'I suppose it depends on the secrets and the impact they'll have on those around us. Some secrets are best buried, while others can heal, allowing one to grow. It's delicate, isn't it? Knowing when to expose and when to safeguard.'

I looked at the couple and asked William, 'Have they found love?'

William stroked his chin, thinking before answering. 'Their faces speak of love lost and found, of dreams chased and abandoned, of the unspoken longing that lingers between two souls bound by fate.'

That's profound, I thought.

I watched the couple clasp hands across the table while I thought about what I would add to their story. 'On their quest, they've found a rare gift, a connection, plus the prospect of love.'

I took a sip from my wineglass as my thoughts wandered back to William's earlier words about hidden truths. For years, I had safeguarded my secrets, but in the presence of William, I had an urge to tell him the truth.

In my mind, but not out loud, I planned what I would say, 'William, there's something I haven't told you. Something about me you should know.'

William would turn in curiosity and concern. 'What is it, Anna?'

Taking a deep breath, I'd speak softly, 'Anna Dupont isn't my real name. It's a name I chose for myself a long time ago, to escape a past I'd rather forget.' William's eyes would widen, but he'd remain silent, willing me to continue.

'My real name is Claire Peis.'

William would nod, absorbing my revelation. 'Thank you for trusting me with this, Claire Peis. Your honesty means a lot to me.'

William's voice snapped me from by fantasy, 'Anna? Anna, are you alright?'

I chuckled. 'I'm sorry William, I was crafting the tale of that couple and I guess I lost myself in a daydream.'

***

Claudia

'Good evening, Stephen. I trust this is a good time to phone?'

'Indeed, Claudia. I know you must wait until your walking partners have retired for the evening. Is Sarria to your liking?'

'It's not raining, Sir, which is a plus.'

'That's good, Claudia. I hear congratulations are in order. You discovered how William was transporting the goods.'

'Yes, Stephen. It was a clever deception, having us focus on the puzzle box.'

'I assume that you have come to the same conclusion as us. Marshal is working for organised crime.'

'Yes, Stephen.'

'That being the case, this becomes a matter for law enforcement and not the security services. If I recall correctly, you suspected this from the beginning, Claudia.'

'He's been manipulating us, Sir, exploiting his position for personal gain in the past. I suspect a considerable portion of his wealth stems from illicit activities.'

'It appears so. Have you figured out how he did this while we were monitoring his finances?'

'I believe so, Sir. Will you refer William Marshal to the Police?'

'Yes. We'll pass on the information. How they handle it is up to them. This is a police matter now, so I have a new assignment for you. You're being sent back to Ukraine. We have identified a plot to assassinate President Volodymyr Zelensky and other top Ukrainian officials. Two officers in the agency responsible for protecting senior government leaders will be arrested tomorrow morning. The suspects are colonels in Ukraine's State Protection Department. They were recruited by Russia's Federal Security Service, the FSB, to provide information about Zelensky and other top officials' whereabouts and to recruit others who could help in the assassinations. You are being sent to Ukraine to assist the State Protection Department.'

'I see, Stephen. Are we aware how the assassinations were to occur?'

'A rocket attack was planned.'

'An effective method.'

'Indeed, Claudia. Also, you will have seen the reports that Russia has threatened to target British military assets in Ukraine and beyond, in response to comments made by our foreign secretary. He told Kyiv that they can use British weapons to strike targets inside Russia. It's important that we have good people on the ground in Ukraine.'

'Yes, Sir.'

'Tensions are escalating, Claudia. Russia is conducting drills simulating the deployment of battlefield nuclear weapons.'

'Do we believe Russia will follow through with its threat to attack British assets?'

'A direct assault on our interests beyond Ukraine is improbable, but a provocative action is likely, one that wouldn't elicit a direct response from the UK.'

'If the situation worsens for Ukraine, do you foresee Britain deploying ground troops?'

'They're decisions best left to politicians, Claudia. But here's what I'll say: With China throwing its weight behind the Russian War Machine, overcoming Russia in Ukraine will be a formidable task, even if the UK and France intervened militarily. Ukraine contends, with compelling justification, that a larger conflict involving Europe is looming. They assert it needs to be halted on their territory.'

'They're grappling with the challenge of replenishing their military forces.'

'We're striving to steer clear of being pulled further into the conflict, but I'm afraid conflict may be inevitable.'

'In the annals of history, Sir, Russia has proven itself impervious to invasion.'

'That truth is as clear to us as it is to Russia. As it stands, the path ahead is shrouded in uncertainty.'

'Is it quiet on the China front?'

'We are at a time when there is no respite on the foreign stage. While cyber threats from Russia and Iran are globally pervasive and aggressive, respectively, China is our top priority. China's recent pattern of behaviour is instructional. It includes two malicious cyber campaigns that targeted parliamentarians and Britain's Electoral Commission. In cyberspace, we believe that China's actions weaken the security of the internet for all. We have recently charged three men with assisting Hong Kong's intelligence service, so our diplomatic relationship with the People's Republic is rapidly deteriorating.'

'Is the world already at war?'

'In the future, historians will undoubtedly debate that question.' Stephen paused, inhaling deeply. 'Claudia, how soon can you return to London?'

Inwardly, I smiled. I'd diverted Stephen's attention from how William was compensated for his unlawful deeds. Holding my breath, I prepared to broach the subject of staying in Spain a while longer. 'If I may, Sir. Having come this far along the Camino, I would like to finish the journey to Santiago before returning to the UK. I would need five days, and I still have annual leave owing.' Given the seriousness of our discussions, I waited for Stephen's response, uncertain of what it would be.

'Very well, Claudia. I expect to see you in my office in seven days' time. And, when the right moment presents itself, inform William Marshal that we are aware of his activities. We don't want him to believe he's escaped scot-free.'

Chapter 24
The reckoning

Anna Dupont

On awakening, a dull ache throbbed through my right foot, a forerunner to the challenging day ahead. To my dismay, I discovered a new blister on my little toe and felt a sharp twinge shoot from the tendons—a trifecta of discomfort. With a sigh, I wiped away a stray tear, my uncertainty about the day's walk weighing on me.

William greeted me cheerfully as I descended the stairs, followed by the familiar welcome of Claudia and Jonathan, each geared up for the twenty-five-kilometre trek to Portomarin. Despite my discomfort, I plastered on a smile and exchanged waves of greeting, keeping my turmoil concealed.

'It's not raining,' Jonathan said with a grin.

At least that is one good thing.

'That's great,' I said.

Leaving Sarria, we encountered the preparations for the foot race, organisers bustling about hanging banners and marking the start line. A morning mist hung low over the town, and if it wasn't for the throbbing in my foot, it would have been picturesque. Unaware of my discomfort, Claudia set a fast pace and four kilometres on we were at the outskirts of Barbadelo, a sleepy hamlet nestled amidst rolling hills. At its heart stood the weathered stone church, Glesia de Santiago de Barbadelo, its bell tower reaching for the sky. Claudia told us it was one of the most renowned churches along "The Way", having been declared a National Monument in 1976. She regaled tales of its connection to legends and folklore, hinting at enigmatic symbols hidden within its walls. Images of lions, birds, and snakes, drawn from medieval bestiaries, adorned its interior, or so she claimed.

We all nodded but it fell upon to me to ask. 'Claudia, what on earth is a bestiary?'

'Oh, sorry, Anna. A bestiary, derived from the Latin term "bestiarium vocabulum". It is essentially a compendium of beasts. A collection of creatures, often depicted with imagery. In medieval times, bestiaries described just a few dozen to well over a hundred animals. These explanations weren't merely about the physical attributes; they also delved into the creatures' symbolic and Christian significance. For instance, the unicorn was often depicted as a symbol for Christ, while others focused on the unique traits of the animals themselves.'

Though I thanked Claudia for her explanation, the feeling of confusion lingered. Claudia's enthusiasm remained undiminished as she continued, 'Here there are peculiar human figures depicted in sections of the church. You'll find them on the tympanum, doorways, windows, and even on a side door.'

We studied the enigmas adorning the church, and William's words about secrets filled my mind again. Claudia carried her own mysteries, reminiscent of the retired French operative who helped me escape the horrors of my relationship. I had doubts about her, but was she a spy? She was fluent in Spanish, smart and had a remarkable memory, traits she'd concealed but which were now revealing themselves.

In the end, does it matter what she does? No, only who she is.

Leaving Barbadelo, we continued our journey. As we neared Mercado do Serra, a police car arrived and blocked the road at the intersection we were about to cross, probably facilitating the passage of runners racing from Sarria to Santiago. Across the road was a little bar, perfect for breakfast, I told the others.

Having ordered my coffee, I returned to our table to rest my foot. I'd abandon the shoes William gave me in favour of my old pink sandals, a choice that necessitated honesty with my companions. I could no longer conceal the struggles I was facing with each step.

We continued our journey, and I attempted to immerse myself in the beautiful surroundings, yet my unease proved to be a formidable distraction, causing me to worry that I might have overlooked some of the stunning scenery. The path to Vilachá was along country lanes, bordered by stone fences and dotted with farms straight from a bygone era, scenes immortalised in early 20th-century films. Despite their rustic nature, it was clear that these lands were tended by ageing hands, suggesting that the younger generation were reluctant to continue the traditions. To people not accustomed to it, farmyard smells of silage and manure could be overwhelming.

My resolve faltered as the pain in my foot intensified, until finally, in a small bar nestled in Vilachá, I could bear it no longer. Tears gushed from my eyes and I succumbed to a wave of anguish. My companions gathered around me; their concern was obvious. They grappled with how best to help me, but the suggestion of summoning a taxi to ferry me the short distance to Portomarin was met with my stubborn refusal. I swapped my shoes again, clinging to the hope that it would offer a measure of relief. Slowly, we resumed our trek, descending steeply before arriving at the banks of the Rio Miño. Stretching out before us was a sturdy bridge spanning the river's width and ahead, a stone stairwell ascended into the centre of Portomarin, a daunting sight for me, battling my distress. In a moment of levity, Claudia seized upon the opportunity to lift my spirits. Mischievously, she bounded up the stairs with infectious energy, her voice carrying the strains of the Rocky theme, an homage to the iconic scene from the film where the boxer

Balboa concludes his morning run with a triumphant ascent of the steps of the Philadelphia Museum of Art. Returning, Claudia extended her hand, a promise to see me through to journey's end. With her support, I found the strength to face the climb.

Our hotel was easy to find, yet first, as was our custom, we found a bar to kill time until we could check in. This one, in the middle of town, overlooked the Church of San Xoán, a temple fortress consisting of a single nave and a semicircular front originally built to protect the pilgrims on The Way. Claudia informed us that the church had its roots as a humble chapel from the early medieval period. Apparently, because of the flooding of the Rio Miño, the church was moved to its current location, stone by stone, in 1962. To our delight, some of our young friends arrived at the bar and joined us until it was check-in time. Federica gave us all a big hug.

My room was small but comfortable. Lying down, I drifted off instantly. Waking an hour and a half later, I tended to my blisters before heading downstairs to meet the others. Hungry and relieved to find a nearby restaurant, we enjoyed a meal of pizza and gnocchi. Back in my room, I hoped my blisters would improve overnight for the following day's walk. As I checked William's updates on my phone, the distant sound of bagpipes echoed from the street below.

William's Social Media Post

Embarking on the last leg of our journey, which we've divided into five stages, the Camino experience has once again transformed. We are greeted by ideal walking conditions, making the storms of our mountain crossing feel like a distant memory. Leaving Sarria, we share the trail with hikers engaged in a cross-country event, their gear strapped to their backs. Some are running, while others walk with great enthusiasm. Even at road crossings (deserted country lanes) the police are there to ensure our right of way. I shared a smile with Anna, reminiscing about the times we had to navigate busy freeway interchanges with nothing but a green line painted on the tarmac to separate us from traffic.

The trail from Sarria to Portomarin feels like it's straight out of a picture book. Old stone wall fences embrace us on both sides, and the path meanders through farmlets that have remained unchanged by the passage of time. Surrounded by the distinctive scent of cattle, farmers diligently milk their thirty or forty head in old stone dairies. I feel a touch of sadness, knowing that they may be the last generation to carry on this way of life. After walking through many nearly deserted villages in the weeks prior, it seems unlikely that the next generation will continue these old traditions. Our experience of today, with its sights and smells, may soon be lost to time.

Our companions on this leg of the journey are all unfamiliar faces, and I feel the loss of our familiar Camino friends. As if sensing my nostalgia, a man resting on the side of The Way beckoned me. He produced a large chocolate bar and broke me off a piece, offering it with a warm "Buen Camino".

***

Claudia

We gathered in the lobby of our accommodation, ready to embark on the journey to Palas de Rei, a stretch spanning 24.8 kilometres. I was pleased that Anna was with us, though her apprehension was obvious. We had barely ventured 100 metres from our Pension, down the hill towards the river, when Anna halted, a tough decision weighing on her.

'I'm sorry,' she said, her voice strained. 'My foot... it's too painful. I'll have to take a taxi and meet you later.'

I wasn't surprised, but was stunned when William volunteered to accompany her. Gratitude flickered in Anna's eyes, but she was adamant that William continue the journey with Jonathan and me. Despite her protests, William shook his head resolutely, refusing to budge. Privately, I suspected Anna was relieved, though she pretended otherwise.

Jonathan and I watched Anna and William retrace their steps before we commenced our journey.

'The hike to Palas de Rei is supposed to be difficult,' Jonathan said with a smile.

'If you started in Sarria, it would be. Funny, now twenty-four kilometres sound like a pleasant morning stroll.'

We followed the road out of town and across the Rio Miño, though not via the same bridge we'd arrived on, before joining a trail that ascended steeply. Shrouded in heavy mist, there were no views to speak of, obscured by the fog. Jonathan and I walked in silence until we reached the first village of the morning, Gonzar.

'Do you want to look at the Church of Santa Maria?' I asked.

Jonathan pondered for a moment. 'To be honest, Claudia, I'm a bit churched out.'

'Thank goodness. Me too. What about breakfast?'

'Nah. Let's push on to Hospital de la Cruz.'

'Alright.'

With Anna and William absent, Jonathan and I swept forward, our pace brisk, overtaking fellow pilgrims. As we passed two women around his age, I asked Jonathan about his quest to find the future Mrs. Swindon. 'Has anyone caught your eye?'

Jonathan chuckled. 'It all sounds whimsical now, doesn't it, the future Mrs. Swindon?'

'Not at all, Jonathan. Given your spiritual convictions, you're more likely to connect with someone who shares your values along the Camino than anywhere else, especially a dating app.'

'I've found some pilgrims we've met attractive, but a proper opportunity hasn't presented itself.' Jonathan paused, and I sensed he wanted to say more, so I held my tongue and waited. 'Do opposites attract?'

I shrugged, exaggerating the movement of my arms. 'I'm just a single lassie. What would I know?'

'Claudia, I won't pry, but there's another side to you, as there is for each of us.'

Jonathan's comment didn't surprise me and I wasn't worried by his inquisitiveness. I'd experienced an inquiring mind many times in my career and knew how best to deal with it. The solution was a long-winded answer to his question. 'Jonathan, opposites often initially attract, but sustaining a relationship founded on differences is challenging. Picture this: you meet someone who sees the world differently and there's an immediate spark, right? It's like discovering an alternative universe of ideas and perspectives. That initial excitement draws us in. But here's the thing: sustaining a relationship like this hits roadblocks. Communication is trickier when we're coming from opposite ends of the spectrum. Imagine trying to navigate through a forest without a compass or map. That's what it's like when viewpoints differ by a wide margin. Religion, politics, fishing, or how to raise a family, anything can trigger strife. When inevitable conflicts arise, resolving them is like untangling a knot. Relationships are built on sharing and, while diversity adds spice, it's the shared moments, inside jokes, late-night talks, adventures, and everything else we use as equity that glues a relationship together. Without them, foundations are on sand.'

Jonathan nodded.

Keep going, Claudia.

'Emotional connection is another piece of the puzzle. To build a deep bond, we need empathy, the ability to understand another's viewpoint. When differences are vast, it's like communicating in different languages; we struggle to connect. And finally, long-term compatibility: opposites might attract, but for a relationship to go the distance, attraction needs to run deep. We need shared goals, values, and dreams to align. Otherwise, paths will diverge sooner than we want.' Jonathan opened his mouth to speak, but I continued. 'You're not seeking a clone, either. Far from it, Jonathan. Imagine you and your partner have vastly different beliefs on something, like politics or religion. That's okay, as long as your core values align. Values guide us, shape choices, actions, and our priorities. They are the fundamental beliefs like honesty, integrity, respect, and compassion. So, even if you and your partner have different viewpoints, by having shared values, you're both committed to the same principles. This creates harmony in a relationship, which leads to mutual respect and growing closer together. So, while differences can add interest, a solid foundation is needed to weather the storms ahead. Principles Jonathan, they're like the North Star guiding us, ensuring we stay on course even when troubles arise.'

Jonathan chuckled. 'There I was, Claudia, thinking that you were a spy, and it turns out you're a psychiatrist.'

Reaching Hospital de la Cruz, I longed for my first cup of coffee of the day. Jonathan had different ideas and proposed continuing to Ventas de Narón, twenty minutes further along the trail and I didn't argue. He wanted to be in Palas de Rei quickly, so that William and Anna didn't have too long a wait.

In Ventas de Narón, a cross stood by a chapel, beckoning pilgrims like us to stop. Pausing beside a fellow traveller, Jonathan turned to me and said, 'Do you know the story behind this chapel, Claudia?' I shook my head; I was ignorant on this occasion.

A woman, stocky, about my height but in her fifties, leaning on her sturdy walking poles, spoke.

Without moving her eyes from the cross, she said, 'According to local legend, Ventas de Narón was the site of a battle between Christian forces and the Moor Kings during the Moorish advance towards Galicia. The legend recounts that the Christian forces, likely led by local lords or knights, bravely defended the area against the invading Moors. The battle is said to have been fierce, with both sides fighting valiantly for control of the strategic location. Over time, the legend of the battle at Ventas de Narón has become intertwined with the history and folklore of the region. The chapel itself may have been built as a commemoration of the battle.' She paused... 'Or as a place of worship for the Christian community in the area.'

Turning to face us, she smiled. 'The exact truth behind the legend may elude us, but I love the myths, stories, and historical events that make the Camino such a captivating journey.' With a nod of farewell, she left us. Watching her go, she cast a lonely shadow and in her, I could see myself in twenty years' time. We left shortly after to find a bar.

Breakfast and two coffees later, we were refreshed and ready to push on towards Palas de Rei. After Ventas de Narón, the trail wound its way through open forests and then rolling hills. Our journey led us to a traditional village named Lameiros, where we saw the woman we'd encountered in Ventas de Narón, standing in front of another stone cross. It was as if she'd waited for us, or rather waited for me. Without acknowledging our presence, she spoke. 'The Cruceiro de Lameiros, was erected in 1670. At its base, the symbols etched in weathered stone depict the anguish and sacrifice of Jesus Christ. Yet, there is an unexpected juxtaposition atop the cross. Instead of a crucified Christ, there is a symbol of maternity, the Virgin Mary cradling what seems to be Jesus, whether as an infant or the Christ of the Cross. It is a departure from the conventional imagery associated with crucifixes. What might it signify?' Her gaze shifted towards me, signalling that the question was directed at me.

'It is a representation of the Alpha and the Omega, the beginning and the end, encapsulating the cycle of life and death?'

'Maybe,' the woman replied. 'Or perhaps it speaks of the unconditional love of a mother for her son, transcending even the darkest of hours?'

With that, she turned and departed, leaving Jonathan and me to contemplate the cross.

'The beginning and the end,' Jonathan mused. 'Opposites!'

I pondered his observation before responding, 'They aren't necessarily opposites in the traditional sense. Rather than opposing forces, they symbolise the totality and infinity of God's being.' After a pause, I added, 'Shall we continue?'

'Yep, I'm ready.'

As we resumed our journey, I pondered Jonathan's earlier question about whether opposites attract. It wasn't simply a passing inquiry; more, it reflected our own dynamic. Was he asking if our relationship could encompass the breadth of the Alpha and the Omega? I didn't know.

Half an hour on, the overcast sky cleared, and the sun brightened the landscape, casting a golden glow. I was lost in thought, pondering the complexity of falling in love while on holiday, a topic that had been on my mind before the events of that day. When I first joined up with William and Jonathan, I feigned being the ideal companion, someone who embodied the qualities Jonathan sought in a partner. As the days passed, I found my place within the group and the crafted facade fell away, revealing more of the authentic Claudia beneath. It had been gradual, shedding layers and I'd not intended my true self to appear, but it had happened none the less. I wondered whether Jonathan's perception of me had shifted, too. Was he still captivated by the version of Claudia I'd presented initially, or had he grown to appreciate the real Claudia?

The allure of meeting someone new while undertaking a shared adventure is undeniable. The thrill of exploring unfamiliar surroundings together, of overcoming hardships and our shared sense of achievement are like a whirlwind. As he led the way, I studied Jonathan's body, reminiscing over our dinner table conversations, glances exchanged amid cobblestone streets and the occasional blossoming of desire within me. That Jonathan and I would share feelings for each other was no surprise, but the depth of my emotions had been unexpected. I pushed them away; it was easy to be swept up in the moment and overlook the long-term challenges. Our differences would be pronounced once the Camino ended and everyday life set in—I knew this to be a truth. Our beliefs, values, and goals were not compatible, and the Camino had created a fantasy, helped by my early manipulative behaviour. My time on the Camino with Jonathan would not have a fairy-tale ending, of that I was sure, but I would cherish the memories of this journey together and I hope he would feel the same way.

Jonathan pointed to an eagle flying overhead.

'I see it,' I yelled, pondering where this journey would ultimately lead him. I was destined for Ukraine; would he yet stumble upon the future Mrs. Swindon?

We continued our journey for another half hour, the anticipation of our reunion with our fellow trekkers building with each step. Abruptly, Jonathan halted, his eyes bright with excitement. 'We're in!'

'Almost,' I said.

'I'll text the others. Where are we supposed to meet them?'

'Praza do Concello–the council square,' I said. 'I studied the map last night; it shouldn't be hard to find.'

After an exchange of messages, William responded, informing us he and Anna were waiting in a bar overlooking the square. Within fifteen minutes, we were reunited, and Anna asked us whether we'd had our Camino passports stamped. In our eagerness, we had forgotten.

'Our first task is to find the local church and have your passports stamped,' said Anna

Jonathan grinned sheepishly. 'We walked right by it on our way here.'

'Then lead on, Jonathan,' Anna said.

With another Camino stamp secured, my stomach growled. It was lunchtime and my friends agreed. Being a Sunday, the options for food were limited, with many establishments closed. Venturing to the outskirts of town away from the main thoroughfare we stumbled upon a small bar where the sound of chatter spilled out onto the street. Anna, ever adventurous, suggested that we give it a try.

As we pushed open the door, the scene inside resembled something from an American western. Conversations halted, and curious glances were cast our way as we entered, strangers in a foreign land. As we settled at a table, the hum of conversation resumed around us. The lighting was dim, and the rustic décor added to its appeal. We sat back, soaking in the atmosphere, listening to the animated chatter of the locals as they swapped tales, laughter spilling out across the room occasionally. The aroma of home-cooked food wafted from the kitchen. It was a place where time slowed down, inviting us to linger, the perfect spot to enjoy a leisurely lunch of soup, cheeses and fresh bread, washed down with a glass of local red.

During our meal, Anna and William spoke of their plan to take the bus to Arzúa the next day, and then again, the following day, to O Pedrouzo. They wanted to give Anna's foot a chance to heal, to allow her to walk the last stretch into Santiago. Their bond was clear, deepening as the trek was coming to an end. I carried a heavy weight on my conscience, for I knew the scars left by her past mistakes. Anna's life had been irrevocably altered by choosing the wrong partner. Anna was oblivious to William's true nature, one steeped in criminality. William would face certain prosecution if I disclosed what I knew to the authorities. The moral dilemma that had plagued my thoughts ever since I uncovered William's murky connections to organised crime was reaching a crescendo:

Should I warn Anna?

She wasn't at risk of harm, more of disappointment, and if William was arrested, her heart would be broken. I was certain, after Astorga, that William was no longer involved in crime. Their fate rested in my hands. Feeling uncertain, I opted to seek advice from Brother Artōrius, confident that he would offer guidance on the matter.

After lunch, we checked into our hotel. Later, I went out alone, hoping to find Brother Artōrius, but to no avail. He was an enigmatic figure. When you sought him, he was nowhere to be found, but when you least expected it, he appeared.

We met up again for dinner and were lucky to find a seat at one of the few open restaurants. Rob, from Melbourne, whom we hadn't seen in a few days, came in, accompanied by a woman we didn't recognise. The restaurant was full, but the owners allowed us to accommodate him and Valentina from Ukraine at our table. It would have been easy to have talked late into the evening with them, but fellow pilgrims were waiting outside to eat, so we departed shortly after finishing our meal.

Back at our accommodation, I collapsed onto my bed, only to discover it was uncomfortable. The mattress almost folded in two under my weight. 'Well,' I said to myself, 'It seems I'm up for an uncomfortable night.' Resigned, I took to the chair and opened my phone to read Jonathan's latest social media post. It was a departure from his usual travel log style, featuring a poem. Written by Jonathan, I presumed, but I knew its genesis: the mystical woman we met in Ventas de Narón and later in Lameiros.

Jonathan's Social Media Post.

Alpha and Omega

In the beginning, whispers of light,
Alpha's dawn breaks eternal night,
The first breath of a sacred tale,
Life unfurls the Spirit's gale.

Stars ignite in heavens wide,
God's own hand, a cosmic guide,
From dusk to dawn, creation blooms,

In Alpha's heart, all life resumes.

Through valleys deep and mountains high,
The Alpha's love will never die,
In every heartbeat, every sigh,
A trace of grace, a boundless sky.

When shadows fall and dusk descends,
Omega's call, where time suspends,
The last note in life's refrain,
Completes the circle, ends the pain.
Yet in this end, a new beginning,
Omega's dusk is dawn's first winning,
For Alpha and Omega blend,
A seamless flow, no start or end.

In faith we walk, in hope we trust,
From dust to stars, return to dust,
Alpha's dawn and Omega's night,
In God's embrace, we find our light.

I sat back in my chair, my eyes lingering on Jonathan's piece.

The title, "Alpha and Omega", was inspired by the Cruceiro de Lameiros we'd seen earlier. So, just the title alone stirred something within me. As I read the lines, I was lost in the imagery and our journey, a transcendence that the poem evoked.

The opening lines, "In the beginning, whispers of light, / Alpha's dawn breaks eternal night," drew me into the timeless dance of creation—the universe's birth and stars igniting at the touch of a divine hand. I felt a shiver at Jonathan's portrayal of Alpha. The beginning was a literal and spiritual dawn. I wondered if it reflected his search for meaning.

As I continued to read, I reflected on the poem's progression from creation to existence: "Through valleys deep and mountains high, / The Alpha's love will never die." I thought about life's valleys and peaks, the love that sustains people through them. Was Jonathan saying that love and grace were constants, no matter the hardships we face?

When I reached the lines about Omega, the end, "When shadows fall and dusk descends, / Omega's call, where time suspends," I felt sadness mixed with hope. The idea that the end of one journey was merely the beginning of another spoke to his deeply held beliefs about life and death, endings and beginnings.

The final stanza left me in quiet contemplation. "In faith we walk, in hope we trust, / From dust to stars, return to dust," I repeated to myself. The cycle of life, framed within the embrace of divine love, felt like a gentle reassurance. I saw in Jonathan's words a reflection of his faith journey, a path lit by hope and trust.

I closed my eyes for a moment, letting the poem's message wash over me. In Jonathan's eloquent exploration of beginnings and ends, of Alpha and Omega, was a reminder that life, in all its phases, was part of a greater story. For Jonathan and many of those who walk the Camino, it was a divine story.

I opened my eyes again and whispered, 'It's easy to forget that I'm here because of my occupation. For Jonathan, his is a spiritual journey. I hope he discovers the future Mrs. Swindon.' Jonathan had revealed a new side to himself that day. The Camino was touching us each in ways we could never have imagined.

I sighed, then inhaled deeply. 'Okay then. I wonder what William wrote about. I'm sure it won't be religious.'

William's Social Media Post

The Camino de Santiago is a journey of self-discovery, a pilgrimage that often leads to unexpected encounters and cherished memories. Palas de Rei, a picturesque town along the way, proved to be another wonderful experience. Anna and I took a taxi from Portomarin, leaving Jonathan and Claudia to walk this section alone. When we all met again, we were on the lookout for a place to enjoy a simple Sunday lunch.

Many places in Palas de Rei were closed, which left us feeling slightly disheartened. Our growling stomachs echoed the urgency of our quest for a hearty feed. Just when it seemed like our options were dwindling, we stumbled upon an unlikely-looking bar. The lively chatter spilling out from within the cozy establishment hinted that this might be a local haunt.

Curiosity buoyed us as we pushed open the door. The room inside was smaller than my living room. A bar dominating its length. We were met with the sight of weathered yet dignified older men seated around tables and standing at the bar, engrossed in conversations and sipping on vino blanco and vino tinto.

We found a vacant table and observed, trying to decipher the unspoken rules of this hidden gem. Feeling like outsiders, we approached the bar to place our order, leaving a note and coins on our table as per the apparent custom. The friendly barman delivered our drinks and discreetly collected the payment, returning shortly with our change.

As I sipped my vino tinto, I marvelled at the camaraderie and warmth that permeated the room. The locals were generous with their laughter and stories, even though we couldn't understand a word of the conversations swirling around us.

From the menu, we shared a cheese platter, a choice that pleasantly surprised. The portion was abundant, with enough cheese to clog the arteries of even an Olympic athlete.

One patron's kind gesture, covering the next round of drinks for everyone, left us with a profound sense of the shared spirit that defines the Camino de Santiago.

Today, our simple quest for lunch became one of those encounters that make this pilgrimage so special. It reminded us of the beauty of human connection.

***

'Good morning, Claudia,' Jonathan declared. 'Are you ready? It's a big one today, nearly thirty kilometres.'

'Yes, Arzúa. Strangely, Jonathan, I'm looking forward to the walk. Their bus doesn't leave until nine forty-five this morning. Do you think we can beat them in?'

'What's the time now?' Jonathan smiled as he checked his watch. 'It's nearly six. Even if we averaged six kilometres per hour and walked non-stop, we couldn't do it. At best, we could be in by eleven. At the slowest, their bus will arrive at quarter to eleven.'

'Gee, that is close. With wings on our feet, we should make haste! My prediction. We'll be in the church square no later than eleven thirty. What do you reckon?'

Jonathan strode out, calling back over his shoulder with a giggle, 'Not if you hang around outside our Pension, we won't. Are you coming, Claudia, or what?'

The early morning air was crisp, the sky still the darkness of night as we set out from Palas de Rei. Under the light of my headlamp, the trail revealed itself as Jonathan and I pushed forward. The first stretch was gentle through Carballal, the sleepy village just beginning to stir, and then on to San Xulián. As I turned my head,

367

my beam cast like a lighthouse, and I caught glimpses of ancient stone buildings nestled amongst verdant fields. The trail dipped into the dense woods of Coto, where the scent of pine filled the air as we made for what we thought would be a shaded path in the summer.

'It is peaceful here,' I said to Jonathan, the only sounds being the rustle of leaves and the occasional bird as they woke from their slumber. When we emerged from the woods, the small village of Leboreiro appeared, with its stone bridge and medieval Church of Santa Maria, another nod to the centuries of pilgrims who had walked this same route.

'Do you want to stop and look?' Jonathan said.

'No,' I replied. 'We are on a mission.'

He laughed, 'A race more like it.'

Jonathan was right, it was a race. Until I'd resolved my dilemma, I wanted to reduce the time William and Anna spent on their own.

After passing through the hamlet of Furelos, with its picturesque Romanesque bridge arching over the Furelos River, we finally arrived in Melide as dawn was breaking. The bustling town was a contrast to the silence of the countryside we'd traversed. The streets were alive with the chatter of locals and pilgrims alike, plus the aroma of freshly baked bread and roasting coffee beans wafting through the air. We found a cafe in the town centre, rustic wooden beams overhead and modern artwork adorning the walls, and settled in for breakfast.

Jonathan looked at his watch. 'What do you think William and Anna are doing right now?' I smiled and lifted my coffee cup as if it were a wine glass. 'The same as us.'

Having selected our breakfast from pre-prepared options on display and consumed our drinks quickly, I was on my feet, suggesting to Jonathan that it was time to leave. Checking the map of Melide on his phone, Jonathan asked if we could explore the Plaza del Convento and the outside of the Church of Sancti Spiritus as we left town, saying our path led us past them.

'Sure,' I replied. *How could I say no?*

The Camino path led us past a mix of ancient and contemporary architecture, with narrow cobbled streets guiding us to the central square, Plaza del Convento, where the Church of Sancti Spiritus stood. The square was a hive of activity, with market stall holders setting up, gearing up to sell everything from local cheeses to handcrafted souvenirs.

Even though I was in a hurry, I was reluctant to leave Melide, wishing we had more time to explore. The trail took us through the villages of Boente and Castañeda, each with their own unique feel: small chapels and friendly locals offering a warm "Buen Camino!" The path became more challenging as we approached Ribadiso, a hamlet with a medieval bridge and an Albergue that appeared to have been plucked from a storybook. Finally, after several more kilometres, we reached Arzúa. Walking into the town square, the place where we were to meet William and Anna, I felt a sense of accomplishment. Jonathan touched my shoulder. 'Well done,' he said.

I turned to face him. 'Give me a hug.'

We embraced as friends, conquering heroes. I didn't understand why, but tears welled in my eyes. Jonathan's phone buzzed. A text message from William:

Look over your shoulder.

We turned and spotted Anna and William in the window of a cafe, waving to us. We returned the gesture and as we started moving towards them, something in the corner of my eye, near an old oak tree, caught my attention.

Is that Brother Artōrius?

Careful not to signal to the others that I was looking at anything other than where we were going, I turned my head slightly for a better look. Shadows were the only thing to be seen under the oak. I was imagining things, or was I?

***

'Sit, sit,' Anna said. 'I can't believe you're already here.'

Jonathan grinned. 'We didn't want you to have all the fun without us.'

Two coffees promptly arrived. William gestured to the server, signalling that they were for Jonathan and me. 'My treat,' William said.

I said to Anna, 'What have you done since you arrived?'

'Scheduled a physiotherapy session for four thirty this afternoon. I'm hopeful it will aid in healing my foot for the walk into Santiago.'

'And what else?' William prompted.

'I also purchased another pair of shoes.'

'Oh, that's fantastic,' I said.

Anna grimaced. 'I regret the decision already.'

We sat for a while before deciding it was time for lunch. We opted to purchase a selection of treats from the supermarket and enjoyed a picnic in the square next to the church. Afterwards, we checked into our accommodation, which wasn't far away. My room was surprisingly spacious and even boasted a balcony. The bed was luxuriously comfortable; after the ordeal of the previous night's mattress, anything would have felt like an improvement.

The accommodation came with communal washing and drying machines. Meeting the others downstairs, we piled everything in together, men's, women's, colours, and whites, and filled the machine. It is said that walking the Camino is life-changing. Who would have thought that I, Claudia, who always separates her laundry and even puts her delicate things into their own washing satchel, would willingly dump all my clothes in with those of everyone else? We took turns monitoring the washing progress and when it was our turn and the dryer was free, transferred the clothes into it. Supervising the clothes as they tumbled, we had to empty the machine as soon as they were dry to allow the next person their turn.

With the washing done, Anna, accompanied by William, left for her physio appointment. Jonathan went up to his room, and I set out for a stroll to explore the town.

I discovered Brother Artōrius beneath the shade of the ancient oak near the church, his tattered robe blending with the moss-covered trunk. He sat alone, eyes closed in meditation, yet they opened as I neared, as though he expected me.

'I thought I would find you here,' I said.

'Ask and it will be given to you; seek and you will find; knock and the door will be opened to you.'

'Matthew 7:7,' I said.

'For a woman who has lost her way with God, you know your scriptures.'

I smiled. 'I haven't got any special religion this morning. My God is the God of Walkers.'

Brother Artōrius nodded 'Claudia, you quote from *In Patagonia* by Bruce Chatwin.'

'For a man of the cloth, Brother Artōrius, you are well read in the way of travel books.'

'Life is a journey, Claudia.'

There was a lull in our exchange before Artōrius said, 'You seek me!'

How does he know?

'Yes. I'd like your guidance.'

He nodded, a smile playing on his lips. 'Sit, my child. Share your burden with me.'

'It's about William, William Marshal.'

'Ah.'

'Initially, we suspected him of espionage, which was why I was assigned to this mission. He's actually a smuggler for organised crime, though I am sure his operations involve neither drugs nor weapons.'

'What troubles you about this, Claudia?'

'I confess,' I began, my voice trembling, 'William is a good man, despite his actions. He's kind and over these weeks, I've grown fond of him. There's a budding relationship between him and Anna, and you once mentioned that she'd endured immense suffering in her past. Anna remains oblivious to William's nature. The Camino marks the end of William's criminal activities. Yet, with the knowledge I possess, I'm torn. Should I report him to the authorities and also warn Anna? I fear shattering their chance at happiness.'

Brother Artōrius nodded. 'These matters are out of your hands, Claudia. Stephen Walls tells me that MI6 will refer him to law enforcement.'

'Yes, Stephen told me. If I withhold what I know from the police, how his criminal payments evaded detection despite the monitoring of William's finances, he's unlikely to face prosecution.'

'I see. You solved the Bible passage riddle from El Burgo Ranero?'

'I believe so. He also received payments by other means.'

Brother Artōrius closed his eyes for a moment, gathering his thoughts. 'You speak of William's kindness and his intentions to change, yet his wealth has been amassed through the suffering of others. Even if he hasn't directly caused harm, his actions have enabled it. While he may not have trafficked drugs or firearms, consider if it were software or code for cipher for phones, encrypted communication devices shielding drug or human traffickers from police surveillance. William might have enabled criminals to evade justice and perpetuate their misery.'

I nodded, feeling conflicted. 'But people can change, can't they? If he leaves that life behind, doesn't he deserve a second chance?'

Brother Artōrius replied softly. 'Redemption is a path we each can walk, but it does not erase the past. Anna has known the pain of choosing the wrong partner. To withhold the truth from her is to deny her the agency to choose wisely this time. And as for William, he must face the consequences of his actions to truly change.'

'If I report him, his future... and Anna's, would be destroyed. If I say nothing, I feel complicit in his past crimes.'

Brother Artōrius placed a comforting hand on my shoulder. 'The right path is rarely the easiest, Claudia. You must weigh the consequences of your silence against the potential for true justice and the prevention of further harm. The answer lies not in what is easy, but in what is right.'

I took a deep breath, the weight of his words a burden. 'Thank you, Brother Artōrius. I understand now.'

As I rose to leave, Brother Artōrius spoke again, his voice gentle but firm. 'Remember Claudia, our actions define us. Choose with a clear heart, and you will find peace.'

William's Social Media Post

In the heart of northern Spain, under the ever-watchful gaze of the sun and rain, Anna and I met on a pilgrimage along the Camino de Santiago. Our steps fell in perfect harmony, our laughter echoing through the Spanish countryside, as we embarked on this remarkable journey as companions.

For many days, the path weaved its way under our feet as we shared stories, shouldered our backpacks, and marvelled at the breathtaking landscapes. There is an undeniable joy in traversing life's path with a friend, a shared sense of purpose and a trusted companion for moments when the road grows challenging. As Helen Keller wrote, 'Life is either a daring adventure or nothing at all.'

Anna and I will rejoin The Way on our last day so we can stride into Santiago together. We are companions–partners on this shared journey and perhaps on roads still to be travelled.

Chapter 26
Santiago de Compostela

Jonathan Swindon

Our last day: O Pedrouzo to Santiago de Compostela. Walking the Camino with Claudia over the last few days has been a delight. She was wonderful company, but I'm overjoyed that Anna and William will join us for the twenty-four-kilometre trek to the Cathedral. As we gather at the cafe below our Pension for breakfast, we're filled with expectation and excitement. Although Anna is all smiles, I imagine she's worried that her foot will survive the day. I prayed for her last night and, across the table from her as she eats her fresh tomato on toast with a drizzle of olive oil, I whisper another prayer, asking God to ease the pain in her foot and carry her with Him into Santiago.

Putting her empty coffee cup in its saucer, Anna said, 'Are we all ready?'

Together, we replied, 'We are.' Anna moved her hand, hovering above the tablecloth, into the centre of the table, inviting us to place our hands on top of each other. Using a phrase from *The Three Musketeers*, she quoted, 'All for one and one for all.' We repeated it before standing, lifting our packs and stepping into the street. We'd barely cleared the main street when the rain started. On went our wet weather gear.

Much of the early part of the walk involved a trek through eucalyptus forests. After navigating the runway of Santiago airport at eight forty-five that morning as the sun was rising, we trudged into San Paio for coffee. With the excitement of reaching the Cathedral tantalisingly close, we were soon back out in the rain. The walk took us through more eucalyptus plantations and farmland. On a sunny day, the scenery would have been verdant, but in the relentless rain and cold, it felt like a space that had to be endured. Needing a toilet break, we made an unplanned coffee stop and as we left the cafe; the sky cleared. William put his finger in the air and declared that we should pack away the raincoats. A little further on, we arrived at Monte do Gozo, a small hill where we were promised a panoramic view of the city and the Cathedral.

'This is a little disappointing,' Anna said as we surveyed the bronze plates scattered on the ground, remnants of a sculpture that once stood here. 'Where's the renowned view of the city?'

Claudia chuckled as she said, 'Follow me.'

After a 600-metre stroll, we encountered the towering statues of two pilgrims. Encased in bronze, they depicted figures dressed in medieval pilgrim attire. The taller pilgrim raised a hand, shielding his eyes from the sun as he gazed towards Santiago de Compostela, the ultimate destination just beyond the horizon. His companion, shorter and slightly stooped, grasped a staff decorated with a gourd and shell, ageless symbols of the pilgrimage.

I stood back and studied the sculpture. Their robes, the style of ancient travellers, seem to ripple with an eternal wind and at their feet were tokens from modern pilgrims, a scattering of stones, prayer cards, and colourful ribbons. Like the statue of the lady in O'Cebreiro, the bronze has taken on a greenish patina. They were probably by the same artist, though I wasn't sure. The figures depicted anticipation; their long journey was nearing its end.

Sensing our time together was drawing to a close, I called out with excitement, hastily retrieving my phone from my pocket. 'William, Anna, Claudia, stand next to the sculptures for a photo!'

They gathered around the Statue of Pilgrims at Monte do Gozo, mimicking the poses of the bronze figures. William shielded his eyes, pretending to scan the horizon, while Anna and Claudia clutched their imaginary staffs, pointing towards Santiago de Compostela. The sight of my friends against the backdrop of the city and the iconic effigies played with my emotions. Like many on our journey, this was a moment I wanted to hold on to forever. 'Perfect. Now, point towards our destination and I'll snap another.'

'Onward,' I called. We journeyed closer to the city, and we stopped for another photo opportunity by a sign announcing our arrival in Santiago. Following the path for half an hour, we found ourselves piped into the Cathedral square, marking the end of our walk. Bathed in sunlight, we joined the milling throngs, alongside hundreds of non-pilgrims admiring and photographing the church.

'Jonathan,' Claudia yelled above the bustling crowd. 'A woman is calling your name.' She pointed, and I glimpsed someone around my age, examining what seemed like a driver's licence in her hand. She scanned the crowd, searching for someone. I patted my trouser pocket and found that my wallet was missing. It must have slipped out when I retrieved my phone at the Statue of Pilgrims on Monte do Gozo. My credit card, cash, driver's licence, all the essentials were in there. A swarm of people passed between us, and when I looked again, she had vanished.

'Claudia, she's found my wallet. We have to find her.'

Claudia nodded before heading off into the throng of people. I turned, searching for William and Anna, but they were nowhere to be seen. I plunged into the crowd, my heart racing as I scanned the teeming square for any sign of the woman. My eyes darted from face to face. All I saw were many excited pilgrims at the end of their ordeal. I was hoping to glimpse her, the woman with my wallet.

Desperate, I pushed through clusters of people; I had no money other than that in my wallet and I wondered whether she'd found the wallet or only my licence? The cathedral's spires loomed above, casting shadows across the square. I weaved around families and groups, anxiety mounting. Then, through the throng, I spotted

Claudia waving frantically near the steps of the cathedral. Beside her was the smiling woman, holding up my wallet.

'I found her, Jonathan!' Claudia yelled, beaming.

I took the wallet from the woman's offering hand, my relief overwhelming. 'Thank you, thank you so much,' I said, my voice trembling. The woman nodded.

'No problem. I knew it was important. I'm glad I could help.'

'How did you find me?' I asked.

'This morning, I was walking near the Pilgrim statues and I picked up your wallet from the ground and inside was your driver's licence. I put your name, Jonathan Swindon, into Facebook and of the twenty who came up, one was walking the Camino. With your last update from Arca and from the place I found your wallet, I expected you to arrive at the Cathedral. In the spirit of the Camino, I followed my instincts and ventured to seek you out.'

I went to reply but found myself lost for words. Claudia filled the void. 'Excuse our rudeness, we haven't introduced ourselves. I am Claudia, this is Jonathan, as you know, and here come the other two members of our troop, William and Anna.'

I'm very pleased to meet you all. My name is Pip.

Pip, I mumbled silently to myself. What a beautiful name.

Claudia explained to William and Anna what had transpired, and they were overjoyed and humbled by Pip's kindness. William turned to Pip and said, 'If you're not in a rush, would you do us the honour of joining us for lunch? It would be a privilege.'

She hesitated, and I held my breath.

There was wariness in her voice, but she replied with a smile, 'Yes, I would. Are you planning to pick up your Compostela first?'

Our group exchanged glances as Claudia said, 'Does anyone know where the Pilgrim's Office is?'

'I do,' Pip said, 'I'll take you.'

At the Pilgrim's Office, the process was completed with breathtaking efficiency, but we were treated with respect. Each was welcomed and congratulated. We were reminded that we'd joined a community of seekers that stretched back over a thousand years and I had to fight back tears as I realised what I'd achieved.

The lady at the desk stared at me and said, 'Why did you undertake the Camino?'

With a hidden smile, I mused on my mission to discover the future Mrs. Swindon. I answered, 'For spiritual reasons,' which was the truth.

Compostelas in hand, we found a restaurant overlooking a plaza and near the Cathedral.

'I am going to buy a bottle of bubbly to celebrate, perhaps two,' William said. 'Pip, do you partake?'

'Bubbly, that would be lovely.'

I also requested a glass of champagne and none of my friends remarked on my change of heart. Drinking wasn't prohibited in my evangelical church, but it was certainly frowned upon. At that moment, the champagne seemed fitting.

We enjoyed a traditional meal together and Pip engaged in conversation with my friends effortlessly. It was as though we'd known her forever, reminiscent of our daily encounters on the Camino.

Anna's phone buzzed with a text message. 'It's Ana and Ian. They want to know if we'll join them tonight for dinner after the

Pilgrims' Mass. Ana expects everyone to be there, whatever her "everyone" means. She mentioned Chinmay and Baby James too.'

'Absolutely,' Claudia replied and William and I nodded in agreement. I was surprised when Claudia invited Pip.

Pip said, 'You don't want a stranger tagging along!'

Claudia laughed. 'This is the Camino; everyone is a stranger until they're not. We'll look after you, won't we, Jonathan? Join us, Pip, please.'

'Where are you meeting for dinner?'

Anna grimaced. 'That's a challenge as Ana hasn't made the booking yet. She mentioned she'd let us know after Mass, and then we'll walk there together.'

Claudia said to Pip, 'Have you been to a Pilgrims' Mass?'

'No, I haven't.'

'Well, that settles it,' Claudia said. 'Join us for the Pilgrims' Mass and we'll go to dinner from there.'

***

Waiting outside the Grand Cathedral, my eyes flitting from face-to-face searching for Pip, doubt lingered. Would she show up? We were strangers to her, and maybe she agreed to join us out of politeness.

Then, amidst the murmurs of the crowd, Pip's voice reached my ears, slightly breathless yet unmistakably hers.

'Sorry everyone,' she said. 'It was difficult parking, then I had to walk into the heart of the old city. I hope I haven't kept you waiting.'

Speaking for all of us, I said, 'No, not at all.'

Passing through the imposing ornate doors of the Santiago de Compostela Cathedral, a wave of cool air enveloped me, momentarily halting my steps. The grandeur of the interior was exceptional. 'It's breathtaking,' I murmured softly.

'It is breathtaking,' Pip said.

Above me, lofty ceilings soared skyward, their arches adorned with meticulous carvings and gilded embellishments that gleamed in the subdued light. Stained glass panels infused the space with transmitted light of crimson, azure, and emerald, painting the stone walls a kaleidoscope of patterns. Incense hung in the air, sweet and smoky in the presence of ancient stone.

Anna had told us she harboured a hope that we'd witness the grandeur of the Botafumeiro, as did I. Such an event was a rare privilege, reserved for significant religious occasions or at the behest of devoted pilgrims who'd made significant donations. The lingering traces of incense hinted at past swings of the Botafumeiro, but it also carried a risk of disappointment, as the spectacle was unlikely to be repeated during our service. To see the Botafumeiro in action would be to glimpse an age-old tradition spanning centuries. Fellow pilgrims we'd met along "The Way" spoke of it in reverent tones; it wasn't merely a dazzling display; it was more like a transcendent experience.

'It's more than simply an impressive spectacle,' they had said. 'It's profound, a mystical journey. The sight of the giant silver censer soaring through the air, releasing billows of fragrant incense, connects one to the divine, and also to the pilgrims who've trodden this path before us.'

We drifted towards the pews, amidst the murmur of fellow pilgrims as they filled the cavernous space, feet echoing on the stone floor. Ahead, the golden altar glowed, a beacon in the shadowy interior. The figure of Saint James, resplendent in gold and jewels, stood above it, his presence commanding. I took a seat, the wooden bench creaking under my weight.

Claudia gently touched my shoulder. 'Not here,' she whispered. Her finger pointed upwards, towards the Botafumeiro. 'If it swings, it will carry on down the Transept. Let's sit there, beneath its passage.'

She led us to a spot where the swinging censer, if it was used, would hover above our heads.

When the service started, the sound of the organ flooded the cathedral, its rich tones reverberating from the stone walls.

'Beautiful,' I murmured to Pip, who was beside me.

The choir of priests started singing, their voices in harmony, melodies praising the heavens and lifting my soul with them. Lost in the music, I surrendered to its embrace, the unfamiliar Latin lyrics like a lullaby at day's end. There was a depth that I'd not found in the Evangelical Christian music of my church.

When the priest began his sermon, his voice was gentle yet powerful. My Spanish was poor, but I knew he was talking of the journey we'd undertaken, hardships we'd faced, and the faith that had carried us through. Peace washed over me, a sense of completion, something I'd sought since I took my first step on the Camino.

At the end of Mass in the Santiago de Compostela Cathedral, the air suddenly grew thick with anticipation, when eight monks appeared. Eyes turned towards the great silver incense burner, the Botafumeiro, hanging from a pulley system near the altar.

Pip whispered, 'We are going to see it!'

I felt goose bumps.

In rich burgundy robes, the monks took their positions, each grasping a chunky rope that would set the Botafumeiro in motion. They moved with practised grace; their synchronised actions honed by countless repetitions of this sacred ritual. As the lead monk signalled, together they tugged the ropes with measured force. Slowly, the Botafumeiro began to move, tentatively at first in gentle arcs. With each coordinated tug from the monks, the swings grew wider and more powerful and the censer soared higher and higher, reaching a dizzying height, passing just below the ceiling of the transept and above my head. As it swung, releasing clouds of fragrant incense, one monk turned his head. He stared at me, our eyes meeting. Even at that distance, I recognised the eyes of Brother Artōrius and felt a spiritual connection to him. Incense permeated the air, heightening my senses, and a familiar hymn whispered to me:

Be still and know that I am God.

Overwhelmed, tears welled in my eyes, interrupted by a gentle touch from Pip, who inquired about the subtle breeze that accompanied the Botafumeiro's passage overhead. 'Did you feel that?' she asked.

Closing my eyes and drawing a deep breath, I responded, tears wetting my cheeks, 'Yes.' In that instant, I felt the presence of my Saviour and the future Mrs. Swindon.

The monks slowed their pull on the ropes and the Botafumeiro's swings became less pronounced, gradually coming to a rest. The incense continued to waft through the air, a lingering reminder of what had occurred.

Chapter 27
Baby James

Claudia

The restaurant pulsed with energy, populated by the familiar faces from our journey. There were Ian, Catherine, and Baby James, hailing from Richmond in Virginia, Ana, Ian, Chinmay, Isaac, Miriam, Clair, Chuck, and Cathy, among others. Amidst the lively chatter and clinking of utensils, urgency pervaded the air as people exchanged contact information and posed for the last photographs. The moment would be fleeting; paths converging briefly before scattering to the far corners of the globe once the meal was over. Some newfound connections would become little more than memories, while others would endure as lasting friendships.

I seized the opportunity, Anna nursing baby James while engaged in conversation with Chinmay at a neighbouring table, and Jonathan introducing Pip to Chuck and Cathy, to approach William, deciding that directness was the best way, especially as I'd guessed that William knew, from early in the Camino, that I was a British agent. I refilled William's wineglass and said, 'The Bible reading Father Calieo gave you. The chapter and verse serve as a date, an impending event that will negatively affect the stock market. That's how you will receive payment for your role on the Camino.'

William took a sip from his glass. 'That's an interesting theory, Claudia.'

'Analysis following 9/11, showed some made a small fortune profiting from a crash in the stock market. They had advanced knowledge of the atrocity, didn't they? Are you a skilled investor, William, or is it insider knowledge that's the payment? The authorities will know what to look for.'

'It is still an interesting *theory*.'

I contemplated my next move for a moment. 'You've been playing a game, William. Early in our journey you dropped cryptic references like lines from the film "The Mule." You've played the perfect role, protected by the Security Service because of your work in technologies of national importance. After retiring from BAE Systems, it was a stroke of genius, fabricating involvement in espionage, to ensure your safety along the Camino.'

William smiled as he said. 'You know I won't divulge anything, Claudia.'

'This conversation stays between us, William. No recording devices.'

'If you say so.'

'The thing is, William; I've grown quite fond of you.'

'The feeling is mutual.'

'I'm also fond of Anna,' I said.

William's expression tightened. 'Ah, I see where this is going.'

Choosing my words carefully, I said, 'William, I believe you truly loved your wife, Hannah, and that you care for your daughter, Samantha. I believe you were duty-bound to carry the puzzle box on the Camino, a box filled with items precious to Samantha, mementos of her mother.' I paused and took a breath. 'But how desperate does a person have to be to cast suspicion on the daughter he loves? Who would exploit something as sacred as the puzzle box for their own gains? And let's not forget about Hannah's brother!'

William set his wineglass down with a heavy sigh. 'Yes, what kind of man?' he muttered; his expression troubled. 'It just... developed that way. If it matters, know that the weight of that decision burdened me greatly and that the Camino has transformed me into someone different.'

'I've noticed the change in you.'

'None of us are the same as when we began. I want to share what has changed me.'

William told of how the spirit of Hannah had led him to safety during the fierce storm crossing the Pyrenees to Roncesvalles. He reminded me of our encounter with Richard, guiding his visually impaired wife Eleanor along the Camino. 'Claudia, they were not merely travellers on the Camino; they were the very embodiment of the Camino's essence. And when I ran with the bulls in Puente La Reina, that also affected me... In San Juan, I asked Jack, Jack Rabbit, a question. He rephrased the question, and I saw my life in a different light. Do you remember the medieval monastery in Nájera, when Jonathan asked us to stand still? I heard the centuries old chants, Claudia, as if I was transported through time. It spoke to me just as the Selenehelion did, when we stood transfixed, marvelling at the breathtaking spectacle of the moon setting and the sun rising simultaneously.' William sighed... 'Claudia, the singing nuns of Carrion de los Condes, they were singing to me.' He sighed again. 'They were singing to me.'

William brushed away a tear. 'Lorraine and Phil from California, they were meant to cross my path. They taught me the importance of living with compassion for others. Every person we've met on this journey has touched my life in some way.' He inhaled. 'Then there was the Holy Cross of Santo Toribio. I felt it there, the presence of the good people who've walked this path before me. It was Puerto Irago Cruz de Ferro, where I felt the gravity of my sins and then, when I heard the haunting voice in Iglesia de San Juan Bautista, I knew I had to become a better man. Claudia, I know I can be, with Anna by my side.' William's voice became tinged with hope. 'If you'd allow it, Claudia, there could be a future for Anna and me. She could have the bookshop she dreams of.'

I want to highlight that some of the life-changing events occurred before Astorga, yet despite this, he consciously chose to proceed with the wrongdoing… William wanted to engage me in a moral discussion, something I would not allow. Instead, I repeated Brother Artōrius's wise guidance. 'William, redemption is a path we all can tread, but it does not absolve us of our past deeds.'

He nodded, absorbing the weight of my words. 'I understand, Claudia. So, what happens next?'

'Along with your share trading, the police will examine the money you've accrued from your real estate dealings over the past two decades. They will be meticulous too. They'll discover that your buyers consistently paid above market value and sold for a loss, lining your pockets with substantial profits. When they delve deeper, they'll uncover a troubling connection between the buyers and criminal syndicates. At best, you will have your assets seized as proceeds of crime. The worst-case scenario? You might find yourself behind bars.'

William nodded, his expression sombre. 'Will you tell Anna?'

I met his gaze with kindness. 'Do I need to tell Anna?'

William shook his head. 'No. Thank you, Claudia. I will do that.'

As Anna returned to the table, with a heavy heart, I excused myself and strolled towards the bar, seeking the comfort of another drink. As I passed by where Baby James was nestled in his mother's arms, he reached out to me. Catherine gestured to the empty chair, then gently passed Baby James into my arms. Settling the child on my knee, I met his innocent gaze and whispered,

'You know, Baby James, the Camino teaches us something invaluable. Life is all about the people we meet along the way.'

THE END

www.ingramcontent.com/pod-product-compliance
Lightning Source LLC
Chambersburg PA
CBHW050114120726
47904CB00004B/1342